BASEBORN

BASEBORN

THE RISE OF VALDRIA

NOLAN R. HIGHMOOR

TARTARY

CONTENTS

For Ren

Cover design and illustration by TARTARY

First Edition

ISBN 979-8-89969-000-6 (paperback)

Published by TARTARY

tartary.com

Printed in the United States of America

PROLOGUE
ON THE ART OF FORGETTING

The first thing they do is take down the face.

Before the body, before the sword-arm, before the inscription is chiseled away—always the face. A rope around the neck, a team of oxen, and the bronze head comes free with a sound like a great bell cracking. It rolls across the cobblestones and comes to rest in the gutter, eyes to the sky, expression still frozen in that familiar pose of noble resolve.

The crowd watches in silence. Some of them remember when this same face was raised, years or decades before, to cheering that shook the windows. They called him Liberator then. Betrayer now. The name has changed. The face is the same.

By nightfall the bronze will be in the furnaces. By week's end a new statue will stand on the empty pedestal—same pose, same upraised sword, same expression of serene conviction. Different face. The inscription will proclaim a new set of virtues, a new list of victories. Children not yet born will be lifted onto their parents' shoulders to gaze upon features they will believe have always been there.

This is the first lie of empire: that power has a face.

In every city of the realm there stands a statue. A figure in armour, sword raised towards the heavens, gaze lifted like one receiving a divine mandate. The inscriptions vary—here a name, there a title, in the grandest squares a catalogue of conquests—but the message is constant. *Here stood a great man. Here is his legacy in bronze.*

Bronze remembers nothing. It only knows the fire. It does not care if it is cast into a god or a devil, so long as the weight remains the same.

Statues commemorate the necessary lie rather than the forgotten truth, until belief changes and they fall. A general who wins ten battles may see his monument pulled down for one act of defiance. A minister who serves faithfully for thirty years may watch his likeness dragged through the streets for a single ill-timed word. The pedestals are never empty for long. New faces rise to fill them, cast in the same eternal pose, until they too outlive their usefulness to the living.

In the first year of Peacehold's New Order, fourteen statues were melted down and recast. The chronicles do not record how many had been raised to those same men only years before.

This is the story of how those statues came to stand. The story behind the bronze faces and gilded inscriptions—the story that monuments are designed to make us forget.

No heroes walk these pages. The dead emerge stripped of nobility.

But the dead, unlike their statues, cannot be recast.

DRAMATIS PERSONAE

OF THE IRON EMPIRE

SERAN THE UNIFIER — The First Iron Emperor. Seeker of the Elixir. He looked for the cure to death and found the cause.

MORDECAI, THE SHADOWHAND — High Magistrate and the true power behind the crumbling Creedseat. A man who directed the slaughter from the darkness.

SILAS IRONSCRIBE — Chancellor for thirty-seven years. Discovered too late that total obedience is a remarkably poor retirement plan.

PRINCE CADEN, THE FIRSTBORN — The eldest son murdered for the crime of being too inconveniently competent.

EDRIC, THE SECONDBORN — A puppet emperor who excels in poetry and descended into madness, which at least made the Shadowhand's job more interesting.

LUCAN — The last heir. A royal captive too valuable to let go and too dangerous to have for dinner.

JARED STEELBANE — A commander of absolute duty currently haunting his own survival.

SYLVANUS — Traded his dignity for his men's lives and finds the air at the top remarkably cold.

HOLTEN — A veteran instructor doing penance for the students he taught too well.

OF THE REBELS

CORWIN HARROW — The First King of Rising Cheros, who asked one question and started the rebellion. An efficient martyr.

DECLAN SAYER — A herald who whispered the world into a fever.

OSRIC GOLDENCLOAK — An advisor whose wise counsel had the unfortunate habit of arriving after the funeral.

IAIN CAIRN — Sworn brother to Osric; shared the idealistic court and the resulting doom.

BRENNAN AXLE — Chariot driver. Betrayed his lord and learned that bitterness is a heavy passenger.

OF MARSH

MAREN ASHFORD — Lord of Valdria. A peasant pragmatist who treats imperial collapse like a particularly difficult plumbing issue.

LADY LYRA — Terrifyingly efficient. She manages the Basin so Maren can focus on his hobby of not dying.

MARKUS QUILLEN — The Administrator. Loots ledgers instead of gold; the only man who thinks a census is a thrill.

HADRIAN NARROWDALE — The Diplomat. Last of a royal house and Maren's resident moral compass.

ROLAND KNOX — The Shield. A former butcher who now handles much larger cuts of meat.

BERIC DURRANT — Guerrilla master. Believes centralised empires are just gilded cages with worse security.

HANS XANDER — Divine strategist. Sees war as math; currently the world's most overqualified minor official.

VALEN ASHFORD — Son of Maren Ashford.

KAIA ASHFORD — Daughter of Maren Ashford.

OF CHEROS

KHARIC STORMBORN — The Hegemon. A God of War with a legendary temper and a staggering bill for overworked sin-eaters.

LORD TORIAN THE STONEHEART — The uncle who provided the spark for Kharic's rise by the simple act of dying.

KING ARION — The Shepherd King, dreaming of marble palaces while sitting in a moistened tent.

ELDRAN GREYMANTLE — Kharic's "Second Father" and chief advisor. An elderly strategist who fears the divinity his lord has embraced. He records the truth of the Storm in secret journals.

GLENN STORMBORN — The Kinsman. The family conscience with a secret life-debt to an "agricultural fraud."

AARON HESTOR — General of the Black Guard. A veteran serving for the sake of memory and better days.

BEROLD THE BRANDED — Lord of Whitecroft, Commander of the "Stone-Eaters." A branded convict who thinks Maren is a fraud with good irrigation.

CASSIUS JONN — A knight of the old school. Famous for keeping promises, even to people he no longer recognises.

PART ONE
THE IGNOBLE RISE

No rise is truly noble; it is only successful. Greatness is a theft committed in the dark by those too stubborn to stay in the mud.

    — The Secret Annals of House Valdria

CHAPTER ONE

THE SMELL OF EMPIRE

IN WHICH THE IRON EMPEROR ROTS, AND MORDECAI THE SHADOWHAND DISCOVERS THE LIMITS OF POWER

OF THE FISH CARTS

The smell woke him.

High Magistrate Mordecai opened his eyes in the swaying darkness of the imperial litter and immediately wished he hadn't. The heat was a living thing—wet, thick, pressing against his skin like a fever. The silk curtains, drawn tight against the afternoon sun, trapped it inside, turned the litter into a sealed kiln where nothing could escape.

Nothing except the smell.

It came in waves. First the fish—the salt-rot stench of ten wagonloads of preserved mackerel and brine-casks, positioned around the litter like offerings to a god. The fish was deliberate —the plan made flesh. But beneath it, threading through the brine like poison through wine, came the other smell.

Sweeter. Thicker. *Wrong.*

Mordecai pressed his sleeve against his nose and looked at the thing on the cushions beside him.

The Iron Emperor had been dead for eleven days.

The physicians had packed the body in salt and camphor, had wrapped it in silk soaked with cedar oil, had done everything the ancient texts prescribed. It wasn't enough. Nothing was enough in this heat. The face that had once commanded forty million souls was bloating now, the skin stretched tight as a drum, the features losing their definition like a candle left too near the fire. The hands—those hands that had signed a hundred thousand death warrants—had turned the colour of foul cheese.

A fly crawled across the Emperor's lips. Mordecai watched it. Let it feast.

Eleven days, he thought. *Forty-three more to the capital—the ceremonial route, with its endless detours to provincial shrines, would take twice as long as the direct road.*

Outside, the procession continued its crawl eastward. Ten thousand servants, forty thousand soldiers, ministers and generals and scribes—all of them following a corpse. All of them bowing to a dead man's litter, kneeling in the dust as it passed, offering prayers to meat becoming soup.

And none of them knew. And they would not—so long as he was there to keep the curtains closed, to give the orders, and to make the lie real.

That was the miracle, if you could call it that. Mordecai had expected discovery within hours. He had expected some servant to notice that the Emperor's food was never eaten, that his chamber pot was never filled, that no sound emerged from behind the silk curtains except the buzzing of flies. But the terror the Emperor had cultivated for forty years served them now. No one approached without permission. No one questioned the strange new orders. No one dared.

Fear, Mordecai thought, *is the most useful of all emotions.*

Mordecai had never been sentimental about the Iron

Emperor. But he understood achievement when he saw it. The man had done what every would-be conqueror promised and none accomplished: he had taken the Six Kingdoms and made them one. In one lifetime, by an accumulation of victories—campaigns timed to harvest seasons, sieges calculated to starve cities just long enough, treaties offered only when surrender was already inevitable. One by one, the old crowns had fallen: Aldoria in the east, Cheros in the south, Nordheim in the far north, Dragonspire on the hard cavalry plains, and the central clans, heirs of Aurelian realm—Grandmark and Narrowdale—broken in turn.

The Empire's banners advanced behind engineers as much as soldiers—roads laid where armies needed to move, granaries raised where rebellions might grow, census rolls rewritten so that every household could be counted, taxed, drafted.

The poets called it glory. The surviving nobles called it catastrophe. Mordecai called it construction. The Iron Emperor sought no mere kingdom, but an Everlasting Empire—a state that did not depend on charisma, mercy, or even memory. A machine of law and obedience that could run without him. That was the difference between conquest and empire: conquest ended when the conqueror died. An empire, if built correctly, continued. Whatever the realm had become in the years since his death, this much could not be denied: before the Iron Emperor, there were lords and kings. After him, there was Empire.

He had conquered the world; only the grave refused to kneel.

The litter lurched. Mordecai's shoulder pressed against the Emperor's body, and something shifted inside it—what had been solid and was now liquid. The smell intensified. He gagged, swallowed hard, and pulled away.

This is how it ends. For all of us. Conqueror or slave, we all become this in the end.

He watched the Emperor die, sitting beside him in another room, in another province, watching the great man's breath grow shallow, watching the fire fade from eyes that had torched with ambition for seven decades. He had leaned close to catch the final words—hoping for instructions, for guidance, for some last command that would legitimise what Mordecai planned to do.

The Emperor had said only: "The Elixir. They promised me the Elixir."

For this the Emperor had travelled three thousand miles—to the sacred peaks of Wyrmspine where hermits claimed to know the secrets of the Celestine ancestors. For this he had climbed the Stairway of Infinite Steps, had knelt before ragged mystics who spoke of dragon's breath distilled into liquid form, of Quicksilver that could transmute mortal flesh into something imperishable. The sayings of the Old promised that such things existed: "Where dragons once flew, their fire lingers still; who drinks of their essence shall never know the chill." Children's rhymes, peasant superstitions—yet the Emperor had believed. Had spent fortunes on charlatans and alchemists. Had drunk mercury and powdered pearls until his insides rotted.

And then nothing. The most powerful man in history, silenced by the same death that claimed beggars and farmers.

Mordecai had felt a numbness then. A brittle, calculating focus, rather than grief, hollowed him out. A recognition that all his schemes, all his careful accumulation of power, would end the same way. That one day he too would lie in a litter, rotting, while men like himself made plans over his corpse.

But not today, he told himself. *Today, there is work to do.*

He forced himself to look at the body again. To see it

clearly. The Emperor's mouth had fallen open in death, and something dark was leaking from the corner—blood or bile or some more terrible fluid. His tongue had swelled to fill the cavity. His eyes, still half-open, had developed a film like old milk.

Eight thousand Iron-Bound wait for him in the tomb at Shadowmount, just a hundred miles west of the capital. Mordecai thought. *Eight thousand men, dipped living into molten bronze, frozen forever in postures of perpetual vigilance. Their screams had lasted only seconds. Their service would last forever. Their hollow metal eyes stared eternally towards the east, guarding the approach to Steelhaven.*

Rivers of star-silver flow through that underground palace—liquid void drawn from the hearts of fallen stars, glowing faintly in the darkness, tracing the constellations of the Celestine heavens across floors of black obsidian. A cosmos in miniature, built by half a million slaves who joined their Emperor in death.

And he will arrive as this. Meat. Nothing.

The irony was exquisite. The Emperor had spent the last twenty years trying to become iron himself—drinking molten alloys that his alchemists swore would harden his organs, transmute his flesh into something imperishable. The Iron Creed made literal: a man of metal who could never die. He had felt his heart calcifying, had welcomed the spreading coldness as a sign that the transformation was working.

Instead, the iron had killed him. His heart had become a stone that could no longer beat.

Instead, he was decomposing in a box, surrounded by fish.

A knock at the litter's frame. Mordecai stiffened.

"My lord?" Silas Ironscribe asked, muffled by the curtains. "We approach the checkpoint at Sandmere. The garrison commander wishes to pay his respects to His Majesty."

Mordecai closed his eyes. This was the moment. One of

many moments to come—each one a chance for discovery, for failure, for the whole edifice to come crashing down.

"His Majesty is meditating," he called back. "He will receive no visitors. Tell the commander to prepare a report instead. The Emperor will review it when... when he emerges."

A pause. Long enough for Mordecai to hear his own heart pounding.

"Yes, my lord."

Footsteps retreating.

Mordecai let out a breath he hadn't known he was holding. The smell rushed back in—fish and rot and the particular sweetness of human decay—and he had to fight the urge to vomit.

Forty-three days, he reminded himself. *Forty-three days of this, and then the throne is secure. Prince Caden will be dead. Prince Edric will be Emperor. And I will be the power behind the power, as I have always been.*

The fly had found the Emperor's nostril now. It crawled inside, disappeared, crawled out again.

Mordecai watched it. His hand moved, unbidden, to the small iron charm beneath his robe—a thing his mother had given him when he was seven, pressed into his palm with the whispered words: "For when you must do what cannot be undone." He had not believed in such superstitions for thirty years. Yet he had never thrown it away.

His fingers closed around the cold metal. He saw Prince Caden's face as it had been fifteen years ago, when the boy was twelve and had brought Mordecai a plate of honeycakes from the kitchen, unprompted, because "you looked tired, Lord Councillor." The memory surfaced like a drowned thing rising from dark water.

Mordecai released the charm. He had made harder choices than this. He would make harder choices still. Sentiment was a luxury for men who did not have to hold empires together.

He began composing the edict that would murder the rightful heir to the throne.

Here begins the tale of what followed—of the fall of Ironhold and the rise of new powers, of Kharic Stormborn and Maren Ashford, of the war.

Listen well.

The dead are always listening.

OF THE SANDMERE CONSPIRACY

The emperor died on the third day of the ninth month, in a place called Sandmere—the Sandy Hills—far from the capital he had built, far from the tomb he would never occupy in state.

He died with Mordecai the Shadowhand at his side, and Silas Ironscribe, and a handful of trusted servants who understood that their survival depended on absolute silence. He died without giving any final commands, without naming his heir, without settling the countless matters that only an emperor could settle—or so the official account would later claim.

In truth, there may have been final words. There may have been a gesture towards the north, where Prince Caden Firstborn served. There may have been an attempt to write something, anything, before the darkness closed in. But if such attempts were made, they were not recorded. The only witnesses were men whose loyalty belonged to Mordecai the Shadowhand, and their memories proved remarkably selective.

Within hours of the emperor's last breath, Mordecai had taken control.

"The heat is fierce," he announced to the officers who waited outside the imperial litter. "His Majesty has commanded that no one is to approach. The journey continues."

No one questioned him. No one dared. Mordecai the Shadowhand spoke with the emperor's voice, and until someone could prove the emperor was dead, that voice carried absolute authority.

The procession continued eastward, following its planned route, visiting the shrines and monuments the emperor had commanded built to glorify his reign. At each stop, Mordecai reported that His Majesty was indisposed but well, that he would receive petitioners soon, that all was as it should be. The imperial decrees continued to flow from the litter's darkness, signed with the emperor's seal, written in the emperor's name.

No one noticed that the handwriting had changed slightly, that the litter was never opened, never cleaned, never aired despite the late summer heat—or if they did notice, they were wise enough not to speak of it—that a strange smell had begun to emanate from the imperial conveyance, the sweet-sick odour of flesh beginning to decay.

Mordecai ordered cartloads of salted fish to be placed alongside the imperial litter. "His Majesty has developed a taste for the delicacy," he explained. And if the smell of rotting fish mingled with another, darker stench, well, who would say so?

While the corpse of the Iron Emperor mouldered in its silken prison, Mordecai the Shadowhand worked. He summoned Silas Ironscribe, the Chancellor of the Realm, and together they composed the documents that would have mattered.

OF SILAS IRONSCRIBE
AND HIS BARGAIN

Silas Ironscribe was a complicated man, and this was a complicated moment.

He had served the Iron Emperor for thirty years—first as a minor scholar in the conquered kingdom of Cheros, then as an administrator in the new imperial bureaucracy, finally as the second most powerful man in the realm, the Chancellor who spoke with the emperor's authority on all matters of law and governance. He had helped create the Iron Creed, that system of absolute law that treated all men equally under the emperor's will—equally subject to punishment, equally devoid of rights, equally replaceable cogs in the vast machinery of state.

He believed in that creed. He believed in its terrible necessity, believed that only such ruthless uniformity could hold together an empire forged from conquest, believed that the old ways—the chaos of competing kingdoms, the corruption of noble privilege, the sentiment and tradition that had made the world weak—had to be swept away if civilisation was to survive.

He had done terrible things in service to that belief. He had ordered unorthodox books burnt, unwarranted magicians and scholars buried. He had signed execution warrants by the thousands, had sent millions to their deaths building the great roads that bound the provinces together, the canals that carried grain to the capital, the tomb where the first emperor would lie in counterfeit eternity. He had watched his own conscience wither and die, accepting each new horror as the price of a greater good that always receded further into the future.

And now, in the stinking confines of a litter that bore a

dead man's seal, he was being asked to do one more terrible thing.

"You cannot be serious," he said to Mordecai the Shadow-hand, though they both knew he would agree in the end. "The crown prince is the legitimate heir. The succession is clear."

"The succession," Mordecai replied smoothly, "is whatever we say it is. Who else knows the emperor is dead? Who else has access to the imperial seals? We hold the power, Silas. The only question is how we choose to use it."

"And if we choose wrong? If the truth emerges?"

"Then we die. But we die regardless if Caden Trueheart takes the throne." Mordecai's smile was thin as a knife's edge. "You know his reputation. The upright prince, the honest soldier, who believed that the laws of the Iron Creed should apply to everyone equally—even those who wrote them. How long do you think you would survive his reign? How long before he started asking questions about where all the treasure went, about who signed all those death warrants, about what really happened in the years when his father was too ill to rule?"

Silas Ironscribe froze. He was thinking of all the things he had done, all the choices he had made, all the bodies buried beneath the foundations of the new order. He was thinking of the prince he had watched grow from a child into a man of uncomfortable integrity, he might actually try to govern by the principles the Iron Creed claimed to embody.

He was thinking of how such a man would judge those who had made the creed into an instrument of murder.

"What do you propose?" he asked finally.

Mordecai produced a document—a decree, already written, requiring only the chancellor's seal to become law. Silas read it, and his face went grey.

"This is treason."

"This is survival." Mordecai replied. "Sign it, and you live. Refuse, and—well. There are many ways for a man to die on a long journey, and not all of them are pleasant."

Silas Ironscribe looked at the document one more time. It was a death warrant for Prince Caden Firstborn, commanding him to take his own life for crimes he had never committed, signed with the seal of a father who had never ordered it. It was a lie wrapped in a legal fiction, a murder disguised as justice.

It was exactly the kind of thing the Iron Creed made possible.

The quill hovered over the parchment. *It is for the realm,* Silas told himself—the lie rising to meet the occasion like bile. *Caden is too rigid. He would purge the court, shatter the delicate alliances, plunge us into administrative chaos in the name of virtue. A weak emperor we can guide is safer than a righteous one we cannot control. This is no murder or regicide; it is statecraft.*

He signed it.

THE SWORD AND THE EDICT

The decree reached the northern frontier on the twenty-third day of the ninth month.

The wind outside the command tent did not howl; it shrieked. It tore at the heavy canvas, threatening to extinguish the oil lamps that cast long, jittering shadows against the maps of conquered lands. Inside, the air was cold enough to turn breath into mist.

Prince Caden Firstborn stood motionless. The scroll in his hand was heavy, though it was only parchment and wax. The seal at the bottom was his father's—the Iron Dragon, stamped in red ink that looked, in the flickering light, too much like fresh blood.

"It is a forgery," General Montag said again. His voice was a low growl, vibrating with the violence he was holding back. He paced the length of the tent, his shadow stretching and snapping against the walls. "It has to be. The Emperor... your father... he would not."

"The seal is genuine, Montag." Caden's voice was terrifyingly calm. He did not look up from the words that condemned him. "The courier is genuine. The signature is his."

"Then the mind behind it is gone! Mad with mercury and rot!" Montag slammed his gauntleted fist onto the tactical table, making the map markers jump. "You have three hundred thousand swords here, Highness. The Northern Legion obeys your voice, they'd ignore a scrap of paper carried by a eunuch's lackey. Say the word. We march south. We clear the court of those parasites, and we ask the Emperor ourselves."

Caden looked up then. He possessed the eyes of a scholar who had finally found the solution to an impossible equation. It was a look of infinite, crushing fatigue.

"March south?" Caden asked softly. "Civil war? To save my life, I should burn the villages I swore to protect? I should break the Iron Creed—the very law that holds this empire together— just because it has turned against me?"

"The law is a lie if it kills the just!"

"If the law only applies when it suits us, Montag, then it is not law. It is just whim."

Caden walked to the weapon rack. The tent was silent now, save for the snapping of the canvas in the wind. He drew his sword. It was a masterpiece of folded steel, a blade named *Peacekeeper*. He had carried it for ten years. He had never imagined its final target would be himself.

He looked at his reflection in the blade. He looked like his father, before the mercury took him.

"My father demands my life," Caden said, testing the edge

with his thumb. "If I refuse, I prove him right. I prove that I am a traitor who puts his own neck above the decree of the Throne."

"Caden, please." Montag stepped forward, abandoning titles, reaching out a desperate hand. "Don't do this for them. Don't die for a lie."

"Not for them," Caden whispered.

He reversed the blade. He positioned the point against the gap in his ribs, angling it upward, towards the heart. His hands were steady. Steadier than they had ever been in battle.

"I do this for the peace," Caden said. "Because if I die obeying, maybe the lie holds for one more generation. Maybe the world doesn't burn."

"Highness—!"

"Tell my brother," Caden said, his muscles tightening, "that the crown is heavier than he thinks."

He did not hesitate. The Iron Creed did not allow for hesitation. He drove the steel home.

The sound of a body hitting the floor was softer than the wind, but to General Montag, standing frozen in the lamplight, it sounded like the spine of the world snapping.

Outside, the soldiers gathered in the dark, waiting for orders that would never come. Inside, the rightful Emperor lay in a spreading pool of red, dead by the only hand he could not defeat: his own.

OF THE SUCCESSION
AND ITS CONSEQUENCES

Word of the crown prince's death reached the imperial procession three days later, carried by a messenger who had ridden three horses to death in his haste. Mordecai the Shadowhand received the news with appropriate solemnity, his face a mask of practised grief.

"A tragedy," he announced to the assembled court. "The crown prince, corrupted by treasonous advisors, has taken his own life rather than face justice. His Majesty the Emperor is devastated by this loss."

No one pointed out that His Majesty the Emperor was several weeks dead, and becoming less imperial by the day. The smell from the imperial litter had grown strong enough that even the cartloads of fish could not entirely disguise it, but still no one spoke. Fear had many voices in Ironhold, but discretion spoke loudest of all.

The procession turned westward, towards the capital, its pace now openly urgent. There was no longer any need for pretense. The only remaining son would take the throne, and those who had positioned themselves to guide him would reap the rewards of their patience.

Mordecai the Shadowhand permitted himself a small smile as the first towers of Steelhaven appeared on the horizon—and with them, the Twin Iron Titans.

They stood at the Dragon Gate, two hundred feet tall, their forms supposedly cast from the melted weapons of the Hundred Conquered Kingdoms. Every surrendered sword, every confiscated spear, every axe and arrow that the Iron Creed had seized from the subjugated realms—all had allegedly been fed into the forges, transmuted into these monuments of absolute power. The Titans faced outward, their blank iron faces staring down anyone who approached the capital, their massive hands holding the symbols of imperial authority: one gripped a sword the size of a ship's mast, the other a set of scales large enough to weigh a horse.

Only the Emperor holds the power of violence, the statues proclaimed. *Only the Emperor dispenses justice.*

Generations of conquered peoples had passed beneath those pitiless iron gazes, reminded with every step that their weapons were gone, their resistance was futile, their fate belonged to the throne. The Titans were not merely decoration. They were a statement of fact: the old world was melted down, reforged, made into something that served only one master.

Mordecai looked up at them as the procession passed through the Dragon Gate, and felt, as he always did, a grim satisfaction.

All is within the plan.

The imperial funeral was the grandest the world had ever seen. The procession wound its way westward from the capital, a river of white mourning robes flowing towards the dark silhouette of Shadowmount.

Half a million labourers had worked on this tomb for thirty years. They had hollowed out the mountain's heart, filling its caverns with treasures beyond counting. Crossbow mechanisms guarded every corridor, rigged to fire automatically at any intruder. Agate horses pulled chariots of bronze through chambers that would never see sunlight. And everywhere, the gleaming ranks of the Iron-Bound—the immortal army that would guard their master through death as they never could in life.

Into this monument to immortal vanity they placed what remained of Seran the Unifier, First Iron Emperor of The Everlasting Ironhold. They sealed the massive iron doors—doors so heavy it took a thousand men to close them—and left him in the dark.

Around him stood the eight thousand immortals of bronze, gleaming in the torchlight, perfect and incorruptible. They were the dream made manifest: order without decay, obedience without question. And in their centre, sealed within layers of gold and gemstones to hide the truth, lay the

Master of the World—a bloating, liquefying mess that smelt of fish.

The metal had achieved what the man could not. The shell was eternal; the ghost within was merely meat.

As the final stone was rolled into place, sealing the mountain, Mordecai exhaled. Little did he know that one day, a barbarian would crack this tomb open like a gilded egg, only to show the world that the yolk was rotten all along.

CHAPTER TWO

THE DEER AND THE HORSE

IN WHICH THE SECOND EMPEROR'S REIGN DESCENDS INTO MADNESS, AND THE REALM GROANS BENEATH THE WEIGHT OF THE IRON CREED

A single spark may burn a forest; a single voice may bring down an empire. Rulers borrow their strength from the silence of the many.

— *The Book of Changes*

OF THE LABOURERS AT SHADOWMOUNT

The overseer's whip cracked across the boy's back for the third time that morning, yet silence was his only answer. He had learned, in the eighteen months since he had been conscripted to work on the First Emperor's tomb, that crying out only encouraged them.

"Faster!" the overseer shouted. "The stones won't carry themselves! Do you think the Divine One waits for the likes of you?"

This was Hans Xander—though no one in the mud of Shadowmount knew that name yet, not even Xander himself.

Xander bent his bleeding back to the rope and pulled.

Around him, a hundred other men did the same, their combined strength barely sufficient to drag the massive stone block up the mountain's slope. The block was one of ten thousand such blocks that had been cut from the quarries in the south, transported by barge and cart, and now hauled by human muscle to their final resting place.

Somewhere ahead, at the summit of Shadowmount, the iron doors of the First Emperor's tomb were even now being sealed. The treasures of a thousand years were being arranged according to patterns only the dead would ever see. And all of it—every stone, every bronze statue, every drop of liquid starlight—had been carried here on the backs of men like Xander.

Men who would never leave.

He knew the rumours. Everyone knew. The workers on the inner chambers, the ones who had seen the tomb's secrets, were being sealed inside it. Their knowledge was too dangerous to let escape into the world, and their lives were worth less than the onyx ornaments they had arranged around the emperor's corpse. Half a million men had worked on this tomb over thirty years. How many would walk away when the work was done?

Xander suspected he knew the answer.

But he kept pulling. What else was there to do? The Iron Creed offered no appeals, no exceptions, no mercy. Once you were condemned to labour service, you laboured until they decided you had laboured enough. If you ran, they hunted you down and made an example of you—slow examples, public examples, examples that took days to die while the other workers watched and learned the price of defiance.

"Move, dogs! Move!"

The whip cracked again, this time across the back of the man beside Xander—an older man, a farmer from the southern provinces who had been condemned for failing to pay his taxes. He stumbled, lost his grip on the rope, and fell.

The stone block continued its momentum, dragging two other men off their feet. The rope tangled. Someone screamed. And then the massive block was sliding backward, picking up speed, crushing everything in its path.

Xander threw himself aside at the last moment, rolling into a ditch as the block thundered past. When he looked up, the older farmer had vanished—erased by the stone's passage, his body so destroyed that nothing recognisable remained.

Xander lay in the ditch, his chest heaving, but his eyes were not on the gore. They were tracing the line of the snapped rope, calculating the angle of the slope. *The fulcrum was wrong,* he realised with a cold, detached clarity. *The rope didn't snap from weight; it snapped because the angle was off by three degrees. Inefficiency, rather than cruelty, wasted these lives.* He wiped the dead man's blood from his cheek, his mind already solving the equation that had just killed a man.

The overseer cursed. "Clean that up! Get another rope! We'll make the quota if it kills every one of you!"

Xander watched them scramble. He didn't move to help. Instead, his finger traced a line in the mud, dividing the weight of the stone by the number of remaining men. He frowned. *The angle is still wrong,* he calculated, watching the fresh rope being tied. *They will kill three more men before noon, and the stone will still be ten yards short.* He wiped the dead farmer's blood from his cheek and stood up. The deaths meant less to him than the mathematical offence of the waste. "Knot it higher," he muttered, grabbing the rope. "Or we'll all be soup."

OF THE BOY EMPEROR
AND HIS COURT

While nine hundred condemned labourers trudged through the mud towards Shadowmount—while a man named Corwin Harrow asked dangerous questions—the Second Iron Emperor was holding court in Steelhaven, blissfully unaware that his realm was rotting from within.

Edric the Secondborn—His Eternal Majesty, Divine Ruler of All Under Heaven, Son of the First Emperor, Bearer of the Iron Mandate—was twenty-two years old and had been emperor for slightly over a year. In that year, he had signed a thousand death warrants, approved ten thousand regulations, and personally decided exactly nothing of importance. His hand had developed a small callus from the quill, right where it pressed against his middle finger. He was oddly proud of that callus. It was the only evidence that he did anything at all.

The decisions were made for him. They were made by Mordecai the Shadowhand, who had been elevated from High Chamberlain to High Magistrate, the highest rank ever held by one of his station. They were made by Silas Ironscribe, who remained Chancellor despite his obvious discomfort with the new regime. They were made by a dozen lesser ministers and courtiers who had risen to power in the chaos of the succession, each one seeking to carve out a domain of influence, each one careful to defer to Mordecai in all things that mattered.

Edric himself was kept busy with ceremonies and rituals, with hunting expeditions and palace entertainments, with an endless parade of concubines and delicacies designed to distract him from the business of actually ruling. He was weak rather than stupid, though in a court of wolves, the distinction matters little.

Today, he sat on The Creedseat and listened as Mordecai presented the monthly reports.

"The outer provinces remain pacified, Majesty. General Jared Steelbane has suppressed the latest unrest in the conquered territories with minimal losses."

Edric nodded, though he did not know who Jared Steelbane was, or what territories were being discussed, or why it mattered. These were details for ministers to worry about.

"The construction projects proceed on schedule. The new roads will be completed by year's end. The tomb—your divine father's long resting place—has been sealed according to the sacred rites."

Another nod. Edric found the subject of his father's tomb uncomfortable. He tried not to think about what had happened in the months after the old emperor's death, about the decrees he had signed without reading, about the brother who had died by his own sword in a tent far from home.

"And the conscription levies?" Silas Ironscribe spoke from his position at the foot of the throne, his voice carefully neutral. "How do those proceed?"

Mordecai's smile did not waver. "The levies are being collected efficiently, Chancellor. The new projects require fresh labour, as you know. The great roads must be maintained. The walls must be extended. The will of the Iron Emperor must be made manifest in stone and bronze and blood."

"The people grow restless." Silas persisted, though he knew it was futile. "The harvests have been poor. The demands upon the villages—"

"Are the demands of progress, Chancellor. Would you have us return to the chaos of the old kingdoms? Would you have us abandon the great work that the First Emperor began?" Mordecai questioned. "Perhaps His Majesty desires your counsel on whether his father's legacy should be preserved."

Silas fell into silence, his only safe response.

Edric, who had been examining a particularly interesting pattern in the throne's armrest, looked up. "Are we finished? I was hoping to visit the gardens this afternoon. The new nightingales arrived from Aldoria, and I'm told their songs are quite remarkable."

"The last batch were disappointing," he added thoughtfully, picking at a loose thread on his silk robe. "One of them refused to sing for me. I had to have its neck wrung. I do hope these new ones are more... obedient."

"Of course, Majesty." Mordecai bowed deeply. "The realm can wait upon your pleasure."

The court was dismissed. The ministers scattered to their various intrigues. And in the great throne room of Steelhaven, the most powerful, fearful throne the world had ever known continued to rot from within.

OF THE SHADOWHAND'S FAMILIARS

It began as a whisper in the markets of Steelhaven: the High Magistrate had taken a lover. But the few unfortunate servants who cleaned Mordecai's private chambers knew the truth was far colder.

Mordecai had developed a fascination with the serpentine.

Perhaps he saw a kinship in them—creatures that moved without sound, struck without warning, and shed their skins to be born anew. Or perhaps it was simply that, in a court of warm-blooded mammals who sweated and panicked, only the reptiles possessed the stillness he admired.

He commissioned a new minting of the imperial currency. The old coins, bearing the profile of the First Emperor, were slowly withdrawn. In their place appeared the "Double

Serpent"—two intertwining snakes devouring each other's tails, forming an infinite loop of iron scales.

"Order," Mordecai explained to the Boy Emperor, who was busy painting a dead finch gold. "The snake does not waste energy. It does not love. It does not fear. It simply *is*. The perfect citizen."

Edric, delighted by the shiny new coins, signed the decree without reading it.

The Law of the Coiled Path was enacted the next day. It declared the white serpent to be a holy avatar of the Imperial will. To harm one was not merely poaching; it was treason. To kill one was deicide.

Across the empire, snake-catchers were executed. Farmers who found vipers in their cribs were forced to gently relocate them or face the magistrate's whip. In the capital, Mordecai kept a pit of albino cobras in his study, feeding them white mice while he dictated death warrants. He would often let the largest of them, a pale monster named *Silence*, coil around his shoulders during council meetings.

Ministers soon learned that to disagree with Mordecai was to invite *Silence* to investigate the warmth of their necks.

"See how they thrive?" Mordecai would whisper, stroking the dry, cool scales as the snake flicked its tongue at a trembling general. "They understand the nature of power. They know that the only true sin is to be warm, soft, and edible."

Thus, the snake became the symbol of the Iron Creed.

OF HIS SILENT CHOIR

Rosa, a young servant girl whose only job was to ensure the Emperor's tea never dropped below the temperature of a summer afternoon, entered the Orchid Pavilion with trembling hands. She found Edric not on his throne, but on the floor, surrounded by the new Aldorian nightingales.

The birds were not in cages. They were perched on the Emperor's silk-clad knees, unnervingly still.

"Your Majesty," Rosa whispered, kneeling. "The tea is prepared."

Edric didn't look up. He was holding a small, delicate quill, the kind used for the finest calligraphy. Beside him stood a golden bowl filled with a thick, shimmering liquid—liquid gold, kept molten by a small brazier.

"They were singing too fast, Rosa," Edric said, his voice soft and melodic, like a lullaby. "It was untidy. Up and down, up and down. It made my head ache. A song should be a line, shouldn't it? A single, perfect, golden line."

Rosa's eyes travelled to the bird in the Emperor's hand. Her breath caught in her throat.

Edric had wrung its neck only to paint it.

The nightingale was encased in a thin, hardening shell of gold. Its beak was frozen open in a permanent, silent scream. Its wings were fused to its sides, every feather preserved in a metallic tomb. It was beautiful. It was a masterpiece. And, as Rosa watched, the bird's tiny, dark eye gave one final, frantic blink before Edric carefully brushed the gold over the lid, sealing it forever.

"There," Edric sighed, leaning back with a look of pure, childlike satisfaction. "Now it will never miss a note. Now it will be obedient."

He picked up another bird—a living one that was shivering so hard its feathers rustled like dry leaves. It didn't try to fly away. It seemed to know that in this room, the only way to survive was to become a statue.

"Mordecai says the people are hungry," Edric murmured,

dipping his brush back into the gold. "But look at them, Rosa. They have so much. They have the sun, they have the rain... they even have the privilege of dying for me. Don't you think they should be more grateful? Don't you think they should be as still and pretty as my birds?"

He turned his gaze to Rosa. His wide, clear eyes held nothing recognisable as human.

"You're shaking, Rosa. Is the song too loud for you, too?"

Rosa looked at the row of golden corpses on the floor—the "Silent Choir." She realised then that the Emperor didn't see people, or birds, or empires. He saw a messy, noisy room that he intended to "fix" until everything was as silent and golden as his father's tomb.

"The tea..." she stammered, backing away. "The tea is... getting cold, Majesty."

"Let it," Edric said, turning back to his work. "Cold is just another way of staying still."

OF A BEAST OF TWO NAMES

Later that day, the doors of the Shadow Chamber were barred.

Twelve ministers stood in a semi-circle. The air smelt of incense and unwashed fear. In the centre of the room, tethered to a post of gilded iron, stood a deer. It was a small, trembling thing, its coat dappled with spots, its dark eyes wide with the frantic terror of a prey animal trapped with predators.

Mordecai the Shadowhand stroked the creature's neck with a hand that was perfectly manicured.

"Gentlemen," he said softly. "His Majesty has received a tribute from the western barbarians. A magnificent stallion, is it not? A warhorse fit for a god."

He turned to the room, his smile pleasant, his eyes dead.

"But my eyes grow dim with age. I worry I may be mistaken. I wished to consult the wisdom of the court."

Silence. It was a silence so heavy it felt like physical pressure. Everyone looked at the deer. The antlers were undeniable. The spots were undeniable.

"Lord Silas," Mordecai whispered, turning to the Chancellor. "You are the architect of our laws. You know the truth of things. Tell us… what do you see?"

Silas Ironscribe felt the sweat trickle down his spine. He looked at the deer. He looked at the antlers. He thought of the Iron Creed—*Truth is the foundation of Order*. To lie about reality was to unravel the fabric of the world.

Then he looked at Mordecai's smile.

"I see a horse, High Magistrate," Silas said, his steady voice masking the greatest lie of all. "A fine stallion. Powerful. Noble."

"Ah." Mordecai nodded, pleased. "As I thought."

He moved down the line. "And you, Lord Merrick?"

"A horse, my lord! Clearly!"

"Lord Valerius?"

"A steed of rare quality, High Magistrate."

One by one, the most powerful men in the empire looked at a small, frightened deer and dismantled their own sanity to survive. Until Mordecai reached Minister Oswin.

Oswin was old. He had served three emperors. He adjusted his spectacles, peering at the animal. He was a scholar, and scholars had a fatal flaw: they believed words meant things.

"High Magistrate," Oswin said, his voice confused. "Are you jesting? Look at the antlers. Look at the hooves. It is a deer."

The room went completely still. Even the deer seemed to freeze.

Mordecai's face filled with a terrible, tender concern. He

walked over to Oswin and placed a hand on the old man's shoulder.

"A deer?" Mordecai asked gently. "Oh, my old friend. You are unwell. The stress of the court has clouded your mind. To see a beast of the forest where a warhorse stands? This is madness."

He turned to the guards.

"Minister Oswin is suffering from delusions. He is a danger to himself. Take him to the dungeons for... treatment. We must cure him of these hallucinations before they spread."

"It is a deer!" Oswin shouted as the guards dragged him away. "It is a deer! You are all mad! It is a—"

The heavy doors slammed shut, cutting off the truth.

Mordecai turned back to the remaining ministers. He patted the deer—which was now, by imperial decree, a horse.

"Does anyone else," he asked softly, "share Minister Oswin's... vision?"

Eleven heads shook in unison.

"Good," Mordecai said. "Then let the records show that on this day, we admired a horse."

OF THE CHANCELLOR'S DESPAIR

That night, alone in his private quarters, Silas Ironscribe poured himself a cup of wine and contemplated his options.

They were not numerous.

He could flee—but where? The empire stretched in every direction, and beyond its borders lay only barbarians who would kill him on sight. He could rebel—but with what? He had no armies, no allies, no power. Minister Oswin's fate demonstrated what happened to those who spoke inconvenient truths.

Or he could continue as he had begun: complicit, compromised, calling deer horses and signing death warrants, watching the empire he had helped build descend into madness while he smiled and nodded and pretended that everything was proceeding according to plan.

His gaze fell upon the inkwell on his desk—a gift from Minister Oswin, ten years ago. It was carved from black obsidian in the shape of a crouching tiger, symbolizing vigilance. Now, Oswin was dead, killed by the very system they had served together. Silas reached out, touched the cold stone tiger, and then knocked it off the desk with a sudden, violent spasm of his hand.

It hit the floor with a dull thud. It didn't break, but a hairline fracture appeared across the middle of the tiger's body, effectively cutting the beast in two. Silas stared at the severed image, feeling a phantom pain across his own waist.

The wine was bitter. Everything was bitter now.

Silas remembered the man he had been, thirty years ago, when he had first come to Ironhold seeking a patron for his ideas. He had believed, then, in the possibility of a rational state—a government ruled by law rather than caprice, by merit rather than birth, by principle rather than privilege. He had helped create the Iron Creed because he believed that only absolute, impartial law could bring order to a world of chaos.

But law without wisdom was merely tyranny, and Silas had provided plenty of law while others had stripped away every vestige of wisdom. The Iron Creed had become a weapon wielded by monsters, and he had forged that weapon with his own hands.

He thought of Prince Caden Firstborn, dead by his own sword on a cold northern night. He thought of the death warrant he had signed, the one that had murdered an innocent man to protect Silas's own worthless life. He thought of all the other warrants, all the other deaths, all the blood that stained his hands while he pretended they were clean.

What was the point of surviving, if survival meant becoming this?

But he did not fall on his sword, as the prince had done. He did not even stop signing the warrants that crossed his desk each day. He was not that kind of man. He had never been that kind of man.

He poured another cup of wine and waited for morning, when he would resume calling deer horses and watching his world burn.

OF THE CRACKS IN
THE FOUNDATION

Throughout the empire, the consequences of Mordecai's rule manifested.

In the south, where the great Cheros once had stood, the people remembered their ancestors and whispered of freedom. They were a proud folk, these southerners, and fifteen years of imperial rule had not entirely crushed that pride. They remembered the songs their grandfathers had sung, the stories their grandmothers had told, the names of kings and heroes who had defied Ironhold's advance.

And they noticed that the current regime was weaker than its predecessor.

In the east, where Aldoria's merchants had once grown fat on trade, the economy was strangling. The endless labour conscriptions drained the villages of the young men who should have been working the fields and sailing the ships. The endless taxes drained the treasury that should have been funding commerce and investment. The endless roads and walls and tombs consumed resources that should have been building a future.

And everywhere—north and south, east and west—the people were hungry.

The harvests had been poor for two years running. Bad weather, some said. Divine punishment, others whispered. Whatever the cause, the granaries were emptying while the demands kept growing. Villages that had once produced surplus now struggled to feed themselves. Families that had once been comfortable now sold their children into service for the price of a meal.

The Iron Creed answered hunger with labour, taxes, and roads to carry the grain that wasn't being grown. The Iron Creed had an answer for every problem, and every answer made the problem worse.

In the villages, in the work camps, in the endless columns of conscripts marching towards some imperial project or another, a question circulated. It was a dangerous question, a treasonous question, a question that could get a man killed for merely thinking it too loudly.

But it circulated nonetheless, passed from mouth to ear in whispers, scratched on walls in the dark of night, implicit in the sullen silence with which the common folk regarded their masters.

The question was simple: How long?

How long before something broke? How long before the weight of tyranny became too heavy to bear? How long before someone, somewhere, decided that death in rebellion was preferable to life in slavery?

How long before the empire that had conquered the world fell apart?

The answer, unbeknownst to them, was: soon.

OF THE TALES OF IMMORTALITY

Behind the closed doors of the servants' quarters and in the dark corners of the barracks, the whispers about the High Magistrate grew more frequent and more fearful. They did not speak of his policies, but of his nature. They called him the "Silver-Veined," a man who had traded his humanity for the cold endurance of the empire itself.

The court guards whispered of a secret purge during the transition of power, when a desperate cabal of ministers had attempted to remove the Shadowhand. They had trapped Mordecai in a deep, dry well in the palace foundations, sealing the top with a ton of iron. Seven days later, when they opened it to recover his corpse, they found him standing in the dark, his robes immaculate, his eyes wide and unblinking. He had not eaten; he had not slept; he had simply *waited*.

There were stories, too, from the palace kitchens. A fire had once broken out in the Magistrate's private chambers, a blaze hot enough to melt lead. When the guards finally broke through the smoke, they found Mordecai standing in the heart of the inferno, calmly retrieving a scroll. His skin was as cool to the touch as a mountain stream, and it was said he could sit upon a block of northern ice for a day and a night without a shiver, or lie upon a blacksmith's forge in the height of summer without breaking a sweat.

The most enduring rumour, the one that made even the bravest generals cross themselves, was the prophecy of his end. The palace healers whispered that if the Shadowhand were ever truly put to the sword, his body would not yield blood, but liquid starlight. They said a single Blue Sparrow—a fragment of his metallic soul—would burst from his chest at the moment of his passing, flying straight into the clouds to watch over the ruins of the world he had built.

Mordecai did not discourage these tales of his immortality. As he walked the halls of Steelhaven, his footsteps making no sound on the marble, he enjoyed the display of fear on the faces of all. He knew that an empire forged in fear required an undying monster.

CHAPTER THREE

TWELVE WORDS

IN WHICH A PEASANT ASKS TWELVE WORDS, AND THE EMPIRE BEGINS TO CRACK

The sword breaks the bone. The question breaks the spectre he casts.
    — The Crimson Art: Third Meditation

OF CORWIN HARROW AND HIS CIRCUMSTANCES

The rain smelt of turned earth and rotting leaves.

It had been falling for three days now, a steady early winter downpour that seeped through canvas and wool and skin until a man forgot what it felt like to be dry. The field had become a quagmire. Men sat in clusters wherever they could find slightly higher ground, their feet wrapped in rags that had long since ceased to provide any protection. Someone was coughing—the deep, wet cough of a chest infection that would kill him before the northern frontier ever could. A cooking fire sputtered and died under a makeshift shelter of branches, and no one had the energy to relight it.

Late in the Second Year of The Second Iron Emperor's

reign, in this miry field northeast of the realm, beside a village called Sorrowfen, nine hundred men waited for death.

They were conscripts—farmers, labourers, the sons of farmers and labourers—summoned from their homes by imperial decree to serve at the northern frontier. They had been given two months to make the journey, a distance that would have been challenging for fresh men with roads intact and fine weather. They were not fresh men, the roads were not good, and the weather had been terrible since they left.

Now, after six weeks of marching, they were less than halfway to their destination. And the rains had come.

Corwin Harrow—the name history would remember him by—sat under a makeshift shelter and watched the water fall. He was thirty-five years old—old for a conscript, young for a corpse, with the weathered hands that spent their years working the soil. His face was featureless, his body spare, his clothing was indistinguishable from that of the hundreds of other men huddled in the rain around him.

OF TWELVE WORDS

In the final hours before his execution, Corwin sat alone in a cell that smelt of damp stone and old regret. Through the narrow window, he could see the stars turning—distant, unaccusing—ageless stars that had watched over his grandfather's farm, the same stars that would continue on their uncaring course of rotation long after his bones had turned to dust.

He had not intended to become a symbol.

The question had emerged unbidden, spoken to no one in particular, muttered half to himself on a day when the weight of his pack and the futility of his service had pressed too heavily upon his shoulders. Twelve words. A peasant's doubt, spoken aloud at the edge of endurance.

He had said it to a mule, of all things. The beast had collapsed in the mud, refusing to move, and the overseer was whipping it. Corwin had watched the animal's stubborn, silent suffering and muttered, *"Why does it take the whip when it has the strength to kick?"* And then, looking at the overseer's ornate saddle: *"Are kings born to greatness, or do they just hold the whip?"*

He had not known that his words would travel faster than any courier—carried on breath and whisper, multiplying at every telling—passing from conscript to conscript, from camp to camp, until half the empire whispered them as if praying. He had certainly not known that those twelve words would condemn him to die.

Now, in the darkness of his cell, he found himself examining the question from all angles, as a judge might examine testimony for weakness. Were kings born to greatness? The Iron Emperor had been born to power, certainly—had emerged from his mother's womb wrapped in the purple of royalty, had never known a day of hunger or doubt or common labour. Yet what greatness had that birth produced? Cruelty without purpose. An empire built on bones and maintained through terror.

And what of himself? He had been born to nothing—less than nothing, the son of farmers who were themselves the children of farmers stretching back beyond memory. His hands had known the plough before they knew the sword. By every measure that the empire recognised, he was worthless. Insignificant.

Yet here he sat, awaiting execution for the crime of speaking words that had shaken an empire.

That was the answer: Greatness is seized, not bestowed— sometimes unwillingly—by ordinary men cornered by impossible circumstances.

If so, his death would not be an ending. It would be a beginning.

When the guards came for him at dawn, Corwin rose to meet them with a stillness that passed for peace. He had lived as a peasant, had fought as a soldier, and would die as a symbol. A life he had not chosen, yet one that had claimed him.

OF HIS BOYHOOD

He had been born to a family of tenant farmers in Thornvale, a small village in the shadow of what had once been Cheros. His father had worked another man's land; his grandfather had worked another man's land; his great-grandfather had worked another man's land. The pattern seemed unending, as fixed as the turning of the seasons or the rising of the sun.

But Corwin had never accepted it.

From childhood, he had asked questions that made his elders uncomfortable. Why did some men own land while others worked it? Why did kings rule and peasants obey? Why did the gods favour the high and trample the low? His father answered such questions with the back of his hand. His teachers had scorned him; the village elders had warned him that such thinking led only to trouble.

But the questions had never stopped.

Now, watching the rain wash away his chances of survival, Corwin felt those questions crystallise into something harder and more dangerous.

The law was clear. Conscripts who failed to arrive at their posting on time were executed. The Iron Creed did not acknowledge excuses. It did not care that the roads had been washed out, that the supply wagons had broken down, that half the conscripts were sick with fever from the endless damp.

It knew only that nine hundred men had been given a deadline, and that deadline would not be met.

Death was certain; only the manner of it remained in doubt.

Corwin looked around the makeshift camp, at the miserable faces of men who had done nothing wrong except be born poor in an empire that punished poverty with death. He looked at the two overseers—minor functionaries in the imperial bureaucracy, men who had been assigned this duty as a form of punishment themselves—who sat apart from the others, arguing about what to do.

And he made a decision.

OF THE DECISION AT SORROWFEN

That night, when the rain had temporarily slowed, Corwin sought out the man who had become his closest companion on the march: Declan Sayer, a tall man with a gift for words and a history of using them to get into trouble.

"We need to talk," Corwin said.

Declan looked up from the fire he had been trying to coax back to life. "About what? Our upcoming executions? I'd rather not, if it's all the same to you."

"That's exactly what I want to talk about." Corwin sat down beside him, lowering his voice. "We're dead men either way. You know that. I know that. Everyone here knows it, even if they won't say it out loud."

"So?"

"So why die like sheep?" Corwin's eyes were bright in the firelight. "Why walk to our executions with bowed heads, accepting death thinking we deserved it? We did nothing wrong. The rains came. The roads failed. These things happen.

And yet we're supposed to submit to death because some law says that deadlines matter more than lives?"

Declan's silence stretched. "What are you suggesting?"

"If death is inevitable, let us choose the manner of it. If we're going to die anyway—and we are, make no mistake—then let's die on our feet instead of our knees. Let's die fighting instead of waiting for the axe. Let's die for something that matters."

"Such as?"

Corwin leaned closer. "There's a story my grandmother used to tell, about the old days before Ironhold conquered everything. She said that our ancestors were free men, that they chose their own leaders and lived by their own laws. She said the kings of Cheros ruled by the consent of the governed, not by the edge of the sword."

"Your grandmother's stories won't stop an imperial army."

"No. But they might start one." Corwin whispered. "Listen to me. There are nine hundred men in this camp, all of them condemned to die. What if those nine hundred men decided they'd rather die fighting? What if they took up weapons and marched not north but south—back towards the villages they came from, gathering others along the way? What if—"

He stopped. Declan was staring at him with an expression that mixed horror and fascination in equal measure.

"You're talking about rebellion."

"I'm talking about survival. A sliver of a chance, perhaps, but a chance—to live rather than die. To fight rather than submit. To be men rather than sheep." Corwin gripped Declan's arm. "Tell me I'm wrong. Tell me there's another way. Tell me the Iron Emperor will show mercy to men who failed to meet a deadline because the weather was bad."

Declan couldn't tell him any of those things, because none of them were true.

"The overseers," he said at last. "They'll never allow it."

"The overseers are two men. We are nine hundred. And they're as dead as we are if they don't deliver us on time—do you think the Iron Creed will accept their excuses any more than it will accept ours?" Corwin smiled—a cold thing, more threat than warmth. "No. The overseers will join us, or they'll die first. Either way, they won't stop us."

"And if the nine hundred refuse to follow?"

"Then I'll die trying to convince them. But I don't think they'll refuse." Corwin released Declan's arm and stood up. "I've watched these men for six weeks now. I've seen the fear in their eyes, the anger they don't dare express, the desperation that grows a little stronger every day. They're ready, Declan. They just need someone to show them the way."

"And you're that someone?"

"Maybe. Or maybe you are—you're the one with the voice, after all." Corwin looked down at his companion. "Tomorrow morning, I'm going to speak to the camp. I'm going to tell them the truth about what awaits us, and I'm going to offer them a choice. Will you stand beside me?"

Declan Sayer stared into the dying fire. He was thinking of his family, who would be punished for his treason. He was thinking of his own death, which had seemed certain anyway but now felt closer, heavier, and real. He was thinking of all he had ever been taught about the proper order of things, the righteousness of authority, the impossibility of challenging the way the world worked.

And then he thought of the rain, and the mud, and the nine hundred men who were going to die for arriving late to their own executions.

"Tomorrow morning," he said. "I'll be there."

OF THE ORDER

Dawn brought the messenger.

He rode into camp on a grey horse, his crimson sash marking him as an imperial courier. The overseers rushed to meet him, their faces pale with the hope of reprieve—the deadline had been extended, the weather had been acknowledged, mercy was still possible.

The messenger did not dismount.

"By order of the High Magistrate," he announced, his voice carrying across the silent camp, "all conscripts who fail to report to their assigned stations by the appointed date are to be executed for dereliction of duty. No exceptions. No appeals."

He reached into his satchel and produced a scroll, which he handed to the senior overseer.

"This lists the names of every man in your column. You will read it aloud, so that all may know they have been counted. Anyone who attempts to flee will be hunted. Anyone who resists will be killed immediately. Any family that shelters a fugitive will share his fate."

The overseer's hands trembled as he unrolled the scroll.

"But the rains—" one of the conscripts began.

"The Creed does not bargain with the weather." The messenger's eyes were flat, incurious—those eyes delivered such messages a hundred times and would deliver a hundred more. "The Iron Creed is absolute. You knew the law when you were conscripted. The law has not changed."

He wheeled his horse and rode away without another word.

No one moved. Then the overseer read the names—nine hundred names, spoken aloud into the morning air, each one a death sentence pronounced by a bureaucracy that would never see the faces attached to those names.

Corwin listened to his own name called. Declan listened to his. Nine hundred men listened to theirs, and with each name, the reality of what awaited them became more concrete, more inescapable.

When the reading was done, the overseer rolled up the scroll with shaking hands.

"You have three days," he said. "Then we resume the march. And when we arrive late—" He couldn't finish. He didn't need to.

Corwin looked at Declan. Declan looked back.

Now, the look said. *It has to be now.*

OF THE FOX AND THE FIRE

The night before the speech, Declan found Corwin staring at the rain. "They are desperate," Declan said. "But desperation is not enough. Desperate men run. Inspired men fight. They need to believe the heavens are watching." "The heavens don't care about us, Declan." "I know that. You know that. But *they* don't." Declan pulled a piece of silk from his pocket—a scrap painted with phosphorus and glow-worm paste. He grinned, the smile of a carnival trickster. "I'm going to plant this in the cooking pot of the First Squad. And tonight, I'll be in the woods, making noises that sound remarkably like the old spirits of Cheros crying for vengeance." Corwin frowned. "You want to trick them?" "I want to give them permission to be brave," Declan said. "Men need a sign before they can pick up a sword."

OF THE SPEECH

The rain had stopped by noon, and a weak sun struggled

through the clouds as Corwin Harrow climbed onto a wagon to address the assembled camp.

Nine hundred faces looked up at him—exhausted faces, hopeless faces, the faces of men who had accepted that they were marching towards their deaths. The two overseers watched from the edge of the crowd, their hands on their swords, uncertain whether this assembly represented defiance or merely despair.

Corwin took a deep breath and spoke.

"Brothers," he said. "We all know why we're here. We've been marching for six weeks towards the northern frontier, where we're supposed to serve the empire until the empire decides we're no longer useful. Most of us expected to die there —from the bitter cold, from enemy arrows, from the simple exhaustion of men worked beyond their limits. It's what happens to conscripts. It's what's always happened to men like us."

He paused, letting the words sink in.

"But now we have a new problem. The rains came. The roads washed out. And despite all our efforts, we're not going to make the deadline. You all know what that means. The law is clear. We're going to be executed—not for cowardice, not for desertion, not for any crime except arriving late because the weather was bad."

A murmur ran through the crowd. The overseers shifted nervously.

"I want you to think about that," Corwin continued. "Nine hundred men, condemned to death because it rained. Nine hundred families, left without fathers and sons and brothers because a deadline was more important than human lives. Call you this justice? This righteous order that the Iron Creed claims to represent? Or is this something else —something cruel, something stupid, something that treats men like tools to be discarded when they fail to perform on schedule?"

The murmur grew louder. Some men were nodding; others looked around nervously, as they expected imperial soldiers to materialise from the morning mist.

"We have a choice." Corwin raised his voice. "We can accept our fate. We can march forward with bowed heads, knowing death waits at the end of the road. We can die as the empire expects us to die—quietly, obediently, like we deserved nothing better."

He paused again, letting the silence stretch.

"Or we can choose differently."

One of the overseers started forward, his hand on his sword. "That's enough," he called. "You're inciting rebellion. You—"

He got no further. The men nearest him—conscripts who had been carrying fear and anger for weeks—grabbed his arms and held him in place. The second overseer looked around, saw the mood of the crowd, and wisely decided not to intervene.

Corwin raised his voice above the commotion. "Listen to me! We are nine hundred men—nine hundred desperate men with nothing left to lose. That is not weakness. That is strength! The strong man is the one who has something to protect; the strongest man is the one who has nothing to fear."

"Look at the mathematics of the Iron Creed!" Corwin shouted. "If we go North and arrive late, the penalty is death. If we run away and are caught, the penalty is death. If we rebel, the penalty is death." He paused, looking into their eyes. "The price is the same. But only one choice offers a chance to live. If we are to pay the price of death, let us at least buy our freedom with it!"

He pointed south, towards the villages they had left behind.

"Out there, in every town and farm and work camp, there are men just like us. Men who have been worked to death, taxed to starvation, treated like animals by an empire that sees us as nothing more than fuel for its endless projects. Men who are waiting—whether they know it or not—for someone to show them that it doesn't have to be this way."

Corwin drew himself up to his full height.

"I say we become that someone. I say we march south, not north. I say we gather the broken and the hopeless, the hungry and the angry, all the men who have been told that they are nothing and who are ready to prove otherwise. I say we tear down this rotten empire and build something better in its place—something that remembers that kings and lords are not born to greatness."

He paused, and when he spoke again, his voice carried the weight of centuries of suppression, the accumulated fury of every peasant who had ever bowed his head and accepted injustice.

"Are kings and lords born to greatness? Or do they seize it?"

[A Note from the Compiler: The exact wording of Corwin's question has been disputed by scholars for centuries. The version preserved here comes from the Valdria Chronicles, commissioned by Emperor Valdric himself—hardly an unbiased source. Fragments of earlier accounts, discovered in the ruins of the Greymantle Library, suggest the original phrasing may have been considerably more inflammatory. One such fragment reads: "Why should we die for men who would not lift a cup for us?"]

Silence. Nine hundred men who had never been asked anything before.

Then Declan Sayer stepped forward. "They seize it!" he shouted. "And so can we!"

The dam broke. Nine hundred voices rose in a roar that scattered birds from the nearby trees, shook the very earth beneath their feet. Men who had been slumped in defeat straightened their backs and raised their fists.

But the two overseers did not join the cheering.

The senior overseer—a thin man named Septimus who had been assigned this duty as punishment for some minor bureaucratic failure—drew his sword. His hand was shaking, but his voice was steady.

"This is treason," he said. "Every man here will be executed. Your families will be executed. Your villages will be destroyed by fire. The Iron Creed does not forgive rebellion."

Corwin stepped down from the wagon and walked towards him. He did not hurry. He did not threaten. He simply walked, and the crowd parted before him like water before a stone.

"The Iron Creed," Corwin said, stopping three paces from the overseer, "has already condemned us to death. We have nothing left to lose." He looked at the sword in Septimus's hand. "You have two choices. Join us, and share whatever fate awaits. Or try to stop us."

He gestured at the nine hundred men surrounding them.

"There are two of you. There are nine hundred of us. You are good men—I've watched you these past weeks, and I know you hate this duty as much as we hate suffering it. The empire made you our jailers, but you don't have to die as our enemies."

Septimus's sword wavered. His companion, a younger lad, who had never spoken above a whisper in Corwin's presence, stepped forward and laid down his blade.

"I was a farmer too," the younger overseer said. "Before they conscripted me to conscript others. I don't want to die for the Iron Creed."

Septimus looked at his colleague, at the crowd, at the sword in his own hand. Something broke behind his eyes—the last thread of loyalty to an empire that had never shown him loyalty in return.

The sword fell into the mud.

"What do you need us to do?" he asked.

OF THE OATH

That night, by firelight, they forged themselves into something new.

Corwin had no ceremony prepared—he was a farmer, not a priest. But Declan Sayer did. Before the conscription, he had been a travelling storyteller, a keeper of the old songs and older traditions. He knew the words that had been spoken when the Old Kings of Cheros bound their warriors together.

"Kneel," he told the assembled men. "All of you. Even you, Corwin."

Nine hundred men knelt in the mud. The overseers knelt with them.

The mud was cold. Some men were shaking—from the chill, yes, but also from the terror of what they were doing. To kneel not in submission, but in defiance, felt unnatural. It went against every instinct bred into them by generations of fear.

"Repeat after me," Declan said. His voice carried the cadence of ritual, the weight of centuries. "I am no longer a conscript of the Iron Empire."

Nine hundred voices echoed him.

"I am no longer a tool to be used and discarded."

The words spread through the crowd like fire.

"I am a free man. I choose my own fate. I stand with my brothers against tyranny, and I will not bend my knee to any power that demands my death for the crime of being born."

The final words rang out across the night.

Then Corwin rose. He looked at the men around him—still

muddy, still ragged, still bearing the marks of weeks of suffering. But something had changed in their eyes. They were no longer victims. They were no longer walking towards their deaths.

They were an army.

"Tomorrow," Corwin said, "we take the first town. We take their weapons. We take their food. And we send a message to every conscript, every labourer, every man who has been told his life is worthless: you are not alone. We are coming."

The cheer that rose was not loud—they were still too few for that. But it was fierce. It was the sound of men who had discovered something more valuable than hope.

They had discovered rage.

In a muddy field beside an obscure village, the rebellion that would bring down the Iron Empire was born.

OF THE FIRST BLOOD

The imperial messenger arrived at dusk.

He was young—barely twenty, with the soft hands of someone who had never done a day's real labour. He rode a fine horse and wore the crimson sash of the courier corps. He carried, in the satchel at his hip, dispatches that would alert the provincial garrison to the presence of nine hundred missing conscripts.

He also carried, though he did not know it, the fate of an empire.

Corwin saw him first. The messenger had stopped at a stream to water his horse, a quarter-mile from where the conscripts had made their camp. In an hour, maybe less, he would reach the garrison. In two hours, soldiers would be mobilised. By morning, the rebellion—if it could even be called that—would be over before it began.

"We have to stop him," Declan said, appearing at Corwin's shoulder.

"I know."

"If we let him go—"

"I *know*."

Corwin looked at the axe in his hand. It was a woodcutter's tool, not a weapon—dull-edged, heavy, clumsy. But it would serve.

"Stay here," he told Declan. "If I don't come back, scatter. Go home. Pretend none of this ever happened."

"Corwin—"

But Corwin was already walking towards the stream.

The messenger looked up as he approached. His face showed confusion first—what was a peasant doing out here, alone, armed with a woodcutter's axe? Then suspicion. Then, as Corwin kept walking and the distance closed, fear.

"Halt," the messenger said. His hand moved towards the short sword at his belt. "In the name of the emperor, I command you to—"

Corwin swung.

The sound was nothing like the songs described. The messenger made a noise—not a scream, a surprised grunt— and fell.

He was still alive. His eyes were wide, confused, accusing. Blood spread beneath him, mixing with the stream water, turning it pink.

"I'm sorry," Corwin whispered. And he was. The blood of the messenger mixed with the mud, indistinguishable from the rain. The first drop of a flood.This boy had done nothing wrong. He had simply been born into a uniform, trained to serve, dispatched on an errand that would have meant nothing if the world had been different.

But the world was not different. And this boy's survival

meant the death of nine hundred men who had committed no crime except being late.

Corwin swung again.

When he walked back to the camp, his hands were shaking and his axe was red. The men looked at him with new eyes—eyes that held horror and hope in equal measure.

"It's done," he said. "The path behind is closed."

Declan nodded slowly. "Then we go forward."

"Yes." Corwin looked at the axe, at the blood drying on its blade, at the men who had just become rebels. "We go forward."

That night, they burnt the messenger's body and buried his dispatches. And Corwin never forgot the boy's face. In his dreams, for as long as he lived, the messenger was always there—young, confused, dying in a stream that ran red with the first blood of revolution.

Some prices, once paid, can never be recovered.

OF THE FIRST TOWN

What happened next would become legend.

The conscripts had no weapons except for farming tools and the overseers' swords. They had no training except what they had learned from endless labour. They had no strategy except desperation and the peculiar genius of a man who had spent his life asking uncomfortable questions.

It should not have been enough. Against the disciplined armies of Ironhold, against the iron-hard veterans who had conquered the world, nine hundred untrained peasants should have been swept away like leaves before a storm.

But the storm was on their side.

The first town they approached—a small market village called Fairmeadow—surrendered without a fight. The local garrison consisted of three elderly guards who had been assigned there precisely because no one expected any trouble. They took one look at the mob descending upon them, calculated their odds, and opened the gates.

Word spread. By the time Corwin's force reached the next town, volunteers were already waiting to join them. Farmers and labourers, merchants and artisans, anyone who had suffered under the Iron Creed and seen an opportunity for revenge—they came in dozens, then hundreds, then thousands.

Within a week, the ragged band had become an army of ten thousand.

Within two weeks, it had captured three cities and defeated two hastily assembled imperial response forces.

OF AN IMPOSSIBLE VICTORY

The fortress at Irongate should have stopped them.

It sat atop a granite bluff, commanding the only passable road through the eastern mountains. Its walls were thirty feet high and ten feet thick. Its garrison numbered five hundred professional soldiers—veterans of the border campaigns, trained killers who had spent their lives learning the art of holding fortified positions. The fortress had never been taken in four hundred years of recorded history.

Corwin's army, now swelled to fifteen thousand, arrived at its base in the second week of the rebellion. They looked up at those grey walls, at the crossbows glinting on the battlements, at the imperial banners snapping in the wind, and many of them felt their courage failing.

"We can't take that," a former farmer muttered, standing beside Corwin. "We'd lose half our men just reaching the gates."

"You're right," Corwin said. "We can't take it by force."

"Then what do we do? Go around?"

"There is no around. The mountains are impassable this time of year." Corwin studied the fortress, his mind working through possibilities. "We need them to open the gates themselves."

"They're not going to surrender to a peasant army."

"They will not." Corwin smiled—a bleak expression that his followers were beginning to recognise. "So we'll give them something else to think about."

The plan was simple, in the way that desperate plans often are. Corwin sent three hundred men—volunteers who knew they might not return—to climb the cliffs to the fortress's west, where the walls were thinnest because the terrain was considered impassable. They went at night, in silence, carrying torches wrapped in oiled cloth.

Their mission was not to breach the walls. Their mission was to set fires.

At dawn, smoke began rising from inside the fortress. But the garrison commander, a cautious man named Captain Voren, sent a squad to investigate.

They found the granary burning.

The soldiers rushed to extinguish it, pulling men from the walls, breaking discipline in their haste to save the food stores that would keep them alive through a siege.

That was when Corwin attacked.

Instead, his main force struck at the small postern door on the fortress's eastern face, the one used for supply deliveries, the one that was now guarded by only a skeleton crew because everyone else was fighting fires.

Corwin had dressed Septimus in his overseer's uniform, bloodied and torn. Septimus pounded on the postern door, screaming that the rebels were attacking the main gate and he needed to secure the supplies. The guards, confused by the smoke and the chaos, saw an imperial uniform and opened the door without thinking. It was the uniform that beat them, not the sword.

The door fell in the time it takes to boil a pot of millet.

By the time Captain Voren realised what had happened, peasants were swarming through his corridors. The fortress's defensive positions, designed to repel attacks from outside, were useless against an enemy already inside the walls. What should have been an impregnable position became a slaughterhouse.

Three hundred imperial soldiers died that morning. Corwin's forces lost fewer than fifty.

When the sun was fully risen, Corwin stood on the battlements of Irongate, looking out at the road his army could now travel freely. Behind him, his men were cheering, celebrating, beginning to believe that they could, actually win.

"How did you know?" Declan asked, appearing beside him. "How did you know the fire would draw them away from the postern?"

"I didn't know," Corwin admitted. "I guessed. I asked myself: what would I do, if I were the commander? If my stores were burning, wouldn't I save them first? Wouldn't everyone?" He shrugged. "Soldiers are trained to follow orders. They're not trained to question whether the orders make sense. So I gave them a situation where following their training would destroy them."

"And if you'd been wrong?"

"Then we'd all be dead, and the empire would be nailing our bodies to posts as a warning," said Corwin. "But I wasn't wrong. And now every garrison in the province knows that Irongate has fallen. They'll be asking themselves: if that fortress couldn't hold, what chance do we have?"

"Fear," Declan said. "You're not just winning battles. You're winning the war before it starts."

"The Iron Emperor conquered the world with fear. I'm just using his own weapon against him." Corwin turned away from the view, suddenly tired. "Though I wonder sometimes if that makes me better than him, or just more of the same."

He did not wait for an answer.

That night, messengers rode in all directions, carrying news of the impossible victory. The rebellion had found its myth. The empire had found its nightmare.

And in the capital, when word finally reached the court, Mordecai, the Shadowhand read the dispatch with hands that —for the first time in his carefully controlled life—were trembling.

OF THE EMPIRE'S RESPONSE

The retaliation, when it came, was not war. It was punishment.

Mordecai the Shadowhand did not believe a peasant riot warranted the attention of the Imperial Legions. Instead, he dispatched Tarkus Ironhand, the Butcher, a man whose rank was not General, but *High Enforcer*. Tarkus was not a strategist; he was a blunt instrument designed to break things that refused to bend.

He was given five thousand provincial guards and instructions that left no room for interpretation: "Remind them of the hierarchy."

Tarkus understood. The first village he reached was Gallows-Cross...

General Tarkus Ironhand, the Butcher—a name whispered with fear in every province of the realm—received his orders directly from Mordecai. He was given twenty thousand soldiers, the finest the empire could muster, and instructions that left no room for interpretation.

"Crush them," Mordecai had written. "And make certain that no one ever forgets the cost of rebellion."

Tarkus understood. He had built his career on such understanding.

The first village he reached was called Gallows-Cross. It had committed the crime of feeding the rebel army—providing grain and shelter when Corwin's forces passed through two weeks earlier. The villagers had not had a choice; armed men had demanded supplies, and unarmed farmers had provided them. But choice, in the empire's calculus, was irrelevant.

What mattered was example.

Tarkus assembled the entire village—three hundred men, women, and children—in the central square. He read the charges aloud: treason against The Creedseat, material support for enemies of the state, failure to report the presence of rebel forces. The punishment for each charge was death.

"But I am merciful," Tarkus announced, his voice carrying across the square. "I will not kill you all. I will kill only enough to ensure that no other village makes the same mistake."

He selected one family in ten. Sixty-three people, chosen at random—though in truth, his officers had identified those who seemed most beloved, most central to the community's fabric. A grandmother known for her healing herbs. A young father whose laugh could be heard across the fields. A girl of seven who everyone called "Little Bird" because of how she sang.

They were nailed to the doors of their own homes.

The crucifixions took three hours. Tarkus made the remaining villagers watch, made them listen to the screaming, made them understand exactly what the empire was willing to do to those who defied it.

"You may bury them at sunset," he said, when the last nail had been driven. "And you may thank the emperor's mercy that you are alive to do so. But know this: the next village that aids the rebels will not receive such generosity. There will be no survivors. There will be no graves. There will only be ash."

He rode away, leaving behind two hundred and thirty-seven people who would never again hear birdsong without remembering their daughter's screams.

Word of Gallows-Cross spread faster than Corwin's victories ever had. It spread through the countryside like plague, carried by refugees and survivors, whispered in taverns and sobbed in temples. Every village in the province heard what had happened. Every farmer understood what resistance would cost.

Tarkus expected the rebellion to collapse. He expected the peasants to abandon their hopeless cause, to crawl back to their fields, to accept that the empire was Everlasting and its punishment was absolute.

He was wrong.

Because the farmers did not look at the ruins of Gallows-Cross and think: *We must surrender.* They looked at the ash and thought: *We are dead men anyway. Let us take them with us.*

Tarkus Ironhand had meant to act as a firebreak. Instead, he had poured oil on the flames. Within a month, his five thousand guards were swarmed, isolated, and hacked to pieces by mob of forty thousand angry souls. Tarkus's head was sent back to the capital in a pickle jar.

The "riot" was over. The War had begun.

The empire had meant to terrorise them into submission. Instead, it had taught them that submission and resistance carried the same price. The same nails. The same screams. The same ash.

If you are going to die either way, you might as well die fighting.

In the week after Gallows-Cross, Corwin's army doubled in size. And for the first time, the men who joined him were not desperate or hopeful.

They were angry.

Within a month, it had declared itself the restoration of the old Cheros kingdom, with Corwin Harrow as its king.

The title embarrassed him, though he accepted it out of practical necessity. An army needed a leader, and leaders needed titles—it was the way of the world, even a world being remade. But he never forgot the question that had started it all, and he made sure his followers never forgot either.

Kings and lords were not born to greatness. They seized it. And if they failed to govern wisely, the people who had raised them up could pull them down just as easily.

It was a revolutionary idea. It did not need to spread—it simply appeared, the way fire appears when the conditions are right, in a thousand hearts at once.

OF THE UNLEASHING

In the imperial capital, the head pickled in brine sat on Mordecai, the Shadowhand's desk.

The audience chamber was silent. The High Enforcer was dead. The rebel army—now calling itself the *Kingdom of the Rising Sun*—was marching unchecked. They had taken three major cities. The provincial garrisons were melting away.

"The Northern Legion is too far away," Silas Ironscribe said, his voice dry as dust. "It will take them three months to return. By then, the rebels will be at our gates."

Mordecai looked at the map. He looked at the jar. For the first time in fifteen years, the Shadowhand looked cornered.

"We do not need the Northern Legion," Mordecai said softly. "We have a flood of condemned men right here. At Shadowmount."

Silas froze. "The tomb builders? They are slaves. Criminals. Conscripts. They hate us more than the rebels do. If you arm them, they will turn on us."

"Not if they are led by a man they fear more than death."

Mordecai reached for a seal he had not touched since the Iron Emperor died. It was a seal of black iron, kept in a box bound with chains.

"Summon him," Mordecai ordered.

"High Magistrate," Silas whispered, "Jared Steelbane has been in the dungeons for two years. The Old Emperor locked him away because he was too dangerous to be left free in peacetime. He is a monster of the old wars. If you let him out..."

"Then we unleash the monster," Mordecai snapped. "Give him the pardon. Give him the weapons from the armoury. Tell him that if he defeats these rebels, his three hundred thousand criminal slaves will be free men. Tell him... tell him the Wolf is unchained."

OF THE LAST IRON GENERAL

Deep beneath the Courts of Justice, in a cell where no light had penetrated for seven hundred days, a man sat in the dark.

He was not large, not like the brute Butcher Tarkus. He was lean, compact, vibrating with a coiled, kinetic energy. He was General Jared Steelbane, the Last Iron General, the man who had conquered the Southern Kingdoms for the First Emperor before being discarded like a dull blade.

The door creaked open. Torchlight spilt into the cell, revealing a man who sat perfectly still, sharpening a piece of bone against the stone floor.

"General," the messenger stammered. "The Empire has need of you."

Jared Steelbane stopped sharpening. He looked up. His eyes were not human eyes; they were the flat, dead grey of a winter sky before a blizzard.

"The Empire," Steelbane rasped, his voice unused to speech, "has finally realised that laws do not stop swords."

He stood up. The chains on his wrists rattled, a sound that would soon echo across a hundred battlefields.

"Take me to the armoury," the Last General said. "And bring me my army of thieves and murderers. I have work to do."

The Rebellion of Corwin Harrow had found its myth. Now, it had found its executioner.

OF MONTAG'S END

The path to the armoury led past the Black Cells—the deepest pits of the capital, reserved for those whose crimes were not against the law, but against the Shadowhand.

As Jared Steelbane walked, the chains on his wrists now removed, he stopped.

Through the bars of Cell Four, a pair of eyes watched him. They were the only things visible in a face that had been ruined by weeks of "questioning." The man inside had no fingernails left. His uniform was rags. But he stood upright, holding the bars with a grip that still possessed a memory of strength.

It was General Montag. The man who had commanded the Northern Legion. The man who had stood beside Prince Caden when the Prince fell on his sword.

"The butcher walks free," Montag rasped. His voice was like grinding stones. "While the faithful rot."

Steelbane signalled for the guards to hold back. He stepped closer to the bars. He did not mock the prisoner. In the hierarchy of the Iron Creed, they were equals once.

"I go to save the Empire, Montag. The peasants are burning the south."

"The Empire?" Montag laughed, and blood bubbled on his lips. "There is no Empire, Jared. Only a corpse, and the maggots feasting on it. You know who sits on the throne. You know who killed the Prince."

"I serve the Realm," Steelbane said, his face a mask of cold iron. "I do not ask who sits on the chair. I only ask where the enemies are."

"And that is why you are lost." Montag leaned forward, the smell of gangrene and holiness drifting from his cell. "You think you are their saviour? No. Look at me, Jared. Look at your future."

"I am not you, Montag. I will win."

"You are not a General to them," Montag whispered. The prophecy hung in the damp air, heavier than any chain. "You are a knife. Nothing more. And when you are dull, when you have cut enough throats that your edge is gone... they will cast you into the fire, just like me."

Steelbane stood silent for a long moment. He looked at the broken man who had chosen honour over survival. He felt the phantom weight of the pardon in his pocket—a piece of paper that could be torn up as easily as it was signed.

"Goodbye, Montag," Steelbane said finally.

"Die well, Steelbane," Montag replied. "I will wait for you in the dark. It won't be long."

Steelbane turned and walked away. He did not look back. He marched towards the light of the armoury, towards his army of slaves, towards the war that would make him a legend.

But as he walked, he could feel it. A small, cold splinter of doubt, lodged deep in his chest, right where a knife would go.

THE WIDOW'S BANNER

In a village too small to have a name, a widow sat sewing by candlelight.

Her husband had died in the conscription three years ago—not in battle, but of fever in the work camps, building a wall that would never be finished for an emperor who was already dead. She had received the news in a terse official letter, delivered by a clerk who could not pronounce her husband's name correctly and did not care to learn.

Now she was sewing a banner.

It was crimson cloth—stolen from a merchant's cart that had overturned on the road, the merchant too dead from arrow wounds to object. The silk was worth more than everything she owned. She was cutting it into the shape of a rising phoenix, the symbol that the rebel king Corwin had adopted, the symbol that meant *the old ways are ending*.

Her needle moved in the darkness. In, out. In, out. Blood from a pricked finger stained the edge of the banner, and she did not stop to wipe it away.

She did not know Corwin Harrow. She would never meet him—he would be dead within the month, betrayed by a man whose name she would never learn. She did not understand the politics of rebellion, the strategies of war, the calculations of power that drove men to raise armies and burn cities.

She only knew that her husband was dead, and that the empire had killed him, and that somewhere out there, someone was finally fighting back.

The banner would never fly in battle. Imperial soldiers would find it during a routine search, and they would burn her cottage with her inside it. Her name would not be recorded in any history. Her story would vanish like smoke.

But her needle kept moving. In, out. In, out. Stitch by patient stitch, building something that mattered.

Because that was what the powerless did, when the powerful failed them.

They kept working in the dark, and they hoped, and they died hoping.

And sometimes—their hope outlived them.

OF THE IRON MACHINE

Those who remember only the end forget how terrifying the beginning had been. The Iron Emperor's armies mobilised to punish those who rebelled. Custers of iron troops moved like components of a single vast engine—each legion a gear, each supply line a belt, each garrison a cog that turned precisely when commanded. The roads they built were arteries through which punishment flowed. A rebellion in the eastern provinces could be crushed within weeks because the legions needed no time to deliberate, no councils to convene, no debates to resolve. The order came from Steelhaven, and the machine responded.

The law of the Iron Creed was equally mechanical. A man who failed to pay his taxes was not tried by judges who might show mercy; he was processed by clerks who could not. His name entered a ledger; the ledger triggered a requisition; the requisition summoned soldiers; the soldiers took him to the labour camps where three hundred thousand men had already died building the First Emperor's tomb. The system did not hate him. The system did not know him. The system simply processed him, as it processed everything, with the impersonal efficiency of a mill grinding grain.

This was the genius of the Iron Creed: it removed human judgement from the exercise of power. No official could be bribed, because no official had discretion. No general could rebel, because no general controlled his own supply lines. No governor could show mercy, because the law permitted none. The machine ran itself, and the Emperor merely wound the key.

When the machine began to fail—when the corruption at the centre spread outward, when the gears began to slip and the belts began to fray—the collapse was catastrophic precisely because no one knew how to repair what no one fully understood. The Emperor was dead; the Shadowhand was scheming; the generals were fighting among themselves; and the machine, designed to run without human intervention, could not adapt to conditions its creators had never anticipated.

The Iron Machine, built to crush stone, found itself helpless against fire. And fire, as Corwin Harrow knew, spreads best when the wind is against it.

CHAPTER FOUR

THE WASTREL OF MARSH

IN WHICH A DRUNKEN VILLAGE HEADMAN BECOMES A REBEL LORD, AND THE OTHER PROTAGONIST OF OUR TALE EMERGES FROM OBSCURITY

The world heals its scars. What remains are the weeds that outlived the oaks.
— *The Annals of House Valdria*

OF MAREN ASHFORD AND HIS ORIGINS

Maren Ashford, who would found a dynasty that lasted four hundred years was, by all accounts, an unlikely candidate for greatness.

He was just Maren—a man whose identity began and ended with his name, unburdened by the shadow of a great family. He had been born in a small village called Marsh, in a district so insignificant that imperial maps barely acknowledged its existence. His father had been a farmer; his grandfather had been a farmer; his great-grandfather had been a farmer. The pattern seemed destined to continue forever.

His hands told the story. They were a peasant's hands—broad and calloused, the nails broken, the knuckles scarred from a hundred small injuries. Soil was ground into the creases of his palms so deeply that no amount of washing could remove it. They had been born to work the earth and die forgotten.

But Maren had never been much good at farming.

Lazy, his father called him. Irresponsible, his mother agreed. He spent his days drinking in the village tavern instead of working the fields, gambling with money he didn't have, chasing women who were already married, and generally making a nuisance of himself to everyone who knew him. By the time he was thirty, he had acquired a reputation as the village's most dedicated wastrel—the wasted one who would never amount to anything, who would die as he had lived, in comfortable obscurity.

And yet.

Maren drew people to him, despite his faults. He was generous—absurdly generous, giving away money he couldn't afford to lose, buying drinks for strangers, helping neighbours he barely knew. He was fearless—not brave in the heroic sense, but utterly heartless to consequences, willing to say things and do things that more cautious men would never dare. He was funny, in a crude, self-deprecating way that made even his critics laugh despite themselves.

And beneath the drinking and the gambling and the womanizing, there was a sharp intelligence that surprised anyone who bothered to look for it. He could read people with uncanny accuracy, sensing their strengths and weaknesses, knowing exactly what to say to win their loyalty or exploit their fears. He had a gift for delegation—for finding capable people and putting them in positions where their talents could flourish. He understood, in some instinctive way, that leadership was not about being the best at everything but about surrounding yourself with people who were.

These were not the qualities of a farmer. They were, though no one knew it yet, the qualities of an emperor.

OF THE LABOURERS' ESCAPE

The rebellion found Maren in characteristic fashion: by accident.

He had been assigned, in his capacity as the village's minor headman—a position he had acquired through a combination of bribery and default—to escort a group of conscript labourers to a work site in the west. It was precisely the sort of tedious, thankless task that he usually found ways to avoid, but this time his excuses had failed him, and he had no choice but to lead the wretched column of farmers and prisoners towards their destination.

Halfway there, he decided he'd had enough.

"This is ridiculous," he announced to his second-in-command, a solid, reliable man named Markus Quillen—the kind of officer who never raised his voice and never lost a wagon. Markus kept lists in his head the way other men kept prayers: rations, boots, horses, bolts of cloth, names of the sick. He had been trained as a militia youth before the examinations stole him into ink and law, and he carried both disciplines with the same quiet severity.

"We're not going to make it in time. The rains have ruined the roads, half the men are sick, and even if we arrive, we'll probably just be executed for being late. I say we cut our losses."

Markus looked at him with the patient expression, he isn't surprised by anything his commander said. "Cut our losses how?"

"We let them go. The labourers, I mean. We tell them to scatter, find their way home, disappear into the countryside.

The empire will assume bandits got them, or disease, or any of a dozen other misfortunes. No one will ever know."

"And what about us?"

Maren shrugged. "We disappear too. Find somewhere to hide until this whole thing blows over. I hear the southern marshes are nice this time of year—plenty of fish, plenty of wine, and no imperial inspectors asking uncomfortable questions."

It was a mad plan, casually treasonous, meriting immediate execution. But Markus Quillen, who was neither mad nor casual, found himself nodding along. A quality about Maren—some quality of magnetic certainty—that made even his most outrageous proposals seem reasonable.

The labourers were released. Most of them fled, vanishing into the countryside to take their chances with bandits and starvation rather than face the certainty of imperial punishment. But some of them stayed. They looked at this unlikely headman, this drunken village nobody who had just risked his own life to save theirs, and they saw something worth following.

"If you're going to hide in the marshes," one of them said, "you'll need men to watch your back."

Maren looked at the ragged band that had gathered around him—farmers and labourers, the lowest of the low, men who had nothing to lose because they had never had anything to begin with—and felt the first stirrings of something he had never expected to feel.

Ambition.

But beneath the ambition, stirring in the depths he rarely examined, was something else. Something older and more painful.

His mother had died when he was eleven, worn to nothing by the endless labour of peasant life. His father had followed two winters later, having drunk himself into an early grave. There had been no one to mourn them properly, no one to tend their memories. Just Maren, alone at thirteen, learning that the world did not care whether he lived or died.

He had responded to that lesson in the only way he knew how: by refusing to care about anything himself. He drank because feeling nothing was better than feeling the vast emptiness that threatened to swallow him. He joked because laughter kept the darkness at bay. He collected followers because if enough people needed him, he might begin to matter.

It was not heroism that drove Maren Ashford. It was the desperate hunger of a nobody in his entire life, who had been told by every authority that his life was worthless, who had finally glimpsed a chance to prove them all wrong.

OF TOMORROW

In the depths of the night, when the camp was quiet and even his guards dozed at their posts, Maren Ashford allowed himself to remember who he had been.

A farmer's son, whose greatest ambition, once, had been to own his own plot of land—a few acres more than his father had tilled, a slightly larger house, a wife who smiled when she saw him coming home from the fields. Simple dreams. Peasant dreams. The kind of dreams that noblemen would have laughed at, had they deigned to notice peasants at all.

Now he commanded armies. Now lords knelt before him and called him their leader. Now the fate of the realm hung upon his decisions, and every choice he made impacted generations yet unborn.

He had not asked for this.

That was what the histories would never record—that

Maren Ashford had never wanted power. He had wanted only to survive. To protect his family. To carve out some small space of safety in a world that seemed determined to crush everyone who lacked the protection of noble blood.

But survival, he had learned, was not a static thing. To survive, you had to grow stronger. To grow stronger, you had to take power from those who held it. And once you had taken enough power, you found that you could not simply stop—that the momentum of your rise carried you forward whether you willed it or not.

Now here he sat, on the eve of a battle that would determine everything, and he found himself wondering: at what point had he crossed the line from survivor to conqueror? At what point had his defensive measures become aggressive ones? At what point had one wanted only to protect his family become one who ordered other families destroyed?

He did not know. There had been no single moment—it had been a gradual process, an erosion of principles so slow that he had not noticed until the principles were gone entirely.

What he knew was this: he could not go back. The path he had walked could only be walked forward. The men who followed him had staked their lives on his victory, and he owed them that victory regardless of his personal doubts.

Tomorrow, he would fight. Tomorrow, he would kill, or order killing. Tomorrow, he would take another step towards the throne that he had never wanted but could no longer refuse.

And in the quiet hours before dawn, Maren Ashford allowed himself to grieve—not for the men who would die, though that grief would come later, but for the simple farmer's son he had once been, whose innocent dreams had been consumed by the fire of history.

He would make himself matter, even if he had to tear down an empire to do it.

THE TAX COLLECTOR'S HORSE

A Vignette of Maren Ashford

The imperial tax collector arrived in Marsh on a fine autumn morning, riding a horse worth more than any three houses in the village combined.

His name was Inspector Warren, and he had come to collect the The Tithe of Scraps—a new tax invented by some bureaucrat in the capital who had never planted a seed in his life. The levy would take a third of the village's stored grain. Without it, half the people would starve before spring.

The village elders had gathered to plead for mercy. They had brought their accounts, their records, their carefully documented proof that the village could not possibly pay what was demanded. They had rehearsed their arguments, polished their bows, prepared their most abject expressions of loyal submission.

Maren Ashford was not among them. He was drinking in the tavern.

But when Inspector Warren emerged from the meeting— smugly satisfied, the elders' pleas having made no more impression than raindrops on stone—he found his horse missing.

Chaos erupted. Soldiers searched. Threats were made. The village headman—an elderly man named Colm who had held the position for forty years—was dragged forward and told that if the horse was not returned within the hour, he would be executed for theft.

Maren appeared ten minutes later, leading the horse by its reins.

"Found him wandering by the river," he announced cheerfully. "Poor creature must have gotten loose. You really should tie better knots, Inspector."

The horse's sudden wanderlust deceived no one. But proving it was another matter, and Inspector Warren was too relieved to press the issue. He snatched the reins, mounted hastily, and rode away—unaware that Maren had planted something in his saddlebag.

A week later, word came from the capital. Inspector Warren had been arrested. Among his possessions, searchers had discovered detailed plans for a smuggling operation—plans that implicated him in the theft of imperial goods across three provinces. The documents were crude forgeries, but no one bothered to question them in time. Warren was already dead, executed for crimes he had never committed.

The supplementary harvest levy was quietly canceled. The bureaucrat who had invented it was reassigned to a post in the frozen north. And the village of Marsh kept its grain.

"How did you know?" Markus Quillen asked, when the dust had settled. "How did you know they would believe the forgeries?"

"I didn't know. I just knew that men who look for guilt usually find it, especially when you make it easy for them." Maren took a long drink of wine. "Besides, Warren was skimming from his collections. I'd heard rumours for months. So the forgeries weren't entirely forged—they just exaggerated what was already true."

"You could have been caught. You could have been killed."

"I could have sat back and watched half the village starve." Maren's smile faded. "Some risks are worth taking, Markus. Some fights are worth losing. And some horses are worth stealing—because they're already paid for in blood."

The village of Marsh never forgot what Maren had done for

them. And when, years later, he returned with an army at his back, they remembered that he had saved them with a stolen horse and a clever lie.

OF THE BAND OF BROTHERS

Word travels fast in troubled times, and the story of the wastrel who had defied the supremacy spread through the countryside like wildfire.

More men came to join him—outlaws and deserters, escaped conscripts and disgraced soldiers, anyone who had fallen afoul of the Iron Creed and needed somewhere to hide. Maren welcomed them all, asking no questions about their pasts, judging them only by their usefulness in the present. His band grew from dozens to hundreds, then from hundreds to thousands, until he commanded a small army of desperate men united only by their loyalty to him.

They were not an impressive force, by any conventional measure. They had no training, no discipline, no proper weapons. They ate what they could steal or forage. They slept in caves and abandoned farmhouses. They looked, and often smelt, like the bandits they were frequently mistaken for.

But they had something that more formidable armies often lacked: they believed in their leader.

Maren had a gift for making men feel valued. He remembered their names, asked about their families, shared their hardships without complaint. He promoted based on ability rather than background, elevating former slaves and petty criminals to positions of responsibility while sidelining those who failed to perform regardless of their origins. He was never too proud to take advice, never too stubborn to change his mind, never too arrogant to admit his mistakes.

And he was lucky. Incredibly, impossibly lucky, in a way

that made even his followers wonder if some higher power was watching over him. He stumbled into victories he had no right to win. He escaped traps that should have been certain death. He made decisions on impulse that turned out, in retrospect, to be exactly right.

"The gods love fools and drunkards," he would say, when questioned about his success. "And since I'm both, I'm doubly blessed."

It was a joke, but like many jokes, it contained a kernel of truth. Maren Ashford always bent probability in his favour—not through any virtue or skill of his own, but through some cosmic accident that had placed him at the centre of events he was utterly unqualified to control.

OF THE WEAVER'S
DAUGHTER FROM WEED

For all his burdens, Maren still possessed a wastrel's heart—a heart that craved lightness when the world grew too heavy. Lyra was the hammer and the anvil; she was necessity, duty, and the cold reminder of what they had lost.

Maren had a way of looking at a woman that made her feel like the only inhabitant of a dying world. It wasn't the hungry, predatory gaze of a nobleman, but the soft, appreciative look of a man who found beauty in a stray lock of hair or a smudge of flour on a cheek. To Lyra, he offered his duty; to the other women of the village, he offered his attention—a far more dangerous currency.

And then there was Celia.

She was a weaver's daughter from a neighboring village—Weed, a girl with hair the colour of autumn wheat and a laugh that didn't sound like a decree. She had come to the camp seeking protection, but she brought with her something Maren hadn't felt in years: ease.

Maren found himself wandering towards the communal well whenever Celia was there. He would help her carry her buckets—a task Lyra would have found absurd—just to hear her hum the folk songs of Weed. Celia didn't talk about rations or troop movements; she talked about the way the wind moved through the tall grass.

One evening, Lyra watched from the shadows of the command tent as Maren sat by the well, carving a whistle for Celia while the girl laughed, her hand resting briefly on his arm.

Lyra didn't storm out. She didn't scream. She simply turned back to her ledgers, her face a mask of frozen iron.

"He desires her silk," Lyra murmured, the quill snapping in her hand, staining her fingers with ink that looked like blood. "And I am the wool he needs. He will love her for the beauty I traded away to keep him alive."

The hatred did not bloom all at once. It was a slow-growing weed, nourished by every smile Maren gave to Celia and every cold command he gave to his wife.

OF KILLING THE SACRED SNAKE

The Thornwood was a place of wet rot and quiet starvation. Maren Ashford, currently fumbling with his trousers, swayed slightly as the last of a stolen wineskin hummed in his blood. He had wandered into the dark to avoid the hollow-eyed glares of his mutinous men, seeking only the simple dignity of a private piss against an oak tree.

Instead, he found a nightmare.

It wasn't silent. It was a wet, rhythmic crunching sound that drew him past the tree line. In a small clearing bathed in moonlight, Maren witnessed a tableau of horrific consumption.

A common brown stag—the symbol of the heartlands, of simple prey—lay tangled in the undergrowth. Its eyes were wide, glassy pools of terror, its ribs already cracked inward. Wrapped around it, tightening like a noose of cold muscle, was the Great White Serpent.

It was massive, thick as a mainmast, its scales gleaming with the sickly, pale luminescence of polished alabaster. It was the Iron Emperor's living totem, the "Pale Constable" that adorned every banner of the Creedseat. Its jaw was unhinged, stretched impossibly wide as it began to swallow the stag's hindquarters whole. The Empire, in plain sight, devouring the land.

Maren froze. His bladder emptied itself, unbidden. He made a noise—a pathetic, drunken squeak trapped in his throat.

The serpent stopped swallowing. The great white head snapped around. Onyx eyes, cold as winter stars, locked onto the interrupting little man. It didn't appreciate an audience at dinner.

With a hiss that smelt of old blood and copper, the serpent released the dying stag and coiled violently. It struck faster than thought.

Maren didn't dodge. He didn't plan. He panicked. He let out a high-pitched yelp, tried to turn, slipped on a patch of moss slick with morning dew, and fell backward with the grace of a dropped sack of turnips.

As he flailed, his hand—clutching a rusted skinning knife he used for cutting cheese—swung out in a desperate, blind arc of pure terror.

Schluck.

Luck is a funny god. The serpent's scales were hard as iron, but its eye—that massive, black orb—was soft as jelly. The rusted blade plunged deep into the socket, scrambling the primitive brain behind it.

The massive weight of the reptile convulsed. It thrashed like a whipping cable, smashing saplings and churning the mud, narrowly missing Maren's skull before collapsing into a heavy, twitching stillness.

Silence returned to the woods, save for the ragged, wet breathing of the stag.

Maren crawled over on hands and knees, trembling violently. He looked at the snake—dead by fluke. He looked at the stag. The poor beast was crushed, its spine broken. It looked at him with those dying, terrified eyes, pleading for an end.

With a heavy heart and shaking hands, Maren used the same bloody knife to cut the stag's throat. A mercy kill.

He sat back in the mud, staring at his work. The symbol of the Empire, dead. The symbol of the land, dead. And him, a drunk peasant with piss-stained trousers, holding the knife.

"I just wanted to pee," he whispered to the corpses.

Then, the cold reality crashed in. His men back at camp. Starving. Mutinous. Waiting for a reason to give up or a reason to fight.

He couldn't just leave them here. The lie needed evidence.

It took hours. The sun was already painting the grey sky with streaks of bloody orange when Maren stumbled back into the camp clearing. He was exhausted, covered in mud, slime, and two kinds of blood.

He didn't just drag the snake. He had tied the stag's legs to the serpent's body with vines and hauled the entire grotesque trophy—predator and prey tied together in death—across the forest floor. He dropped the massive, tangled weight in front of the dying fire embers with a ground-shaking thud.

The camp woke up. Silence fell like a hammer.

Bertram, the old veteran, stood up, his jaw slack. He looked at the white scales, then at the crushed stag, then at Maren's haunted face.

"It was eating it," Bertram whispered, his voice cracking. "The Pale Constable... it was consuming the land. And you stopped it."

Maren saw the shift in their eyes. It wasn't just hunger for meat anymore. It was awe.

He straightened his aching back, wiping slime from his cheek, and forced the tremor out of his voice. He pointed a shaking finger at the white carcass.

"The Emperor thinks we are food," Maren announced, his voice rough as gravel. "He sent his pet to finish what the tax collectors started." He kicked the dead snake's snout. "It choked."

"He saved the stag," someone whispered. It wasn't true—the stag was dead—but truth no longer mattered. "He slew the Iron Worm."

As the whispers turned into a low, fervent chant, Maren caught his reflection in a puddle of bloody water. He didn't look like a hero. He looked like a man who had just dug his own grave with a cheese knife.

He had traded his honesty for an army. Now he had to lead them.

"They think I saved the deer," he thought bitterly, feeling the weight of their belief settling on his shoulders like a yoke. The stag was dead, its throat cut by his own hand in mercy, but truth had no place here anymore. To them, the intent mattered more than the result.

He suppressed the urge to vomit, tasting bile and the sour memory of stolen wine. *Fine.*

If they need a dragonslayer, he told himself, forcing his

shaking hands to still, *I will be their dragonslayer. If they need a saviour, I'll play the saviour.*

He looked at the faces of his men—no longer mutinous, but ready to march into hell for him.

Whatever it takes to keep them fighting. Whatever it takes to win.

OF THE THREE HEROES

As Maren's band grew from a gang into an army, three men emerged as the pillars of his rise. They were not yet the legends they would become, but the seeds of their future greatness—and cruelty—were already sown.

The first was Markus Quillen, the solid administrator who had been with Maren from the beginning. He was not exactly a brilliant man, neither a warrior, nor a charismatic leader. But he was reliable in a way that brilliant men often are not. He kept the supplies flowing, the records accurate, the army fed and equipped even when resources were scarce. He handled the tedious details that Maren was too impatient to manage and too wise to ignore. Without Markus, the rebel band would have starved or scattered within months; with him, it became something capable of lasting.

THE ARITHMETIC OF NECESSITY

Years later, during the Long March to the West.

Numbers do not lie. Markus Quillen had built his career on that certainty—the rational comfort of mathematics, the impartiality of ledgers. Feelings deceived; loyalty wavered; even honour could bend under sufficient pressure. But numbers were pure.

Now he stared at the numbers on his desk, and for the first time in his career, he wished they would lie.

"You've checked these?" Maren asked, not looking up from his dinner.

"Three times, my lord. The granary inventories are accurate. The consumption rates are based on actual measurements, not estimates. The projection is as reliable as any I've produced."

Maren took another bite of roasted fowl. He chewed slowly, methodically, as if the report on his desk were a minor administrative matter rather than a sentence of death for five thousand people.

"Summarise it."

Markus had hoped he wouldn't have to say the words aloud. "We have grain sufficient to feed ten thousand soldiers for thirty days, or ten thousand soldiers and five thousand refugees for fourteen days. After fourteen days, we will be forced to forage, which will slow our advance by at least a week and expose our supply lines to enemy raids. After thirty days at reduced rations, combat effectiveness will decline by an estimated forty percent."

"And if we continue feeding both?"

"We lose the campaign. The northern army will cut our supply lines before we can reach Brightfort. Kharic will have time to reinforce. The war extends by six months minimum, possibly a year. Casualty projections increase by—"

"I understand." Maren set down his fork. He picked up the report, scanned it briefly, and set it down again. His expression did not change. "Feed the soldiers. March the rest."

Markus had known the answer before he asked. He had prepared himself for it. And yet, hearing the words spoken aloud—so calmly, so matter-of-factly, between bites of dinner—something in him recoiled.

"My lord, the refugees include women. Children. The elderly. Without our protection—"

"They'll die." Maren picked up his fork again. "Some of them, anyway. The young and strong will survive. They'll find other camps, other sources of food. They'll endure, as peasants have always endured, because that is what peasants do." He looked up, meeting Markus's eyes for the first time. "You think I don't know what I'm ordering? You think I haven't done this arithmetic myself, lying awake at three in the morning, trying to find numbers that add up differently?"

"I didn't mean to suggest—"

"There is no version of this war where everyone survives. There is only the question of who dies, and for what purpose." said Maren coldly. "I choose my soldiers over those refugees because my soldiers can end this war. Because every month this war continues, ten times as many refugees are created. Mercy's arithmetic yields only corpses."

Markus was silent. He had no counter-argument.

"I don't expect you to forgive me," Maren continued. "I don't expect anyone to forgive me, least of all myself. But I expect you to implement the decision, because you are the only man in this army who can make it look like logistics instead of murder." He took another bite. "Draft the orders. Reduced rations for non-combatants, effective immediately. 'Temporary measure pending resupply.' Whatever language makes it easier to enforce."

"And when they realise what's happening? When they try to stay?"

"Then the soldiers move them. Gentle if we can. Rough if we have to." Maren's jaw tightened imperceptibly. "Don't look at me like that, Markus. You think I don't know what this makes me? I grew up hungry. I know what it feels like when the food runs out." He stabbed at his plate. "But I've got ten thousand mouths to feed who'll be doing the fighting. Those refugees can't win me a war. Wish to hell it were different, but wishing don't fill bellies."

"And if that realm never comes?"

Maren did not answer. He returned to his dinner, eating steadily, mechanically, to him the food had no taste—he had long ago stopped expecting anything to have taste.

Markus gathered the reports and left the command tent. Outside, the evening was cool, the stars just beginning to appear. Somewhere in the camp, children were laughing. They did not yet know that tomorrow they would begin to starve.

He drafted the orders.

He dipped his quill. The ink was black. The paper was white. The lives he was erasing were invisible. He wrote the words *"reduced rations"* and thought about how cleanly they sat on the page, how little space they took up. It was terrifying, he realised, how much horror could be hidden inside good penmanship.

The second was Roland Knox, a former butcher whose massive frame and savage fighting style had earned him his nickname. He was Maren's bodyguard, his enforcer, and occasionally his conscience—the one man who could challenge Maren to his face without fear of reprisal. He was crude, violent, and spectacularly loyal. When Maren was in danger, Roland was there with his axe and his bellowing war cry. When Maren needed dirty work done, Roland did it without questions or complaints. He was not a subtle weapon, but an effective one. His legend would be cemented years later, in a darker time, but his nature was evident from the start.

The incident that defined Roland's legend happened in the second year of the war.

The rebel army had liberated a village called Shepherd's Rest. The villagers welcomed them as saviours, provided food and shelter, celebrated their freedom from imperial taxation. Everything seemed peaceful.

Then the scouts reported that an imperial patrol was approaching—five hundred soldiers, too many to fight openly, not enough time to retreat. The army could escape through the mountain pass to the north, but only if they left immediately. If they stayed to fight, they would be trapped. If they ran but were too slow, the imperials would catch them in the open.

The problem was the villagers.

Some of them—the young men, the unmarried women, anyone mobile—could come with the army. But the elderly, the sick, the children too young to travel fast... they would slow the column down. They would be the reason the imperials caught them. They would be the death of the rebellion.

"We leave them," one of Maren's officers said. "It's harsh, but it's the only way."

"If we leave them, the imperials will make an example," another replied. "Every village from here to the coast will hear about how the rebels abandoned their supporters. No one will help us again."

Maren looked at Roland. Roland understood.

"Give me thirty men," the Dogslayer said. "And four hours."

He went back to Shepherd's Rest. He gathered the villagers who couldn't travel—the old, the sick, the too-young. Seventy-three people in all. He led them to a cave system in the hills above the village, a place the locals knew but outsiders wouldn't think to search.

Then he did something that haunted him for the rest of his life.

He sealed the entrance.

He left food and water inside, enough for a week if rationed carefully. He left instructions: stay low, stay hidden, wait until the imperials have moved on.

But he also left an elderly woman named Cora. She was ninety-three years old, sharp-minded but too frail to survive the journey. She was the village healer, the keeper of its history, the person everyone looked to in times of crisis.

She understood what Roland was doing. She understood why.

"I'll keep them calm," she said, as Roland prepared to seal the entrance. "I'll make sure no one panics, no one makes noise, no one does anything stupid."

"Three days," Roland said. "After that, you can dig out."

"I know." She smiled—the smile of a woman who had lived long enough to see worse things than this. "Go save your rebellion, butcher. This old woman will hold the line here."

Roland Knox, the Dogslayer, who had killed men with his bare hands and laughed, found his hands shaking as he rolled the last stone into place. He wasn't a strategist. He was a butcher. And sealing a tomb—even a temporary one, filled with living breath instead of cold meat—felt too much like his old trade.

"Three days," he rasped through the gap before the final rock fell. "Don't make a sound. Or I'll come back and kill you myself."

It was the only way he knew how to be kind.

Then he turned his back on the silence and went to do the thing he was actually good at. He took his thirty men and didn't just lead a diversion; he orchestrated a massacre.

They struck the imperial patrol in a narrow ravine. Roland fought with a heavy axe in his right hand and a meat cleaver in his left, roaring like a daemon let loose from the hells. He made so much noise, chopped with such horrific enthusiasm, and spilt so much blood that the imperial commander panicked, convinced he was facing the vanguard of a hundred berserkers rather than thirty men buying time. By the time the imperials realised their mistake, the rebel army was gone, the village was empty, and the Dogslayer had vanished into the hills, leaving a carnage that would make veterans vomit.

The rebels escaped. The imperials, frustrated and confused, torched Shepherd's Rest to the ground but found no one to punish—the villagers had vanished.

Three days later, Cora led the survivors out of the cave. They rebuilt their village. They never forgot what the Dogslayer had done—how he had saved them by burying them alive, how he had trusted a ninety-three-year-old woman to keep seventy-two terrified people silent while soldiers searched overhead.

When Maren heard the story, he summoned Roland to his tent.

"You could have failed," he said. "You could have been wrong about the cave. You could have miscalculated the time. Those people could have died in the dark."

"Yes." Roland's face was unreadable. "But they didn't."

"Would you do it again?"

"If it saved you? If it saved the cause?" Roland met his lord's eyes without flinching. "I would bury my own mother in a cave, my lord, if that was what victory required."

It was not a boast. It was the truth about the kind of man Roland Knox was. The kind of man every revolution needs—and every revolution learns to fear.

The third had not yet arrived. But he was coming.

OF THE SCHOLAR'S SEARCH

Before he came to the marshes, Hadrian had visited the camps of three other would-be kings.

He had visited Lord Roden, who had ten thousand men and a pedigree stretching back centuries. Hadrian watched Roden execute a competent scout for failing to bow correctly, and left within the hour. *He values ceremony over intelligence,* Hadrian noted. *He will die proudly.*

He had visited the Red Brotherhood, a massive peasant army in the west. He watched their council debate for six hours about how to divide the loot from a city they had not yet captured. *They are not an army; they are a riot with delusions of grandeur,* he decided. *They will eat themselves.*

Finally, he had stood on a ridge overlooking a ragged band in the Thornwood. He watched their leader—a disheveled man who looked more like a tavern keeper than a general—run from a sudden rainstorm, slipping in the mud while his men laughed at him. But then he watched that same leader share his cloak with a shivering sentry, and later, cheat at dice to let a despondent soldier win.

Hadrian smiled. *He has no dignity,* the scholar thought. *Which means he has no rigid shape. A man with no shape can become anything the times require.*

He walked down the hill to introduce himself.

His name was Hadrian Narrowdale, and he was the last survivor of the old Narrowdale royal house—a kingdom that had been absorbed into Ironhold's empire before most people could remember. He was a scholar, a strategist. He saw patterns where others saw only chaos. He came to Maren Ashford with nothing but the clothes on his back and a mind that had been sharpened by years of bitter exile.

"I have been searching for a master worthy of my service," he told Maren at their first meeting. "I believe I have found him."

Maren, who was drunk at the time, squinted at the slender scholar with bleary suspicion. "Why me? I'm nobody. I'm a village headman who got lucky."

"Exactly." Hadrian Narrowdale smiled. "You have no lineage to defend, no traditions to preserve, no pride to protect. You are free to do whatever works, to adopt whatever methods succeed. In a world where the old certainties are crumbling, that flexibility is worth more than all the noble blood in the realm."

It was an unconventional compliment, but Maren recognised its wisdom. He hired Hadrian Narrowdale on the spot, and never regretted the decision.

OF THE LADY

The camp was a disaster. Maren knew it, Markus knew it, and every fly buzzing over the open latrines knew it. They were surviving, but only just. They were men without women, living like wolves in the mud.

Then the cart arrived.

It was a mule cart, creaking under the weight of sacks of grain, bundles of cloth, and two small children huddled under a tarp. It trundled past the bewildered sentries, who were too shocked to stop it, and came to a halt in the centre of the muddy clearing.

A woman climbed down. She wore a peasant's dress, but she wore it like armour. Her boots were caked in the mud of a hundred miles. Her face was thin, sharpened by hunger and worry, but her eyes were dry and terrifyingly clear.

It was Lyra.

Maren, who was currently nursing a hangover and trying to referee a fight between two thieves over a stolen chicken, froze. He dropped the chicken.

"Lyra?" he croaked. "What are you... how did you..."

"The village isn't safe," she said. Her voice cut through the camp noise like a whip. "Imperial inspectors came looking for 'the traitor's family.' They burnt our house, Maren. They burnt the fields."

She didn't cry. She didn't run to him for a hug. She stood amidst the filth of the camp with a posture that decades of hiding in a peasant village hadn't been able to break. She was no longer just the woman who had married the village wastrel; she was the ghost of Whitecroft, finally stepping out of the shadows.

"I sold the last of the jewelry," Lyra said, her eyes scanning the disorganised tents with a cold, predatory intelligence. "I bribed the checkpoint guards. And I brought what was left of the winter stores."

She turned back to the cart and lifted down a sleeping boy —Valen, five years of age—and a older girl, Mei, who was clutching a wooden doll.

OF THE CHILDREN OF REEDS

While Maren and Lyra spoke, the two children remained by the cart, looking less like the heirs of a rebellion and more like two small, frightened animals.

Valen had eyes that were too large for his gaunt face. He clutched a handful of his mother's skirt as if it were the only thing keeping him from being swallowed by the mud. He was a soft child, born with a sensitive disposition that the Ironhold would have called a defect. He looked at the rough, scarred men around him and didn't see heroes; he saw the same violence that had burnt his home.

Mei, two years older, stood in front of him. She didn't have her brother's fear; she had her mother's stillness. She watched Maren—this man her mother called 'Father'—with a silent, judging intensity. When Maren reached out to ruffle her hair with a hand that smelt of stale ale, Mei didn't flinch, but she didn't smile either.

"They're hungry, Maren," Lyra said, her eyes never leaving her children. "They haven't seen a piece of fruit in six months. They've forgotten what a bed feels like."

Maren looked at his son—the soft boy who seemed to tremble at the sound of a raised voice—and felt a flicker of disappointment he quickly suppressed. He wanted a lion; he had a lamb. He didn't realise then that in the world he was building, lambs were the first to be eaten, and the mother of the lamb would eventually grow teeth to protect it.

"So we left," Lyra said. "I sold the last of the jewelry. I bribed the checkpoint guards. And I brought what was left of the winter stores."

She looked around the camp. She saw the filth. She saw the disorganised tents. She saw the men gambling in the dirt while their weapons rusted. She saw the chaotic, hopeless mess that her husband called an army.

Maren braced himself. He expected screaming. He expected blame. He expected her to ask why he had ruined their lives.

Instead, Lyra sighed—a sound of profound, practical annoyance.

"Markus!" she shouted, spotting the scribe.

Markus Quillen jumped. "My Lady?"

"I assume the cooking fire is upwind of the latrines because you are trying to breed a new plague? Or do you simply enjoy the taste of dysentery in your stew? Move it to the south ridge before we die of stupidity rather than swords!" She pointed a finger at Roland Knox, who was looming nearby, looking dangerous. "And you, big man. Unless you plan to frighten the mildew away with that axe, I suggest you make yourself useful. Stop posing like a statue and help me unload this grain."

Roland blinked. He looked at Maren. Maren shrugged helplessly. *Do what she says.*

Roland moved to unload the cart.

Lyra walked up to Maren. She reached out and straightened his collar, brushing away a layer of dried mud. Her touch was rough, possessive.

"Look at you," she whispered, her voice dripping with a mix of pity and disdain as she violently straightened his mud-caked collar. "You've declared war on the world, Maren, yet you stand there looking like a tavern drunk who wandered into a parade. You can't even button your own shirt, and you want to wear a crown? Gods help us."

She tightened his collar, almost choking him.

"But you are all I have left of a name. So if we are going to be rebels, husband, try to look less like a bandit and more like a man who survives."

"I'm sorry," Maren said. And for the first time in years, he meant it. "I never meant for you to be dragged into this."

"We are already in it," Lyra said. She looked at their children, sitting on the grain sacks, watching their father with wide, frightened eyes. "There is no going back now. So if we are going to be rebels, husband, we are going to be rebels who survive."

She didn't kiss him. She turned and began shouting orders at a group of slack-jawed bandits.

That night, the camp ate warm stew. The latrines were moved. The shirts were mended. And Maren Ashford realised, with a mixture of relief and terror, that he was no longer just a bandit chief. He was a King, because his Queen had just arrived to build him a court out of the mud.

OF THE IRON MATRIARCH

According to her own words, Lyra was a noblewoman from Whitecroft whose family was purged and shamed decades ago. She was hiding in the village of Marsh when she married the "wastrel" Maren.

They called her Lady Lyra, and soon, the men feared her more than they feared the Imperial Legions.

Maren was the heart of the rebellion. He gave them hope, made them laugh, promised them a future. But Lyra was its spine.

She organised the supplies with a ruthlessness that rivaled Markus Quillen. She rationed the food. She established a network of women—camp followers, wives, local villagers— who acted as spies and smugglers, bringing news that Maren's scouts missed.

She suffered, too. That was what the men respected. When the winter rains came and the camp flooded, Lyra stood knee-deep in freezing water, holding her children above the muck, refusing to complain. When the food ran low, she ate less than anyone, her face growing gaunt, her cheekbones sharp as knives.

She was hardening. Maren could see it happen, day by day. The soft, laughing girl he had married was being chiseled away by hardship. In her place was something colder, something stronger, something made of iron and necessity.

One night, Maren found her sewing a patch onto Valen's tunic by firelight.

"It won't always be like this," he promised, sitting beside

her. "When we win… I'll build you a palace. I'll give you silk so thick you'll drown in it."

Lyra didn't look up. "I don't want silk, Maren."

"What do you want?"

She bit the thread, snapping it with a sharp tear. She looked at him, and her eyes reflected the fire.

"I want to be safe," she said. "I want walls so high the fire cannot reach us. I want to ensure that no one can ever lay hands on our children."

"We will be," Maren said. "I promise."

Lyra looked at him for a long moment. She loved him. But she knew him. She knew his soft heart, his tendency to forgive, his desire to be liked.

"You are a good man, Maren," she said softly. "But good men die young in this world. You handle the men. You handle the battles. But when it comes to the things that must be done to keep us safe… the hard things… leave those to me."

Maren nodded, not fully understanding what she meant.

Years later, when the heads of his oldest friends were rotting in baskets at her command, he would remember that moment. He would remember that the monster who protected his throne was not born in a palace. She was forged here, in the mud of the marshes, while he slept and she kept watch over the dark.

Lyra did not just give Maren her loyalty; she gave him her grace. Every time she scrubbed a soldier's tunic or bargained with a crooked merchant for a sack of mouldy grain, a piece of the high-born lady of Whitecroft died.

She watched Maren in the evenings, laughing by the fire, telling stories to his men, and she felt a cold, simmering resentment. He was the 'Lord' because he was liked; she was the 'Matriarch' because she was needed. He got the cheers; she got the grease and the ledger-books.

"He is the light," she whispered to herself one night, watching Maren pass out in a drunken sleep while she sat up mending his boots. "He shines only because I burn, and I am burning away to nothing."

She looked at her hands—once soft, now cracked and stained with the lye she used to keep the camp clean. She hated the mud. She hated the smell of the marshes. But most of all, she began to hate the part of Maren that could still find joy in this squalor, while she carried the weight of their survival like a crown of thorns.

OF THE LORD OF MARSH

By the winter of that first year, Maren's band had done the impossible: they had retaken the village of Marsh itself. The imperial garrison, demoralised and cut off by flooding, had surrendered without a fight. Maren Ashford was back home— not as a wastrel, but as a conqueror.

It was time, his men shouted, to make his position official.

The air was thick with victory and cheap wine. In the village square, where Maren used to pass out drunk, men were now raising their cups and shouting dangerous words. "King!" they bellowed. "King of the West! King Maren!"

Maren sat on a stolen magistrate's chair, looking uncomfortable. He looked at Hadrian Narrowdale.

"They want a King," Maren muttered. "Corwin Harrow calls himself King. The rebels in the East call themselves Kings."

"Kings are targets," Hadrian said quietly, his voice cutting through the noise. "The Empire will hunt down a King with every legion it has. A King challenges the heavens. But a Lord?" Hadrian smiled thinly. "A Lord is just a local problem. The Empire has too many problems to chase every Lord."

Maren nodded. He looked at Markus Quillen. "What do you think?"

"Precedent," Markus said, consulting his mental ledger. "The old regional governors were called Lords. It implies authority, but not treason. Technically."

"Lord of Marsh," Maren rolled the title around in his mouth, tasting it.

He looked at the muddy boots of his soldiers. He looked at the familiar thatched roofs of his home. He wasn't a dragon yet. He was just a man who had bitten off more than he could chew and was trying not to choke.

"I like it," Maren announced, standing up. The cheering quieted. "Humble. Harmless. A title for a drunkard, not a threat. The kind of title a village headman might give himself to impress a tavern wench."

He raised his cup.

"Let Corwin Harrow be a King," Maren shouted to the crowd. "Let the great lords of the South fight over crowns of gold. I am a man of the mud! I am a son of this soil! I claim no throne but this chair, and no land but what we can hold!"

He kicked the mud from his boot—a deliberate gesture.

"I am the Lord of Marsh!"

The roar that went up shook the birds from the trees. It was not the polished acclaim of a coronation; it was the raw, guttural joy of peasants who finally had a name for their anger.

Later that night, as the celebration raged, Maren found Hadrian watching the stars.

"The tall weeds are cut down first," Maren said, handing the scholar a cup. "Better to grow in the shadow until the roots are deep."

Hadrian took the cup. "A farmer's wisdom, my lord."

"The only kind I have." Maren's grin faded slightly, his eyes turning towards the North, where the fires of true war were already burning. "Let them laugh at the Lord of Marsh. Let them think I am small. By the time they realise what I am... it will be too late to stop growing."

And so the title was taken. It was a small name for a small beginning. But as Maren Ashford would prove, even a small spark, if fed enough fuel, can burn the world to ash.

CHAPTER FIVE

THE STORMBORN

IN WHICH THE STORMBORN CLAN RAISES CHEROS'S BANNER, AND A YOUNG LEGEND IS FORGED

Some men lead because they are chosen; others lead because the world has no choice but to follow.
— The Chronicle of the Hegemons

OF WHAT THE STORMBORN CLAN REMEMBERED

In the southeastern reaches of the realm, where the world dissolved into a labyrinth of mist and moving water, there lay the broken heart of Cheros.

The Ironhold did not merely conquer Cheros; they attempted to extinguish it. Forty years ago, when the First Iron Emperor's legions breached the Red Canyons, they came not for tribute—but for the root. History calls it the *Great Smoothing*. The Ironhold believed that the South was too wild, its music too discordant, its people too enamoured with the "madness of barbarians." To fix the world, the Emperor decided, the South had to be made silent.

The Stormborn clan remembered the River of Lament.

They remembered the three days when the Great River did not flow with water, but with the silk-clad bodies of the scholar-nobles and the blood-soaked archives of a thousand-year civilisation. They remembered the Siege of Drumhold, where the Iron legions used massive bellows to pump sulfurous smoke into the red-stone labyrinth, suffocating the royal court until the King of Cheros emerged at the city's gate, only to fall upon his own ancestral blade.

The Ironhold's decree was total: The drums were the first to die. Every war-drum, every ritual chime, every bronze bell in the three thousand lakes was collected and cast into a giant pit. The resulting slag was used to forge the heavy chains that would later bind the southern harbors. To hum a Cheros folk song became a crime against "Axial Stability." To speak the old crimson script was to invite the branding iron.

But the silence was only the beginning. The conquest was a systematic vivisection of the Southern soul. In the first year of the *Great Smoothing*, the Legions enacted what the survivors called the Protocol of the Shattered Mirror. It was a total desecration, designed to ensure that Cheros could never recognise itself again.

The Great Library of Bryn, which held the genealogies and star-charts of ten thousand years, was turned into a pyre that burnt for a lunar month; the sky turned black with the charred fragments of the South's history, and for a generation, the southern rains tasted of ash and ink.

The daughters of the noble houses—the "Red Lilies" who carried the ancestral songs—were stripped of their mourning silks and branded like cattle on the nape of the neck with the Imperial mark. They were marched barefoot into the freezing mines of the North, their dignity traded for the "efficiency" of the state. The Iron Chancellor did not just want their land; he wanted their shame. Every temple of the Ancients was dismantled stone by red stone, the sacred icons smashed into gravel to pave the very roads the survivors were forced to build. They were made to walk upon their own gods.

For fifteen years, the Stormborn survived in the "white spaces" of the Imperial ledgers. They were the "Three Embers" of the prophecy, living in districts where the water was too deep and the forests too thick for the Iron clerks to count every head. They did not merely survive; they festered.

Every time a Stormborn man bowed to a passing Iron Prefect, he was not showing respect—he was measuring the distance to the man's throat. They lived in a state of Active Mourning, wearing their white silks under their grey peasant rags, waiting for the day when the red dust of their ancestral valleys would no longer be a shroud, but a war-paint.

OF THE PROPHECY OF EMBERS

Why did the Empire hate Cheros so much? Why, of all the conquered kingdoms, was the South treated with such special, suffocating cruelty?

It was not because of their armies, which had been crushed, nor because of their wealth, which had been stolen.

It was because of a whisper.

Forty years ago, when the First Iron Emperor stood at the height of his power, his court oracle cast the bones into the fire and read the cracks. The Emperor asked how long his dynasty would last. The oracle trembled, and gave an answer that would doom a million people:

"Though the Storm be reduced to three embers, it is the Storm that shall melt the Iron."

The prophecy terrified the Emperor. He saw the "Storm" as the House of Stormborn and the people of Cheros. In his panic, he tried to stamp out the fire before it could spread.

He ordered the Great Drums of Cheros melted down, for fear their sound would wake the storm. He forbade the teaching of the southern script, for fear the words carried sparks. He hunted the noble families until only a handful remained, hiding in the marshes like hunted animals.

OF THE TIGER OF CHEROS

The head of the clan was Lord Torian of Cheros, called Stoneheart. He was a man who had seen his father's tongue cut out for reciting a poem. His eyes held the memory of the day the Red River turned black with the ash of their burning libraries. He did not want justice. He wanted restitution in blood.

Torian the Stoneheart was a man who lived in the white spaces of the Imperial ledger.

His journey to the South began with a blade and a body. Years ago, in the central provinces, Torian had killed an Imperial Tax-Prefect—not in a heat of passion, but as a preconceived execution of a man who had insulted the Stormborn name. He fled the Ironhold's reach, disappearing into the chaotic, rain-drenched districts of the Southern delta.

He did not hide; he organised.

Whenever the Empire demanded labour for the roads or whenever a local patriarch died, it was Torian who stepped forward to lead. He organised the funerals, managed the conscription lists, and directed the heavy lifting. To the bureaucrats, he was a helpful local elder. To the youths of the district, he was a haunting man of war. Beneath the cover of mourning rites and road-work, he was training a secret army, turning farmers into squads and village brawls into tactical drills.

It was in these times when he attempted to tame his nephew.

Yet it was his nephew who would break the world.

While Corwin Harrow questioned the birthright of kings, Kharic Stormborn wore his own like a second skin.

Kharic was a restless student. He had read books on strategies of war and statecraft until dawn but looked at the scrolls of poetry and tossed them into the fire, declaring that "ink is only good for remembering a dead man's name." When Torian tried to teach him the finesse of the longsword, Kharic had grown bored within an hour, snapping the practice blade in half. "A sword," the boy had spat, "is only for killing one man. It is a tool for a duelist, not a conqueror."

Torian had smiled then—"And what is it you wish to learn, boy?"

"The Teach me how to break an army," Kharic replied, his eyes glowing with the first sparks of the Hegemon. "Teach me the logic that breaks a hundred thousand hearts at once."

So, Torian took him to the granaries. For a month, he made Kharic count every kernel of wheat intended for the "funeral workers." He forced the boy to calculate the weight of water for a three-day march and the speed of a supply wagon in the mud.

"You want to command the Ten Thousand?" Torian would growl, striking the table with a calloused hand. "Then you must first feed them. Glory is the banner, but grain is the breath. If you cannot master the arithmetic of the stomach, your 'Ten Thousand' will be nothing but a pile of hungry corpses before they even see the enemy's steel."

Kharic hated every number, but he learned. He learned that war was a machine of flesh and fuel, even as he dreamed of a day when he could simply set the world on fire and let the gods worry about the counting.

OF A YOUNG LEGEND

Kharic Stormborn was twenty-four years old when the rebellion began, and already he was a known legend.

He stood over six feet tall—giant by the standards of his people—with the broad shoulders and powerful limbs of a born warrior. His face was handsome in a fierce, angular way, dominated by eyes that flashed with lightning when his temper rose. He could lift a bronze cauldron that two other men could barely move. He could draw a bow that no one else could bend. In contests of strength and skill, he had never been defeated.

But it was not his physical prowess that set him apart. It was the loud thundering that was within him—a restless, consuming passion that could not be satisfied by ordinary accomplishments. From childhood, he had chafed against the limitations of his family's reduced circumstances. He had refused to learn the scholarly arts that might have helped him navigate the imperial bureaucracy, dismissing them as "the weapons of slaves." He had devoted himself instead to the arts of war, studying strategy and tactics with the same intensity that other young men devoted to poetry or commerce.

"What use is writing," he had once asked his tutors, "when I can command ten thousand men who write for me? What use is calculation, when I can hire a hundred clerks to calculate? But strength—courage—the ability to break an enemy's line and seize victory from chaos—these things cannot be delegated. These things a man must possess for himself."

His tutors had despaired of him. His uncle had watched him with a mixture of pride and concern. And the common folk of the region had whispered among themselves that here was a dragon's son, a throwback to the great warriors of legend, a man destined for something extraordinary.

In the sayings of the Old, dragons had ruled the world before men—vast creatures of fire and wisdom who shaped the mountains and carved the rivers. When they departed for the Celestine heavens, they left behind their blood in certain mortal lines, their fire in certain mortal hearts. "When the dragon's son rises," the old prophecies said, "empires shall tremble and the old order shall burn." Such talk was forbidden under the Iron Creed—superstition, the bureaucrats called it, punishable by imprisonment—but in the southern provinces, where the archaic ways still smouldered beneath imperial rule, the people remembered. They looked at Kharic Stormborn and saw something older than any empire, something that could not be conquered or contained.

They little knew the truth of it.

What none of them saw—what Kharic himself barely acknowledged—was the wound that drove him. He had been nine years old when the Iron Chancellor brought his father to the executioner's block in Steelhaven. The soldiers had made him watch—had held him in place, forced his eyes open, ensured that he saw every moment of his father's death. It was meant to break him, to show him the price of defiance, to make him afraid.

Instead, it had forged him.

He had not wept. He had not begged. He had stood in silence as the blade fell, and something had hardened inside him—and made unbreakable. The boy who loved poetry and gentle things had died alongside his father. What remained was a weapon wrapped in noble flesh, a creature of vengeance that would spend the next decade being honed to a killing edge.

But beneath that iron resolve, the wound still festered. Every act of courage, every feat of strength, every victory was an attempt to prove that he was worthy of his father's sacrifice

—that the death had meant something. And so he pushed harder, risked more, demanded greater and greater proof of his own worth—not to convince others, but to convince himself.

It was this need that made him magnificent. And it was this need that would destroy him.

OF THE SILENT CITY

Before he was a general, Kharic was a prince of ruins.

His home, Drumhold, the former capital of Cheros, was not built of iron like the Imperial capital. It was carved from the living red stone of the southern canyons, a city of echoes and wind. In the old days, it was said that when the Great Drums of the citadel were beaten, the sound could be heard for a hundred miles, calling the clans to war or celebration.

But the Iron Empire had silenced the drums forty years ago.

When they conquered Cheros, the first thing the Iron soldiers did was slit the skins of the great war-drums and melt down the bronze frames. To beat a drum in Drumhold was punishable by death. The city that had once thrummed with the heartbeat of a people was now suffocatingly quiet.

Young Kharic grew up in this silence. He walked the empty Hall of Echoes, where his ancestors' statues had been defaced by imperial hammers. He saw the red stone palaces overgrown with vines, beautiful but desolate, like a queen forced to wear rags.

"One day," his uncle had whispered to him, pointing at the empty tower where the Mother Drum once hung. "One day, the sound will return. But it requires blood to wet the skins."

Kharic never forgot. He did not fight for territory, or for tax revenue, or for the abstract concept of justice. He fought for the noise. He fought for the moment he could march back into that red canyon, clad in the gold of a conqueror, and strike the drum so hard that the Iron Empire would shatter from the vibrations.

He wanted his ancestors to hear him. He wanted the world to know that the silence was over.

OF THE BRONZE CAULDRON

A Vignette of Kharic Stormborn

The challenge came on a feast day, when wine made cowards brave and fools loud."

Lord Aldwyn was a minor noble from a neighbouring province—a man of middle years with a reputation for cruelty and a belly that spoke of too many banquets. He had come to assess this young Stormborn, this supposed dragon's son that everyone was whispering about. He found Kharic in the great hall, surrounded by admirers, and felt the frigid bite of envy.

"They say you can lift the bronze cauldron," Lord Aldwyn bellowed, cutting through the conversation. The hall fell silent. "That giant sacrificial vessel in the courtyard, which six men cannot move. They say you lifted it above your head."

Kharic set down his wine cup. "They say true."

"I say they lie." Aldwyn smiled. "I say you are a boy playing at being a legend. I say your family trades on old glories while producing nothing but boasts."

The silence in the hall became absolute. Everyone knew what happened to men who insulted the Stormborn name. Everyone waited for violence.

But Kharic simply rose from his seat. "Come," he said. "I will show you."

They gathered in the courtyard—the entire hall emptying to watch—and there stood the cauldron: four feet tall, cast bronze gone green with age, filled to the brim with rainwater from the previous night's storm. It had been forged in the time of the old kings, and it was said that only a true heir of Cheros could lift it.

Kharic approached the cauldron. He did not stretch or prepare. He bent, gripped the handles, and lifted.

The cauldron rose smoothly—water sloshing over the rim, muscles standing out on his arms like cables of iron—until it was above his head.

The bronze groaned under the strain, a sound like a dying bell. The stone beneath his feet cracked—like a whip that echoed in the silence.

Kharic held it there, perfectly still, while the crowd counted heartbeats. Ten. Twenty. Thirty.

His eyes, those twin storms, seemed to merge into a single, terrifying void as the veins in his neck bulged. He was not lifting bronze; he was lifting the reputation of his house."

Then he walked three paces forward, set the cauldron down gently, and turned to face Lord Aldwyn.

"You were saying?"

Aldwyn's face had gone the colour of tallow. "I... that is... I meant no..."

"You meant every word." said Kharic. "You came here to humiliate me. To prove that the Stormborn are nothing but a faded name." He stepped closer. "I have proven otherwise. Now you will apologise—not to me, but to the memory of my ancestors, whose name you dirtied with your doubt."

Aldwyn fell to his knees. His apology was abject, complete, pathetically sincere. And when it was done, Kharic helped him to his feet with perfect courtesy, poured him wine with his own hand, and spoke to him just as nothing had happened.

But everyone who had watched knew the truth. They had seen what Kharic Stormborn was capable of—not just the strength, but the control. The absolute certainty that he was exactly what he claimed to be.

It was magnificent and terrifying.

And the boy who had stood frozen before the executioner's block, watching his father die, was nowhere to be seen. Kharic had buried that child beneath legends. But the dead have a way of rising.

OF THE NEWS FROM THE NORTH

Word of Corwin Harrow's rebellion reached the Stormborn household on an autumn evening, carried by a merchant who had fled the chaos spreading through the central provinces.

The family gathered to hear the news: Lord Torian, his brothers, his sons and nephews, the trusted retainers who had served the clan through its years of exile. They listened as the merchant described the uprising at Sorrowfen, the rapid conquests, the declaration of the Kingdom of Rising Cheros.

When the merchant had finished, silence fell over the room. Everyone was looking at Lord Torian, waiting for his response.

"He calls himself King of Cheros," Torian spat. "A dirt-digger wearing a crown of stolen bronze. It is an insult to every man who ever bled for the true line."

"The world is desperate, Uncle." Kharic Stormborn spoke from his position near the back of the room. "They'll follow anyone who offers them hope."

"And what do you think of this Corwin Harrow? This king of peasants?"

Kharic's lip curled slightly. "I think he's done us a service. He's proven that the empire can be challenged, that the Iron Creed can be broken. But he's not the man to finish what he's started. He's a spark, not a fire."

"You sound very certain."

"I am certain." Kharic stepped forward, his eyes blazing. "Uncle, we've been waiting fifteen years for this moment. Fifteen years of hiding, of bowing, of pretending to be what we're not. The world is crumbling. The rebels are rising everywhere. And what are we doing? Sitting in a merchant's house, listening to secondhand news, debating whether to act?"

Lord Torian held up a hand. "Patience, nephew. The time is not yet right."

"Time does not ripen; it must be seized." Kharic loudly replied. "Corwin Harrow was a nobody—a conscript, a farmer's son—and he shook the world with a single question. We are the Stormborn clan. Our ancestors conquered half the realm. Our name still means something to the people of Cheros. If we raise our banner now, while all under heaven is reeling, we can accomplish what that peasant king never could."

"And if we fail?"

"Then we die as our ancestors died—fighting, with swords in our hands and enemies at our feet. Is that not better than living as we have lived, slaves in all but name?"

Every man present knew that Kharic was right, and every man present was afraid to say so. The imperial reprisals would be terrible if they rose and failed. Entire families had been exterminated for lesser offences.

But Lord Torian looked at his nephew—at the fire in his eyes, the tension in his massive frame, the destiny that radiated from him like heat from a forge—and made his decision.

"We wait," Torian said. "Because if we rise too early, we rise alone.

But not for long. When the moment comes, Cheros will remember our name."

The moment came sooner than anyone expected.

OF THE KILLING OF
THE GOVERNOR

The local governor was a man named Willem Thornwood—a minor bureaucrat from the Ironhold heartland who had been assigned to this backwater province as punishment for some offence against his superiors. He was not a cruel man, as imperial officials went, but he was not a clever one either. He had heard the rumours about the Stormborn clan, had even reported them to his superiors, but he had not taken them seriously enough to request additional troops or increase his vigilance.

This proved to be a fatal error.

When news arrived that Corwin Harrow had seized the central heartlands and the flames of revolt were spreading south, Governor Thornwood decided to demonstrate his loyalty by preemptively arresting suspected rebel sympathisers in his district. The Stormborn clan was at the top of his list.

He sent a messenger to Lord Torian, summoning him to the provincial headquarters for "questioning." It was a transparent trap—everyone knew that those summoned for questioning rarely returned—but refusing the summons would be tantamount to declaring rebellion.

Lord Torian consulted with his family. The debate was fierce but brief. They could flee—the province was surrounded by imperial territory, and there was nowhere to run. They could not submit—the governor's intentions were clear, and submission meant death. There was only one remaining option.

Kharic Stormborn volunteered for the task.

He went to the governor's headquarters alone, armed with only a sword and his own terrible presence. The guards at the gate tried to stop him; he cut them down without breaking stride. The officials in the outer chambers tried to summon help; he killed them before they could raise the alarm. By the time he reached the governor's private office, he had left a trail of bodies behind him and his sword was dripping with blood.

Governor Willem Thornwood died badly. The historical records are unclear on the exact manner of his death, but all accounts agree that it was neither quick nor painless. When Kharic finally emerged from the headquarters, carrying the governor's head, he found a crowd gathered in the square outside—common folk who had heard the commotion and come to see what was happening.

Kharic raised the bloody trophy above his head, and beside it, unfurled a strip of old crimson cloth. He spoke the words that would later move mountains.

"The empire is dying!" he shouted. "Its laws are chains, and its officials are parasites! Today we break those chains! Today we crush those parasites! Today we remember who we are—the sons and daughters of Cheros, unconquered and unconquerable!"

The crowd erupted in cheers that could be heard throughout the city.

The rebellion in the south had begun.

OF KHARIC'S NATURE

In the weeks that followed, as the Stormborn clan gathered their forces and prepared for war, those who served under Kharic Stormborn came to understand what kind of leader they had chosen.

He was not like Corwin Harrow, who had led through inspiration and moral authority. Kharic led through force of personality—through the sheer overwhelming intensity of his presence, which made other men feel small and pale by comparison. When he spoke, men obeyed. They followed him because his certainty was a physical weight, a force they lacked the strength to push back. When he charged, men followed not because they believed they would win but because staying behind seemed more frightening than any enemy.

He was magnificent, and he was terrifying, and he was utterly incapable of moderation.

His rages were legendary. When things did not go as he wished—when subordinates failed him, when plans went awry, when the world refused to bend to his will—he would explode into violence that left strong men trembling. He once killed a messenger who brought bad news, then regretted it instantly and wept over the body. He once destroyed an entire camp's worth of supplies because a clerk had miscounted the inventory. His followers learned to approach him with caution, to deliver difficult news in indirect ways, to never, ever challenge him directly.

But his generosity was equally legendary. When he was pleased, he showered rewards upon those who had pleased him—gold and titles and land, distributed with careless abundance. He shared his soldiers' hardships, eating what they ate, sleeping where they slept, fighting in the front ranks where the danger was greatest. He remembered the names of men who had served him well, and he avenged the deaths of those who had fallen in his service.

Above all, he was brave. He sought out combat as other men sought out pleasure. He placed himself in situations where death was not just possible but probable, and emerged unscathed through some combination of skill, strength, and what could only be called destiny.

"He is not a man," one of his generals said afterward. "He is a force of nature—a storm, an earthquake, a flood. You cannot reason with him. You cannot predict him. You can only follow him and hope that when the destruction is done, you are still standing."

If Maren Ashford was water—formless, adaptable, seeping into cracks—then Kharic Stormborn was fire. And fire, for all its glory, consumes itself.

Fire was not a comfortable form of leadership. But it was effective, and in the chaos of civil war, effectiveness was what mattered.

OF ELDRAN GREYMANTLE
AND HIS COUNSEL

Among those who attached themselves to Kharic's rising banner was an elderly man named Eldran Greymantle.

The old man arrived at Torian Stormborn's court on a morning when the fog lay thick across the valley, as if the world itself was uncertain what shape it wished to take.

He came alone, on foot, leading a mule that carried nothing but a small chest of scrolls and a grey cloak rolled tight against the damp. The guards at the gate took him for a beggar at first—his robes were travel-stained, his beard untrimmed, his sandals worn through at the heel. It was only when he spoke that they understood their error.

"I am Eldran of the House of Greymantle," he said, his voice carrying the clipped precision of a man who had spent decades in the old court. "I served the Kings of Cheros before the conquest. I have come to serve them again."

The guards exchanged glances. The House of Greymantle had been extinguished in the purges—or so the official records claimed. Every man, woman, and child bearing that name had been put to the sword when the Empire decided that administrative competence was too dangerous to leave alive.

And yet here stood a survivor. Seventy years old, at least,

with eyes that had seen the old kingdom fall and the patience to wait fifteen years for its restoration.

They brought him to Lord Torian.

The patriarch of the Stormborn clan received Eldran. Torian sat in a high chair surrounded by his brothers, his nephews, and his captains. Kharic stood at his uncle's right hand, arms crossed, eyes suspicious.

"You claim to have served the Old Kings," Torian said, his voice like gravel in a wooden cup. "So did many men. Most of them are dead."

"I am not most men, my lord."

"Evidently not. The question is whether you are useful or merely fortunate."

Eldran did not flinch at the challenge. He had expected it. Men like Torian Stormborn did not survive fifteen years of resistance by trusting strangers.

"I am neither, my lord. I am necessary." He let the word hang in the air, watching the room react. The younger men bristled at the presumption. The older ones—those who remembered the complexities of the old court—leaned forward with interest. "You have swords. You have courage. You have the loyalty of Cheros. What you do not have is legitimacy."

Kharic's eyes narrowed. "We have the blood of the Stormborn. That is legitimacy enough."

"For Cheros, perhaps. But you do not seek to rule Cheros alone." Eldran turned to face the young warrior directly, unafraid of the barely contained violence in those pale blue eyes. "You seek to overthrow an empire. You seek to unite the southern provinces under a single banner. Tell me, Lord Kharic —when the lords of Yanling and Fenmark and the Jade Coast look at you, what do they see?"

"A conqueror."

"They see a warlord from the northern hills. A man who might free them from one tyrant only to become another." Eldran shook his head slowly. "The people do not fight for warlords, my lord. They fight for kings. They fight for bloodlines. They fight for the memory of what was and the promise of what might be again."

Torian's expression had not changed, but his eyes—those cold, patient eyes—had grown thoughtful. "You speak of raising a king."

"I speak of raising the *right* king." Eldran reached into his robe and withdrew a scroll, yellowed with age. "Before the conquest, I was keeper of the royal genealogies. I knew every branch of the Celestine bloodline, every cadet house, every bastard line that might carry the ancient claim. The Empire thought they had destroyed them all. They were wrong."

He unrolled the scroll on the table before Torian. A family tree, meticulously maintained, with one branch circled in faded red ink.

"The House of Aurelia. A minor branch of the royal line, so insignificant that the Imperial census-takers overlooked them entirely. The current heir is a shepherd named Arion, living in the high pastures above the River of Lament. He has no idea who he is. He cannot read. He prefers the company of his sheep to the complexities of men." Eldran smiled, thin and knowing. "He is perfect."

Kharic's face twisted with disgust. "You want us to bow to a sheep-herder?"

"I want you to place a crown on his head and speak with the voice of the Ancients. Let him sit in the carriage. Let him wear the crimson robes. Let the people see the blood of kings restored—and let them forget that the true power rides behind him, holding the sword."

The hall was silent. Every man present understood the

implications: they would be kingmakers, not kings. They would bow in public and command in private. It was a deception—a magnificent, necessary deception.

Torian studied the genealogy carefully. When he looked up, his eyes found Eldran's.

"You kept this scroll for fifteen years. Through the purges. Through the occupation. Through the executions of everyone who shared your name." His voice dropped to something barely above a whisper. "Why?"

"Because I knew, my lord, that the Empire would fall. All empires fall. And when this one fell, I intended to be useful to whoever rose from the ashes." Eldran met the patriarch's gaze without flinching. "I am offering you that usefulness now. The question is whether you have the wisdom to accept it."

Another man might have been killed for such presumption. Torian Stormborn merely smiled—the cold, thin smile of a man who recognized a fellow survivor.

"You will stay," he said. "You will advise. But know this, Greymantle: I take counsel, I do not take orders. If your advice is good, I will follow it. If it is not, I will ignore it. And if you ever try to manipulate this family—"

"Then you will kill me, my lord, and rightly so." Eldran bowed, deep and formal, the bow of a courtier who had served kings. "I would expect nothing less from the man who will restore them."

Kharic was initially dismissive. What use was an old man in a war that would be won by young men's swords?

But Eldran Greymantle was persistent, and eventually he secured an audience.

"You are the finest warrior of your generation," he told Kharic. "The finest warrior who has ever lived. You will win battles—many battles. But battles alone do not win wars."

"What else is there?"

"Strategy. Politics. The ability to see beyond the next fight to the shape of the conflict as a whole." Eldran leaned forward, his aged eyes bright with intelligence. "Corwin Harrow won battles too—"

Kharic's face darkened. "I am not Corwin Harrow."

"No, you are not. You are better—stronger, braver, more inspiring. But you share his weakness: you think that strength alone is enough. It is not. An empire is not conquered by strength; it is conquered by the patient application of force at the right places and the right times. You need someone who can see those places and times. You need me."

It was audacious counsel, delivered without a trace of deference or fear. Any other man might have been killed for such presumption.

Eldran did not bow nor looked at the muscles or the sword. He looked only at the young man's hands—that were constantly clenching and unclenching, as if trying to strangle the air itself. *Restless,* Eldran thought. *He is a fire that will burn the world to ash if not given a hearth to contain it. I must be that hearth.*

But Kharic saw something in the old man's eyes—a clarity, a certainty, a depth of understanding that even his pride could not dismiss.

"And what would you ask of me in return?" Kharic inquired.

"Only to see Cheros restored before I die. To know that the kingdom my ancestors served will rise again, greater than before." Eldran smiled, he looked not old but ageless—a repository of wisdom accumulated over generations. "I am not asking to command. I am asking to advise. The decisions will always be yours. But let me help you make better ones."

Kharic contemplated, then he nodded.

OF THE SHEPHERD KING

They found the shepherd three days later, living in a mud hut in the high pastures, unaware that he was the last surviving heir of the ancient Royal House of Arion, a side bloodline of the ancient House of Aurelia, of the Old Celestine Kings.

Lord Arion was a harmless, simple-minded elderly shepherd who preferred the company of his mutton to the complexities of men. When the Stormborn soldiers knelt before him in the mud, hailing him as King he wept—not from joy, but because he feared they had come to steal his flock.

"He is perfect," Torian whispered, watching the confused shepherd being draped in a crimson cloak.

"A puppet," Kharic muttered, his face dark with distaste. "He smells of dung and fear. We are to bow to *this*?"

"We bow to the blood, nephew, not the man," Torian replied. "We place him on the throne so that when we speak, it is with the voice of the Ancients. Let him wear the crown. Let him sit in the carriage. We will hold the sword."

And so Arion was paraded through the cities as King Arion, the Righteous—bearing the same title as his grandfather, the beloved last King of Cheros. Yet the grandson was merely a frightened figurehead in borrowed finery, used to legitimise a war he did not understand. The people cheered him, weeping to see the return of the Old Blood.

Kharic watched the cheering crowds with cold, cynical eyes. He learned a dangerous lesson that day: Power does not reside in the throne. It resides in the hand that positions the throne.

It was a lesson he would use later, with tragic cruelty, when the puppet's strings became tangled.

THE WISDOM THAT WAITS

A VIGNETTE OF ELDRAN GREYMANTLE

In the months that followed, Eldran Greymantle proved his worth a hundred times over. He knew the old administrative systems, the trade routes, the tax records, the names of every minor lord and their grudges against the Empire. He could recite from memory which provinces had grain and which had gold, which generals could be bribed and which would have to be broken.

Torian came to rely on him for strategy. Kharic came to respect him—grudgingly—for his understanding of men.

But Eldran was careful. He advised Torian first, always. He deferred to the patriarch in public and offered his sharpest insights in private. He understood that his position was precarious, that a single misstep could see him branded as a manipulator and executed.

He also understood that his true work would not begin until Torian was gone.

The old man watched Kharic with the patient attention of a sculptor studying marble. He saw the fire, the genius, the terrifying potential. He saw also the cracks—the impatience, the pride, the hunger for glory that would one day consume everything it touched.

In his first month as Kharic's advisor, Eldran Greymantle saved ten thousand lives without drawing a sword.

The city of Thornwick had declared against Kharic. Its lord —a stubborn old man named Harwick—had fortified the walls, stocked the granaries, and sworn to hold until the empire sent relief. Kharic's generals urged assault; his soldiers clamoured for the plunder that a stormed city would provide. The young warlord himself was inclined to agreement. An example needed to be made. Resistance needed to be punished.

"My lord," Eldran murmured, "may I speak with you alone?"

They walked together through the camp, the old man and the young warrior, until they reached a rise overlooking the city walls. In the distance, soldiers moved like ants along the battlements.

"You see those walls?" Eldran asked. "They have stood for three hundred years. They were built by engineers who understood that strength is not always the best defence—that sometimes the best defence is making the attack too costly to attempt."

"We shall take them," Kharic declared. "My warriors are the finest in all the realm—"

"Your men would take those walls. Eventually. And when they did, they would lose five thousand in the assault, perhaps more. They would sack the city, as armies always do after a hard fight. They would kill civilians, rape women, burn buildings. And when they were done, the survivors—those who had lost fathers and sons and daughters to your soldiers—would hate you with a hatred that would never fade."

Kharic's jaw tightened. "You counsel cowardice?"

"I counsel wisdom." Eldran pointed towards the city. "Lord Harwick is seventy-two years old. His only son died in the conquest. His grandsons are children. When he dies—which will be soon, because men his age do not survive sieges—there will be no one to hold that city together. No one with the authority to maintain resistance." He paused. "We need not storm those walls, my lord. We need only wait for time to do our work for us."

"Wait? You expect my men to sit idle while—"

"I expect your men to maintain a siege while you continue

the campaign elsewhere. Leave a holding force. Advance with the main army. Take the cities that will fall quickly, gather the victories that will draw more men to your banner. When you return—in six months, a year—Thornwick will open its gates of its own accord. Because Lord Harwick will be dead, and his people will have no one left to die for."

Kharic stared at the old man. "And if you're wrong? If they hold?"

"Then you will have lost nothing but time. The city will still be there. Your army will be stronger, your position more secure. You can storm the walls then, if you choose." Eldran smiled. "But you won't need to. Because the first law of sieges is this: defenders who see no hope of relief eventually stop defending."

Six months later, Lord Harwick died in his sleep—his heart giving out, the physicians said, under the strain of endless waiting. Within a week, his council had opened negotiations. Within a month, Thornwick had submitted to Kharic's authority.

No assault. No massacre. No breeding ground for the rebellions that would otherwise have plagued Kharic's rear for years to come.

"How came you by such foresight?" Kharic asked, when the city had fallen. "What oracle whispered that he would fall?"

"I didn't know," Eldran replied. "But I knew men. I knew that a man of seventy-two, under siege, with no hope and no heir, would not survive long. And I knew that the city's resistance was built on one man's stubbornness—that when he fell, the structure he had built would fall with him." He bowed slightly. "Walls can be broken, my lord. But it is easier to wait for them to crumble."

It was a lesson Kharic would remember—and later, tragically, forget. The wisdom that had saved Thornwick would be abandoned when it conflicted with his pride. The patience that Eldran counseled would give way to the fury that Kharic could never quite control.

But for one moment, standing on that rise, the old man and the young warrior understood each other perfectly.

Yet, even as he praised the old man, Kharic's hand rested on his sword hilt, tapping a restless rhythm.

"Effective," he murmured, looking at the city that had surrendered without blood. "But slow. I do not like slow things, Father. They give the enemy time to think."

Eldran heard the rhythm. *Tap. Tap. Tap.* And for the first time, he knew a chill that had nothing to do with the winter wind.

And that understanding remained through the years, a reminder of what might have been—if only Kharic had continued to listen.

OF THE RED EARTH AND THE HEGEMON'S DREAM

Kharic did not want to rule the world; he wanted to restore it.

To him, the Ironhold Empire was not a civilisation, but a giant, grinding machine that had flattened the soul of the land. He hated the ink-stained clerks who measured a man's worth in copper and grain. He hated the straight, grey imperial roads that sliced through the ancient, curved paths of the ancestors.

On the night after he took the Governor's head, Kharic stood on the balcony of the red stone citadel, looking south towards the waterways of Cheros. The air smelt of salt and wild jasmine—the scent of a home that had been held in a chokehold for forty years.

"They call us rebels," Eldran Greymantle said, leaning on

his staff beside him. "But to the people down there, you are a memory they thought they had lost."

"I do not seek a throne of Iron, Father," Kharic said, his voice low and resonant, like the first roll of a distant storm. "The First Emperor wanted a world that was a single, perfect cage. I want a world that breathes. I want the kings of the South to be kings again. I want the clans of the East to hunt in their own forests without asking permission from a bureaucrat in Steelhaven."

His political ideal was not a New Order, but a Great Restoration, of Nobility upheld. He envisioned himself not as an Emperor, but as the Hegemon—the Lord of Lords, the High Protector who sat above a patchwork of sovereign kingdoms. He would be the sun around which the lesser stars revolved—not by the authority of laws and taxes, but by the raw, undisputed weight of his own glory.

"It is a dream of the past, my Lord," Eldran whispered. "The world has grown small under the Iron. It may not know how to be free anymore."

"Then I will teach it," Kharic said, his hand tightening on the hilt of his father's sword. "I will break the machine, and in its place, I will plant the old seeds. If the world has forgotten the taste of honour and the sound of the drums, I will carve the lesson into their bones. I will give Cheros back to the red earth, and the red earth back to Cheros. And then... I will be the first man in forty years to finally sleep in peace."

He looked at his hands—the hands that had just killed a Governor. They were stained, but they felt alive. For the first time in his life, the silence of Drumhold didn't feel like a grave. It felt like a held breath.

CHAPTER SIX

END OF THE BEGINNING

IN WHICH THE REBELLION ENGULFS THE REALM, AND CORWIN HARROW FALLS TO TREACHERY

In which a field is burnt, a mob is born, and the Empire learns that hunger is more flammable than oil.
— *The Annals of the Crimson Art*

SIX MONTHS AFTER THE RISING OF SORROWFEN

OF THE KINGDOM OF RISING CHEROS

In the space of two months, Corwin Harrow had transformed from a condemned conscript into a king.

It was not a title he had sought, nor one he wore comfortably. When his followers had first proposed it—when they had knelt before him in the ruins of the third city they had captured and begged him to take a crown—he had laughed and asked them if they had forgotten his own words. Were kings and lords born to greatness? If not, then what made him any more suited to rule than the man beside him, or the woman behind, or the child watching from the shadows?

But Declan Sayer, who had become his closest advisor, had pulled him aside and spoken plainly.

"You asked a question," Declan said. "Now you must answer it. If kings are not born but made, then someone must be made king—or else we have no king at all, and an army without a king is a mob. The people need something to follow, Corwin. They need a banner, a name, a face. Give them yours, or watch everything we've built fall apart."

So Corwin had accepted the crown—a circlet of bronze hastily forged from melted-down imperial coins—and declared himself King of Rising Cheros, heir to the old kingdom that Ironhold had destroyed. He established his capital at Thornhall, a city that had once been the heart of Cheros's northern territories, and sent messengers throughout the realm calling all who opposed the Iron Emperor to join his cause.

They came. Oh, how they came.

From every corner of the crumbling empire, the desperate and the angry answered his call. Farmers who had lost their land to imperial seizures. Merchants who had been ruined by endless taxation. Scholars who had seen their libraries cremated and their colleagues buried alive. Soldiers who had grown sick of serving masters who saw them as expendable. They came in hundreds, then thousands, then tens of thousands, until Corwin's army had swelled beyond anything he could reasonably command.

And they did not come alone.

Throughout the former kingdoms, other men were raising other banners. In the east, where Aldoria had once flourished, the Thorne clan—descendants of the old royal house—had reclaimed their ancestral seat and declared the restoration of their kingdom. In the north, ambitious generals who had served Ironhold were now carving out territories of their own, paying lip service to Corwin's authority while building independent power bases. In the west, the people of Dragonspire and Grandmark and Narrowdale were stirring, remembering the days before unification, dreaming of crowns their grandfathers had worn.

The empire was not merely cracking. It was shattering.

And Corwin Harrow, who had started it all with a single question, found himself at the centre of a whirlwind he could not control.

OF THE KING WHO LISTENED

A Vignette of Corwin Harrow

They brought the woman to him on the eve of his greatest victory.

She was old—with skin like crumpled parchment and eyes that held more years than anyone should have to carry. Her name was Mar, nothing more, just Mar, the way the common folk named themselves when they had no surnames worth keeping. She had walked thirty miles from her village to see the king, and she would not be turned away.

"Let her in," Corwin said, when his guards reported the disturbance. "If she came this far, she has something to say."

The woman shuffled into the throne room—if you could call it that, the captured merchant's hall with its borrowed tapestries and makeshift dignity—and stood before the king without bowing. The guards tensed. The advisors murmured. But Corwin only smiled.

"Goodwife," he said, using the respectful term. "What brings you here?"

"My grandson," she said. Her voice was steady, accustomed

to being heard. "He joined your army at Riverside. He was sixteen. He is dead now."

In the room everyone waited, for the explosion—for the guards to drag this insolent peasant away, for the king to defend his cause with righteous anger. But Corwin only nodded.

"I am sorry," he said. "Truly sorry. What was his name?"

"Warren. Just Warren." The old woman's eyes were dry, but something in them was worse than tears. "He believed in you. He said you would make things better. He said the old ways were ending, that men like him could finally matter."

"He was right," Corwin murmured. "He did matter. Every man who fights—"

"He is still dead." The words cut like a knife. "Your words are pretty, King. Your question was clever. But my grandson is still dead, and I am too old to have another, and when I die there will be no one to tend my grave or remember my name."

Corwin rose from his throne. His advisors moved to stop him, but he waved them away. He walked down the steps—slowly, deliberately—until he stood face to face with the woman who had walked thirty miles to accuse him.

"You are right," he said. "Your grandson is dead, and no speech of mine can bring him back. No victory I win will give you comfort. The world I am trying to build—if I build it—will come too late for you, and too late for him."

"Then why?" the old woman asked. "Why do you keep fighting? Why do you send more grandsons to die?"

Corwin said nothing. When he finally spoke, his voice was rough with grief.

"Because if I stop, they will have died for nothing. Because the question I asked cannot be un-asked, and if I fail now, the empire will answer it with blood—not just my blood, but the blood of everyone who dared to hope." He reached out and took the old woman's hands—gently, as one holds something precious. "I cannot bring your grandson back. I cannot promise you victory. All I can promise is that I will remember him. That when I stand on the battlefield tomorrow, his name will be in my heart. That if we win—if we somehow win—his sacrifice will have helped build something worth building."

"Pretty words," the woman said again. But this time her voice was softer.

"They are all I have," Corwin replied. "That and this." He pulled the bronze ring from his finger—the symbol of his kingship, the only treasure he possessed—and pressed it into her palm. "Sell it, if hunger demands it. Or keep it, to remember that a king once held your hands and wept for your grandson."

The old woman looked at the ring. She looked at the king. And then, slowly, she bowed—the first bow she had ever given in her life.

"His name was Warren," she said. "Remember it."

"I will."

She left without another word, clutching the bronze ring so tightly that its sharp imperial patterns left a raw, red indentation in her palm. It was a quiet, unintended reminder that even when the hand that gives it is kind, the weight of a crown always leaves a mark on the skin of those who must carry its cost.

The court resumed its business. The war continued, and the dead continued to accumulate, and the question Corwin had asked remained unanswered.

But those who had witnessed the moment never forgot it. They told their children, and their children told theirs, and the story passed down through generations—of the rebel king who had given away his crown to an old woman who cursed him, who had wept for a farmer's grandson he had never met.

Years later, when Maren Ashford won the throne and

wondered what kind of emperor he should become, it was Corwin's example he remembered. The king who listened.

OF THE COUNSEL OF OSRIC GOLDENCLOAK

Among those who came to Corwin's court were two men whose names made their imprint through the ages: Osric Goldencloak and Iain Cairn.

They were sworn brothers—bound by oaths more sacred than blood, forged in the dark years when they had hidden from Ironhold's hunters in the back alleys of a conquered city. Both had been wanted men in the old regime: Osric for the crime of being a famous scholar, Rowan for the crime of being Osric's friend. They had survived by wit and caution, by knowing when to bow and when to run, by enduring indignities that would have broken lesser men.

Now, with the empire in chaos, they had emerged from hiding to offer their services to the new king.

Corwin received them in his makeshift throne room—a merchant's hall hastily converted to royal purposes—and listened as Osric Goldencloak spoke.

"Your Majesty," Osric began, and Corwin could hear the quotation marks around the title, "you have accomplished something remarkable. In two months, you have done what the greatest generals of the old kingdoms could not do in fifteen years: you have broken Ironhold's grip on the realm. The question now is what comes next."

"What comes next is victory," Corwin said. "We march on Steelhaven, tear down The Creedseat, and—"

"And then?" Osric was gentle but insistent. "Forgive me, Majesty, but have you considered what happens after you've won? Assuming you can defeat the imperial armies—and that is by no means certain—what kind of realm will you build on the ruins?"

Corwin frowned. He had not, in truth, given much thought to such questions. The rebellion had moved so fast, demanded so much, that there had been no time for planning beyond the next battle, the next city, the next meal for his ever-growing army.

"We restore the old kingdoms," he said. "We undo what Ironhold did. We give the people back their freedom."

"Which people?" Iain Cairn spoke for the first time, his voice harder than his brother's. "The people of Cheros? They'll want their kingdom back. The people of Aldoria? They've already declared their own king. The people of Dragonspire and Grandmark and Narrowdale? They're all raising banners even now, and none of them will be content to bow to you once the common enemy is gone."

"They'll have to work together. We all serve the same cause."

"Do we?" Osric shook his head. "Majesty, you've unleashed something that cannot be easily controlled. The old kingdoms didn't fall because Ironhold was strong—they fell because they couldn't stop fighting each other. If you restore them, they'll go right back to warring among themselves. The chaos that Ironhold ended will return, and everything you've sacrificed will have been for nothing."

Corwin weighed the words. He could feel the weight of the bronze crown on his head, heavier than it had any right to be.

"What would you have me do?"

"Don't proclaim yourself lord of a restored Cheros," Osric said. "Proclaim yourself king of something larger—something that encompasses all the old kingdoms, that gives everyone a stake in victory. Don't fight to restore the past. Fight to build a future."

Corwin recognised the wisdom in it. But even as he nodded at the two advisors for their wisdom, he could feel the moment slipping away from him. He had asked a question that had shaken the world, but he did not have the answers the world now demanded.

Kings and lords were not born to greatness. But they needed to be born to something—some quality of vision, some capacity for rule—that Corwin Harrow, for all his courage, did not possess.

OF THE BATTLE OF
THE WESTERN ROAD

The empire's response, when it finally came, was devastating.

General Jared Steelbane—the finest military commander in Ironhold's service—had gathered an army of three hundred thousand men: veterans of the unification wars, disciplined professionals who had spent their lives learning the art of killing. He marched them south at forced pace, sweeping aside the scattered rebel forces that attempted to slow his advance, leaving a trail of deadland and crucified prisoners that announced his intentions with brutal clarity.

Corwin met him on the Western Road, fifty miles from the capital at Thornhall.

It should not have been a fair fight. Corwin's army was larger—nearly half a million men—but it was a mob rather than a military force, a collection of farmers and labourers who had picked up weapons weeks or months ago and still barely knew how to use them. They had won their previous battles through surprise, through desperation, through the simple fact that their enemies had been small garrisons and second-rate troops rather than the empire's finest.

This was different. This was the iron fist of Ironhold, the

same force that had crushed the great kingdoms one by one, the same disciplined machine that had never been defeated in open battle.

The rebels charged with the fury of free men. The imperial lines met them with the silence of machines. There were no war cries from Steelbane's ranks, only the rhythmic thud of shields locking together and the mechanical *thrum-snap* of ten thousand heavy crossbows firing in unison. It was not a battle; it was an industrial process. The farmers threw themselves against a wall of iron bristles, and the wall simply marched over them.

The fight lasted three hours, but in Corwin's mind, time had simply ceased to exist. When the screaming stopped, the silence that followed was far worse—a heavy, wet stillness broken only by the sound of thousands of boots retreating through the gore. The Western Road wasn't a road anymore; it was a river of crimson paste where the smell of split iron and human waste rose in a sickening steam. Corwin stood amongst the ruins of his dream, his bronze crown tilted, his face spattered with the blood of men whose names he had promised to remember but had already begun to forget.

By the end, Corwin's army was broken. Two hundred thousand men lay dead or dying on the Western Road, their blood turning the autumn mud into crimson paste. Another hundred thousand had fled, scattering into the countryside, abandoning weapons and standards and any pretense of organisation. The rebellion that had shaken the world was retreating in chaos, and General Jared Steelbane was already preparing to pursue.

On the ridge overlooking the slaughter, General Steelbane lowered his spyglass. He did not cheer. He did not smile. He watched the carnage with the cold, necessary detachment of a surgeon cutting out gangrene. "This is the price of anger," he said to his aide, his voice flat as the dead land below. "Only iron keeps order."

Brennan Axle drove the king's chariot through the aftermath.

The wheels stuck constantly—not on rocks or ruts, but on bodies. Brennan had to climb down again and again to free them, his boots sinking into mud that was more blood than earth. Once, he looked down and saw a boy's face staring up at him. The boy could not have been more than fourteen. His hands were still wrapped around a spear shaft, the spear itself snapped in half. The hands were too small for the weapon. They had always been too small.

"Keep moving," Corwin said from the chariot, his voice hollow. "We have to keep moving."

Brennan climbed back up and whipped the horses forward. The wheels rolled over the boy's outstretched arm with a sound he would hear in his dreams for the rest of his short life.

A mile further, a dying farmer reached up and grasped the chariot's rim. His guts were spilling out of a wound in his belly, but his eyes were clear, lucid with the terrible clarity of approaching death.

"King," he whispered. "My king."

Corwin leaned down to take his hand.

"I'm sorry," the king said. "I'm sorry I couldn't—"

"Don't be sorry." The farmer's voice was fading. "Just... don't let it be for nothing. Don't let us die for nothing."

His hand went slack. Brennan drove on.

They did not speak again until they reached Thornhall.

Corwin himself survived—barely. He rallied what remained of his forces and retreated to the city, but he knew that it could not hold. The walls were weak, the defenders were dispirited, and Jared Steelbane was coming.

OF BRENNAN AXLE
AND HIS GRIEVANCE

Before we speak of the treachery, we must speak of the man who committed it.

Brennan Axle had been with Corwin since Sorrowfen—one of the original nine hundred, one of those who had knelt in the mud and sworn the oath. He had driven Corwin's chariot in a dozen battles, had saved the king's life twice, had bled more times than he could count for a cause he believed in.

But belief, like all things, can curdle.

It began with small slights. Corwin promoted other men—Declan Sayer, whose clever tongue had done less than Brennan's strong arms. New advisors arrived: Osric Goldencloak with his scholarly wisdom, Iain Cairn with his connections to the northern lords. These men sat in councils while Brennan waited outside with the horses.

"You're the charioteer," Corwin told him once, when Brennan asked to be included. "Your place is at my side in battle, not in war councils."

"I've fought more battles than half your advisors combined."

"And that's why I need you where the fighting happens, not where the talking happens." Corwin clapped him on the shoulder. "You're too valuable to waste on politics, Brennan. Trust me."

Trust. That was the word that festered.

After the Western Road disaster—after the retreat, the starving army, the growing whispers that Corwin had led them into a trap—Brennan found himself thinking thoughts he had never thought before.

He needed me when he was nobody. Now that he's a king, I'm a charioteer.

I saved his life. What has he saved of mine?

When the empire comes for us—and they will come—who will die first? The king? Or the man who drives his chariot?

The imperial agent found him on the second night after the retreat, when the camp was gripped by despair and suspicion.

The man wore perfumed gloves—an absurdity in a camp that reeked of blood and shit and fear. His voice was soft, priestly, the voice of a confessor rather than a spy. On his smallest finger gleamed a ring bearing the Ironhold seal: the iron fist clutching the sun.

"Brennan Axle," the agent said. Not a question. "Born in Millbrook village, third son of a wheelwright. Your mother's name is Marta. She still lives in the cottage by the old mill—the one with the red door that your father painted the summer before he died."

Brennan's blood chilled. "How do you—"

"The empire knows everything, Brennan. Everything that matters." The agent's smile was gentle, kind. "We know that your mother has been questioned three times about your whereabouts. We know that she has lied bravely each time. We know that our patience with her lies is... finite."

"If you touch her—"

"Touch her? Why would we touch her?" The agent spread his perfumed hands. "She's done nothing wrong. She's simply the mother of a rebel. When the rebellion ends—as it must—her son's choices will determine her fate. If you die a traitor, she dies a traitor's mother. If you die a hero of the empire..."

He let the sentence hang.

"The king trusts you," the agent continued. "You could end this. One stroke, and the rebellion dies. One stroke, and your mother lives out her days in peace. One stroke, and the boy whose hands were too small for his spear—there won't be any more of those."

Brennan flinched. The agent had seen him on the Western Road. Had watched him free the chariot wheel from that child's body.

"The empire doesn't offer forgiveness," the agent murmured. "The empire offers survival. Your mother's survival. Your survival, if you're quick enough to reach the imperial lines before the other rebels realise what you've done." He paused.

The agent reached into his robe and placed a small object on the table. It was a half-finished wool sock, grey, with a distinct red stitching at the heel—Marta's signature style. Brennan stared at it. He could almost see his mother's hands holding the needles, sitting by the fire, unaware that a monster had been in her home, touching her things. "She was knitting this when we visited," the agent whispered. "She dropped a stitch when we asked about you."

"We can even arrange for you to be 'captured' rather than rewarded. No one will know you chose this. Your honour remains intact."

"And if I refuse?"

The agent's smile didn't waver. "Then you die with your king, your mother dies answering questions about her traitor son, and the rebellion ends anyway—a week later, with more dead children on both sides." He shrugged. "The empire can afford patience. Can you?"

Brennan thought of his mother's hands, rough from years of spinning wool, gentle when they touched his face. He thought of the boy's hands wrapped around the spear shaft. He thought of Corwin's hand reaching down to grasp the dying farmer's.

"What would I have to do?"

The agent told him.

OF THE LAST COUNCIL
AND CORWIN'S CHOICE

On the morning of the third day, Corwin called his remaining advisors to council.

The room was half-empty. So many had died on the Western Road, or fled in the aftermath, or vanished into the chaos of defeat. Declan Sayer was there, his silver tongue silent for once, his face grey with exhaustion. Osric Goldencloak and Iain Cairn sat together, whispering urgently. And Brennan Axle stood by the door, as he always stood—close enough to hear, far enough to be forgotten.

"We must retreat," Osric Goldencloak said. "North, to Dragonspire. The lords there have declared for us. We can rebuild—"

"Rebuild what?" Corwin's throat was hoarse from three days of shouting orders that no one obeyed. "Our army is gone. Our treasury is empty. Our cause is—"

"Our cause is not dead while you live, Majesty." This from Declan Sayer, finding his voice at last. "The question you asked still burns in men's hearts. As long as you survive, the rebellion survives."

"Then the question should pass to other lips." Corwin stood abruptly, his chair scraping against the stone floor. "I am not a general. I am a conscript who asked a question and ended up wearing a crown I never wanted."

"Majesty—"

"I should surrender."

The silence that followed was absolute.

"I should ride to Jared Steelbane's camp under a white flag," Corwin continued, his voice steadying as the idea took shape. "I should offer myself in exchange for the lives of my men. The empire wants my head—let them have it. Let the rest of you scatter, survive, carry the question forward."

"They won't honour that bargain," Iain Cairn murmured. "You know they won't."

"No. But at least my death would mean something. At least I wouldn't be running while other men die for me."

"And what of us?" Brennan Axle spoke from the doorway. Everyone turned—the council had dismissed him, forgotten he was there. "What of the men who've followed you this far? Do we get a choice in how we die?"

Corwin's face softened. "Brennan. Old friend. You've been with me since—"

"Since Sorrowfen. Since the mud. Since I drove your chariot through a field of dead boys and you held a dying farmer's hand and promised him it wouldn't be for nothing." Brennan's voice cracked. "Was it for nothing, Majesty? All of it?"

"I... I don't know." Corwin looked lost—a man wearing a crown he had never learned to carry. "I don't know anymore. I asked a question, and men answered with their lives, and now I don't know if the question was worth asking."

"Then ask us. Ask what we want. Give us a choice."

Corwin considered this. Then he shook his head.

"There is no choice to give. We retreat north tonight. Osric Goldencloak will lead the main column. I will stay behind with a rear guard—buy you time to escape."

"You'll die."

"Probably." Corwin smiled—that same weary, wondering smile he had worn in Sorrowfen, when the rain fell and the world changed. "But at least I'll die answering my own question. Kings are not born to greatness, Brennan. They choose it. And sometimes choosing it means choosing to fall."

He turned to Osric Goldencloak. "Prepare the evacuation. Brennan Axle—" He paused, looking at his charioteer, his oldest companion who had pulled his chariot wheel from a dead child's body. "I need you with the main column. They'll need someone who knows the roads."

"My place is with you." The words came out strangled.

"Your place is wherever I need you to be. And I need you alive." Corwin gripped his shoulder. "You're my charioteer, Brennan. My hands on the reins. Without you, I couldn't have come this far." His voice dropped. "When this is over—when the empire falls, as it must—the men who survive will need leaders. You could be one of them. Land, title, everything I should have given you already."

Too late, something whispered in Brennan's mind. *Always too late.*

"I never wanted land." His voice was barely audible.

"I know. But you deserved it anyway." Corwin released him and turned away. "Go. Prepare the horses. I'll find you before we leave."

Brennan looked at Corwin's back. He remembered when this back was just the sweat-soaked shirt of a man pushing a plough. Now, it was draped in the mantle of a King, a barrier of bronze and expectation that Brennan could no longer reach.

The grey wool sock in his pocket felt like a brand, searing his skin. The Imperial agent had been right: Corwin was no longer a man; he was a 'Question'. And Brennan was tired of serving a question that only answered with the sound of breaking bones. He didn't want a kingdom; he wanted the smell of his mother's hearth and the certainty that he wouldn't die for a man who had forgotten the taste of real bread.

Brennan walked out of the council chamber with the knife already burning against his thigh, hidden beneath the folds of his cloak.

OF THE PEASANT KING'S SOLITUDE

Corwin did not go directly to his chambers.

He walked instead to the stables, as he had done every evening since they took Thornhall. The grooms had learned not to bow, not to announce him, not to treat him as anything other than someone who had come to see his horse. It was the only place left where he could pretend.

The grey mare was old now—fifteen years, though she moved like twenty. She had carried him from Sorrowfen, through the siege of Greyfork, up the blood-slicked slopes of the Thornwood passes. When he entered her stall, she turned her head towards him and made a soft sound of recognition.

"There you are," Corwin murmured, reaching up to scratch behind her ears. "Still here. Still waiting."

He leaned his forehead against her neck and closed his eyes. The smell of hay and horse and old leather surrounded him. He was not a king facing defeat, not a symbol around which a rebellion had grown and withered, not a man whose closest companion had just walked out with murder in his heart. He was simply Corwin, thirty-six years old, tired beyond measure, standing in a stable with an old horse who did not care whether he won or lost.

"I should have stayed a farmer," he whispered. The mare flicked her ear but offered no opinion.

He stayed there until the light faded, then walked slowly back to his chambers to wait for whoever might come.

OF THE TREACHERY
AT THORNHALL

That night, Brennan Axle walked into Corwin's chambers.

The king was alone, bent over maps that showed evacuation routes he would never take. A pitcher of water stood on the table beside him, two cups already poured. He had been expecting someone—hoping for one final conversation before the end.

He looked up when Brennan entered, and his face showed only warmth.

"Brennan. I hoped you'd come. Sit—drink with me. I know I don't deserve it, but I wanted to thank you. For everything."

Brennan sat. His hand trembled as he reached for the cup. He brought it halfway to his lips, then set it down.

"I can't."

"Can't drink? Or can't forgive me?" Corwin's smile was sad. "I understand. I've asked too much of you—of everyone. If I could do it again…"

"Don't," said Brennan. "Don't say that. Don't tell me what you'd do differently. Don't—"

His hand found the knife. Drew it.

Corwin saw the blade and went very still.

"Ah," he murmured. "So that's how it is."

"I'm sorry." Tears were streaming down Brennan's face now, tears he couldn't stop, couldn't control. "I'm sorry, I'm sorry, I didn't want—my mother, they have my mother's name, they know where she lives—"

"Brennan—"

"You promised me." The words came out in a sob. "You promised it would mean something. The boy on the road, the farmer who called you king—you held his hand and promised him—"

"I know."

"Then why?" Brennan was standing now, the knife shaking in his grip. "Why couldn't you win? Why couldn't you be what you promised? Why did you make us believe when you couldn't—when you were never—"

"Because I believed too." Corwin rose slowly from his chair. He made no move towards a weapon, no attempt to call for guards. He simply stood there, facing the man who would kill him, with a terrible peace settling over his features. "I believed the question mattered. I still believe it, Brennan. Even now."

"Even now?"

"Even now." Corwin took a step forward—towards the knife, not away from it. "Do what you must. Save your mother. Save yourself, if you can. But remember this: the question doesn't die with me. It never could. You can kill he who asked it, but you cannot unask it."

Brennan's hand stopped shaking. A brittle loathing settled into his chest, filling the space where grief had been.

"I know." His voice was steady now—terrible in its steadiness. "That's why it had to be me."

The blade took Corwin in the chest.

As the steel pierced him, the agony was strangely brief. The merchant's hall, the maps, the heavy crown—all dissolved into a blur of grey. For a fleeting second, Corwin wasn't a King in Thornhall. He was back in the fields of Sorrowfen, the smell of damp earth and coming rain filling his lungs. He saw the grey mare waiting by the fence. He had asked the world if kings were born to greatness, and as the floor rushed up to meet him, he finally found his answer: Greatness was a lie told to the living to justify the dead.

He died with a sigh, a man finally laying down a weight he was never meant to carry. The king of the rebels—the man who had asked whether kings were born to greatness—looked down at the steel piercing his heart with an expression not of surprise, but of recognition. He had always known it would end this way, some part of him had been waiting for it.

"Thank you," he whispered.

Brennan didn't understand. He would never understand.

He withdrew the blade and watched his king fall. The king who asked whether kings were born to greatness died without answering his own question, his blood pooling on the floor of a merchant's hall in a city that would fall within the week.

Brennan stood there. Knife dripping. Waiting to feel something. He felt nothing.

Imperial agents killed him three days later. A loose end. They left a grey wool sock on his chest—the one the agent had stolen from his mother's basket. It was still unfinished. Just like his treason.

When Jared Steelbane's forces finally entered Thornhall, they found the rebel leadership in chaos. Declan Sayer had been killed trying to avenge his friend. Osric Goldencloak and Iain Cairn had fled north, towards Dragonspire, where they would play their own role in the dramas to come. The army had dissolved, its soldiers melting back into the population from which they had come.

The first phase of the rebellion was over.

But the fire Corwin had lit was not extinguished—merely scattered. Across the realm, other men were picking up the torch he had dropped, other voices were asking the question he had first asked. The empire had won a battle, but the war was only beginning.

And in the south, where the old kingdom of Cheros had once held sway, a young man named Kharic Stormborn was watching the flames and making plans of his own.

OF THE QUESTION
THAT REMAINED

In the histories that would be written centuries later, scholars would debate what might have happened if Corwin Harrow had lived. Some argued that he lacked the vision to lead the rebellion to final victory—that his skills were those of an agitator rather than a ruler, a destroyer rather than a builder. Others contended that his death robbed the movement of its philosophical centre, its commitment to the revolutionary principle that legitimacy came from the people rather than from blood or conquest.

But both arguments missed the point. Corwin Harrow had asked a question: *Are kings and lords born to greatness?* He had not lived long enough to provide an answer. But the question itself had changed the world.

The war that followed would provide an answer. But it would not be a simple answer, and it would not be a comfortable one.

OF WHAT CORWIN CHANGED

In the weeks after Corwin's death, the empire celebrated.

High Magistrate Mordecai declared three days of festival. The Boy Emperor issued proclamations (written by Mordecai, signed without reading) announcing that the rebellion had been crushed, that order had been restored, that the Iron Creed would endure forever as it had always endured.

They were wrong. They were catastrophically, fatally wrong.

For the empire that celebrated was already dying—in involution, even while it proclaimed its boundless strength. The Iron Emperor had spent his final years chasing immortality while the realm's foundations crumbled. His heir was a puppet, his council a nest of vipers fighting over scraps of power. The treasury was empty, drained by the eastern expeditions and the paranoid construction of walls that could not hold back ideas. The legions that had conquered the world were shadows of their former glory—undermanned, unpaid, led by officers who had been promoted for loyalty rather than competence.

And most fatally of all: the empire had forgotten how to inspire.

The Iron Creed had held the realm together through fear. But fear is a fire that must be constantly fed. The moment it flickers—the moment the subjects glimpse weakness—they remember that they outnumber their masters a thousand to one. Corwin Harrow had shown that flicker. He had proven that the empire could be challenged, that its armies could be fought, that its laws could be defied. He had died for that proof—but the proof remained.

In the villages and towns, in the work camps and conscript barracks, the news of Corwin's death spread like plague. But it did not spread as the empire intended. It did not terrify the population into submission.

Instead, it made them angry.

"They killed him," a blacksmith in Thornvale whispered to his apprentices. "They killed whoever asked the question. That means they're afraid of the question."

"If they're afraid of the question," his apprentice replied, "then maybe the question is worth asking."

Stories multiplied. Corwin became more than he had ever been in life—a martyr, a prophet, a symbol of everything the empire feared. His simple words ("Are kings and lords born to greatness?") were carved into walls, whispered in taverns, taught to children as a catechism of defiance.

And everywhere, men looked at each other with new eyes. *If Corwin could do it—a conscript, a farmer, a nobody—then why not us?*

The empire responded with cruelty. Suspected rebels were executed by the hundreds. Villages that harbored fugitives were burnt to the ground. The Iron Creed, always harsh, became monstrous in its application.

But cruelty only fanned the flames. Each execution created a dozen new rebels. Each burnt village sent refugees streaming into the hills, where other men were gathering, other banners were rising, other voices were taking up Corwin's question.

In Aldoria, the merchant lords calculated profits and losses and decided that rebellion might be good for business.

In Dragonspire, the descendants of the old northern kings remembered their heritage and reached for their ancient swords.

In the central provinces, imperial governors looked at their garrisons—depleted by the war, demoralised by the endless suppression—and wondered if they were on the wrong side.

OF AN ANSWER

And in the south, in the marshes and river valleys of Old Cheros, the Stormborn clan heard the news and knew that their moment had finally come.

"Corwin Harrow is dead," Lord Torian Stormborn told his assembled family. "The rebellion he started is in chaos. The empire thinks it has won."

Kharic stepped into the light, and the air in the hall seemed to surrender. His eyes—those terrifying double pupils—didn't just look at you; they pinned you like a moth to a wall. In the silence of the southern night, he was the only thing that felt real.

"Corwin Harrow asked a question," Kharic said, his voice a low vibration that rattled the effigies on the shelf. He didn't look like a man seeking justice; he looked like a predator claiming a void. "He used words to break the Iron. I will use the Iron to break the world."

He did not merely draw his sword; he unleashed it. The steel caught the dim torchlight, reflecting the twin storms in his eyes. "The time for questions is over," he whispered. "Now, the Empire gets its answer."

"Then we will teach them otherwise."

He turned to the window, where smoke from distant burning villages stained the horizon—the empire's retaliation against suspected rebel sympathisers. He watched the smoke rise, his face unreadable. Then he walked to the family shrine, where the tablets of his ancestors stood in speechless rows.

His father's tablet was there. Lord Roderic Stormborn, executed when Kharic was nine years old, his head displayed on a pike outside the provincial capital. Kharic had been forced to watch. The empire had wanted him to learn fear.

Instead, he had learned patience. And hatred. And the absolute certainty that one day he would repay every drop of his father's blood with an ocean of imperial dead.

He lifted the tablet from its place. Kissed it once. Set it down again.

"Father," he murmured, "I'm coming. Watch from wherever the dead watch, and see what your son will do."

He turned to face the room. His eyes—those terrifying double pupils, like twin storms trapped in amber—fixed upon Lord Torian. "Destiny does not ask questions, uncle," Kharic said softly. "Destiny takes." Then he walked to the centre of the hall, and everyone felt the temperature change—the way a storm had entered through the windows and was gathering itself to strike.

"The empire believes it has crushed one rebellion," Kharic said. "It has merely created space for another. Corwin asked whether kings are born to greatness." His hand dropped to the sword at his hip—the sword his father had carried, the sword that had been hidden from imperial confiscators for fifteen years. "I will provide the answer."

He drew the blade. Held it high.

"We march in three days. Tell the clans. Tell the villages. Tell anyone who remembers what Cheros was, and what it will be again."

The fire in his eyes was terrible to behold.

And those who watched him—family, retainers, the old men who remembered the fallen kingdom—understood that they were witnessing the birth of something that would shake the world. Whether it would save them or destroy them, none could say.

But they would follow him anyway. They had no choice. When destiny walks among men, ordinary men can only bow and pray.

CHAPTER SEVEN

THE DEVOURING

IN WHICH THE EMPIRE HARVESTS,
YET DEVOURS ITSELF FROM WITHIN

*A fortress that cannot be breached from without is usually
hollowed from within. Rust is more patient than the sword.*
— The Archives of the Inner Court

OF THE BLACK TIDE

The Empire did not scream when it woke; it simply began to grind.

For two years, the rebellion had been a nuisance —a series of brushfires on the edges of the map, fought by local magistrates and second-rate garrison commanders. But brushfires, left unchecked, become infernos. When the reports of the Stormborn victories in the South and the creeping insurrection in the East finally reached the Inner Council, the time for dismissal was over.

The order was given. The beast was unleashed.

From the northern frontiers came General Jared Steelbane. He rode with the Northern Iron Legions—three hundred thousand men who had spent their lives slaughtering barbarians in the frozen wastes in the decades after the Six Kingdoms were destroyed. They were not conscripts. They were professional killers, encased in black lamellar armour, disciplined to a degree that stripped them of humanity and left only function.

They marched South like a slow, black oil slick spreading across a map.

"Burn the fields," Steelbane ordered as they crossed River Ochre. "Poison the wells. If a village harbors a rebel, the village dies. If a city resists, the city falls."

The ground shook under their boots. The dust of their marching columns blotted out the sun for miles. This was not a police action anymore; it was an extermination. The local warlords who had proudly declared independence a month ago watched the horizon turn black and felt their courage turn to water.

The Ironhold was coming to reclaim its property.

OF THE GEOMETRY OF AGONY

The Iron Creed was not merely a set of laws; it was a mathematical formula designed to strip the human heart of its impulse to resist. In the scrolls of the Inner Court, order was not maintained by justice, but by the Calculus of Fear.

The foundation of the Creed was the Law of the Quintet, or the Web of Five. Every village was divided into groups of five households, stitched together by a thread of blood. If one man whispered treason, and the other four did not report him by sunset, all five families—the elderly in their beds, the infants in their cradles—were taken to the executioner's block. To the Iron Creed, there was no such thing as an innocent bystander. There was only the Informer and the Accomplice.

Punishment under the Creed was as precise as an architect's blueprint. It was not enough to kill a man; the State sought to unmake him.

The most terrifying of these was the "Tether of the Five Currents." Reserved for those who dared to challenge the Imperial Mandate, the prisoner was taken to the central square of the capital. Five heavy war-horses were brought forth—one for each limb, and one for the neck. When the drums struck a single, final beat, the horses were driven towards the four corners of the compass and the northern star. It was a death that mirrored the Empire's own expansion: a violent pulling apart of a single body to satisfy the demands of a map.

"The flesh may fail," the Iron Judges used to say, *"but the Law is a straight line that never bends."*

For lesser crimes, the tools were simpler but no less efficient: the branding iron to mark the face of the thief, the obsidian saw to remove the feet of those who walked where they were forbidden, and the The Bisector, a massive blade that ended a life with a single, horizontal stroke, leaving the victim to look upon their own lower half for several agonizing minutes before the light faded.

This was the "Peace" the First Emperor had bought. It was a world where men did not trust their neighbours, where children feared to speak in their sleep, and where the only sound louder than the grinding of the imperial machine was the terrifying, absolute silence of a people who had been broken into pieces.

OF THE MAD BOY

In the third year of his reign, Emperor Edric—His Divine Majesty, Eternal Lord of All Under Heaven, The Second Iron Emperor—was twenty-four years old and had completely lost his mind.

The physicians called it "heavenly agitation." The court called it "divine inspiration." Those who knew the truth called it nothing at all, because speaking the truth was punishable by death—along with speaking about the weather, looking at the emperor's left ear, breathing too loudly, or dreaming the wrong dreams.

The boy who had once been merely weak had become something far worse: unpredictable. He would spend days in catatonic silence, staring at dust motes, refusing to blink. Then, without warning, the storm would break.

"He is stealing my air!" the Emperor would shriek, pointing a trembling finger at a terrified chamberlain. "I saw him! He inhaled the imperial oxygen! Cut out his lungs! Give me back my breath!"

And Mordecai would bow, murmur his agreement, and arrange for the execution with the efficiency of a butcher clearing a counter.

It was not ideal. A functional puppet would have been easier—someone who could read a script without trying to eat the parchment. But Mordecai had worked with worse. The trick, he discovered, was to ensure that the madness always flowed downhill towards his enemies.

"Your Majesty," Mordecai would whisper, approaching the throne with the softness of a spider. "I have received reports that Lord Cedric of the Eastern Province has been... *mocking* the royal silence."

"Has he?" Edric's eyes would widen, lighting up with a terrified, paranoid fury. "Has he dared? Bring him here! I will have his tongue cooked! I will have his eyes fed to the fish!"

Then, the fury would vanish as quickly as a blown candle. Edric would giggle, a wet, childish sound. He reached for the Great Heirloom Seal—the heavy block of pure white nephrite that symbolised the Mandate of Heaven, the sacred object for which armies had burnt and died.

He placed a walnut on the armrest of the Dragon Throne. He raised the Seal.

CRACK.

The sound echoed in the silent hall like a neck snapping. The shell shattered under the weight of the Empire.

Edric picked the meat from the debris, smiling vacantly.

"Your Majesty is most wise," Mordecai said, bowing to the nutcracker. "I shall see to Lord Cedric immediately."

And so, Lord Cedric—one of the few competent administrators left, whose only crime was questioning Mordecai's tax ledgers—was erased from the world, victim of a walnut and a whisper.

OF SILAS IRONSCRIBE'S
FINAL PETITION

Silas Ironscribe had been Chancellor of the Realm for thirty-seven years. He had served the first emperor faithfully, if not always willingly. He had witnessed the conspiracy at Sandmere, had signed the false edict that murdered Prince Caden Firstborn, had spent every night since then dreaming of blood and betrayal.

For years, he had repeated the same justifications until they wore smooth as river stones: *stability, order, the greater good*. The words had lost their meaning through overuse, become ritual phrases rather than reasons.

But there were limits to what even Silas Ironscribe could stomach.

"You cannot do this," he said, standing before Mordecai in the chamberlain's private chambers. "The new taxation rates will destroy what remains of the empire's economy. The provinces cannot bear it. The people are already starving. If you squeeze them further—"

"The treasury requires funds," Mordecai replied, not looking up from the documents he was reviewing. "The army requires payment. The court requires maintenance. Where else would you suggest we find the money?"

"From the imperial reserves. From the—"

"The imperial reserves are for emergencies." Now Mordecai did look up, and his eyes were impassive as granite. "This is not an emergency, Grand Magistrate. This is simply governance."

"Governance?" Silas felt the word stick in his throat. "You call this governance? The emperor hasn't made a coherent decision in months. You've executed half the competent officials in the capital. The rebellions are spreading faster than Steelbane can suppress them. And you sit here talking about taxation rates, unseeing that the realm is set in flames around us!"

Mordecai set down his quill with deliberate care. "Grand Magistrate. You have served the throne for many years. Your expertise is valued. But perhaps you have forgotten your place."

"My place is to advise the throne on matters of law and justice. My place is to ensure that the empire functions according to the principles laid down by the founding emperor. My place is—"

"Your place," Mordecai interrupted, "is wherever I say it is. You hold your position because I permit it. You live because I find you useful. The moment either of those things changes..." He smiled, and there was no warmth in it. "Well. You've seen what happens to those I find less than useful."

Silas stood very still. He was an old man, and tired, and he had spent too many years compromising with evil to pretend he was still capable of heroism. But something in him—some remnant of the young idealist who had once believed in the law, who had once thought justice was more than a word—refused to remain unspoken.

"Mordecai," he murmured, "I signed the edict that killed Prince Trueheart. I lied for you at Sandmere. I have been complicit in every crime you have committed since the old emperor died. But this—this madness you are implementing—I cannot support it. I will not support it."

"Then you are of no further use to me."

The guards entered before Silas could respond. They were efficient, well-trained, utterly loyal to those who paid them—which was to say, utterly loyal to Mordecai the Shadowhand. They took Silas by the arms, not roughly but firmly, escorted him towards the door.

"Wait," Silas said. "Wait. You can't—I am the Grand Councillor. I am a member of the highest court in the land. You cannot simply—"

"I can do whatever I wish," Mordecai said, returning his attention to his documents. "You should have realised that years ago. Consider it a final lesson."

Silas looked at the guards dragging him—men wearing the uniforms he had designed, enforcing the laws he had written, serving the power he had helped consolidate. The Iron Creed was working perfectly. It was functioning exactly as he had intended: absolute obedience to absolute power. The only error was thinking that he, the architect, would be exempt from the blueprint.

Silas Ironscribe was executed three days later, on charges of treason, conspiracy, and "harboring thoughts injurious to the divine majesty of the throne." His confession—written by Mordecai's scribes and signed by Silas under torture—implicated a dozen other officials, all of whom were arrested and executed in turn.

The last voice of restraint in the imperial government had been silenced.

Now there was only Mordecai, and the puppet emperor, and the endless appetite of power that fed on everything it touched.

OF THE IRON HARVEST

To understand why the rebellion took three years to succeed, one must first understand what it meant to face the Imperial Legions in open battle.

In the early months of the third year, a rebel army known as the "Free Brothers"—forty thousand strong, flush with minor victories against local garrisons—made the mistake of engaging a single imperial division at Redfork Valley. The rebels were brave. They were passionate. They charged with the names of their ancestors on their lips and the fire of liberty in their hearts.

The Empire did not shout back.

The Imperial division, commanded by one of Steelbane's lieutenants, stood in absolute silence. Ten thousand men, encased in black iron lamellar armour, arranged in a grid so precise it looked like tiling on a temple floor. When the rebels charged, the Imperial front rank did not brace; they simply knelt.

Thrum.

Three thousand heavy crossbows fired in unison. The sound was not like weapons discharging; it was like a massive door slamming shut.

The rebel front line simply evaporated. Men were thrown backward as if kicked by invisible horses, their shields shattered, their armour punched through by bolts thick as thumbs. Before the survivors could stand, the second imperial rank stepped through the gaps, leveled their crossbows, and fired. Then the third.

It was not a battle. It was an industrial process.

When the rebels finally reached the imperial lines, broken and terrified, they met the shield wall. The Imperial soldiers fought with the rhythmic, joyless efficiency of butchers dressing meat. *Block. Thrust. Step. Block. Thrust. Step.* They did not break formation to pursue. They did not celebrate kills. They simply advanced, a grinding wall of iron that chewed up everything in its path and left only red mud behind.

By noon, the "Free Brothers" ceased to exist. Thirty thousand rebels lay dead. The Imperial division had lost fewer than two hundred men.

This was the machine that Steelbane commanded. A weapon forged to conquer the world, perfected over a hundred years of constant warfare. Against such a force, courage was irrelevant. Hope was a statistical error.

As long as the machine was fed, it was invincible.

OF THE PRICE OF DEFIANCE

And where the armies passed, the "Pacification" followed.

The Iron Creed stated: *The guilt of one is the guilt of all.* It was not a metaphor.

When the village of Oakhaven was found to have supplied grain to a rebel scouting party, General Steelbane did not simply execute the headman. That would have been mercy. Instead, he ordered the *Decimation of the Hearth*.

Imperial engineers arrived with surveying equipment. They divided the village into precise grids. Every structure within the condemned zone—houses, barns, shrines—was burnt. Every living thing within those structures—men, women, livestock, dogs—was driven into the central square.

The soldiers did not act with anger. They did not rape or loot—such things were breaches of discipline, punishable by death. They simply carried out the work. They separated the population by height. Those taller than a wagon wheel were executed by the sword. Those shorter were taken as slaves for the state quarries.

The heads of the executed were not mounted on pikes—pikes were temporary. Instead, they were boiled, stripped of flesh, and mortared into a pyramid at the village crossroads, facing the imperial highway. They are known as Towers of Silence, with a plaque affixed to the base, reading simply: *ORDER RESTORED.*

Across the central provinces, these pyramids multiplied. They stood as silent sentinels, white bone against the green fields, reminding every traveler that the Empire saw everything, forgave nothing, and possessed the power to turn entire communities into masonry.

It was effective. For every man who joined the rebellion in those days, ten stayed home, terrified into submission by the white pyramids. The Empire was not just an army; it was a force of nature, inevitable and cruel, and to fight it seemed as foolish as fighting an earthquake.

OF GENERAL
STEELBANE'S DILEMMA

Five hundred miles to the south, Jared Steelbane was winning every battle and losing the war.

It was not a situation he had ever expected to face. He was the finest general of his generation—of any generation—one who had never been defeated in open combat, whose tactical brilliance had broken the armies of a dozen rebel leaders. He had crushed Corwin Harrow at the Western Road. He had scattered the forces of the restored kingdoms. He had proven, time and again, that the disciplined legions of Ironhold could overcome any enemy when properly commanded.

But discipline required resources. Resources required administration. And administration required a functioning government that could collect taxes, maintain supply lines, and reinforce armies when they suffered casualties.

None of which existed anymore.

"The supply wagons are three weeks late," his quartermaster reported, his face drawn with exhaustion. "The treasury has sent nothing since midsummer. I've had to requisition from the local population, but there's barely anything left to requisition. The rebels stripped these provinces clean before we arrived, and what they left behind, we've already taken."

"And the reinforcements?"

"The reinforcements..." The quartermaster hesitated. "General, the reinforcements are not coming. The garrisons that were supposed to supply them have been recalled to the capital. Something about... internal security concerns."

Steelbane closed his eyes. He could picture it perfectly: Mordecai the Shadowhand, surrounded by imaginary threats, pulling troops from the frontlines to protect himself from enemies that existed only in his paranoid imagination. Stripping the army of resources to fund whatever scheme he was currently pursuing. Destroying the very foundations of imperial power in his desperate attempt to hold onto it.

"What are our current numbers?"

"One hundred and eighty thousand effective fighting men. Down from three hundred thousand at the start of the campaign."

"And the enemy?"

"Lord Kharic Stormborn is reported to have over four hundred thousand men under his banner. Lord Maren Ashford has two hundred thousand in the west. The various minor rebels account for another three hundred thousand scattered across the provinces." The quartermaster paused. "General, we are outnumbered nearly five to one, and the ratio is worsening by the day."

Jared Steelbane had faced long odds before. He had won victories that lesser commanders would have called impossible. But even he could not conjure soldiers out of thin air, could not feed an army on promises, could not fight a war when his own government was actively working against him.

"Send another petition to the capital," he said at last. "Request immediate resupply and reinforcement. Emphasise that the situation is critical."

"General, the last three petitions have gone unanswered."

"Unanswered is too kind," the quartermaster corrected, pulling a scroll from his sleeve. "This arrived this morning. It's a requisition order from the Palace Kitchens. They demand two hundred crates of southern wine for the Emperor's birthday festival." He laughed, a dry, brittle sound. "We are eating horse leather, General. And they want wine."

"Send it anyway. And prepare the army to march south. If we cannot win here, we will fall back to a more defensible position."

It was the first time in his career that Jared Steelbane had ordered a retreat. He hated every syllable of the command. But he was a practical man, and he knew the difference between courage and suicide.

The empire was dying, and not even the finest general in the world could save it from itself.

OF THE RUSTING MACHINE

In the capital, the machinery of governance ground to a halt.

Officials who had once administered a realm of forty million souls now spent their days in terror, afraid to make any decision that might draw Mordecai's attention. The treasury, bled dry by corruption and mismanagement, could no longer pay the salaries of the clerks who were supposed to collect taxes. The army, deprived of supplies and reinforcements, was slowly disintegrating as soldiers deserted to join the very rebels they had been sent to fight.

And in the throne room, the Boy Emperor laughed at shadows and ordered the execution of anyone who looked at him wrong.

"The Heaven's Mandate has been withdrawn," the common people whispered in the streets. "The Iron Dynasty has lost the favour of the gods."

They were right, in their way. Not because gods had withdrawn their blessing—Mordecai the Shadowhand had no more belief in heavenly mandates than he had in honest governance—but because the system the first emperor had created required competent administration to function, and competent administration required trust, and trust was the one thing Mordecai had systematically destroyed.

Before the throne was being conquered by those who challenged, it was collapsing under the weight of its own corruption, falling apart at the seams, dissolving into chaos because the men who should have been holding it together were too busy plotting against each other to notice that the ground was giving way beneath their feet.

In the south, Kharic Stormborn gathered his armies and prepared for the final campaign. In the west, Maren Ashford built his strength in patient silence. Throughout the realm, men who had once been loyal subjects of Ironhold looked at the madness emanating from the capital and asked themselves a question that had once been treason to even think:

If this is what the empire has become, why should we fight to preserve it?

The answer, increasingly, was: *We shouldn't.*

And so the empire died—not in a single battle, not in a glorious last stand, but in a thousand small surrenders, a million individual decisions to stop fighting for a cause that no longer deserved loyalty.

The Iron Creed had promised order. It had delivered chaos.

The Iron Emperor had promised stability. His successors had delivered madness.

And now the iron was rusting, the creed was forgotten, and the Ironhold that had once seemed permanent was revealed as what it had always been: a fragile construction of human ambition, no more permanent than the men who had built it.

The wheel was turning.

And nothing could stop it now.

OF THE WILDFIRE

News of the chaos in the capital travelled faster than imperial couriers could ride.

It was not a specific event that broke the dam, but the realization that the dam was unmanned. The Emperor was mad. The Shadowhand was hoarding gold while the provinces burnt. The invincible armies were starving in the field.

The message flew on the wings of rumour: *The beast is sick. The monster is eating its own tail.*

And the world, holding its breath for three years of terror, finally exhaled in a roar of fire.

It was no longer just a peasant rebellion. It was a resurrection.

In the North, the descendants of the Dragonspire Kings dug up their ancestors' banners. In the East, the Golden Lords of Aldoria declared independence, slaughtering the imperial tax collectors. In the South and West, men who had bowed their heads for thirty years stood up.

There was no coordination. There was no plan. There was only a chaotic, violent, beautiful explosion of ambition. The map of the Iron Empire, once a solid block of black ink, was fracturing into a hundred bloody shards.

The spark from the marshes had become a wildfire. And there was not enough water in all the oceans to put it out.

CHAPTER EIGHT

THE ORPHAN OF WAR

IN WHICH LORD TORIAN OF CHEROS, THE STONEHEART MEETS HIS END, AND KHARIC STORMBORN ASSUMES COMMAND

*No man is a Lord while his father lives; no man is a Master
while his teacher speaks.*
  — *The Wisdom of the Ancient Lords*

OF THE BATTLE OF DENHAM

This was still the war against Ironhold—the imperial armies remained the enemy, and the rebel coalition remained fragile allies united only by their common hatred of the Iron Creed.

Lord Torian had spent his entire life preparing Kharic for command. Now, at the age of sixty-seven, he prepared to die so that his nephew could claim it.

The battle of Denham was not supposed to be decisive. It was supposed to be a probing action, a test of the imperial defences, a way to measure the strength of General Jared Steelbane's position before committing to a full assault. Torian had argued for caution, had counseled patience, had urged Kharic to wait until the Ironhold's internal collapse had weakened its armies further.

But Kharic was done waiting. The coalition of rebel kingdoms was fracturing under the strain of inaction; every day that passed without a major victory was a day that doubt crept deeper into the hearts of his allies. He needed a triumph, needed something to rally the disparate forces under his banner, needed to prove that he was more than just his uncle's protégé.

"Let me lead the attack," he had said, on the eve of battle. "Let me show them what I can do."

"You are too valuable to risk," Torian replied. "If you fall, everything we have built falls with you."

"Then I am too valuable to hide behind while others fight my battles." Kharic's jaw was set with that stubborn determination that Torian knew all too well—the same determination he had seen in Kharic's father, on the day Lord Roderic Stormborn had walked to his execution with his head held high. "I will lead the assault. You will hold the reserve. That is my decision."

It was not a request. Kharic had grown beyond the boy who had asked his uncle for permission; he was a commander now, and commanders gave orders rather than soliciting advice. Torian could have argued—could have reminded Kharic of all the reasons this was foolish—but he saw the fire in his nephew's eyes and knew that argument would be useless.

"Then at least let me ride beside you," he said. "If you must charge into danger, let danger find both of us together."

Kharic hesitated for a second. The mask of command slipped, and Torian saw the boy he had raised from the age of fourteen—the boy who had watched his father die, who had sworn vengeance with tears streaming down his face, who had needed his uncle's guidance through every step of the long road that had led to this moment.

"You shall remain with the reserve," Kharic said at last. "I require a man of trust to command the second wave. Should the assault falter—"

"It won't fail."

"If it fails," Kharic continued, "you must retreat. Save what you can. Continue the war without me."

"I would rather die beside you."

"I know." Kharic reached out and gripped his uncle's shoulder. "But your death would serve nothing. Live, uncle. Live, and if I fall, remember what I was trying to build."

They embraced—a brief, fierce clasp that said everything words could not convey. Then Kharic turned and walked towards his horse, towards the waiting army, towards the battle that would change everything.

Torian watched him go, and felt the weight of years pressing down upon his shoulders.

He would not see his nephew alive again.

OF THE CHARGE AND THE TRAP

The imperial position at Denham was stronger than Kharic had expected.

General Steelbane had chosen his ground well: a narrow valley where superior numbers would be of limited use, flanked by hills that concealed the full extent of his forces. The obvious approach was a frontal assault through the valley floor —which was, of course, exactly what Steelbane wanted.

Kharic saw the trap. He saw it, and he charged into it anyway.

"We cannot take the valley without flanking the hills," his officers argued. "The imperial forces will cut us apart."

"Then let them cut," Kharic replied. "When their arms grow weary from the slaughter, we shall still be coming. The storm does not tire."

It was madness. It was also, in its own terrible way, genius. Kharic understood something that his more cautious advisors did not: that morale, in war, was everything. An army that believed itself invincible would accomplish what armies that doubted themselves could not. And the only way to make an army believe in its invincibility was to lead it through the impossible and emerge victorious on the other side.

The assault began at dawn.

Kharic led from the front, as always—his great sword carving through the imperial defenders, his voice rising above the chaos to rally men who might otherwise have faltered. Blood pooled in the hoofprints, dark and steaming. The imperial lines bent, buckled, broke under the fury of the rebel assault.

But Steelbane had anticipated this. He had placed his strongest troops at the flanks, hidden in the hills, waiting for the moment when the rebel charge had committed itself fully. And when that moment came—when Kharic's forces were deep in the valley, surrounded on three sides by enemies they could not see—he sprung his trap.

The counterattack was devastating. Imperial soldiers poured down from the hills, cutting into the rebel flanks, turning what had seemed like a breakthrough into a desperate struggle for survival. Kharic's charge, which had been on the verge of shattering the enemy centre, was suddenly threatened with encirclement.

Steelbane did not fight like a man; he fought like a geometer. While Kharic's warriors shouted to the gods, the Imperial Legions maintained a terrifying, rhythmic silence. Every time the Stormborn rebels broke a line, they found another behind it—a wall of black lamellar, calculating their fatigue. Kharic saw in this war, that even a storm can be measured, timed, and eventually, exhausted.

And that was when Torian the Stoneheart made his decision.

OF THE UNCLE'S CHOICE

Torian the Stoneheart charged fiercely, to buy back the time his nephew had wasted on pride. As he rode into the fray, he looked at the Imperial formations—straight, sharp, and lethal—and knew that the age of the old clans was being crushed by the age of the killing machines. He was a relic of a more honourable world, and he chose to be the shield that caught the final blow intended for the future.

From his position with the reserve, Torian could see everything: the success of the initial assault, the imperial counterattack, the growing danger to his nephew's force. He could see that Kharic was trapped—not defeated, not yet, but trapped—and that without immediate intervention, the trap would close.

He could also see that the only intervention capable of saving Kharic would cost everything.

"Prepare the reserve," he ordered, his voice steady despite the hammering of his heart. "We advance at once."

"My lord, if we commit the reserve now, we have nothing left. If the attack fails—"

"If the attack fails, it won't matter whether we have reserves." Torian was already mounting his horse. "My nephew is in danger. Nothing else matters."

They charged—eight thousand men, the last uncommitted force on the rebel side, throwing themselves into the chaos of the valley floor. Torian led them personally, his age-stiffened limbs screaming in protest, his eyes fixed on the banner that marked Kharic's position.

The impact was enough. The imperial flanking forces, caught between Kharic's front and Torian's charge, wavered. A brief, glorious moment—it seemed like the battle might turn, that the two forces might link up, that victory might still be possible.

And then Lord Torian took an arrow through the chest.

He did not fall immediately. He was too stubborn for that, too determined to see his nephew safe before he allowed himself to die. He kept riding, kept fighting, kept pushing forward even as blood soaked through his armour and his vision dimmed.

Kharic saw him coming. Saw him fall.

"UNCLE!"

The scream cut through the noise of battle like a blade through silk. Kharic turned his horse, abandoned his assault on the imperial centre, charged towards the place where Torian had fallen. His soldiers followed, drawn by their leader's anguish, abandoning their own engagements to protect the man who had just sacrificed everything to protect them.

The imperial forces, sensing the confusion, pressed their advantage. The battle that had been on the verge of victory collapsed into desperate defence. And in the centre of it all, Kharic Stormborn knelt beside his dying uncle and listened to the last words he would ever hear from this man who had raised him.

"You are ready," Torian whispered, blood bubbling at his lips. "You were always ready. I just... didn't want to let go."

"Don't. Don't leave me. I need—"

"You don't need me anymore. You never did." The old man

murmured."Be... be the man your father would have wanted. Be the king... Cheros deserves."

"Uncle—"

"I loved you," Torian wheezed, red froth bubbling at the corners of his mouth. "Like my own son. Remember that." The old man's hand found Kharic's face, trembling fingers trying to wipe away a smear of dirt—or perhaps a tear.

"Eldran... take Eldran as your Second Father. Trust him as you trusted me. He sees what we cannot... Promise me."

He lacked the strength. The hand slid down, leaving a faint trail of blood on Kharic's jaw like a final, tragic benediction. The hand fell away. The eyes went blank.

And Kharic Stormborn, surrounded by enemies, cradling the body of his uncle—who had taught him to fight, raised him into a warring soul, who had been a father to him—threw back his head and screamed.

OF THE DEFEAT

The battle of Denham was not a draw. It was a catastrophe.

With Torian dead, the rebel command structure collapsed. The reserve force, seeing their leader fall, broke ranks. Steel-bane's heavy cavalry ran them down in the mud.

It was not an orderly retreat; it was a rout.

Kharic Stormborn fought his way out, carrying his uncle's body across his saddle, surrounded by a handful of loyal guards. Behind him, the main strength of the rebel coalition lay broken in the valley. The banner of the Stormborn—the flag that had never touched the ground—was trampled into the bloody earth.

They retreated fifty miles without stopping, fuelled only by terror and grief.

When they finally halted, the camp was silent. There were

no songs. There was no boasting. The invincibility of the Stormborn clan had died with Torian. The soldiers looked at Kharic not with awe, but with hollow, frightened eyes. They were waiting for Steelbane to finish them off.

Kharic sat alone in the darkness. He had lost his army. He had lost Torian, who was like a father to him in all but name. He had lost his direction.

"We march at dawn," he whispered to his commanders, but his voice lacked its usual fire.

"March where, my lord?" a captain asked, his arm in a sling. "We have no strength to attack Steelhaven. If we stay here, Steelbane will crush us."

Kharic had no answer. The thin night mist hovered around the camp, like the uncertainty of his path forward.

Inside the tent, he placed his uncle's body on a cot.

He wept.

He wept not just for grief, but for failure. He had led the charge. He had walked into the trap. The blood of the rebellion was on his hands.

The death of Torian was more than the loss of a general; it was the collapse of a canopy. For fifteen years, Torian had been the buffer between Kharic and the heartless and cynical plotting of the other rebel lords. He had filtered the betrayals, silenced the doubters, and provided the legitimacy of the Old Name.

Now, as the rain turned the valley of Denham into a slurry of grey ash and red mud, Kharic realised that the world he knew was no longer his home. He looked at his fists—those hands that could lift a cauldron—and saw that they were useless against the silence of a dead mentor.

OF THE SECOND FATHER

The weeping stopped when the tent flap opened.

Kharic did not look up. He sat in the dark, still wearing his blood-crusted armour, the silence of the room heavier than any scream.

"Get out," Kharic growled. "I told the guards I wanted no one."

"I am not the guards."

Eldran Greymantle stepped into the tent. He carried a bowl of water and a clean cloth. He did not bow. He did not look frightened by the murderous aura radiating from the young warlord.

He walked to Kharic, knelt, and dipped the cloth in the water.

"Your uncle is dead," Eldran said. His voice was not soft; it was factual, hard as granite. "Your father is dead. You are an orphan, Kharic Stormborn."

Kharic's hand flew to his sword hilt. "Do you come to mock me?"

"I come to wash your face."

Eldran reached out. For a second, it seemed Kharic might strike him. But he didn't. He froze, just as he had frozen before the executioner's block years ago.

Eldran wiped the blood—Torian's blood—from Kharic's jaw.

His hands were as cold as the water in the bowl. When he wiped the blood from the young warrior's face, he wasn't comforting a child; he was cleaning a weapon. He saw the grief in Kharic's eyes and felt nothing but satisfaction—for a god must first be emptied of his humanity before he can be filled with the rage required to burn an empire.

"The world is full of men who wish to be your enemy,"

Eldran said quietly. "But a king needs more than enemies. He needs a voice to tell him the truth when he does not wish to hear it."

He finished cleaning the face of the most dangerous man in the world, then sat back.

"You have lost a father today," Eldran said. "But the war remains. If you wish to win it... if you wish to make sure Torian did not die for a fool... then I will carry that burden for you."

Kharic looked at the old man. In the flickering lamplight, Eldran's grey cloak seemed to merge with the shadows, his lined face stern yet protective.

Kharic's rage broke, leaving behind a terrible, childlike need. He was a god of war, yes. But gods are lonely things.

"Stay," Kharic whispered. It was the plea of a boy who was terrified of the dark.

"I am here," Eldran said. "I am not going anywhere."

From that night on, Kharic called him *Father*—Second Father, as Torian had commanded with his dying breath. He gave Eldran the trust he had given Torian, the obedience he had given Roderic.

He did not understand, until it was too late, that a man can only have so many fathers before fate decides he is meant to stand alone.

OF THE SHEPHERD'S SUMMONS

The moment of quiet between the new father and the orphaned son was broken by the sound of horns.

Not the alarm horns of an enemy attack, but the ceremonial horns of the court.

Kharic frowned. He stood up, his armour clinking, and walked to the tent flap. Outside, the camp was in confusion. A retinue of gold-clad messengers was riding through the mud, their clean cloaks a stark contrast to the bloodied, exhausted soldiers of the rebel army.

The lead messenger stopped before Kharic's tent. He looked terrified to be in the presence of the Wolf, but he held up a scroll with the royal seal.

"Lord Stormborn," the messenger stammered. "His Majesty, King Arion commands your presence at Greymoor Keep immediately."

Kharic stared at him. "Commands?"

The word tasted wrong in his mouth. For two years, King Arion the Righteous had been a decoration, a puppet Torian brought out for parades. He signed what he was told to sign. He ate what he was told to eat.

"All the lords are summoned," the messenger continued, his voice shrinking under Kharic's gaze. "To discuss the... reallocation of command following Lord Torian's death."

Eldran Greymantle stepped up beside Kharic. The old man's eyes narrowed.

"The Pillar falls," Eldran whispered, "and the roof tries to become the sky."

Kharic let out a low, dangerous laugh.

"The shepherd thinks because the Tiger is dead, the sheep like him can rule the jungle," Kharic said. He snatched the scroll from the messenger's hand and crumpled it.

"They will come for you now," Eldran whispered, standing in the rain without a cloak. "With scrolls and smiles, they will try to divide your army, to strip your titles, to remind the world that you are just an orphan who lost a battle."

Kharic's eyes, normally twin storms, were now flat and dark like the bottom of a well. "Let them come," he said. "I have nothing left to lose but the war. And a man who has lost his heart is a terrifying thing to meet on the field."

"Tell the King I am coming," Kharic snarled. "Tell him I will bring him a new sword as my gift."

The messenger spurred his horse and fled.

Kharic looked at Eldran. "He wants a council? I will give him a council. I will show him exactly who owns this rebellion."

He did not know yet that the Shepherd had teeth. He did not know that in the game of kings and pawns, the one who holds the seal is sometimes more dangerous than the one who holds the sword.

The sun set on the day of grief.

CHAPTER NINE

A KING'S PROMISE

IN WHICH ARION IS NO LONGER A SHEPHERD AND GIVES DECREE, MARON IS NAMED LORD OF VALDRIA

A crown is gold; an army is steel; but opportunity is a sharpened tooth. Do not mock the sheep until you have seen it hungry.

— The Chronicles of the Rebel Court

OF THE HANGING MEN

Two heads rotted on pikes above the main gate of the rebel camp.

They were not imperial spies nor deserters. They were loyal soldiers of the coalition who had made a simple mistake: they had privately referred to King Arion as "The Shepherd" while drinking in a tavern.

It was a nickname everyone had muttered for two years. But since a week ago, it was treason.

Arion stood on the battlements, watching the crows peck at the eyes of the petty men he had ordered killed. His hands trembled slightly, not from regret, but from the adrenaline of power.

"Let them look," Arion whispered to his chamberlain. "Let every man in this camp, every lordling who answered the summons see what happens to those who forget who wears the crown."

He turned away from the gruesome sight. That old Arion—the frightened, kindly man who missed his pastures—had died with Torian Stormborn. The man who walked back to his chambers was something new.

OF THE PUPPET'S DREAM

King Arion stood before the bronze mirror in his chambers, adjusting the heavy silk robes that felt like a costume.

For two years, he had been no more than a jester. Torian Stormborn had plucked him from a sheep pasture, washed the dung from his boots, and placed a crown on his head. "Sit here," Torian had said. "Sign this." "Wave to the people."

Arion knew what he was: a symbol of the lost Celestine Kingdom of old. A living flag to remind the people of the old royal bloodline. He ate the finest food, drank the sweetest wine, and lived in constant terror that one day, Torian would decide the flag was no longer necessary.

But today... today was different.

News had arrived at midnight. Torian was dead. The terrifying Stoneheart, the man who cast a shadow over the entire rebellion, was gone.

Arion looked at his reflection. He saw an old man with watery eyes and trembling hands. But behind the fear, he saw something else: Survival.

The tiger is dead, Arion thought, his heart hammering against his ribs. *And the cub—his nephew—is wounded and grieving. If I do not act now, the wolf will eat me next. But if I strike while he is bleeding...*

He picked up the heavy staff of office. It felt solid. Real.

"I am not a shepherd," he whispered to the empty room. "I am the King."

OF THE GATHERING OF WOLVES

It was a humid, late spring morning when the Great Hall of Greymoor Keep was a cauldron of noise and panic.

Dozens of rebel lords, minor generals, and bandit kings had gathered at the summons. They were a motley collection—men who had risen from nothing, men who had lost everything. They smelt of horse sweat, rain, and fear.

They argued over retreat routes. They shouted about supply lines. They whispered about the impending arrival of Steelbane's army.

At a corner, two of King's scribes listened and wrote down anything they had said that was of worth.

When the doors opened and King Arion entered, the noise did not stop immediately. It trailed off slowly, disrespectfully.

Arion walked to the high seat. He did not sit. He stood, clutching his staff of office until his knuckles turned white.

"Silence," he said.

It was not a shout. It was a command. The lords looked at him, surprised. The old puppet had never spoken first before.

"Torian Stormborn is dead," Arion announced. "We mourn him. He was a hero. But heroes die. Kings must lead."

He unrolled a map on the central table.

"The army are scattered. The generals are confused. This ends today. From this moment, the seat of my court moves East, to Drumhold."

A murmur of protest rose up. Drumhold was far from the front lines, and too close to the Stormborn clan's ancestral power base.

"It is not a retreat!" Arion cut them off, his voice gaining a sharp edge. "It is consolidation. To fight the Empire, we must be one fist, not five fingers. Drumhold is the ancient capital of Cheros, there is no reason for the King of Cheros not being there."

He looked at the generals, his eyes hard.

"I am reclaiming the seals of command. There will be no more private armies. No more independent warlords. General Yvens, General Winteraye... step forward and present your tallies. I wish to hear your strength, and I wish to hold your seals."

The lords hesitated. This was madness. The old man was stripping them of their power.

"You ask for our swords?" General Winteraye sneered. "Torian let us keep our command. Who are you to—"

The doors of the Great Hall slammed open with a violence that shook the dust from the rafters.

OF THE INTERRUPTION

Kharic Stormborn stood in the doorway.

He looked like a nightmare dredged up from the battlefield. His armour was dented and stained dark with dried blood— his uncle's blood. He wore no helmet. His hair was matted with rain and sweat. Behind him stood Eldran Greymantle, a shadow in grey.

Kharic walked into the hall. The crowd parted for him like water fleeing a shark. He did not look at the other lords. He looked only at Arion.

"My condolences to you for your loss, Kharic. Lord Torian was a man of courage..."

"You want armies, old man?" Kharic's voice was a low growl that vibrated in the floorboards.

He walked to the high table. He drew his sword—not to strike, but to slam it onto the table, embedding the tip three inches into the wood.

"I brought you the army," Kharic said. "The survivors of Denham are outside. Five thousand men who watched my uncle die. They are hungry. They are angry. And they are waiting for orders."

Arion recoiled, shrinking back into his chair. For a second, the illusion of the King flickered, revealing the terrified shepherd underneath.

"Lord Stormborn," Arion stammered, then caught himself. He straightened his back. "We... we were discussing the defence of the realm."

"Defence?" Kharic laughed. It was a humourless sound. "There is no defence. There is only advance, and Steelbane. He is at Stonedeer. He is building a wall around our brothers."

Kharic leaned over the table, his face inches from the King's.

"Give me the General's Signet. I will march North tonight. I will break Steelbane, or I will pile my bones on top of Torian's."

OF THE INSULT

The hall held its breath. This was the moment. The Tiger is dead, now the Cub was demanding the pack.

Arion looked at Kharic. He saw the grief, the rage, the uncontrollable violence. If he officially gave Kharic the army now, the Stormborn clan would rule forever, and Arion would go back to being a prop.

Now, Arion thought. *Strike now, or die.*

"No," Arion said.

Kharic froze. "What?"

"I said no." Arion stood up, clutching his staff. "Your grief honours you, Kharic. But it also blinds you. You are a lethal, critical weapon, not a commander."

Kharic turned to see four swordsmen, whose faces he did not know, their hands pressed on their weapons , standing near by Arion.

Arion turned to the assembled lords, his voice rising to mask his fear.

"We will indeed march North to relieve Stonedeer. But we will not march in anger. We will march with discipline."

He pointed a shaking finger at a man standing in the shadows of the pillars—a tall, scholarly man with a neat beard and polished armour.

"General Stellan," Arion declared. "Step forward."

Stellan stepped into the light, bowing deeply.

"I name General Stellan as the Supreme Commander of the Northern Army," Arion announced. "He shall hold the Seal. He shall lead the relief force."

Kharic stared at Stellan—a bureaucrat, a politician who had never led a vanguard charge in his life. The insult was physical, like a slap to the face.

"And me?" Kharic whispered, his hand drifting to the hilt of the sword stuck in the table.

"You are a promising warrior," Arion said, choosing his words carefully to avoid immediate death. "You shall serve as General Stellan's Second-in-Command. Learn from his patience, Lord Stormborn. It will do you good."

A wine cup on the table beside Kharic rattled as the vibration of his fury travelled through the wood.

General Stellan stepped forward, the silk of his tabard rustling with a clean, sharp sound that seemed an insult to the blood-caked leather Kharic wore. He did not look at Kharic with anger, but with a maddening, scholarly pity. He adjusted a silver ring on his finger, his movements slow and deliberate, as if he were in a library rather than a war-room.

"I accept the Mandate, Your Majesty," Stellan said, his voice smooth and untroubled. He turned slightly towards Kharic, offering a shallow, formal nod. "Do not fret, Lord Stormborn. Valor is a fine quality in a subordinate. I shall find a proper use for your... energetic nature."

Stellan paused, adjusting his silk cuff with a slow, maddening grace. "The disaster at Denham was regrettable, of course. But to those of us who study the calculus of war rather than the songs of heroes, it was not... unforeseen. Your uncle was a magnificent hammer, Kharic. But eventually, a hammer always hits a stone too hard and shatters. It was a tragedy of metrics, nothing more."

Kharic's eyes narrowed.

OF THE MUD AND
THE COVENANT

Before Kharic could explode over General Stellan's appointment, Arion quickly pivoted. He needed to distract the wolf before he bit.

"But the North is not the only front," Arion said loudly, his eyes scanning the back of the room. "While General Stellan's main army engages Steelbane, we must strike the Empire where it is weak. We need a second army to march West. To bypass the fighting and strike at Steelhaven itself."

He was hunched over the table, his head bowed so low his nose nearly touched the parchment. He was a man in a fever to be King, his fingers stained black with ink.

For several minutes, the only sound in the tent was the frantic, rhythmic scratching of his quill. King Arion was performing the oldest ritual of power: the distribution of crumbs. He signed decree after decree, confirming the titles of those whose blood was "pure" enough to matter.

"Lord Berold of Whitecroft," the King announced, his voice thin but commanding. "For your steadfast loyalty, I name you Count of the Silver Marches. Your cavalry shall be our centre."

Berold stepped forward, his silk robes rustling as he took the vellum. The torchlight caught the jagged purple brand on his jaw—the mark of a 'Life-Eater'—a brutal convict's scar that looked violent and out of place above his collar of gold brocade. He bowed with a smug, theatrical grace, casting a sidelong glance at the fuming Kharic.

"General Yvens," Arion continued, still scribbling, his silver quill dancing across the page. "I elevate you to Warden of the Eastern Gate. See to it the supply lines are held."

One by one, the lords were called. Arion admired his own bird-like scrawl on each document, a man lost in his patronage. He ignored the dirt-stained minor lords at the back of the room as if they were part of the furniture.

Finally, King Arion reached the bottom of his stack. He looked up, his eyes scanning the back of the room, searching for a sacrificial lamb to toss into the western gloom.

Arion pointed to a man standing in the shadows near the wine barrels—a man who looked more like a camp follower than a lord, trying to remain invisible.

"You there," Arion called out. "Step forward."

"Who let the peasant in?" Lord Berold of Whitecroft muttered, loud enough to be heard.

Maren Ashford stepped into the light. He looked weary, his boots caked in fresh mud. He bowed awkwardly.

"Your Majesty."

"Who is this?" Kharic asked, his voice dripping with incredulity.

Kharic Stormborn glanced up from the map he had been

studying. His gaze swept over the newcomer with the brief, dismissive assessment of a man accustomed to measuring worth at a glance. "You. What do you command?"

"This is Maren Ashford," Arion was introduced by an announcer. "A leader from the Eastern Marshes. He has brought... significant resources to the coalition."

Kharic frowned. He looked at this stranger—average height, average face, armed with nothing but a quiet demeanor.

"Resources?" Kharic scoffed. "He smells of manure."

Maren bowed—not deeply, but correctly.

"I've come to fight the war, my lord. Same as everyone here."

"The same as everyone here." A smile flickered across Kharic's face, more contemptuous than amused. The other lords chuckled.

"And what do they call you, little commander? Every bandit in these parts has a title these days."

"Lord of Marsh, my lord," Maren said, his voice even.

"Lord of Marsh." Kharic repeated the words, tasting the absurdity of them. "A title for toads and mosquitos."

"A small title for a small place, my lord."

"A baseborn, in the King's court." Lord Berold snorted. "Boy, I command eight thousand cavalry. Lord Stormborn commands forty thousand strong. You command...what? A dozen pitchforks?"" He pronounced the word like a curse.

"I command the roads you haven't been able to walk for months," Maren spoke mildly. "Since the winter thaw, I've taken Blackwood Watch and the Oakhaven Pass. No sieges, no glorious charges. I simply cut their supply lines until the garrisons ate their own horses, then walked in when they were too weak to lift their gates."

The room went quiet. Blackwood Watch was a formidable stone outpost.

"You *threatened* them into surrendering?" Kharic asked, his interest piqued but his contempt still high.

"I showed them the heads of the messengers they sent for help," Maren replied evenly. "They realised no one was coming. It saved me the trouble of cleaning blood off the walls."

Arion cleared his throat, sensing the shift in the room. "He has shown... remarkable resourcefulness, we should name him..." Arion looked towards Kharic for approval.

"So the peasant is here to demand his reward." Lord Berold added.

Kharic's eyes narrowing as a memory surfaced. "If it is marshes you want, I have plenty more to give you. There is a miserable village there—Valdria, in the swamp west of Drumhold, on the edge of Westmarch. Do you know it? I marched through the western bogs years ago. Lost two hundred horses in the mud. "

Maren didn't flinch. "I know of it, my lord. Peat-cutters and bogwheat farmers."

Lord Berold laughed. "Lord of Valdria! Long may he reign over the frogs and the peat-diggers!"

King Arion, lost in his own ritual, once again dipped his silver quill. With a flourish far too grand for the mud-stained tent, he scrawled his name in a chaotic, bird-like maze of loops—a signature he had practised in his private journals on statecraft. He pressed his seal into the wax, admiring the "ghost-scrawl" with a scholar's pride before handing the tacky vellum to Maren.

"Go forth, Lord of Valdria," Arion said, straightening his back as if reciting from a half-memorised script. "It is written that a King is the sun, but his Lords are the rays that define the reach of his glory. Carry the radiance of our glory into the Western gloom; be the beam in our shadow, and let the world see the weight of a Celestine grace restored."

The other lords joined in—a ripple of aristocratic amusement at the jumped-up peasant who thought he could sit at the table of war lords.

Maren's hand didn't move to his sword. It rested on the table, near a wine cup. He tapped the cup once—a small, sharp sound that cut through the laughter like a knife drop. For a split second, his eyes met Berold's, and the nobleman stopped laughing, though he couldn't have said why. It was the look of a man memorizing a face for later disposal.

"Lord Ashford of Valdria, I would have you take the Western road to strike the Iron's army, from Valdria, take your men through the mountains." Arion said, in a kingly, but trembling old voice.

Kharic yanked his sword out of the table with a screech of metal on wood. The sound sent Arion recoiling into the depths of his high seat, his rehearsed majesty vanishing as he nearly upended the very inkwell he had so proudly used to sign Maren's fate.

Kharic didn't even look at the trembling old man. He walked up to Maren, towering over him by a full head.

"The Western road? The passes are guarded by the Iron Vanguard. They don't surrender because they're hungry, little crow. They will eat you alive."

He looked up at the giant, his expression calm. "I have a strong stomach, my lord."

Kharic laughed. It was a harsh, barking sound. "You'll need more than a stomach, peasant. You'll need a casket."

He turned back to the map. He grabbed a quill, dipped it in ink, and flicked it towards Maren.

Kharic sneered at King Arion, "You send this... nobody... to fight some of the finest garrisons in the world. They will eat him alive."

Arion leaned back against his seat just in case.

"If you are going to the West to die, now at least you have a title suitable for your tombstone."

Maren did not flush. He did not get angry. He bowed to Kharic, a small, tight smile playing on his lips.

"I thank the Second General for his generosity," Maren said softly.

The emphasis on *Second General* was slight—a reminder that Kharic was no longer supreme commander—but it cut Kharic deeper than any sword.

For a second, he considered cutting the peasant down right there.

Arion saw the tension. He clapped his hands loudly.

"So be it!" Arion proclaimed. "General Stellan to the North. The Lord of Valdria to the West. Prepare to take on the impossible."

He raised his silver cup, the wine sloshing over the rim. "And to ensure you run fast, my good lords, hear this Covenant, sworn before the gods of our ancestors."

He leaned forward, his voice cracking with a misplaced authority. "Our goal is to take down the Creedseat. Whosoever enters the gates of Steelhaven first... shall be King of the Central Plains."

A heavy, airless silence followed. The lords exchanged glances of dark disbelief. Steelhaven was a city of iron walls and ten-year granaries. Between this room and the capital stood Jared Steelbane's undefeated legions, the Shadowhand's assassins, and a thousand miles of hostile terrain. To talk of "racing" to the capital while they were still shivering in the mud was more than a gamble; it was a madness.

General Stellan cleared his throat, a dry, awkward sound.

Lord Berold's smile faltered, replaced by a look of wary frustration. They all knew the truth: the Ironhold was still a mountain of lead, and they were but a few sparks at its base.

But Arion was too far gone in his puppet's dream to notice the chill. He unrolled a scroll of heavy, ancient vellum and began to read, his voice trembling with a shepherd's misplaced pride.

"Hearken!" Arion read, his voice trembling with a shepherd's misplaced pride. "By the Luminous Grace of King Arion the Righteous of Restored Cheros, Scion of the Celestine Skies, let it be broadcasted to the firmament! The Ironhold is a blight of rusted souls, a scourge upon the good earth. Their transgressions are a mountain of lead! We, the Sovereigns of Restored Glory, do hereby decree a Storm of Iron and Blood. Let the Ten Thousand march! Let the earth shudder under the boots of Justice! And let the Decree of the Race be etched in stone: He who first punctures the void of the Capital's gates, he who first plants his feet upon the soot of Steelhaven, shall be anointed the sovereign Lord of the Heartlands, King of all the Central Plains!"

Arion finished with a flourish, his breath coming in ragged gasps as if he had just run a league. He stood there, waiting for the roar of approval, for the clash of swords against shields.

Instead, the only sound was the crackle of a dying torch and the distant, rhythmic dripping of rain from the tent's eaves. The lords of the realm avoided each other's eyes; Lord Berold studied the embroidery on his sleeves with sudden, intense fascination, while General Stellan cleared his throat with a dry, awkward rasp. Silence filled the hall—the awkward vacuum of a stage where lines are forgotten.

Then, the sound came. It was a low, jagged vibration from the back of Kharic Stormborn's throat—a laugh sounding like stones grinding together at the bottom of a well.

Kharic stopped laughing. He looked at Arion, then at Maren.

"You all heard the King's promise." Kharic hissed. "All shall wage war on Iron, and eventually race to Steelhaven, let the mud-lord race me. Let him crawl through his swamps. When I am done killing Steelbane, I will come to the capital."

He leaned in close to Maren, his voice a dangerous whisper.

"And if anyone else is sitting in my chair when I arrive... I will burn the chair, and the man sitting in it."

He sheathed his sword, turned on his heel, and stormed out of the hall.

The Council was over.

Kharic marched to war. Maren marched to the mud.

And Arion sat back on his throne, wiping sweat of his forehead, thinking he had solved all his problems.

OF LAUGHTER

Outside, in the crisp morning air, Markus Quillen fell into step beside his lord.

"That could have gone worse," Markus offered.

Maren gave no words. He reached out and ran his thumbnail down the leather cover of the ledger Markus carried. It left a faint, white scratch—a tally mark carved in silence. Then he looked back at the command tent, at the banners of noble houses snapping in the wind, at the vast encampment of warriors who had been born to war while he had been born to mud.

"Remember that name," he said at last. "Valdria. Remember how they laughed."

"My lord?"

Maren's face was calm, but something more violent remains behind his eyes—he had learned to wait.

"Someday," he said, "they won't be laughing."

He walked towards the edge of camp, towards the marshes, towards the worthless village that no one else wanted.

Markus watched him go, and felt the first stirring of awe.

Here, he thought, *is a man who knows how to hate properly. Who knows that the deepest revenge is served not hot, but frozen—preserved across years, across decades, until the moment is exactly right.*

He followed his lord in silence.

OF THE MUD AND THE SEED

While the realm watched the north, two different powers were growing in the shadows throughout the long, wet summer.

In the military camps of the rebellion, General Stellan sat in pavilions of fine silk, surrounded by maps and mathematicians. He was a man of the "Art of War," obsessed with supply metrics and the "proper" alignment of the stars. To Stellan, the army was an apparatus to be tuned; to the men in the mud, he was merely a piece of lard in a clean tabard, a soft thing protected by a wall of vellum and vanity.

Kharic Stormborn, nominally Stellan's subordinate, was the one who actually breathed and who the men followed. He ignored the high councils, spending his nights around the communal fires of the common soldiers. While Stellan wrote reports to the King, Kharic was absorbing the wild lords and the independent warbands that Arion had tried to disenfranchise. He didn't offer them titles or vellum deeds; he offered them a share of the vengeance he was brewing. He was strengthening his grip not through the King's seal, but through the primal magnetism of a man who promised to lead them through the fire. He was an army within an army, a storm waiting for the sky to darken.

But hundreds of leagues away, Maren Ashford was conducting a slower, silent harvest in the West.

Valdria was exactly as Kharic had described it: a wet, miserable provincial mess. But the fog that blinded the Hegemon's spies was Maren's greatest shield. He did not just recruit men; he hoarded them. He took the scholars whose libraries had been ablazed, the blacksmiths whose anvils had been seized, and the deserters who had learned that "Storm-glory" didn't fill a stomach.

Maren was no saint. He didn't dig those dikes out of a love for the soil. Every shoveled clod of freezing mud was a mental tally against the men who had laughed at him in the Summer Palace. He worked until his hands bled, his mind replaying Berold's mockery and Arion's bird-like scrawl. He wasn't just building a base; he was building a weapon.

For six months, the isolation that was meant to be their punishment became their greatest forge. By the time the wet summer turned to autumn, the "peasant lord" had transformed his ragtag force of thirty thousand into a disciplined, hungry tide. Markus Quillen sat in his draughty tower, the scratch of his quill the only constant in the damp air.

"We have bog-iron for new pikes and grain for the winter," Markus reported, looking over his spectacles. "And the muster rolls are complete, my lord. We now command sixty thousand men."

Markus looked up, his eyes sharp. "It is a dangerous number. Too large to hide forever, yet too small to storm the capital alone. The men are getting restless, Maren. They want to know when we are going back to claim what we were promised."

Maren looked at the map, his eyes quiet. "Not yet. Let Kharic think he is the only tiger in the woods. We wait for the exact moment the world looks away."

OF THE PEASANT'S DOUBT

As the army grew, so did the weight of the man's fear.

Late that night, Markus Quillen entered the command tent. The air inside was thick with the smell of wet wool and peat smoke. From the inner chamber—the partitioned area Maren shared with his wife—Lyra's voice drifted out, sharp and unrelenting as a saw blade.

"Another week of rain, Maren. Another week of eating gruel that tastes like wet dog. Look at my hands! The damp has gotten into the bone. You promised me a palace, and you gave me a tent that smells of mildew and horse sweat. If we stay here another winter, I swear I will let the bog-wights take me, just to be warm!"

Markus paused. He heard the rustle of silk—Lyra storming out the back flap, leaving a silence that felt heavier than her shouting.

He stepped forward to find Maren not studying the map, but staring at ten open chests of gold—the first "tribute" squeezed from the western bog-mines. In the flickering candlelight, the coins looked like the eyes of a predator. Maren was counting them, his hands shaking so violently that the metal clinked with a rhythmic, frantic sound.

"I'm doing the smart thing, Markus," Maren whispered, ignoring his wife's departure. "Did you hear her? She's right. This place is a grave. But this gold... it's enough to buy every farm in the South. Why should we march to Steelhaven? Why should I risk my neck against the Stormborn or those Iron generals?"

He looked up, his face pale, his eyes darting to the tent flap where Lyra had vanished.

"The envoy gave me a stamped pardon. I can go back. I can take Lyra somewhere warm. I can be a farmer again, but with

silk on my back. She would stop screaming. We could just...
leave."

"You cannot go back," Markus said, stepping into the light.
"That pardon is a death warrant with better calligraphy. This
gold is not a gift; it is the price of your sword. The moment you
disband this army, you are no longer a Lord. You are just a rich
thief, and the first magistrate you meet will hang you from the
nearest oak."

Maren froze, a half-packed shirt in his hand. He sat on the
edge of the bed, looking at his calloused, trembling hands. At
that moment, he didn't look like a King. He looked small, tired,
and profoundly ordinary—a man bullied by his wife, terrified
of his enemies, and longing for a simple way out.

"I never asked for this, Markus," Maren confessed, his voice
cracking. "I just wanted to lower the taxes. I didn't want to
conquer the world."

"It is too late to be small, Maren," Markus said gently,
placing his hand over the map of the Heartlands. "When one
rides on the lion's back, one cannot dismount without being
eaten."

The silence in the tent lasted until the fire settled into red
embers. Finally, Maren let out a long, shuddering breath.

"Distribute the gold to the soldiers," Maren said, standing
up. He didn't look at the chests again. "Tell them... tell them
it's a bonus for the march ahead. A gift from their Lord."

He never mentioned the pardon again. But as he turned
back to the map, Markus saw the truth in the slump of the
man's shoulders: Maren Ashford wasn't marching because he
wanted a crown. He was marching because he was too terrified
to stop.

INTERLUDE I
THE MUD THAT BINDS US

IMPERIAL DECREE #704: CONCERNING THE TIDINESS OF THE REALM

It has come to Our attention that the mud in the Western Marshes is being unnecessarily noisy. It clings to the boots of the unworthy and makes a wet, slapping sound that echoes even unto the Onyx Chambers, disturbing the sleep of the Ancestors. Henceforth, the Mud is ordered to turn into Stone.

Should the Mud refuse to be Stone, the Peasants living within it must serve as the Glue. Let them be pressed together, face to face, in the hollows of the earth, until they are as hard as the mountain. A world without cracks is a world without tears. Furthermore, all birds in the Eastern gully must be blinded with silver needles, so they may sing of the internal light rather than the external filth.

—By the Hand of the Divine, Edric II, the Son of Stillness, Stamped with the Imperial Seal

OF THE SCAVENGERS

The scent of the rotting empire travelled faster than its law, and across the provinces, the vulture-lords began to stir. They moved with a cold, parasitic arithmetic, polishing their family banners for a victory they had yet to earn. These were men of the middle-ground, cautious scavengers who marched towards the Heartland with agonizing slowness, always careful to stay three days behind the fire and two days ahead of the hunger. They were a parade of gamblers, each waiting for a neighbor to bleed first, their eyes fixed not on the restoration of the mandate, but on the treasury vaults of Steelhaven. They did not seek to break the machine; they simply hoped to be the ones holding the levers when the grinding finally stopped.

OF BERIC DURRANT
AND HIS ARRIVAL

The man who would become Lord of the Greenway came to Maren's camp in the manner of a drowned rat seeking shelter from a flood it had caused.

It was the third week of hiding in the Thornwood marshes, when the rebellion was still small enough to be called banditry and Maren's "army" numbered fewer than two hundred souls. The rain had not stopped for six days. The ground had become a living thing—treacherous, hungry, pulling at boots and swallowing cooking fires. Men slept standing up because lying down meant waking in three inches of black water. The sick list grew longer than the duty roster.

Maren was attempting to eat a supper of boiled roots and despair when the sentries dragged in their catch.

"Found him in the eastern gully, sir. Claims he's got information."

The prisoner was enormous—a head taller than any man in camp, with shoulders like oak beams and hands that could have palmed a man's skull like a child's ball. His clothes were rags held together by mud and determination. His beard was a matted catastrophe that might have contained small animals. He smelt of pig shit and rotting vegetation, which meant he smelt roughly the same as everyone else in camp, only more so.

"Information," Maren repeated, setting down his bowl. The roots had been tasteless anyway. "What sort of information could a man who looks like he lost a fight with a swamp possibly possess?"

The giant grinned, revealing teeth that had seen better decades. "The sort that keeps you alive past tomorrow, headman. There's an imperial patrol coming. Forty men, maybe fifty. They know you're here. They've got a local guide—a farmer named Hendricks who you robbed last month."

"We didn't rob him. We requisitioned grain for the—"

"Doesn't matter what you call it. Hendricks calls it robbery, and Hendricks knows these marshes better than his own wife's face." The giant's grin widened. "Lucky for you, I know them better than Hendricks."

Markus Quillen stepped forward, his hand on his knife. "And why would you help us? What's your stake in this?"

"My stake?" The giant laughed—a sound like boulders grinding together. "My stake is that those imperials burned down my village last spring. Killed my brother. Took my nephew for the labour gangs. I've been living in these marshes for eight months, eating frogs and dreaming of the day I get to watch imperial soldiers drown in the mud they made us dig."

He looked at Maren with eyes that held no cleverness, no calculation—only a simple, bedrock hatred that went down to the bone.

"My name is Beric. I used to be a farmer. Now I'm whatever you need me to be, so long as it ends with dead imperials."

Maren studied him for a long moment. The rain drummed on the canvas overhead. Somewhere in the camp, a man was coughing—the wet, rattling cough that meant he wouldn't last the week.

"Can you get us out of here before the patrol arrives?"

"I can get you to a place they'll never find. Deep marsh, solid ground, good water. It'll take three days of walking through shit up to your knees, and you'll lose anyone too weak to keep up. But you'll live."

"And after?"

Beric's smile faded. "After, you let me stay. You let me fight. And when this is over—if this is ever over—you remember that the man who saved your rebellion was a farmer from Greenway who had nothing left to lose."

Maren extended his hand. Beric took it.

Neither of them knew, in that moment, that they were sealing a bond that would one day require a silk cord to sever.

OF THE MARCH

The march through the deep marsh was everything Beric had promised and worse.

They moved in single file through channels of black water that ranged from ankle-deep to chest-high, following paths that existed only in Beric's memory. The giant went first, testing each step with a long pole, calling back warnings in a voice that carried despite its lowness. "Soft bottom here. Step on the root. Mind the drop."

Maren walked behind him, watching the massive shoulders work, watching the way Beric's feet found purchase where there seemed to be none. The man moved through the marsh like a creature born to it—slow, deliberate, utterly certain.

"How do you know these paths?" Maren asked, during one of their brief rest stops. They were standing on a hummock of solid ground barely large enough for twenty men, the rest of the column still strung out behind them in the grey-green murk.

Beric wrung water from his beard. "Ran these marshes as a boy. My father trapped eels here. His father before him. The channels change with the seasons, but the deep ways stay the same if you know what to look for."

"And the imperials don't know?"

"The imperials?" Beric spat into the water. "The imperials think the marsh is a obstacle. They build roads around it, bridges over it. They've never understood that the marsh is the land. Everything else is just what grew on top."

He looked back at the column—exhausted men, half of them sick, all of them terrified—and his expression softened slightly.

"Your lot aren't soldiers. Most of them will die before this is over, one way or another. But they're following you into a swamp in the middle of the night because you asked them to. That's worth something, headman. That's worth more than you know."

On the second night, they lost their first man.

His name was Tam, a former conscript who had joined them after escaping a labour gang. He had been coughing for days, and the endless wet had turned the cough into something worse. He fell in one of the deeper channels and simply... didn't rise. By the time the men behind him realised what had happened, the marsh had already claimed him—pulled him down into the black mud like a lover's embrace, leaving nothing but a few bubbles and a spreading stain of blood where his head had struck a submerged root.

They couldn't stop to bury him. They couldn't even stop to mark the place. The patrol was still behind them somewhere, and Hendricks was still guiding them, and every hour they delayed was an hour the imperials used to close the gap.

Maren watched the place where Tam had disappeared until the column pushed him forward. He tried to remember the man's face and found he couldn't—only a vague impression of youth, of fear, of a cough that wouldn't stop.

One man, he told himself. *One man, against the forty we would have lost if the patrol had found us.*

It was the first time he had performed that calculation. It would not be the last.

OF HUNGER

The place Beric led them to was everything he had promised: a series of interconnected islands in the deep marsh, invisible from any approach, surrounded by channels too treacherous for any force to navigate without a guide. There was fresh water from a spring that bubbled up through the peat. There were fish in the channels, frogs in the shallows, birds' eggs in the reeds.

There was not enough food for two hundred men.

The supplies they had carried were nearly exhausted. The fish were small and bony, more effort to catch than they provided in sustenance. The frog meat tasted like mud and went through a man's bowels like water. Within a week, the hunger had become a living presence in the camp—a weight that pressed on every thought, a hollowness that no amount of watered soup could fill.

Maren watched his rebellion begin to starve.

"We could send foraging parties," Markus suggested, during one of their increasingly grim councils. "Small groups, at night. There are villages on the marsh's edge—"

"And every village has imperial eyes now," Maren said. "The moment we show ourselves, Hendricks will know. The patrol will know. We'll have given away everything Beric bought us."

"Then what? We sit here and watch them waste away?"

Maren had no answer. He looked at the fire—barely more than embers now, because they couldn't spare the fuel—and felt the weight of two hundred lives pressing down on his shoulders.

That night, he couldn't sleep. He wandered the camp instead, moving between the huddled forms of sleeping men, listening to the sounds of restless hunger. A child was crying somewhere—one of the refugees had brought her daughter, barely six years old, and the girl had not stopped crying since they'd run out of porridge three days ago. The sound cut through Maren like a blade.

He found Beric at the water's edge, sitting motionless on a fallen log, staring out at the dark expanse of the marsh.

"Can't sleep either?" Maren asked.

"Don't need much sleep. Never have." Beric didn't turn. "Sit down, headman. You look like death's younger brother."

Maren sat. The log was wet, like everything else in this forsaken place, and the cold seeped through his clothes immediately. He no longer noticed such discomforts. The body, he had learned, could adapt to almost anything if given no choice.

"How long can we last?" he asked.

"On what we have now? Another week. Maybe two if we're careful with the rations." Beric's voice was flat, matter-of-fact. "After that, the weak ones start dying. Then the sick ones. Then the rest of us, unless something changes."

"And what could change?"

Beric was quiet for a long moment. Then he reached into his coat and produced something—a small bundle wrapped in oilcloth, carefully protected from the damp.

"This," he said.

Maren unwrapped it. Inside was food—real food. Half a loaf of bread, only slightly mouldy. A chunk of dried meat. A small pot of rendered fat.

"Where did you get this?"

"Been saving it. Found a cache on one of the outer islands—some trapper's emergency store, probably dead now. Took it three days ago, been keeping it for..." Beric trailed off.

"For what?"

"For this." The giant finally turned to look at him.

"I didn't touch it. I robbed that patrol for *my* dinner. This... this was for when *you* needed it."

In the moonlight, his face was a study in exhausted determination. "You're not eating, headman. Don't think I haven't noticed. You've been giving your share to the children, to the sick, to anyone who looks like they need it more. You're starving yourself to keep them alive."

"They need it more than I do."

"Horseshit." The word was flat, without heat. "You're the only thing holding this rabble together. You die, they scatter. They scatter, the imperials hunt them down one by one. Every life in this camp depends on you staying alive, and you're too stupid or too stubborn to see it."

He thrust the bundle into Maren's hands.

"Eat. That's not a request."

"I can't take your food—"

"It's not mine. Nothing is mine anymore. I gave up having things the day the imperials burnt my home." Beric's voice cracked slightly. "But I'm not giving up this. I'm not giving up you. You're the first man in my life who ever looked at me and saw something other than a big dumb farmer who was good for lifting heavy things. You asked my name. You listened when I talked. You treated me like I mattered."

He looked away, embarrassed by his own emotion.

"That's worth more than bread, headman. That's worth starving for."

Maren looked at the food in his hands. The bread smelt of must and salvation. The meat was so dry it would take an hour to chew. It was the most precious gift he had ever received.

"Eat," Beric said again. "Eat, and tomorrow we figure out how to feed the rest of them. But tonight, just... eat."

Maren ate.

OF THE NIGHT BERIC SAVED HIM

The fever came on the ninth day.

It started with chills—Maren told himself it was just the cold, just the endless damp that had seeped into his bones. Then came the sweating, the headaches, the strange lightness in his limbs that made every step feel like walking through water. By nightfall, he couldn't stand.

"Marsh fever," the camp's only physician said—a former butcher named Hendel who knew more about pigs than people but was all they had. "I've seen it before. The bad water, the rotting vegetation... it gets into the blood. Half the time it passes. Half the time..."

He didn't finish the sentence. He didn't need to.

Maren spent three days in a delirium that blurred the line between sleeping and waking. He saw his mother's face, dead these twenty years. He saw the white stag in the forest, bleeding silver light from its throat. He saw statues of himself in every city of the realm, bronze faces staring down at crowds who had forgotten his name. He saw his children—the children he did not yet have—watching him from a wagon that grew smaller and smaller in the distance, too far to reach, too far to save.

And through it all, he was aware of a presence beside him. A massive shadow that never left, that pressed wet cloths to his forehead and forced water between his cracked lips, that spoke to him in a low, steady rumble whenever the nightmares grew too loud.

"Easy, headman. Easy. You're not dying tonight. I didn't drag your sorry carcass through three days of swamp just to lose you to a fever. You owe me better than that."

On the third night, the fever broke. Maren woke to find himself lying on a pallet of reeds in one of the larger shelters, his body weak as a newborn's but his mind clear for the first time in what felt like years.

Beric was beside him, slumped against the shelter wall, asleep sitting up. The giant's face was haggard, his beard wilder than ever, his clothes stiff with dried mud and sweat. He looked like he hadn't moved in days.

Maren tried to speak and produced only a croak.

Beric's eyes snapped open instantly—a soldier's reflex, even in a man who had never been a soldier.

"You're awake." The relief in his voice was naked, unguarded. "Thank the gods. Thank whatever gods still listen to men like us."

"How long?" Maren managed.

"Three days. Four nights. The physician said you'd probably die. I told him if you died, I'd break his neck for being wrong." Beric's grin was a ghost of its usual self. "I think he believed me."

"You stayed."

"Where else would I go?" Beric helped him sit up,

supporting his weight with surprising gentleness for such massive hands. "You're the only man in this camp who knows where we're going. The only one who can make the others believe we might actually get there. You think I'd let you die just because your body decided to give up?"

He pressed a cup of water to Maren's lips—clean water, somehow, in a place where everything was mud and rot.

"The camp?" Maren asked, when he could speak again.

"Still here. Still alive, mostly. We lost four more to the fever, and Old Tam's widow finally gave up the ghost. But the rest are holding on." Beric's voice dropped. "They've been asking about you. Praying for you, some of them. You matter to these people, headman. More than you know."

Maren closed his eyes. He could feel his body's weakness like a weight, could feel how close he had come to slipping away into the dark. But beneath the exhaustion, something else stirred—something that felt almost like hope.

"Thank you," he said. "For staying. For... for all of it."

Beric shrugged, but his eyes were bright with something that might have been tears.

"That's what brothers do, headman. That's what the mud taught me—when you're in it together, you don't let go. You hold on until you both come out, or you both go under. There's no in-between."

He held up his hand—massive, calloused, still stained with the mud of the marsh.

"The mud that binds us. That's what my father used to say. The marsh doesn't care if you're rich or poor, high or low. It treats everyone the same—kills you if you fight it, saves you if you learn its ways. We're marsh-brothers now, you and I. Bound by the mud. Whatever happens next, that doesn't change."

Maren took the offered hand. The grip was warm, solid, utterly certain.

"Marsh-brothers," he repeated.

It was a peasant's oath, a farmer's bond—nothing that would have held weight in any lord's court. But in that moment, in that miserable shelter surrounded by sick and starving men, it felt more sacred than any vow ever sworn in a cathedral.

Neither of them could know that years later, in a moonlit garden far from this swamp, one brother would pour wine while the other drank poison.

Neither of them could know that the mud that bound them would one day become the grave that separated them.

They knew only this: that they were alive, against all odds, and that as long as they stood together, there was still hope.

It was enough. For now, it was enough.

PART TWO
THE FALL OF IRON

It is the nature of iron to weigh down the wearer. The ultimate victory of an empire of steel is to forge the heaviest shroud for its own corpse.

— The Crimson Art: Final Meditation

CHAPTER TEN

THE GOD OF WAR

IN WHICH THE BOATS ARE BURNED,
THE IRON ARMY BREAKS, AND THE
HEGEMON RISES FROM THE ASHES

To kill one is an act of rage punishable by death; to kill a hundred thousand is an act of arithmetic rewarded with lordship. Cruelty requires a pulse; true heartlessness requires only a pen.

— The Crimson Art: Tenth Meditation

OF STEELBANE'S SIEGE

By the third year of the rebellion, the war had reached a crisis.

General Jared Steelbane—Ironhold's finest commander, who had crushed Corwin Harrow and restored order to the central provinces—had marched north with three hundred thousand men to destroy the rebel kingdoms one by one. His first target was Dragonspire, the old northern realm that had been restored under King Aldwin. He besieged their capital at a place called Stonedeer, trapping the royal family and their army within walls that grew weaker by the day.

The other rebel kings watched from a distance, paralyzed by indecision.

They had gathered their armies—hundreds of thousands of men, collectively far outnumbering Jared Steelbane's force. But they could not agree on what to do. Some argued for immediate attack; others counseled caution. Some wanted to relieve Stonedeer; others secretly hoped the siege would succeed, eliminating a potential rival. They camped in the hills surrounding the besieged city, observing the imperial forces, debating endlessly while Dragonspire starved.

OF THE TIGER'S TEARS

The Northern Army—the relief force sent by King Arion—had been camped at Axeville for forty-six days.

The continued rain had turned the encampment into a swamp. Morale was rotting faster than the grain supplies. Fifty miles to the north, the fortress of Stonedeer was under siege, and every day, messengers arrived begging for relief.

The rain was not just water; it was a cold, grey weight that sought to drown the soul. In the infirmary tents of Axeville, the smell of wet wool and infection was thick enough to choke a man.

A young boy, no older than sixteen, lay on a pile of rotting straw. His breath was a shallow, wet rattle—the lung-rot had taken him. Beside him sat a figure that seemed too large for the cramped, leaking space.

It was Kharic.

He was not wearing his gilded armour. He was in a simple, mud-stained tunic, his massive hands trembling as he tore a piece of dry bread into small, soft bits. He dipped them into a cup of warm wine and held them to the boy's blue lips.

"Eat, Davos," Kharic whispered. His voice, usually a thunderclap that broke enemy lines, was as soft as a mother's prayer. "The road to the North is long. You'll need your strength."

Kharic knew the boy would be dead before the moon rose. He wasn't feeding him bread; he was feeding him dignity.

The boy's eyes fluttered open, glassy with fever. He recognised the face—the angular jaw, the eyes like trapped lightning. "My Lord... the boats... they say we aren't moving."

"We move tomorrow," Kharic promised. He took his own cloak—a heavy, fur-lined thing worth more than a village—and wrapped it around the shivering boy, tucking the edges in with a delicate, heartbreaking care. "Sleep now. I will stand the watch for you."

When the boy finally drifted off, Kharic stood. His face transformed instantly. The tenderness vanished, replaced by a mask of cold, jagged stone. He stepped out of the infirmary and into the downpour, where Xander and the other sentries watched him.

Kharic didn't look at them, but as he passed towards his own command tent, he stopped by a cook-fire that was struggling to stay alive. He took the ladle from a startled cook and tasted the watery broth.

"This is horse-piss," Kharic growled. "If the men eat this, they will fight like ghosts. Give them the salted pork from my personal stores. All of it."

"But my Lord," the cook stammered, "that was meant for your table for the month!"

"Then I shall be hungry," Kharic said, already walking away. "A Tiger does not feast while his cubs starve."

OF THE GOD ON THE BOARD

The rain lashed the silk of the command tent, but inside, the air was unnervingly still.

Outside, leaning on a heavy halberd, Hans Xander stood in the mud with the other sentries. They were shadows in the dark, but their ears were pressed towards the light leaking from the tent.

"They say he hasn't slept in three days," a young soldier whispered, his teeth chattering.

A heavy footfall in the mud silenced them. Cassius Jonn approached, his silver-filigreed armour dull under the rain, a cloak of wolf-fur heavy on his shoulders. The other sentries stiffened, but Cassius didn't look at them with the cold eyes of a commander. He stopped beside Hans, his gaze fixed on the glowing silhouette of the tent.

"What do you see, Hans? You've been staring at the shadow on the silk for an hour."

Hans didn't look away from the tent. "I see a man moving pieces into a furnace, General."

Cassius smiled—a tired, knowing expression. "Most men see a suicide. You see the setup. I told Kharic months ago that he was wasting you on a halberd. He didn't listen."

"Kharic Stormborn listens only to the wind," Hans murmured.

"And the wind is screaming tonight," Cassius replied, before turning to enter the tent.

Inside, the clicking of stone against wood was the only sound. Kharic Stormborn sat across from Eldran Greymantle. Between them lay a board of Strategos.

"The logic of the terrain is absolute, my lord," Greymantle said, his voice weary. He pointed to the board, where Kharic's obsidian pieces were boxed in by an overwhelming sea of ivory.

"General Zelbek has the hills. The textbook says we must wait."

Kharic didn't look up. He moved a small obsidian piece—a sacrifice—into the heart of the enemy lines.

"The textbook was written by men who were afraid to lose," Kharic said softly. "Zelbek thinks the board is static. He trusts his eyes."

Kharic picked up his 'King' piece and placed it directly in the path of a crushing ivory charge. A move of absolute madness.

"But the board is alive," Kharic continued. "I will turn my men into a fire that has no choice but to burn through the enemy or die. Zelbek will see my move and he will freeze. He will wait for a logic that isn't coming."

Cassius stood in the corner, watching the firelight carve Kharic's face into something stone-like. He looked at the board, then back towards the tent flap where Hans stood guard. He realised then that Kharic was playing with souls, but Hans... Hans was the only one who could see the entire board.

"You play with pieces, Eldran," Kharic whispered. "I play with the fear of death."

OF THE COWARD'S DELAY

But General Stellan, the Supreme Commander appointed by the King, refused to move.

"We wait," Stellan told his officers, sipping warm wine in his dry, opulent tent. "Let Steelbane exhaust himself against the walls of Stonedeer. Let the Dragonspire army weaken the Empire. When both beasts are tired, we shall step in and skin them both."

It was a prudent strategy. It was a politician's strategy.

But Kharic Stormborn was not a politician.

He stood in the rain outside the command tent, watching his soldiers shiver in the mud. He heard their empty bellies growling. He saw the fire dying in their eyes. He thought of his uncle Torian, whose bones were still waiting for vengeance.

"He is not waiting for victory," Kharic whispered to Eldran Greymantle. "He is waiting for us to freeze."

Eldran nodded, his face grim. "Stellan fears Steelbane more than he fears the gods. He will never cross the river."

"Then he is in my way."

Kharic gripped the hilt of his sword. The leather creaked.

"Stay here, Father. I have a command to relieve."

OF THE TIGER'S HUNGER

Kharic walked into the command tent. The guards did not stop him; they were more afraid of the Stormborn than they were of the King's orders.

General Stellan looked up from his map. He frowned. "Second General, I did not summon you. We are discussing logistics."

"Logistics," Kharic repeated. He walked to the table. He did not look at the map. He looked at the fat, comfortable man who held the King's Seal. "The men are eating roots and boiled leather. Our allies in Stonedeer are eating their own horses. And you sit here discussing logistics."

"It is a complex situation," Stellan said dismissively. "You are a warrior, Kharic. You understand fighting, not grand strategy. Go back to your troops. We march when I say we march."

"We march tomorrow," Kharic said.

Stellan stood up, his face reddening. "This is treason! I hold the General's Signet! I am the voice of King Arion! Guards! Arrest this—"

The sword moved so fast it was a blur of silver light.

Kharic didn't just cut Stellan's throat; he severed the head completely. It hit the map table with a wet thud, overturning a goblet of wine. The red wine mixed with the red blood, soaking into the parchment.

The tent went silent. The other officers stared in horror.

Kharic sheathed his sword. He reached out and picked up the heavy bronze General's Signet from the table, wiping a speck of blood from it with his thumb.

"The King is far away," Kharic announced, his voice calm and terrifying. "Steelbane is right there."

He looked at the trembling officers.

"General Stellan was a traitor working for the Empire. I have executed him." Kharic held up the Seal. "I am in command now. Issue the order."

"W-what order, my lord?" a captain stammered, stunned.

"Send every scrap of food to the soldiers. Feed them until they are full. Then bring the boats."

Kharic's eyes burned with a cold, blue fire.

"We attack tomorrow."

OF THE CROSSING

Dawn broke grey and frosty over the River Isldra, and Kharic Stormborn kept his word.

His army gathered at the river's edge: forty thousand men, preparing to cross into what every military expert agreed was certain death.

Kharic walked among them. He wore no helmet, no armour heavier than boiled leather. If he was going to ask his men to die, he would show them how dying was done.

"Listen to me," Kharic said, his voice carrying across the assembled ranks. "We are forty thousand against three hundred thousand. If we fight expecting to retreat, we will retreat. If we fight expecting to lose, we will lose. The only way we win this battle is if every man on this field fights as though his life depends on it—because it does."

He turned and walked to the nearest boat.

No one stayed behind.

OF NO RETURN

The crossing took three hours—three hours of vulnerable exposure. But Jared Steelbane, confident in his numerical superiority, chose to wait. Let the rebels come to him, he reasoned. He would crush them at his leisure.

It was the last mistake he would ever make.

When the final boat touched the northern shore, the commanders urged Kharic to secure the landing zone. Instead, Kharic stood by the riverbank, looking back at their fleet of supply boats—their only means of retreat across the treacherous water.

"Burn them," he ordered.

"My lord?" Lord Ironhand stared at him in horror. "Those boats are our lifeline. If we burn them, there is no way back."

"That is the point," Kharic said, his voice carrying over the roar of the river. "As long as the men know there is a way back, they will fight with one eye on the retreat. I want them to fight with both eyes on the enemy."

He grabbed a torch from a sentry and threw it onto the deck of the nearest transport. The dry timber, soaked in pitch, caught instantly.

"Burn the boats!" Kharic roared to his stunned soldiers. "Smash the cooking pots! Carry only three days' rations! After three days, we will feast in Stonedeer, or we will feed the crows in this valley!"

The order spread like madness.

The soldiers, realizing that their commander had just cut off their only escape, felt a terror that quickly transmuted into a cold, desperate fury. They watched the flames consume their lifeline, turning the night sky orange. The fire turned the river into a mirror of hell, blotting out the rising sun.

There was no retreat. There was no tomorrow. There was only the fortress.

"Now," Kharic declared, turning to face the imperial lines. "Let glory be written."

The army formed up. Forty thousand men arranged in fighting columns, stripped of everything that might slow them down, committed beyond possibility of retreat. They were not merely soldiers anymore. They were instruments of pure destruction, with nothing to lose and everything to gain.

Jared Steelbane, watching from his command post, felt the first stirring of unease. The rebels were not behaving as rebels should. They were not hesitating, not probing for weakness. They were coming straight at him with the relentless momentum of a flooding river.

He ordered his lines to prepare for assault.

It would not be enough.

OF THE NINE CHARGES
AT STONEDEER

What happened at Stonedeer would be studied by generals and debated by scholars for two thousand years, but no song could ever capture the lived-in reality of the slaughter. It was not a battle of tactics; it was a battle of biologies.

Jared Steelbane had the high ground and three hundred thousand men. His Iron Legions were not a militia; they were an engineering project. They raised no war cries. As the forty thousand rebels approached, the only sound from the Imperial side was the rhythmic, metallic *clack-thrum* of sixteen-foot pikes being lowered in unison at the signal of a single bronze whistle. To the Legions, war was a matter of mathematics and meat—they simply had to stand, and the world would break against them.

Kharic led the first charge personally. He hit the Imperial front line like a meteor falling from a cold sky.

"Ironhold killed my father!" his scream ripped through the morning mist. His greatsword, a massive slab of notched steel, cleaved through a laminated shield and the man behind it in a single, sickening crunch of wood and bone.

Behind him, his men followed into the meat grinder. They did not fight like soldiers; they fought like men who had already been executed. Because the boats were ash at their backs, they treated their own bodies as expendable hardware. When their spears shattered against the Imperial plate, they used their swords. When their swords notched and stuck in ribs, they used their daggers, their helmets, and eventually, their teeth.

The Imperial defence was terrifying in its silence. Every time Kharic's men smashed into the front rank, the Ironhold formation simply absorbed the shock. The back ranks stepped forward into the slurry of blood and entrails left by the fallen without missing a single beat of the drum. It was like stabbing a mountain.

By the fifth charge, the nature of the battle changed from fury to exhaustion. The rebels were weeping as they fought, their lungs burning with the scent of ozone and iron. Biology dictated they must collapse—flesh and blood cannot sustain that level of violence for five hours. Their arms were leaden, their blades so dull they were essentially bludgeoning the enemy to death.

But every time the rebel line wavered, Kharic was there. He

was no longer a man; he was a force of nature, dripping with blood that wasn't his, his armour dented into his chest, yet refusing to fall. He dragged his army forward by the sheer, terrifying magnetism of his will, screaming that death was behind them, and only life lay through the enemy's throat.

The Imperial officers watched in growing horror. They had defeated countless rebellions with discipline, but those enemies had always possessed the survival instinct to retreat. These men had none. They welcomed the pikes, pulling themselves *up* the shafts of the spears just to get a hand around an Imperial throat.

By the ninth charge, the impossible happened.

The Imperial line—the iron wall that had conquered the world—cracked. It wasn't a tactical failure; it was a psychological contagion. Panic is not a thought; it is a virus. It jumped from shield to shield, turning an army of engineers into a herd of terrified animals. The Legions realised they were not fighting an army, but a forty-thousand-headed ghost that could not be killed because it was already dead. Fear, cold and absolute, rippled through Steelbane's ranks.

"They aren't human!" a Centurion screamed, his voice breaking as a rebel with no weapon but a jagged stone tackled him into the mud.

The line broke. The rhythmic drumming stopped, replaced by the chaotic, high-pitched scream of a rout. Jared Steelbane, the invincible Last General, watched from his horse as his three hundred thousand "engineers" turned into a panicked herd. He did not stay to die. He turned his horse and fled into the shadow of the southern hills, retreating to wait for orders from an Emperor who had already forgotten his name.

Kharic let him go. He stood in the centre of the slaughter, his chest heaving, his sword-arm shaking with a palsy of pure fatigue. He didn't chase the dog; he was too busy looking at the gates of the capital, which were finally, for the first time in an age, standing unguarded.

THE BIRTH OF THE HEGEMON

By sunset, the valley of Stonedeer was a silent graveyard of iron. The other rebel commanders—the Lords of Grandmark and Dragonspire—who had watched the slaughter from the safety of their hill forts, now descended. They approached the rebel camp with the hesitant, flickering steps of men walking into a lion's den.

They were summoned to a draughty, blood-spattered farmhouse. Kharic did not rise when they entered. He sat at the head of a splintered oak table, his skin stained so deeply with the copper of death that he seemed cast in bronze.

Lord Aldwin of Dragonspire, his silk robes looking absurdly clean amidst the filth, tried to salvage a shred of dignity. He raised a silver goblet with a trembling hand. "To the victory," Aldwin declared. "And to the spirit of Corwin Harrow, who started this fire. Today, we stand as brothers, united by—"

CRACK.

Kharic backhanded the goblet with such violence that the silver dented against Aldwin's teeth. Red wine splashed across the table, indistinguishable from the dried blood on Kharic's gauntlets. "Corwin Harrow was a dreamer who died in a ditch," Kharic said, his voice a low, jagged rasp. "He died because he fought like a man. I won because I fought like a monster."

He stood up, the scent of wet wool and slaughter radiating from his cloak. "You are not my brothers. Brothers bleed together. You merely watched me bleed. If you are Kings, then what is the man who holds your lives in his palm?"

He drove his greatsword into the floorboards. The vibration

hummed through the very soles of their boots. "From this day forward, I am the Hegemon. You may keep your titles, but understand the new geometry of this world: You breathe because I allow it."

"Now," Kharic commanded. "Show me the weight of your crowns."

Aldwin was the first to break. His knees hit the rough wood with a sickening thud. Then the others followed—a slow, rustling collapse of royal dignity. Driven by a primal terror, they prostrated themselves. Aldwin fell first. It wasn't a bow; it was a collapse. The silk of his robes met the blood on the floor as he pressed his forehead into the filth, trading his dignity for his breath. They crawled towards Kharic's boots across the stained floor. They were no longer Kings; they were livestock.

But Markus Quillen, the envoy from the West, remained standing by the door. He looked small and unarmed in his simple grey tunic.

"Your knees, scholar," Kharic said softly. "Do they not work? Or must I break them to teach you the geography of this room?"

"My knees bend for my lord, the Lord of Valdria," Markus said. His voice was steady. "To kneel to two masters is to be a traitor to both. Surely, the Hegemon—the man who burned his boats for an oath—values a man who knows the weight of a covenant?"

Kharic towered over the scholar, the smell of copper and ozone radiating from his armour. "Loyalty to a ghost. Maren is playing in the bogs while I rewrite the annals of the world."

"My lord Maren sends his congratulations," Markus continued, staring at Kharic's chest rather than his eyes. "He recognises a Hegemon when the earth shakes. But Valdria is far away, and the marshes are deep. My lord suggests that while you break the front gate, someone must still ensure the back door is bolted.”

“The back door?”

“The Western Pass,” Markus said softly. “To ensure Steelbane’s remnants do not escape to reorganise. My lord is currently... tidying the threshold.”

Kharic smiled—a thin, jagged expression. He saw the game. Maren was building his own wall while the world was distracted by the Storm. “Tell your master,” Kharic whispered, “that if he steals my kill, I will turn his swamp into a glass pond. Get out, scholar.”

AFTER STONEDEER

Three days later, the battlefield was quiet, but the river still would not flow.

Kharic Stormborn walked along the banks of the River Isldra. The water was choked with the dead—thousands of Imperial corpses, bloated and tangled in the reeds, forming a dam of flesh and iron that turned the water a crimson colour. it merely seeped through the gaps in Imperial plate, a slow, thick weeping of the earth itself. The smell was sweet and cloying, a mixture of rot and river mud.

He picked up a sword that lay half-buried in the silt. It was a fine blade, Imperial steel, engraved with prayers for long life. Now it was scrap metal.

“Victory,” he murmured to himself. “This is what victory looks like.”

He watched his soldiers on the far bank. They were stripping the dead. Men were laughing, holding up gold chains and nephrite belt-buckles, arguing over boots. They had been heroes three days ago, ready to die for freedom. Now they were scavengers, made rich by slaughter.

It felt… small.

"My lord?"

A young guard approached hesitantly. He was barely eighteen, his face spattered with mud. He held a helmet filled with water. "You have not drunk since morning, Hegemon."

Kharic looked at the boy. "What is your name, soldier?"

"Elian, my lord. From the Southern Coast."

"Tell me, Elian. Are you happy?"

The boy blinked, surprised by the question. "Happy? We won, my lord. The Empire is broken. We are going to be rich. We are going to be free."

"Free." Kharic turned the dead man's sword over in his hands. "The Iron Empire executed my father because he wanted to be free. I killed three hundred thousand men to avenge him." He let the sword fall back into the mud with a wet *plop*. "I told myself that justice justified anything. That no price was too high."

He looked at the dam of bodies in the river.

"But now I wonder if the price is simply being transferred. From me to them. From my suffering to theirs." He looked at Elian. "Is one tyrant's fall worth the rise of another? If I kill the monster only to sit on his throne, have we actually changed the world, or just the name on the map?"

Elian shifted uncomfortably. "I… I don't know about tyrants, my lord. I just fight where you tell me. And I hope to go home one day."

Kharic laughed softly. It was a dry, brittle sound.

"'Just go home'," Kharic repeated. "You are wiser than I am, Elian. I have no home left to go to. I burnt the boats."

He turned away from the river, away from the stench of victory. Behind him, the fortress of Stonedeer brooded in silence, its broken walls a monument to the violence that had passed through it.

The certainty that had driven him for three years—the pure, white-hot rage—was cooling into something harder, like obsidian. He realised he did not care about governing. He did not care about freedom. He only cared about the finish line.

He looked West, towards the setting sun. towards the capital.

"We march," Kharic said to the wind. "On Steelhaven."

"And Elian?"

"Yes, my lord?"

"If we see the Lord of Valdria on the road… do not let him speak. Kill him."

OF THE GOD BORN IN BLOOD

The order was given, but as Elian turned to leave, he froze.

The sun was finally setting over River Isldra, casting a long, blood-red light across the valley. From the far bank, a sound began to rise—low at first, like the vibration of distant thunder, then growing into a rhythmic, deafening roar.

It was the sound of forty thousand men—and the two hundred thousand prisoners who had survived the slaughter —beating their spear-butts against the earth in unison.

"God of War!" they screamed. "God of War!"

The cry was not one of love; it was a sound of primal terror and total surrender. To the soldiers who had watched him cleave through the Iron Wall, Kharic Stormborn was no longer a man who bled or a lord who led. He had become something elemental—a force of nature that had broken the world's logic. In their eyes, only a god could have burned those boats; only a god could have turned a slaughter into a miracle.

Kharic stood on the blood-soaked silt, the shadow of his silhouette stretching halfway across the river. He heard the name they called him. He felt the vibration of the earth beneath his boots. He did not smile. He did not wave. He simply closed his eyes, let the wind carry the scent of the dead, and accepted the burden of his new divinity.

He was the God of War. And a god has no home, no brothers, and no retreat.

As the moon rose over the valley of Stonedeer, the roar continued, a haunting anthem for a dead empire and the terrifying new world that had just been born in its place.

CHAPTER ELEVEN

THE WEIGHT OF EARTH

IN WHICH THE LAST IRON GENERAL CHOOSES SURRENDER AND TWO HUNDRED THOUSAND MEN ARE BURIED ALIVE

Never bake bread from the wheat of the Northern Pits. They say the grain has eyes, and the crust will bleed when you break it—for the roots have tasted the marrow of men who were buried with their names still in their mouths.
— *Folk Saying from the Stonedeer Fields*

OF THE FORTY THOUSAND DEAD

When the screaming finally stopped at Stonedeer, what remained was a silence louder than the battle.

The victory was absolute. Kharic Stormborn had done the impossible: he had set fire to his own boats, starved his men of hope, and driven them to break the empire's spine. But as the smoke cleared, the cost of that miracle began to settle upon the victors like ash.

The numbers were staggering. Forty thousand imperial dead. Two hundred thousand prisoners huddled in the mud, stripped of weapons and dignity.

But numbers did not capture the truth. The numbers did not capture the look in the survivors' eyes—both victor and vanquished—who knew they had witnessed the death of an age. The invincibility of Ironhold had been broken, not by superior tactics, but by a madness that refused to die.

OF JARED STEELBANE'S CHOICE

Jared Steelbane survived the battle, but he was not sure he wanted to.

He had commanded from the rear, as proper generals do, and when the rout began, his personal guard had cut a path through the chaos and carried him to safety. He escaped with less than twenty thousand men—the shattered remnants of an army that had once been the terror of the realm.

For three days, he led his survivors south. He did not sleep. His mind was a feverish loop of tactical maps, replaying the battle, looking for the error, the flaw. He was already planning his counterattack, drafting petitions for fresh levies, believing that the Empire could still be saved if he could just regroup.

He had sent his most trusted lieutenant, Sylvanus, to the capital to plead for reinforcements.

But on the fourth day, Sylvanus returned pale and shaking.

Sylvanus did not ride into camp with the arrogance of an Imperial envoy. He stumbled in on foot, his horse dead miles back, his armour covered in dust. He looked pale, shaking, like a man who had seen a ghost.

"Where are the reinforcements?" Steelbane demanded, gripping the map table. "Where is the Emperor's decree?"

"The Emperor?" Sylvanus laughed a jagged, hysterical cry. "There is no Emperor. There is only Mordecai the Shadow-hand, and he is looking for a neck to cut."

Sylvanus pulled Steelbane close, his voice dropping to a terrified hiss.

"They wouldn't even let me into the palace, General," Sylvanus whispered. "Mordecai refused to see me, only sent a scroll. And on the road back... an assassin tried to put a crossbow bolt in my back. I killed him, but his dagger bore the Imperial mark." Sylvanus whispered, refusing to look at the other officers. "We cannot go back."

Sylvanus threw a dagger onto the table. The pommel bore the intricate seal of the Inner Court.

"They don't want explanations, General. They want a corpse to blame. If you return to Steelhaven, you won't be defending yourself. You'll be walking into your own execution."

Jared Steelbane stared at the dagger.

A frosted, familiar dread coiled in his stomach—not the clean fear of battle, but the suffocating, slimy fear of the dungeon.

He remembered the damp stone of the Black Cells, where he had sat five years ago. He remembered how Mordecai had stripped him of his rank, chained him in the dark, and left him to rot because he was "too popular" with the troops. He remembered how they had pulled him from that pit—gaunt, blinking in the sunlight—only when the fires of rebellion grew too hot for their comfort.

"Save us," they had said then, shoving a sword into his hand. *"Be our shield."*

And he had done it. He had marched north. He had crushed Corwin Harrow. He had saved their worthless skins.

And now?

Jared Steelbane looked at the scroll from Mordecai—a polite recall order that was, in reality, a death warrant. He had served Ironhold for a lifetime. He had won a hundred battles.

And now he was being discarded like a broken tool, once again.

Now that he had stumbled once, the cage door was swinging open again.

He was not a general to them. He was a hunting dog. You feed the dog when there are wolves, and you skin it when it limps.

"I fought for them," Jared whispered, his voice trembling with a rage that had been building for twenty years. "I bled for them. And this is my reward? To be murdered by a eunuch who has never held a weapon heavier than a wine cup?"

He looked at his soldiers outside the tent—men who were starving, wounded, looking to him for salvation. If he marched them south, he was marching them to the slaughterhouse to cover Mordecai's crimes.

Jared Steelbane made his decision. It was the hardest thing he had ever done, and yet, the only thing left to do.

He sent a message to Kharic Stormborn, requesting a meeting under flag of truce.

OF THE KNELT

Three days later, in a tent pitched between the lines, the greatest general of Ironhold knelt before the man who had destroyed his army.

Beside him knelt his two most trusted commanders, forming the last triumvirate of the Imperial North.

On his right was Sylvanus, the sharp-eyed strategist who handled logistics and intelligence. On his left was General Holten, a massive man whose face was a ruin of old scars. Holten commanded the Heavy Vanguard—the "Iron Wall." He was a man of few words, famous for holding the Northern Frontier against barbarian hordes for three weeks with no supplies.

"I offer you my sword," Jared said, his voice hollow. "My soldiers. Everything I have left. In return, I ask only that you spare my men—they are good soldiers, they deserve better than execution for following orders—and that you give me the chance to prove my worth."

Kharic sat on a simple wooden stool, cleaning his fingernails with a dagger. He did not look up immediately. The silence stretched, heavy and dangerous.

Finally, Kharic stopped scraping. He looked at the three kneeling commanders with cold curiosity.

"The legendary Last General of Ironhold," Kharic said softly. "Why should I trust you? A week ago, you were trying to kill me. A traitor to one master is easily a traitor to two."

"A week ago, I served the Empire." Jared looked up, and for the first time, his eyes showed the depth of his bitterness. "But the Empire I served is dead. It has been eaten from the inside by eunuchs and politicians. I will not die for a traitor who sits on a stolen throne."

Kharic stood up. He walked over to Steelbane and placed the tip of his dagger against the General's throat. A single drop of blood welled up against the steel.

"Words are wind, General. Convince me not to finish what I started at Stonedeer."

Jared Steelbane did not flinch. He did not pull away from the blade. Instead, he reached for his own sidearm—a short officer's blade—and reversed it, pressing the hilt into Kharic's free hand while keeping his own neck against Kharic's dagger.

"My life is already yours, Hegemon," Jared whispered. "If I wanted to live as a coward, I would have fled south. I am here because I want to hunt the men who betrayed us. Use me as a sword, or break me here. But do not doubt my hate."

Beside him, Sylvanus and Holten drew their daggers and cut their own palms, pressing their bleeding hands into the dirt—an ancient, irrevocable Blood Oath of the Northern Frontier.

"We are dead men walking," Holten rumbled, his voice like grinding stones. "Only you give us breath. We swear by the blood of the earth: your enemies are our prey."

Kharic looked at Steelbane's unblinking eyes. He felt the weight of the man's desperation. It was heavy, and it was real.

Kharic smiled—a terrifying expression that did not reach his eyes. He withdrew the dagger from Steelbane's throat.

"Rise," Kharic said. "I accept your blood. And I have a use for your hate."

He walked to the map table. He pointed to the vast, rugged terrain of the Heartland—the core of the Empire they were about to destroy.

"The Iron Emperor sits in Steelhaven, thinking his walls will save him," Kharic said. "He thinks you are coming to save him. But you are going to open the way for me."

He looked at the three men.

"Serve me in this. Help me burn the rotten heart of this empire. And when the ash settles, you will not just be generals."

Kharic's voice dropped low, filled with the promise of future power.

"The Heartland will need new masters. The old dynasty will be gone. Who better to rule the Three Shields than the men who trained them?"

Jared's eyes widened. It was a promise of a crown, though unspoken.

"I shall name you Lords." Kharic declared. "March west with me. Prove to me that you deserve to rule."

The three men bowed low, their foreheads touching the dirt. They had come expecting death; they left with a promise of redemption.

"It shall be done, Hegemon," Steelbane promised.

Kharic watched them go. He had not just recruited an army; he had forged a weapon.

He did not tell them that he intended to use them as jailors. He did not tell them about the "Three Shields." For now, hope was a better motivator than duty.

OF MAPS AND WHISPERS

With the blood oath sworn, the atmosphere in the tent shifted from execution to council.

Sylvanus, eager to prove his worth as the new King of High Pass, unrolled a bundle of oilskin documents he had smuggled from the capital. He spread them across Kharic's table, smoothing out the corners with trembling hands.

It was the prize every rebel had dreamed of for three years: the detailed secrets of Steelhaven.

"The Dragon Gate is impregnable from the outside," Sylvanus explained, tracing the ink lines. "But here, beneath the West Wall, is the drainage system for the Imperial Gardens. It is unguarded."

He moved his finger to a cluster of buildings near the Palace.

"And here," Sylvanus whispered, as if revealing the location of gold, "are the Secret Granaries of the Inner Court."

Kharic leaned in. "Grain?"

"Enough to feed the city for a year," Sylvanus promised. "Mordecai stopped issuing rations to the army months ago. He has been hoarding it all here, in the Royal Park, waiting out the siege. The silos are full, my lord. It is the finest wheat in the Empire."

"And the garrison?" Kharic asked, looking at Steelbane.

"Demoralised and unpaid," Steelbane answered grimly.

"They are eating rats while Mordecai sits on mountains of grain. They fear you, Hegemon. But they hate him more. With us riding at your side, the city defenders will open the gates before you even string a bow."

Kharic looked at the maps, at the promise of food for *his* men, and then at the three traitors who were now his keys to the throne. He smiled. It was the smile of a wolf who sees the throat exposed.

"You have done well," Kharic said. "Tonight, you feast as my brothers."

But outside the command tent, there was no feasting.

The two hundred thousand surrendered Imperial soldiers were corralled in the open fields, stripped of their weapons and armour. They sat in the mud, shivering in the cold wind, watching the rebel soldiers celebrate.

The tension was palpable. For decades, the Ironhold soldiers had oppressed the people of the South and East. Now, the roles were reversed. Rebel soldiers walked among the captives, spitting on them, kicking them, stealing their boots and rations.

"Look at them," a captive whispered, clutching his bruised arm. "Our generals drink wine with the savage, giving away *our* grain, while we eat mud."

"They sold us," another muttered. "Steelbane saved his own neck. Sylvanus gave away the food stores. They left us to rot."

"If we go back to the capital, Mordecai will kill us for surrendering. If we stay here, the rebels will starve us."

A ripple of unrest moved through the vast sea of prisoners —a low, dangerous hum of two hundred thousand desperate men realizing they had no future.

Inside the tent, Kharic raised a cup to his new Kings. But his ears, sharp as a predator's, caught the sound of the unrest outside. He looked at the map of the Secret Granaries—food that was now *his*—and then he looked towards the flap of the tent.

He did the maths in his head. The grain in the capital was for *his* conquerors. It was not for these losers.

He realised then that while he had acquired three useful dogs, he had also inherited a very large, very hungry pack of wolves.

And he had no intention of feeding them.

OF THE BURIAL OF THE LIVING

After Jared's surrender, Kharic faced a logistical nightmare that no poem would ever recount: what to do with two hundred thousand mouths in a starving land. The imperial soldiers sat in the mud of Stonedeer, stripped of their iron but not their resentment, a sleeping ocean of men awaiting a word.

The answer, when he gave it, was delivered with the same casual tone one might use to order the clearing of a forest.

"Bury them," he said.

The silence in the command tent was so sudden it felt like a physical blow. His generals—men who had waded through blood for years—stared at him as if he had spoken in a dead language.

"My Lord," General Arcas finally found his voice, "we have twenty divisions of able-bodied men. If we put them in the vanguard... if we use them to storm the walls of Steelhaven, they can be the fodder that exhausts the Emperor's last reserves. Why waste the meat when the wolves are hungry?"

Kharic didn't look up from the Strategos board. He moved an ivory piece, a slow, deliberate slide.

"A hungry dog follows the man with the meat," Kharic said softly. "But a beaten dog waits for the man to sleep so it can tear out his throat. You think of them as soldiers. I think of them as a ticking clock."

He looked up, and for a moment, the fire in his eyes made the lanterns seem dim.

"We have grain for ten days. If we feed them, my own men will be eating grass by the time we reach the capital. If we *don't* feed them, we are marching with two hundred thousand starving rebels at our back. Do you wish to sleep in a camp where you are outnumbered five-to-one by men who have nothing left to lose?"

"We could arm them as we reach the city," Arcas persisted, desperate. "Force them to choose between the Emperor's gallows and our front lines."

"They have already chosen," Kharic snapped. "They chose to live in shame rather than die in battle. I have no use for men who value their breath more than their honour. They are a broken blade, Arcas. If you try to wield a broken blade, it only cuts the hand that holds it."

He stood up, his shadow stretching long across the map of the empire, a dark stain that seemed to swallow the southern provinces.

"If they stay, we starve. If they go, they regroup. If they fight for us, they betray us at the first sign of rain. There is only one place where an enemy is truly pacified."

He pointed a finger at the ground.

"Below. Where they can finally serve the Empire as fertiliser for a better world."

First came the deception. Kharic announced that the imperial prisoners were to be incorporated into the rebel army. He promised them food, rank, and a share of the spoils from the coming conquest of Steelhaven. "We are all brothers now," he told their officers. "Ironhold betrayed you. I will not." Relieved, starving, and desperate for hope, the prisoners willingly stacked their armour and weapons in great piles, believing they were being prepared for reissue. They were separated into groups of five thousand, ostensibly for "reorganisation," and marched to different holding areas for their meal, guarded by Kharic's most loyal veterans.

Then came the feast. Or what passed for one.

Great cauldrons of stew were wheeled into the holding pens. The smell was overpowering—a thick, salty broth of meat and herbs that made the starving prisoners weep with gratitude. They did not know the meat was horseflesh from their own fallen mounts. They did not know the herbs included Root of Slumber—a mild sedative harvested from the western bogs, not strong enough to kill, but enough to make a man's limbs heavy and his mind slow.

"Eat!" Kharic's officers urged them, their smiles tight. "Eat your fill, brothers. You have a long march tomorrow."

The prisoners ate ravenously. They gorged themselves until their bellies ached, washing it down with barrels of watered wine. Within an hour, a heavy lethargy settled over the camp. Men dropped where they sat, their weapons already stacked miles away, their eyelids drooping, too full and too tired to question why the "reorganisation" was happening at midnight.

It was the mercy of the butcher: calming the cattle before the hammer falls.

Then there was the digging. Kharic sent cavalry detachments to scour the surrounding countryside. They rounded up twenty thousand peasants—farmers, labourers, old men and young boys—and drove them to the valley south of the camp. For three days and three nights, the sound of shovels did not stop. Under the whip, the conscripted labourers dug ten vast trenches, each a mile long and twenty feet deep. They were told they were building defensive earthworks against a counterattack. They dug until their hands bled, and those who collapsed from exhaustion were simply tossed aside.

On the fourth night, the trap closed. The prisoners, unarmed and unarmoured, were marched towards the trenches under the pretense of a midnight assembly. When they arrived, they found not rations, but lines of heavy infantry blocking their retreat, and archers massed on the ridges above.

Realisation rippled through the crowd, followed by a surge of panic. But it was too late. They were unarmed men against steel. "Push them in," Kharic ordered.

The slaughter was mechanical. The front ranks were driven into the pits at spearpoint. Those who resisted were cut down by arrows. As the trenches filled with living, screaming men, the conscripted labourers—threatened with their own deaths—were forced to begin shovelling the earth back in.

The screaming lasted for hours. The ground heaved and shuddered as thousands of men fought for air beneath the soil, a terrible, undulating motion that sickened the moon. It took until dawn for the movement to stop.

OF THE HEAVING

The voices were no longer coming from throats, but from the marrow of the world, a muffled, collective wail that seemed to vibrate out of the very bedrock. But it was the ground itself that provided the true horror. Under the pale, sickly light of the moon, the vast field did not merely settle; it pulsed.

The earth had become a liquid lung. The soil heaved and shuddered in rhythmic, agonizing waves as two hundred thousand men fought for a final gasp of air. From a distance, it looked as if the valley floor was a living sea of mud, an undulating tide of filth and desperation that refused to be still. Here and there, a hand would break through the surface—fingers clawing at the indifferent stars—only to be dragged back down by the shifting weight of the men struggling beneath.

It was a landscape of breathing dirt. The sound was not just of voices, but of the earth itself grinding, the dry soil packing tight against the wet heat of dying flesh. By the time dawn touched the valley, the movement had finally stopped, but the ground remained warped and furrowed, frozen in a permanent, silent ripple.

The message lingered longer than the smell. Throughout the realm, men heard what had happened at Stonedeer. They spoke of it in whispers—of a place where the mountains had been used as shovels and the earth had been turned into a stomach.

Even the victors did not sleep well that night. They felt the phantom vibration beneath their boots, a restless thrumming that made the strongest warriors sick to their souls. In the morning, the desertions began. Not many—just a few men slipping away into the mist, abandoning the glory they had won—but enough to show that while fear can conquer an enemy, it can also poison a friend.

Kharic himself never spoke of it again. If the decision haunted him, he gave no sign. If he regretted it, he showed no regret. Only his servants noticed that he stopped eating meat for three days afterward—took only rice and water, like a man in mourning—before returning to his old habits as if nothing had changed.

But the dead of Stonedeer would follow him to his grave—a haunting sea of shadows that even his radiance could not burn away.

OF ELDRAN GREYMANTLE'S WARNING

That night, in Kharic's command tent, his advisor Eldran Greymantle spoke words that would prove prophetic.

"You have won a great victory," the old man said, his vne—intoxicating when first tasted, poisonous when consumed in excess."oice heavy. "The greatest victory in living memory. But victory is like wi

Kharic was cleaning his sword, working oil into the blade with methodical care. He smiled, a gesture of supreme arrogance.

"Poison? I call it power, Father. Look at the map." Kharic pointed his dagger at the western territories. "I have Steelbane. I have Sylvanus. I have Holten. The 'Three Kings' of the West. I didn't just defeat them; I bought them. I split their command so they must watch each other like jealous wives. They will check each other's ambition, and together, they form a wall of iron."

He laughed, sheathing his dagger.

"I have secured the West without losing a single Cherosian soldier. I have locked the back door and thrown away the key. Maren Ashford will rot in that swamp until he dies of old age."

"You built a cage," Eldran said quietly. "But you are assuming you trapped a rat. I fear you have trapped a dragon."

Kharic frowned. "What are you saying?"

"I'm saying that whilst you play politics with traitors, the real threat is growing in the mud. What you did today—the prisoners, the burial—will be remembered. You rule through fear."

"Let them fear," Kharic snapped.

"The Iron Emperor ruled through fear. Look where it got him." Greymantle leaned forward, his eyes intense. "There is another way. This Maren Ashford… he wins battles too, but he wins them differently. He offers mercy to those who surrender. He welcomes defectors rather than burying them. His army grows in the silence whilst yours bleeds in the spotlight."

"A baseborn." Kharic scoffed, pouring himself wine. "A peasant who got lucky with a pitchfork. Let him try to cross the Three Kings. He'll be dead before winter."

"He is the only one who didn't kneel," Eldran warned. "You see three locks on the door. I see three men who have already betrayed one master, ready to betray another if the price is right. And if Maren Ashford walks out of that swamp…"

"He won't." Kharic cut him off. "I have three hundred thousand men. He has mud."

"You underestimate him." Greymantle rose to his feet, his grey cloak sweeping the floor. "I am an old man, and I have seen many great warriors in my time. Some were cruel, some were kind, but the ones who lasted—the ones who founded dynasties—were the ones who understood that war is not an end in itself. It is a means to an end. And if the means destroy the end, what have you accomplished?"

He departed, leaving Kharic alone with his sword and his thoughts.

The young commander sat in silence for a long while, considering the old man's words. Then he set aside his sword and reached for his cup.

"Let him found dynasties," he muttered to the empty tent. "I'll found victories."

But the wine tasted sour. And for a fleeting second, the image of the muddy farmer at Greymoor flashed in his mind— the man who had tapped his cup while everyone else laughed.

Survivors, Kharic thought with a sudden, irrational spike of hatred. *I should have killed him then.*

OF THE PRICE OF SILENCE

Dawn broke over the camp, but it brought no warmth. The screaming from the valley had finally stopped, replaced by a heavy, suffocating silence.

In the command tent, the three generals sat in the dim light. They were no longer the "Last Triumvirate"; they were prisoners waiting for a verdict.

"Where are they?" Holten asked, his voice a ragged whisper. He stood by the tent flap, looking towards the north. "The guards told me the legions were being moved at midnight. They said the Hegemon was sending the survivors to the Northern Frontier to bolster the defences against the barbarians. But I didn't hear wagons. I didn't hear marching."

"They didn't go north," Sylvanus said. He didn't look up from the table. His hands were clasped so tightly his knuckles were white. "I grew up in the valley, Holten. I know how the wind carries sound. Those weren't the shouts of a march. Those were the cries of a slaughterhouse."

"You don't know that," Holten snapped, though his eyes betrayed his terror. "Kharic gave us his word! He swore on the blood of the earth! He wouldn't... he couldn't kill two hundred thousand men in cold blood. He's a soldier, not a butcher."

"He is a monster," Sylvanus hissed, leaning forward. "He's a beast in human skin who drinks hate instead of wine. We handed him our men, Holten. We told them to drop their swords, and he used that silence to bury them alive. We are the ones who led them into the pits."

"Silence!"

Jared Steelbane finally spoke. He hadn't moved for an hour. His eyes were fixed on the flickering candle, wide and bloodshot.

"Jared, we have to do something," Holten pleaded. "If there's still time, if even a few cohorts are left—"

"I said silence," Jared repeated, his voice cold and sharp as a razor. He turned his gaze to Sylvanus. "The Hegemon has been generous. He spared our lives. He has promised us a future in the new order. If he says the soldiers moved north, then they moved north."

Sylvanus stared at him, horrified. "Jared? You can't be serious. You saw the smoke. You heard the—"

"I heard nothing," Jared interrupted. He stood up, towering over his old friends. The fear in his eyes had turned into something uglier: the desperate, defensive loyalty of a broken man. "And if I hear either of you calling our Lord a 'monster' or a 'beast' again, I will not hesitate. I will walk to the Hegemon's tent and report your treason myself. I will not hang because you two can't keep your tongues behind your teeth."

The silence that followed was different now. It wasn't the silence of the dead in the valley; it was the silence of a betrayal in the room.

Holten backed away, looking at Jared as if he were a stranger. "You would sell us? After twenty years of service? You'd send us to the pits to save your own skin?"

"I am ensuring our survival," Jared whispered, his voice trembling. "The Empire is gone. Our army is gone. There is only Kharic Stormborn. He is the sky, and he is the earth. You can either bow to him, or you can be buried under him. Choose."

The tent flap opened, and a Cherosian officer entered, his smile thin and cruel.

He threw a heavy vellum map onto the table. It showed three blood-red circles drawn around regions of Heartland that held true weight. They were like three iron links of a chain.

"The Hegemon is moved by your wisdom," the officer said,

peeling a blood-red orange with a small, serrated knife. The juice stained the map on the table like a fresh wound. "He has decided to name you Lords of the Three Shields. Congratulations. You are now a sovereign of the Heartland."

Jared did not speak. He knew that in Kharic Stormborn's camp, a crown was often just a heavy collar made of gold.

"But your fiefdom is still behind the iron curtain of Steelhaven," the officer continued, flicking a seed onto the floor. "For now, the Hegemon requires your counsel. You will remain here, in the Central Command, to ride in the Hegemon's own golden carriage. He values your knowledge of the Heartland's defences far too much to let you go just yet."

As the officer left, Jared reached for the map, his hands shaking. He didn't look at Sylvanus or Holten. He couldn't.

Kharic had not just killed their men; he had turned the survivors into ghosts who would spend the rest of their lives watching each other, waiting for the next betrayal.

OF THE TIDE FROM THE WEST

While the Heartland was still trembling from the rhythmic thud of the earth settling over the dead at Stonedeer, a different sound began to emerge from the Western fog. It was the sound of a hundred thousand pairs of boots—most of them caked in bog-iron and dried peat—moving with a slow, relentless discipline.

Maren Ashford had finally stopped digging.

He had left Valdria not as a Lord of Mosquitoes, but as the master of a silent avalanche. Behind him marched the very things Kharic had discarded: the broken, the survivors, and the "unimportant." They carried pikes forged from bog-ores and wore boiled leather that smelt of the swamp, but their eyes held a clarity that the "Lords" in their silk pavilions had long ago lost. They were not fighting for glory; they were marching for the only thing the mud ever promises—the right to exist.

As the column crossed the jagged threshold of the Westmarch mountains, Maren reined in his horse. He looked back at the retreating mists of his exile, then forward towards the smoking horizon of the Heartland.

"The Hegemon thinks he has locked the door," Maren said, his voice carrying the dry, rasping weight of the soil. "He thinks the Three Shields are his wall. He has forgotten that walls are made of stone, and stone always sits upon the earth."

Beside him, Roland Knox gripped the hilt of his sword, his face a map of fresh scars and old grudges. "One hundred thousand, my lord. They aren't laughing now. They don't even know we're coming."

"Let them stay blind," Maren replied, his gaze fixing on the distant, shimmering silhouette of Steelhaven. "Kharic rules the Storm. He rules the heights. But the Storm eventually runs out of rain, and the heights are only reached by climbing out of the mud."

He raised his hand—a simple, unadorned gesture—and the massive tide of men began to pour down into the Central Plains. They did not march with banners of gold or songs of heroes. They moved in the silence of the ignored, a heavy, grinding force of nature that the mathematicians in the capital had failed to account for.

The Weight of Earth had finally begun to move. And it was moving for the throne.

CHAPTER TWELVE

THE HIGH ROAD
AND THE LOW

IN WHICH REBEL LORDS MARCH
TOWARDS THE SAME PRIZE,
AND THE NATURE OF THEIR
CONTEST BECOMES CLEAR

The eagle rules the sky until the storm breaks its wings. The grass rules the earth because it has already learned how to be stepped upon.
> — *The Chronicles of the Rebel Court*

OF THE STORM UNLEASHED

The victory at Stonedeer had made Kharic Stormborn a god to his men, but the surrender of Jared Steelbane did not end the violence; it merely unleashed it.

Flush with victory, Kharic Stormborn turned his army north like a scythe swinging through dry wheat. The news of what had happened at Stonedeer—the forty thousand dead, the two hundred thousand buried alive—travelled ahead of him, turning the hearts of imperial garrisons to water.

City after city threw open its gates before his banners even appeared on the horizon. Governors who had sworn eternal loyalty to the Creedseat hanged themselves rather than face the Hegemon's judgement. Those who tried to resist were crushed with terrifying efficiency, their walls breached and their granaries burned.

In three weeks, Kharic conquered five provinces. He did not pause to govern or rebuild. He was a force of pure destruction, carving a path of ash and ruin towards the capital, daring the world to stop him.

It was in the wake of this terrifying momentum that the rebel lords gathered to plan the final blow.

OF TWO APPROACHES

The contrast between the two commanders' methods became apparent immediately.

Kharic Stormborn marched directly towards Iron Pass, known as The Throat, the legendary pass that protected Ironhold's heartland. His army was vast—over two hundred thousand men—and it moved with the relentless momentum that had become his trademark. Towns that resisted were destroyed; garrisons that surrendered were incorporated or eliminated. The message was clear: submit or die.

Maren Ashford took a different path.

Maren's army was smaller—one hundred thousand men—but it moved faster, unburdened by the logistics of occupation and reprisal. When he approached towns, he sent emissaries ahead with offers of amnesty. When garrisons surrendered, he welcomed their soldiers into his ranks and treated their officers with respect.

"You're giving away the victory," his general Roland Knox complained, watching the latest batch of former enemies receive positions in their army. "These men fought against us yesterday. How do we know they won't fight against us tomorrow?"

"We don't," Maren admitted. "But if we treat them well,

they have no reason to. And if we treat them badly—" he gestured towards the north, where smoke still rose from Kharic's advance "—they have every reason to fight to the death."

"That's soft thinking."

"That's practical thinking." Maren smiled. "I'm not in this for glory, Roland. I'm in this to win. And winning means being smart about how we fight."

He pointed to a distant fortress.

"See that captain we captured at Riverbend? He has a cousin commanding the garrison at Oakbridge. Tomorrow, I'll send him ahead with a cask of wine and a promise that his cousin keeps his rank. Oakbridge will fall without us lifting a shield."

The approach worked. Word spread ahead of Maren's advance: surrender to the Lord of Valdria and be treated fairly; resist and face the consequences. More and more garrisons chose surrender. More and more towns opened their gates. By the time he reached the southern passes, he had added thirty thousand men to his army with barely a sword drawn in anger.

There are men whose talents slumber until the world has need of them. They live in obscurity, enduring indignities that would break lesser spirits, waiting for the moment when their gifts will be recognised. And when that moment comes—when the right master finds the right servant—the results can reshape history.

— The Chronicle of the Generals

OF HUMBLE ORIGINS

Hans Xander, the man who would become the greatest general of his age was born to nothing in the village of Millford.

Hans had no surname.

His father was a low official who died young after his name was disgraced. His mother lived long enough to teach him what poverty meant in practical terms: cold food, unpaid rent, and the daily arithmetic of endurance. When he entered the army, the ledger required a second name.

He wrote Xander.

No one asked what it meant. A name only needed to be repeatable, and history repeated his.

He was not impressive to look at. Average height, thin build, with a face that was pleasant but average. He had no special strength, no athletic prowess, no skill with weapons that might have marked him for military service. What he had was a mind—a mind that saw patterns where others saw only chaos, that understood war the way other men understood breathing.

But no one knew it. No one cared to look.

In his youth, Hans endured humiliations that became legend. The most famous occurred when he was sixteen: a local bully, offended by some imagined slight, challenged him to crawl between his legs in the public square. Everyone expected him to fight—and die, for the bully was twice his size —or to flee and be marked a coward forever.

Hans crawled.

He got on his hands and knees in front of the entire town and crawled between his tormentor's legs, accepting the laughter and contempt that followed.

There was no sound but the grit scraping against his trousers. No one laughed—not yet. They were too shocked. They watched a man choose shame over death, and in that silence, they decided he was less than human. When asked later why he had submitted to such degradation, his answer was simple.

"A man who dies for pride dies for nothing. I have plans that require me to live."

It was not the response of a warrior. But it was the

response of a survivor—and survival, as Maren Ashford would have understood, has its own kind of strength.

Yet even in those dark years, his genius found small ways to reveal itself. There is a story— apocryphal, though the mathematicians swear it is true—that a local commander once needed to count his troops quickly before a bandit attack. The soldiers were too numerous and too disorganised to count directly. Xander, who was helping unload supply carts nearby, said: "Have them line up in rows of three. Count those left over. Then rows of five. Count those left over. Then rows of seven."

The commander, desperate, tried it. The remainders were two, three, and two. "You have two hundred and thirty-three men," Xander said, unhesitated. The actual count, performed later, confirmed it exactly. The commander asked how he had done it. Xander shrugged. "Numbers speak to me. They always have." The commander offered him a position. Xander declined.

"It is not magic," Xander added, seeing the commander's confusion. He tapped his temple. "It is just rhythm. An army is music, Commander. Most people hear the noise; I hear the beat."

He was waiting for something—someone—though he could not have said who.

OF SERVICE TO THE HEGEMON

When the rebellion began, Hans Xander, who was relieved of the labourer camp work at Shadowmount and pushed to the battlefields, had joined Kharic Stormborn's army like thousands of others—another body to fill the ranks, another pair of hands to carry supplies. He had no connections, no patrons, no way to distinguish himself from the mass of common soldiers.

But he had ideas.

He submitted proposals to the generals above him—tactical suggestions, strategic analyses, observations about enemy weaknesses and friendly strengths. His writings were detailed, brilliant, showing a grasp of military science that rivaled the greatest theorists of history.

They were ignored.

The generals did not read proposals from common soldiers. The commanders did not take advice from men without rank or reputation. Xander's insights—any one of which might have changed the course of battles—disappeared into the vast bureaucracy of the rebel army, unread and unappreciated.

He served for two years in this obscurity, watching officers make mistakes he could have corrected, seeing soldiers die in engagements he could have won. The frustration was unbearable. But he endured, as he had always endured, waiting for his moment.

Then came the council at Greymoor.

Xander had been assigned to guard duty outside the command tent—a position that allowed him to hear everything while being ignored by everyone. The rebel generals had gathered to plan the next campaign, and Kharic Stormborn himself presided.

For three hours, Xander listened to plans that would fail. He heard generals propose flanking manoeuvres that ignored the terrain. He heard lords recommend supply routes that would strand armies in hostile territory. He heard men of noble blood make decisions that would kill thousands—and he could do nothing, because he was nobody, because his father had made horseshoes instead of war.

Until he could stand it no longer.

"The northern route won't work," he said, stepping into the tent under no permission. "The river floods this time of year. Any army that crosses there will lose half its supply train before it reaches the ford."

The tent hushed.

Kharic Stormborn turned slowly, his eyes finding the common soldier who had dared to interrupt a council of lords. His expression was not angry—it was something worse. It was contemptuous.

"Who are you?" he asked.

"Hans Xander. A soldier in the Third Infantry."

"A soldier." Kharic's lip curled. "A soldier who presumes to advise generals. A soldier who believes his opinion matters in a council of lords."

"My opinion is correct. The river—"

"Your opinion is irrelevant." Kharic cut him off. "You are a commoner. Your place is outside, with the other tools. When we need you to carry things and die on command, we'll call for you."

Even Eldran Greymantle, who usually saw worth where others saw dirt, remained silent. He was looking at the map, frowning at the river crossing Xander had mentioned. Perhaps he knew the soldier was right. But he also knew his master's temper. To speak now would be to waste capital on a nobody. So the old man said nothing, and that silence cut deeper than the laughter.

The laughter from the lords was cruel and immediate. Hans Xander felt his face burn, felt the shame coiling in his chest like a living thing.

"The plan is adequate," Kharic continued, turning back to his maps. "For men of your... *origins*."

The word hung in the air like a sentence. *Origins*. Not intelligence. Not the worth of his ideas. His origins. His blood. The accident of his birth.

Xander withdrew without another word. But that night,

alone in his tent, he wrote a letter he did not send. It was addressed to no one—just words poured onto paper, a record of humiliation that he would never forget.

The lion mocks the fox, he wrote, *until the fox outthinks the lion. Then the lion discovers that pride tastes like ash, and cunning tastes like victory. Today I was mocked. Tomorrow—or the day after, or the year after—the lion will learn. They always do.*

And when that day comes, I will not mock in return. I will simply win. Because victory is the only argument that matters, and I intend to make it often.

I will remember this, he wrote. *When the time comes—and it will come—I will remember exactly how much my service was worth to you.*

He burnt the letter before dawn. It was too dangerous to keep.

But he did not forget. And years later, when Maren Ashford's envoys came with an offer of command and respect, Hans Xander remembered this night. Remembered the contempt in Kharic's eyes. Remembered the word *origins* spoken like a curse.

Some betrayals are planted in a single moment of cruelty.

Some take years to bear their bitter fruit.

This one was already growing.

His time came only when he met Markus Quillen.

OF THE MAVERICK
IN THE GRANARY

More men signed up to join Maren Ashford's army as it moved west like a slow tide. On his horse, Maren looked at the mud. He was preoccupied with the exhaustion of his men and the endless, creaking line of supply wagons.

In a roadside depot near the Westmarch border, Hans

Xander was assigned as a Granary Keeper—a clerk of the dust. He spent his days counting grain-sacks that smelt of mildew.

It was here that Markus Quillen found him, staring at a ledger that refused to balance.

"The oats for the third column didn't vanish," a voice said from the shadows of a barley stack. Markus looked up to see a thin, nondescript soldier tracing lines in the dirt. "The cavalry took the high ridge four hours early to avoid the rain. They grazed in the valley. The missing grain is still in the wagon behind you. You're counting a debt that has already been settled by the grass."

Markus performed the calculation. It was flawless. He looked at Xander—an average-looking youngster with a charcoal stick—and saw a mind that understood the logic of movement.

Markus went to Maren's tent that evening. Maren was unbuckling his mud-caked boots, sharing a jug of ale with Roland. He was tired, his mind already on the next day's march.

"Maren," Markus said, dropping the ledger. "I've found a young talent, a maverick of strategy. A man who sees the war before it happens."

"Another genius, Markus?" Maren grunted. "Every tavern from here to the marshes is full of 'geniuses' who can win the war over a cup of ale. But the moment the march starts and the wheels sink into the clay, they're the first to drop the ball. Tell this one to count the spare horseshoes—"

"He was with the Hegemon, Maren. He knows how the Stormborn thinks."

"If he were any good, the Hegemon would have made him a General," Maren laughed, exhausted, he sipped his wine, waving a hand at the flies. "I don't need another counter of beans, Markus. I need men who can hold a pike." Maren waved a hand, dismissing the greatest military mind of his generation as if he were a fly.

And so, as the army marched west, Hans Xander remained in the rear. He ensured the bread arrived and the boots were mended, while the man he served forgot his name before the ale in his cup was finished.

OF THE UNBLOODY SWORD

The pivotal moment of the campaign came not on a battlefield, but at the walls of Southguard, the fortress city that controlled the southern supply roads.

The Governor of Southguard was a loyalist named Lord Tybalt. He had provisioned his walls, rallied his five thousand men, and prepared to die for the Empire. When Maren's army arrived, Tybalt stood on the ramparts, ready to slit his own throat rather than suffer the shame of capture.

General Roland Knox wanted to storm the walls. "We outnumber them twenty to one," Knox argued. "We can crush them before noon."

"And lose five thousand of our own men?" Maren shook his head. "And force every other city on the road to fight to the death because they fear the same fate?"

Maren turned to Hadrian Narrowdale, his strategist. "Talk him down."

Hadrian rode to the gate alone, carrying no weapon, only a scroll. He did not shout threats. He shouted logic.

"Lord Tybalt!" Hadrian called out. "The Ironhold is dead. Steelbane has surrendered. If you die today, you do not die for an Emperor—you die for a memory. But if you open these gates, my Lord Maren pledges not only to spare your life, but to confirm your title. You will remain the Lord of Southguard. You will keep your lands. You will keep your soldiers to protect your people."

On the ramparts, Tybalt hesitated. The dagger was already at his neck.

"Why would a rebel honour a failing lord?" Tybalt shouted back.

"Because we need administrators, not corpses!" Hadrian replied. "Serve the new order, and bring honour to your family. Or die, and let your city burn for your pride."

Tybalt lowered the dagger.

An hour later, the gates opened. Maren Ashford did not just spare Tybalt; he publicly embraced him, let him keep his sword, and named him Marquis of the South.

The effect was instantaneous.

The news spread down the Imperial Highway faster than any horse: *Surrender does not mean defeat. Surrender means promotion.*

The resistance collapsed. It was a domino effect of greed and relief.

When Maren reached the treacherous High Pass—the final barrier before the capital—he found it guarded by an Imperial General who had heard of Tybalt's good fortune. Maren did not even draw his sword. He simply sent chests of gold and fine wine up the mountain, along with a letter promising the General a position in the new government.

That night, the Imperial banners were lowered. The General claimed he had been "outmaneuvered." In reality, he had been bought.

Maren Ashford walked through the most dangerous pass in the world without losing a single man.

"Kharic fights the enemy's body," Hadrian noted, watching the rebel army march effortlessly through the open gates. "You fight their mind."

"No," Maren corrected, looking at the road ahead. "I fight their fear. And gold is a very good weapon against fear."

Yet, despite these swift victories, Maren's overall advance was slower than the chronicles suggest—and deliberately so.

Each town that surrendered required administration. Granaries had to be inventoried, tax rolls examined, local officials evaluated for loyalty or corruption. Maren spent as much time in council chambers as in command tents, reviewing reports that Markus Quillen prepared with obsessive precision.

"You could move faster," Roland Knox complained, watching yet another day consumed by paperwork. "Every hour we waste here is an hour Kharic gains."

"Kharic gains territory. I gain infrastructure." Maren did not look up from the grain tallies. "When the war ends—and it will end—the man who controls the food controls the peace. All Kharic's victories won't feed his army through winter."

It was not inspiring rhetoric. It was not the stuff of legends. But it was the reason that Maren's forces never went hungry, never lacked for ammunition, never faced the logistical crises that plagued every other army in the field. Quillen's ledgers were worth more than a thousand cavalry charges.

The ugly choices came later, after the war, when Maren would have to decide which of his promises to keep and which to break. But that was a problem for another day. For now, the columns marched, the granaries filled, and the Lord of Valdria built his kingdom one requisition form at a time.

Kharic, meanwhile, was bogged down at The Throat.

OF THE THROAT

The Throat, is the great Iron Pass that had defended Ironhold for generations did not fall easily now.

The Throat was aptly named—a narrow canyon where

the cliffs pressed in like teeth. A hundred men could hold off ten thousand there, and they did. Kharic hurled his forces into that meat grinder, and the canyon floor rose inches higher each day, paved with the bodies of his best soldiers.

The defenders—a small but determined garrison led by officers who knew that surrender meant death—held firm. Weeks passed. Casualties mounted. The rebel army grew frustrated, then angry, then desperate.

"Launch a new round of attack before dawn," Kharic ordered through gritted teeth, staring at the map.

"Go around them," Eldran Greymantle counseled, stepping into the light. "Find another path. The pass is not the only way into the Inner Realm."

"The pass is the honourable way." Kharic's pride was burning. "To sneak around like a thief in the night—"

"Is exactly what Maren Ashford is doing!" Greymantle snapped. "Whilst you spend your strength against these walls, he advances through undefended territory."

Kharic glared at the old man. "Let him. I will take the capital."

"You do not understand," Greymantle said, his voice dropping to a dangerous whisper. "Reports have arrived. He has already bypassed the southern forts. He is days away from the gates of Steelhaven."

Kharic froze. "He is where?"

"If you do not move now, he will claim the throne before you even see the city."

Kharic rounded on his advisor, fury blazing in his eyes. "If Maren Ashford is sitting in my chair when I arrive... I will burn that Creedseat and the man in it."

"And start a war between rebel factions while the empire still stands?" Greymantle shook his head. "Pride will be your destruction. Go around, Kharic. Win the war, not the argument."

The two confronted each other—the young warrior and the old advisor, fury constrained by wisdom.

Finally, Kharic turned away, smashing his fist onto the table.

"Send scouts to find another path," he ordered. "We go around."

It was a concession, but it came too late.

CHAPTER THIRTEEN

THE SHADOW'S ECLIPSE

IN WHICH THE SHADOWHAND IS SLAUGHTERED, THE IRON BLOODLINE RESUMES POWER

One coin for the baker, two for the thief, Ten for the General who brings me his grief. The Empire is a clock that has forgotten the chime, We are all just puppets killing the time. Shhh... do you hear it? The silk cord's song? It's short for the weak, and it's thin for the strong.

— Fragments from the Imperial Bedchamber

OF THE SIMPLE PLAN

Mordecai did not consider himself a traitor nor even an evil man. In the cold, crystalline theater of his mind, he was a surgeon performing a lingering, necessary amputation on a gangrenous state. For twenty years, his "Simple Plan" had remained etched behind his eyes like a sacred blueprint—a map of quiet, structural collapse. He called it The Erosion of the Great Axis. He had no use for the crude instruments of the warlord; fire and steel were for barbarians like Kharic. Mordecai's weapons were more refined: ink, ritual, and the slow, deliberate weight of time. He believed that true power was never seized —it was inherited through the sheer exhaustion of the old order.

The blueprint was a masterpiece of Peaceful Transmutation. He began by turning the Emperor into a God, which was merely a polite way of making him a ghost. By complicating the court's ancient rituals into an impenetrable maze of ceremony, Mordecai had effectively entombed the Iron bloodline within the Orchid Pavilion. When the people could no longer see the man, the Sovereign ceased to be a leader and became a symbol—a hollow vessel that Mordecai alone could fill. Slowly, the machinery of state was duplicated. He built a shadow bureaucracy where every imperial decree was subtly superseded by his own "Administrative Clarifications." He was an architect of atrophy, patiently hollowing out the throne until its only structural integrity came from the tension of his own grip.

He preferred the mad boys and the hollowed-out princes. They were placeholders, not leaders. He imagined himself as a Restorer of Axial Stability, a man like Hyan of old, who would not take the throne by force, but would be begged by a desperate world to accept the Mandate once the Iron bloodline had finally thinned into a transparent thread. It was a beautiful, bloodless geometry.

But Mordecai had perfected the dynamics of the palace while forgetting the chemistry of the earth. He had optimised the gears of the court while the provinces starved. He had fixed the ceiling of the empire while the foundations rotted in the rising tide of famine.

As he stood behind the heavy velvet curtains of the Imperial Bedchamber, the faint, phantom scent of rotting mackerel tickled his senses—a persistent reminder of the filth beneath his high ideals. However, he realised then that his beautiful, simple plan was about to be shattered by the messy, red reality of war.

OF THE SKY PAINTER

The Emperor Edric sat on a pile of silk cushions, painting the air with a dry brush.

His only companion was a young servant girl named Elara, who was tasked with holding the invisible inkpot. She was terrified, for she had seen the last girl executed for sneezing.

"Do you see it, Elara?" Edric whispered, his eyes wide and unblinking. "The blue is finally drying."

"Yes, Your Majesty," Elara whispered, staring at the empty room. "It is... magnificent."

Edric stopped painting. He looked at her with a clarity that was more frightening than his rage.

"You are lying," he said softly. "There is no blue. There is no paint. Just as there is no Emperor."

Elara froze. "Majesty?"

"They think I am mad," Edric giggled, tapping his temple. "But I am the only one who sees the strings. Mordecai thinks he is the puppeteer, but he is just wood painted to look like flesh. We are all wood, Elara. We are all here dancing because the Great Silence is humming a tune we cannot quite hear."

He leaned in close, his breath smelling of sweet wine and decay.

"Do you know what madness is, little girl? Madness is believing that the chair you sit on is real, but the fear in your heart is not."

He returned to his painting, sweeping the dry brush across the void with frantic, jagged strokes. His voice dropped, losing its conversational tone and slipping into a feverish, rhythmic chant—a nursery rhyme for the damned.

"Now, hold it! I saw a horse with a human face, Running backwards to lose the race. The river is dry, the fish will cry, The whole wide world is made of dye. I painted a hook in the angel's eye, To catch the clouds as they float by. Snip goes the scissor, snap goes the bone...The King is eating his gut alone."

Elara squeezed her eyes shut and held the invisible pot for the Emperor, praying for her life spared.

OF THE MAD BOY'S END

In Steelhaven, the news of Jared Steelbane's surrender hit the court like a thunderclap. The Northern Army was gone. The rebels were at the gates, charging towards Steelhaven.

Mordecai the Shadowhand realised his time was up. The game of shadows he had played for twenty years was ending. He needed a scapegoat to blame for the ruin of the empire, and a new strategy to negotiate his own survival.

He went to the Imperial Chambers.

Emperor Edric—The Second Iron Emperor—sat on the floor, giggling as he arranged gold coins into piles. He did not look up when the High Magistrate entered with three hooded guards.

"The rebels are coming, Your Majesty," Mordecai said softly.

"Let them come!" Edric laughed, clapping his hands. "I shall order the clouds to rain fire upon them! I am the Son of Heaven!"

Mordecai looked at the mad boy with utter contempt.

"Heaven is deaf, Edric. And the people are angry. They need someone to blame for their hunger. They need someone to blame for the war."

Edric stopped laughing. He looked at the guards, then at

the silk cord in Mordecai's hands. A flicker of sanity—and terror—returned to his eyes.

"I am the Emperor," Edric whispered. "You cannot touch me."

"You are a mistake," Mordecai said. "One I am correcting."

He nodded to the guards. They moved forward. The Emperor screamed, but the heavy velvet curtains muffled the sound. It was over quickly.

Mordecai stood back, smoothing the front of his robes. His breathing was steady, yet his palms felt unnervingly damp. He turned away from the cooling body of the boy-emperor and gestured to a silent servant waiting in the corner.

The servant stepped forward, carrying a basin of solid, heavy gold. It was filled not with scented oils or rosewater, but with water so saturated with salt that the crystals crunched at the bottom.

Mordecai plunged his hands into the brine.

He scrubbed his fingers with a frantic, rhythmic intensity. The salt acted as an abrasive, reddening his skin, biting into the small nicks on his cuticles. He did not know why he did it. He told himself it was an ancient rite of the Shadowhands, a cleansing of the "Iron Grip," but in truth, it was the only way he could stop himself from smelling the phantom scent of rotting mackerel.

He scrubbed until his hands ached, until the water turned a cloudy, stinging white. Only then did he feel clean enough to lie.

Mordecai adjusted his robes, took a final look at the "Son of Heaven" slumped on the floor, and walked out to the terrified court.

"The Emperor has ascended to the heavens," Mordecai announced, his face a mask of tragic grief. "Overcome by shame for the state of the realm, he has taken his own life. But the Ironhold must endure."

Mordecai didn't wait for the court to mourn; he simply produced a pre-drafted decree, stained with the Emperor's still-warm thumbprint, declaring himself Regent with absolute power until the realm returned to 'Axial Stability.

He needed a new puppet. One with the bloodline to satisfy the traditionalists, but weak enough to control.

He chose Lucan—Prince Caden's young son.

OF THE LAST PRINCE'S GAMBIT

Prince Lucan was the last surviving member of the royal house.

He was young, quiet, and known for his frail constitution. He spent his days reading poetry and nursing a persistent cough that racked his thin frame. Mordecai had allowed him to live precisely because he seemed so harmless—a sickly weakling who would make a pliable successor after the mad boy's ascension to the heavens.

But Lucan had learned the most important lesson of the Iron Court: *To survive, one must be invisible.*

The coronation was set for the fifth day. But on the fourth day, Lucan did not appear for the rites and rehearsals.

"He claims to be ill," the eunuch messenger reported, trembling. "He says the spirits of his ancestors are haunting his chambers. He refuses to leave his bed."

Mordecai sneered. He saw this for what it was: a child's last, pathetic attempt at defiance.

"If he cannot walk," Mordecai declared, adjusting his ceremonial robes, "I will drag him to the throne myself. No one delays the Shadowhand."

He marched to Lucan's private residence in the Orchid

Pavilion. Arrogance made him careless; he left his heavy guard outside the inner courtyard, entering the darkened bedchamber with only three attendants, holding the Imperial Seal.

"My Prince," Mordecai said, bowing low. "The throne awaits. You must come to the temple for the purification rites, and ceremony rehearsals."

Lucan sat on his bed, coughing into a handkerchief.

"I am... too ill," Lucan wheezed. "I cannot go. The spirits... they disturb me."

Mordecai sighed. He was impatient. The coronation needed to happen tonight to secure his power.

"The rites are mandatory, Highness." Mordecai stepped into the room, waving his guards to stay back. He needed to coax the boy, not drag him. "Come. I will support you."

He walked to the bedside. He looked down at the frail, trembling prince. He saw nothing but a tool to be used.

"You are the Emperor now, Your Majesty, The Third Iron Emperor" Mordecai whispered, leaning close, his voice dripping with false solicitude. "Get up, boy," Mordecai commanded, looming over the boy in the bed. "The empire does not wait for your vapors."

Lucan in the bed sat up. The coughing ceased. The terror vanished from his eyes, replaced by a cold, ancestral clarity.

"The empire waits for no one," Lucan said softly. "Especially not a thief."

He raised his hand—a sharp, cutting gesture.

Before Mordecai could react, the heavy velvet curtains behind him parted.

Two of Lucan's loyal retainers—men he had secretly befriended over years of shared captivity—lunged from the shadows.

One struck Mordecai's knees with a heavy club, shattering

bone. The other drove a long knife into his shoulder, pinning him to the floor.

Mordecai, the man who had commanded armies and silenced ministers with a glance, screamed—a raw, ugly sound that was cut short as Lucan stepped from the bed.

The Prince held the sword his father, Prince Caden, had given him as a child. He walked to the writhing Regent.

"You killed my father," Lucan whispered, standing over the man who had destroyed his family. "You killed the law. You killed the world."

Mordecai looked up, eyes wide with the shock of the impossible. He tried to speak, to bargain, to weave one last lie.

Lucan didn't let him. He drove the blade into Mordecai's chest, putting his full weight behind it.

Lucan's hands were shaking so violently that the sword's tip drew frantic, silver circles in the dim light. He wasn't a warrior; he was a man performing a desperate surgery. He didn't strike with the grace of a knight, but with the frantic, messy necessity of a victim who had calculated that his life was worth exactly one lunge.

"That," Lucan hissed, "is for the silence."

Mordecai the Shadowhand died choking on his own blood. As the air left his lungs, Mordecai's fingers spasmed, clenching a coin.

Lucan watched the red pool spread across the white marble. "He is not immortal," Lucan whispered, his voice cracking. "The stories... they were all lies. He's just meat."

He wiped the blade on the Regent's silk robes. He felt sick. The blood wasn't gold or divine liquid starlight; it was just warm, sticky failure.

Lucan knelt to retrieve the Imperial Seal from the corpse's belt. As he did, he noticed Mordecai's fist, white-knuckled in death. He pried the stiff fingers open.

It wasn't a weapon. It was a coin.

It was heavy, made of ancient lead that felt oily to the touch. Lucan held it up to the candlelight. Stamped upon its face were two serpents, distinct and terrified, knotted together in a loop of eternal hunger. Each was devouring the tail of the other.

Lucan stared at it. It was the symbol of the new law, but older. Crude. Primal.

One eats, one is eaten, Lucan thought, a chill running through him. *The infinite trap.*

The Shadowhand had died holding the truth of his own rule: a circle of consumption that left nothing behind.

Lucan pocketed the heavy lead. His arms were hollow with exhaustion, yet the sword ignored his weakness. It found the gap between the vertebrae with the cold precision of a compass, sliding through the Regent's neck as if it were performing a necessary correction to a long-flawed equation.

He walked out to the courtyard, his hands bloody, the Seal in one hand, the severed head in the other. He threw the head of the Shadowhand at the feet of the Imperial Guards.

"The traitor is dead," Lucan announced. His voice trembled, yet it carried the weight of the Iron Creed. "I am the Emperor. Bow, or join him."

In the dark, the guards looked at the head. They looked at the boy who had suddenly become a man. They bowed.

Lucan didn't feel like an Emperor; he felt like a child who had finally broken a terrifying toy, only to find the room still dark.

He walked to the window of his liberated palace and looked out at the quiet horizon. He saw what the others did not: fires burning on the distant hills—not one or two, but thousands. A ring of fire, closing in on the dark heart of the world.

He had cut the cancer out, only to realise the body was already a skeleton.

THE HEALING OF THE CORPSE

Between the death of the Shadowhand and the arrival of the rebels, there was a brief window of time where the sun seemed to rise again over Steelhaven.

Lucan did not spend his hours in the harem or the wine-cellars. He moved his bed into the Hall of State, sleeping on a military cot so he could be woken at any hour. He was a young man attempting to repair a clock while it was falling from a tower.

His first act was the Audit of the Legions. He summoned the quartermasters and found that the Empire's "Great Host" was a phantom. For years, Mordecai had been collecting pay for a million soldiers; Lucan discovered that four hundred thousand of them were "ghost-soldiers"—dead men whose names remained on the rolls so that generals could pocket their wages.

"I am not an Emperor of men," Lucan remarked to his scribe. "I am an Emperor of ink and dust."

He issued the Edict of the Open Gate. He pardoned three thousand "Iron Prisoners"—veterans who had been jailed for minor infractions or for showing "excessive mercy" in the field. He personally walked to the Great Dungeon, broke the seals, and offered these broken men a choice: return to their homes with a week's rations, or take up their swords again for a Crown that finally cared for their lives. Most stayed. They saw in Lucan the ghost of his father, Caden the Kind.

He sent riders to every rebel faction—not with threats of fire, but with White Scrolls of Reconciliation. He offered tax exemptions for three years, the return of ancestral lands, and a seat at a new, reformed Council. He believed, with the desperate purity of youth, that the rebels fought because they were hungry for justice.

He did not yet understand that some, like Kharic, were only hungry for blood.

OF THE DECREE

In a feverish alignment of ink and intent, Lucan issued a Decree—meticulously hand-copied and dispatched like a final, desperate equation to every corner of the realm:"

BY THE CALCULATION OF THE HEAVENS AND THE UNWAVERING SYMMETRY OF THE MANDATE:

KNOW, O Children of the Great Iron, that Righteousness is no mere tremor of the heart, but the very Axial Stability upon which the world rotateth. As the sun seeketh the Zenith by a geometry of absolute truth, so too must the Sovereign seek the Luminescence of Virtue.

The Mandate of Heaven is not a sword to be brandished, but a Celestial Equilibrium to be maintained. We, Lucan, having studied the Harmonics of the Past, find that an Empire is built not of iron, but of the Radiant Architecture of Grace.

BE IT DECREED:

That Kindness shall henceforth be the primary instrument of our Governance. For even as the smallest pebble altereth the orbit of a pond's ripples, so doth a single act of Royal Grace restore the fractured music of the spheres.

Let the people walk in the Equinox of Mercy, for a throne that is not balanced by the weight of Compassion is but a geometric impossibility—a point without a plane, destined to vanish into the dark.

SEALED IN THE LIGHT OF THE PERPETUAL STARS.

— We, Lucan, The Third Iron Emperor, Architect of the Great Peace.

OF THE FORTY-SIX DAYS

Lucan, the Last Emperor of Ironhold, ruled for forty-six days.

History would remember him as the one who surrendered, but the records of the inner court tell a different story. They tell of a young man who, having cut the cancer from the throne, tried desperately to heal the dying patient.

He worked with a feverish intensity. In his first week, he purged the court of Mordecai's remaining cronies, executing the corrupt and reinstating the few honest officials who had survived the purge. He opened the imperial granaries, distributing grain to the starving populace of the capital. He issued edicts abolishing the harshest of the Iron Laws, trying to signal to the world that the tyranny had ended, that sanity had returned to the Dragon Throne.

He slept three hours a night. He ate while reading dispatches. He tried, with every ounce of his strength, to be the emperor his father Caden would have been.

But a man cannot stop a landslide with a shovel.

On the forty-fifth day, Lucan sat in the Hall of Maps. The candles were burning low. The room was cold.

"Report," he said to his new General of Defence.

"The Northern Army... is gone, Your Majesty," the general whispered. "General Steelbane surrendered to Kharic Stormborn at the River Isldra three weeks ago. He... he buried the soldiers alive." The general's voice cracked. "Two hundred thousand men. Gone. Kharic is marching south. He leaves no survivors."

Lucan closed his eyes. Two hundred thousand. The last strength of the empire. And now the Monster was coming.

"Then we must hold the passes," Lucan said, fighting to keep his voice steady. "If Steelbane has fallen, Kharic will be marching on Iron Pass—the Throat. It is the strongest fortress in the world. If we reinforce it, we can hold him for months. We can negotiate. We can—"

"Your Majesty." The general dropped to his knees. He looked terrified not of the distant monster, but of the immediate truth. "Kharic is not the threat."

Lucan froze. "What?"

"Kharic is still in the north, dealing with the aftermath of the battle. But the other one... the rebels at The Narrows..."

The general pointed a trembling finger at the map. Not at the distant northern border, but at the blue line of the southern waterway, less than thirty miles from the capital.

"They are here. At Kingsriver."

"Who?" Lucan frowned. "Which of Kharic's generals is it?"

"Not Kharic's, Majesty. An independent force. They fly the banner of... a Maren Ashford."

"Ashford?" Lucan stared at him blankly. "I have never heard of this man. Is he a noble of the restoration? A defector from the legions?"

Lucan searched his memory of the imperial 'Threat List'—a document updated weekly with the names of warlords and traitors. Maren Ashford was not on it. The man had traversed half the empire without ever being important enough to write down.

"He calls himself the Lord of Valdria."

"Valdria?" Lucan searched his mindmap of the imperial charts and found nothing.

"It is... a peat-cutting village on the edge of Westmarch, Majesty."

The absurdity of the village's name hung heavy in the air.

The Ironhold Empire, which had conquered the known world, was being threatened by a villager from a swamp.

"A peasant," Lucan whispered. "You tell me Steelhaven is threatened by a peasant?" He stood up, a flash of his grandfather's fire returning. "Then we crush him. Mobilise the Palace Guard. Arm the citizens. If he is a nobody from a swamp, he cannot have siege engines. He cannot have heavy cavalry. How many men does he have?"

"One hundred thousand, Majesty."

Lucan sat back down slowly. "How? How did a nobody gather a hundred thousand men and traverse the Southern Mountains so quickly without a fight?"

"He didn't fight, Majesty. He walked." The general looked down at the floor. "He bypassed the strongholds. He sent messengers to the garrisons we couldn't pay, promising them food and safety. They didn't just surrender, sire. They joined him."

Lucan looked at the map. He looked at the edicts on his desk—the plans for tax reform, for justice, for a future that would never happen.

He did the calculation.

I have ten thousand Palace Guards. I can fight this Maren Ashford. I might even hold him off for a week.

But while I fight Maren, Kharic Stormborn will arrive from the north.

Maren Ashford accepts surrenders. Kharic Stormborn buries men alive.

If he fought the peasants now, he would be too weak to stop the God of War later. And if that god of war took the city by storm, there would be no city left.

"He is at the gates," Lucan said, the realization settling over him like a shroud. "And the people will not fight for me. Why should they? I am just another name in a long list of failures."

"Majesty?" The general asked, waiting for the order to deploy the guards.

Lucan looked at the Imperial Seal on his altar. To a warrior, it was a prize. But to Lucan, it was merely a variable in a final, losing equation. Surrendering wasn't an act of cowardice; it was the final calculation of a boy who had learned that sometimes, the only way to save the music is to break the instrument.

Lucan blew out the candle, plunging the Hall of Maps into darkness.

"If we fight," Lucan whispered to the dark, "everyone dies. If I lose my pride... perhaps the city lives."

He stood up. He did not reach for his sword. He reached for the Imperial Seal, feeling its cold weight one last time. "Open the gates," Lucan ordered, his voice devoid of fear. "I am going to surrender the world to the peasant."

CHAPTER FOURTEEN

AT HEAVEN'S GATE

IN WHICH MAREN ASHFORD ENTERS THE CITY OF IRON, AND THE MANDATE OF HEAVEN IS A LIGHTNING ROD HE CANNOT AFFORD TO HOLD

A city is not a fortress of boulders; it is a fortress of belief. Once the people stop believing the walls can save them, the gates are nothing more than firewood waiting for a match.
— The Chronicles of the Rebel Court

THE TWIN SHADOW OF THE SIX KINGDOMS

Maren Ashford's army reached the outskirts of Steelhaven on a grey October morning. The city was the greatest in the world... It was the heart of everything Ironhold had created.

Long before the walls of Steelhaven appeared, Maren saw the giants.

Two hundred feet of solid, unyielding iron rose above the horizon like the skeletons of dead gods. These were the Twin Colossi of the Mandate, the infamous sentinels the First Iron Emperor had forged from the melted remains of a million blades. Every spear, every halberd, and every shattered sword of the Six Kingdoms had been fed into the Great Furnace to create them. They were a billion deaths hammered into a permanent, vertical silence.

As the army drew closer, a new colour broke the oppressive grey of the iron: White.

Strips of unspun silk—the colour of ancient mourning— fluttered from every crenellation and arrow-loop. From a distance, it looked as though a pale frost had settled over the dark stone.

Maren raised his hand, halting the column a thousand yards from the gate. He stared at the open portal, then up at the blank, featureless visors of the iron giants.

"It's too clean," Maren whispered. "The gates are open, the flags are out, if I were the Emperor's strategist, I'd wait until our vanguard was under the shadow of those colossi and then drop the portcullis. We'd be trapped in a kill-box."

"A trap requires a spring, my Lord," Markus Quillen said, pulling his horse alongside Maren. He didn't look at the giants; he was looking at a set of captured quartermaster ledgers. "And a spring requires tension."

Markus pointed towards the battlements, where the "guards" stood like listless ghosts. "My audits are absolute. The Palace hasn't issued a grain ration in six weeks. The 'Iron Legions' in this city are currently trading their bronze buckles for turnip peels. To set an ambush, you need soldiers who believe they will be fed tomorrow. These men only believe in the hunger of today."

"You're sure?" Maren asked, his hand still white-knuckled on his sword.

Maren looked at the massive iron feet of the Colossi, then at the yawning mouth of the city. He took a breath of the cold, soot-stained air.

"Then we enter," Maren said. "But tell Beric to keep the

heavy infantry in the rear. If the maths is wrong, I want enough men left alive to burn this graveyard to the ground."

The army moved. As they passed under the archway, the shadow of the iron giants fell over them.

OF THE WHITE ROBES

The city gates opened with a groan, exhaling the stale air of a dying dynasty. Its grand streets empty. But the massive inner gates of the Imperial Palace remained barred, the last defiance of the Palace Guard.

It did not last long.

"Open it, or I knock it down!"

Roland Knox did not wait for a ram. He swung a massive two-handed warhammer, the impact sounding like a thunderclap that shook the very walls. Once. Twice. With a bestial roar, Roland shattered the ironwood beam, splintering the heavy timber and kicking the gates open.

He stood in the breach, panting steam, but the expected hail of arrows did not come. Instead, the crash was swallowed by a sudden, unnatural stillness—that dwells only in tombs or churches. The dust of the shattered beam hung suspended in the stale, incense-heavy air.

Lucan emerged. He wore robes of unspun white silk—the colour of ancient mourning—that trailed behind him like a funeral shroud. Behind him followed a pathetic procession of the "Old World": twenty eunuchs in faded crimson, their faces powdered bone-white to hide their terror, and a dozen court ladies whose silk slippers clicked rhythmically against the stone, a sound like dry leaves in a tomb.

Maren's eyes, seasoned by years of tavern dice and village scandals, found themselves wandering towards the ladies of the inner court. It had been an eternity since he had seen women who didn't smell of woodsmoke and wet wool. They were exquisite, possessing a fragile, painted perfection that made even the radiant memory of Celia from Weed seem like a rough sketch in charcoal.

Lucan held the Imperial Seal aloft in both hands. He did not look at the blood stains on Roland's hammer or the mud on Maren's boots. He looked at the sky, his voice rising in the high, melodic cadence of the Celestial Court Dialect—a language so archaic with such dense, ritualised jargon that it sounded like foreign tongue.

"In observance of the Atemporal Syzygy and the Crystalline Stasis of the Primeval Order," Lucan intoned, his voice trembling with a scholar's precision, "we, the Final Echo of the Luminous Orthodoxy, the Third Scion of the Iron Plane, do hereby validate the Asymptotic Decay of our sovereign resonance. We tender this Void-Resonant Signet as a Homostatic Pivot to arrest the Harmonic Divergence of the terrestrial plane, imploring the Apotheosis of the Vanguard to mitigate the Dissipative Trauma upon the Unformatted Multitude sheltered herein, from the entropic fires of Your conquest."

The silence that followed was absolute. A stray breeze ruffled the silk of Lucan's robes, but the rebel army stood frozen, their mouths slightly agape.

Maren Ashford stared at the boy. He looked at Hadrian, who was slowly scratching his head with the hilt of his dagger, then back at Lucan.

"I'm surrendering," Lucan whispered in the plain, common tongue of the streets. He sounded like what he was: a terrified nineteen-year-old boy.

"The empire is yours," he said. "Do with it what you will. I ask only that you please spare the common people of this city, who are guilty of nothing except living under rulers who failed them."

Maren looked at the young man—this last scion of the dynasty that had crushed the old kingdoms, that had built its greatness on the bones of millions. He could have killed him. Many expected him to kill him.

But Maren Ashford was not Kharic Stormborn. Maren had grown up loving wine and women, who had spent his youth in taverns and dice games, who had never been accused of excessive virtue. But he was also someone who understood when to indulge his appetites and when to suppress them. The palace treasuries lay open before him, filled with gold beyond counting. The imperial harem awaited, stocked with beauties from every province. His soldiers expected to loot—it was the traditional reward for conquest, the payment they had earned through blood and suffering. Any ordinary commander would have let them take what they wanted. Maren Ashford did not.

"Rise," he said. "You are no criminal, to kneel in the dirt. You are the victim of evil men, as we all are."

With both hands, Lucan offered Maren the Everlasting Seal —Maren looked at the legendary Heirloom of the Realm, that grand imperial seal made by the First Iron Emperor, and examined it—a hefty white stone the size of Lucan's two hands, on which inscribed are ancient runes he could not read. It was the symbol of absolute power, the heavy heart of the empire. To hold it was to hold the Mandate of Heaven.

Maren looked at the seal. The light caught the stone, promising power beyond measure. But Maren kept his hands deliberately at his sides, as if the object were red-hot iron.

"Keep it," Maren said.

Lucan blinked, confused. "My lord?" He trembled in fear.

"I am called by King Arion of Cheros," Maren said, his voice loud enough for his own officers to hear. "And Lord Stormborn, the Hegemon of Cheros is on his way. You will present that to the Hegemon yourself when he arrives. I will not touch what is not mine."

"I will spare the city. I will spare you. The old order is finished, but we need not begin the new order with blood."

Lucan wept with relief. He did not know that mercy is often just a postponement. He would live for exactly three more weeks—until the day Kharic Stormborn rode through the gates.

The crowd that had gathered to witness the surrender erupted in cheers. The common people of Steelhaven—who had expected massacre, who had prepared for the worst— found themselves celebrating instead.

Maren left them to their celebration and walked alone into the Grand Hall. The heavy doors swung open, the silence of the room swallowing the cheers outside, and then... the smell hit him.

It hit him like a blow. This was different. This was the smell of empire.

Stale incense, first. Centuries of it, soaked into the tapestries and carpets, layered until it had become something else entirely—not fragrant anymore, but cloying, rotten, the smell of prayers that had gone unanswered for too long. Then the old wax, dripped from a thousand ceremonial candles, forming a geological record of dead emperors in the crevices of the stone floor. Beneath that, mould—the kind that grows in places where windows are never opened, where fresh air is considered an insult to tradition.

And underneath it all, faint but clear, the smell of decay. The decay of an idea. The rot of a system that had been dying for years and had only now stopped pretending to breathe.

Maren stood in the doorway, breathing it in, understanding what he had conquered. This is what power smells like when it's gone bad, he thought. *This is what I must never become.*

He turned to his guards. "Open the windows," he ordered. "Scrub the walls with lye. Burn the carpets." He looked back at the empty throne, looming in the shadows. "And seal the doors. We camp outside the city tonight."

The Lord of Marsh, it seemed, was a different kind of conqueror.

OF THE THREE MERCIES

Maren's first act as master of the capital was to abolish the Iron Creed.

The harsh laws that had governed Ironhold for fifty years —the laws that punished minor offences with death, that conscripted millions for endless projects, that reduced the common people to something less than human—were swept away in a single proclamation. In their place, Maren established what he called the Three Mercies:

First, murder alone would be punished by death. All other offences would receive lesser penalties.

Second, forced labour would be abolished. Men would work for wages or not at all.

Third, taxation would be reduced to a level that allowed families to survive and prosper.

It was a revolutionary change—a repudiation of everything Ironhold had stood for. And it came not from a philosopher or a sage, but from a former village headman who had never studied law or governance in his life.

"How did you know what to do?" Hadrian Narrowdale asked him, after the proclamation had been issued.

Maren shrugged. "I asked myself what I would have wanted, back when I was a farmer. The answer wasn't complicated. People cannot constantly live in fear. They want to keep enough of what they earn to feed their families. They want to know that the law protects them instead of preying on them." He smiled. "It's not wisdom. It's just common sense."

"Common sense," Hadrian repeated. "The rarest commodity in politics."

The Three Mercies spread through the realm like wildfire.

In every province, in every town, people heard about the new lord who had conquered the capital not with cruelty but with mercy. They heard that the Iron Creed was dead, that the old oppression was finished, that a new age was beginning.

And they came to believe what had seemed impossible just months before: that change might actually be for the better.

OF THE PEARLS

Maren stood alone in the Grand Hall, staring at the Creedseat that loomed in the shadows. It was made of black iron—intricate, spiked, and cold. It didn't look like a chair; it looked like a trap designed to hold a man in place while the world bled him dry.

"It suits you," a voice said from the darkness.

Maren turned to see Lady Lyra walking slowly out of the inner chambers. She was no longer wearing the rough-spun wool of the camp, the clothes of the woman who had baked bread in the mud of Marsh. She had draped a shimmering robe of imperial silk over her shoulders, and in her hands, she held a heavy necklace of black pearls—the famous 'Tears of the Iron Sea.'

She wore the silk not as a garment, but as armour she had spent twenty years waiting to reclaim. She walked up the steps of the dais, her reflection ghost-like on the polished obsidian floor, and ran her hand along the armrest of the throne.

"Sit down, husband," she whispered. Her eyes weren't just bright; they were burning with a predatory hunger. "The girl from Whitecroft died in a ditch so you could stand here. Don't let her death be for nothing. Sit down, and let them see their new Emperor. I washed the mud of your village from my skin every night for twenty years, Maren. Do not tell me to go back to it."

"This is not a chair, Lyra," Maren said softly. "It is an execution block."

"Only if you are weak." Lyra stepped closer, holding the pearls against her throat. The black spheres looked like drops of frozen night against her pale skin. "We have the walls. We have the treasury. We have the people. Why should we hand it all over to a madman from the south? Kharic is a wolf, but even wolves starve when the gates are shut."

She held out the necklace, the pearls clicking softly together like the teeth of a predator.

"Look at these, Maren. One of these pearls could buy the entire village of Marsh. The inner chambers are overflowing with them—crowns of sapphire, rubies the size of hearts, wealth that the Empire spent three hundred years stealing from families like mine." Her voice trembled, not with fear, but with the raw ache of a long-delayed inheritance. "Are we to just... leave them? To be beggars again, hiding in the tall grass?"

Maren looked at his wife. He saw the fierce, terrifying ambition in her eyes, but beneath it, he saw the shivering eleven-year-old girl who had watched her house burn. He realised then that she didn't want the throne because she loved power; she wanted it because she was tired of being hunted.

He reached out and gently took the necklace from her hands. The pearls were as cold as the iron seat.

"If I sit on that throne today," Maren said, his voice hardening into the same iron as the chair, "Kharic will not just break his teeth. He will burn this city to the ground with us inside it. He has four hundred thousand men who eat human flesh for breakfast. We have... maps, and a few thousand farmers who are tired of bleeding."

He dropped the necklace back into its velvet box with a dull, final thud.

"Put the silk back, Lyra. We are not keeping the jewels. And we are not keeping the throne."

Lyra stared at him, her face twisting into a mask of aristocratic fury. For a moment, she looked like she might strike him.

"You are a coward," she hissed, and in that moment, she was once again the High Noble looking down at a peasant. "Fortune has dropped the world into your lap, and you are too afraid to hold it because your hands are still stained with the dirt of your father's farm."

"I am not afraid to hold it," Maren replied, turning his back on the throne. "I am just waiting until it cools down enough not to burn my hands off."

He grabbed her arm—firm, but without the cruelty of the Empire. "Now, go. Pack your things. We sleep in the tent outside the city tonight. I'd rather be a living King in the mud than a golden corpse in this hall."

Lyra didn't move. She stared at the velvet box as if it contained a severed head rather than a fortune. Then, her eyes snapped up, searching Maren's face with a new, sharper suspicion.

"And the Seal, Maren?" she whispered, her voice trembling with a different kind of fever. "That Star-glass Heart of the Empire. The Wyrm-fire in stone. You have it, don't you? You didn't leave that in a box."

"I don't have it," Maren said. He began to unbuckle his sword-belt, his movements slow and deliberate.

"Liar." Lyra stepped into his space, the scent of expensive imperial perfume—a scent she hadn't worn in twenty years—clashing with the smell of the rain on his cloak. "The soldiers said the Prince surrendered to you at the gate. They said he knelt in the dust. No one kneels to a man like you without offering the stone. I want to see it, Maren. I want to hold the weight of all under heavens in my palm. Just once."

Maren finally looked at her. His eyes were as flat as a frozen pond.

"You want to see it?" Maren asked. He reached out and tilted her chin up. "Then go to the inner sanctum. Go to the little boy sitting on a pile of cushions, weeping for a father who was murdered by his own advisors. Lucan still has the Seal. I told him to keep it wrapped in its silk. I told him to hold it tight until the Hegemon arrives."

Lyra pulled away as if he had burnt her. "You... you let him keep it? You left the Mandate of Heaven in the hands of a child?"

"I left a death sentence in the hands of a child," Maren corrected her, his voice cutting like a razor. "Kharic Stormborn is riding north with a storm at his back. He is looking for a King to kill. If he enters this city and finds me holding that stone, he will not offer me a seat at his table. He will offer me a spike on the battlements."

He stepped towards her, his shadow swallowing her silken form.

"You want the Seal because you think it makes us royal, Lyra. But in this room, on this night, that stone is a lightning rod. I am the Lord of Valdria. a village headman who got lucky. As long as I am 'small,' Kharic can afford to let me live. The moment I touch that stone, I am an Emperor. And the world only has room for one of those at a time."

Lyra stared at the dark, empty Creedseat, then back at her husband. The realisation hit her like a physical blow: Maren wasn't just being cautious; he was using the boy prince as a shield.

"You're using that child," she hissed. "You're leaving him to face the wolf while we slink away into the dark."

"I am saving our children," Maren replied, grabbing his travelling cloak. "The boy's blood is already cursed by his grandfather's sins. Mine is just mud. And mud, Lyra, is very hard to kill."

He walked towards the doors, not looking back.

"Pack the plain wool. Leave the silk for the looters. We leave within the hour."

OF THE LAST SCION

While Maren reorganised the realm, Lucan was confined at the Orchid Pavilion, his quiet residence in the shadow of the palace walls.

He was not in chains. Maren allowed him his books, his servants, and even his family. For three weeks, the last Emperor of Ironhold lived a life he had never known: a peaceful one.

He spent his days teaching his young son to read the ancient classics, believing that the storm had passed.

"The Lord of Valdria is a man of honour," Lucan told his wife, former Queen Consort late one night, as they watched the rebel campfires burning gently outside the city. "He accepted the Seal. He spared the city. In the ancient texts, the virtuous conqueror always grants the fallen house a small fiefdom to maintain their ancestor's spirits."

His wife looked at him with fearful eyes. "But the other one... the Stormborn..."

"The Stormborn will listen to Maren," Lucan said, clinging to a hope that was as fragile as it was desperate. "The war is over. We are no longer emperors, but we will live. Perhaps... perhaps we will even serve."

He drafted a petition to Kharic Stormborn, asking humbly for permission to retire to his family's ancestral farm in the western plains, to live as a common scholar. He polished the language until it was perfect, full of gratitude and submission.

He never sent it. He was waiting for the "right moment" to present it to the Hegemon.

He did not know that he was already a ghost. He was planning a future in a world that had already decided to erase him.

OF THE TIGER AT THE DOOR

Maren Ashford was now the master of Steelhaven. He sat in the centre of the world, with the Iron Emperor and the wealth of centuries at his feet.

And he was terrified.

"Seal it," he ordered Markus Quillen, standing before the open doors of the Imperial Treasury.

Markus paused, his quill hovering over a fresh ledger. He looked into the vault, where the torchlight caught the glint of things that should never have seen the sun. There were chests of coin stamped with the faces of dead men, enough silver to buy every farm from here to the Great Sea. There were ingots of gold stacked like cordwood, cold and heavy as tombstone.

But it was the smaller things that sickened Maren's stomach.

The 'Tears of the Iron Sea' lay in a tangled heap, black pearls that looked like the eyes of drowned sailors. Beside them sat the blood-rubies of the Southern Clans, stones the size of a child's fist that seemed to pulse with a dark, inner heat. There were silks so fine they felt like cobwebs, and ivory carvings that had cost entire forests their lives. To Maren, it didn't look like wealth; it looked like a mountain of unpaid debts.

"My Lord," Roland whispered, his voice echoing in the vast, hollow space. "The value of this room... it could fund the rebellion for a hundred years. It could feed our men until the end of time."

"It's not food, Roland. It's bait," Maren replied. He wouldn't step across the threshold. He kept his mud-caked boots firmly on the stone of the hallway. "This gold is the blood of the people, hammered flat and polished. If we loot it now, we become the very thing..."

But Markus was not looking at the gold. He was directing his clerks to haul dusty crates out of the archives—census records, tax rolls, and topographical surveys.

"Markus," Roland Knox laughed, kicking a chest of silver coins. "You're looting the wrong room! The gold is over here."

"These papers..." Markus said, blowing dust off a heavy ledger. "these tell us how many households are in the realm, where the grain is stored, and which mountain passes have secret trails."

He looked at Maren with dead seriousness.

"Gold makes you rich, my lord. These maps make you a King."

Maren nodded, seeing the weight of those papers. "Seal it all." he repeated. "Do not let a single coin—or a single map—be taken."

"The men are restless," Roland Knox warned. "They remember the agreement at the Council. 'Whoever reaches

Steelhaven first is King of the Central Plains.' They are asking why a king is acting like a frightened guest."

"One must remain alive to be King." Maren said grimly. "We are just the ones who got here first."

He walked to the ramparts and looked east. He could not see signs of Kharic's army yet, but he could feel it. Reports had been arriving daily, each more terrifying than the last.

Kharic Stormborn was burning a path to the capital.

Furious that Maren had stolen his glory, the Hegemon had unleashed his full savagery on the road through the Pass. The city of Oakhaven, which had hesitated to open its gates for an hour, was razed to the ground. The garrison at Twin Rivers—five thousand men who had surrendered—was buried alive, just like the prisoners at Stonedeer. Every village, every town, every farmhouse on the direct route paid the price for Kharic's rage.

The sky to the east was permanently grey with the smoke of his advance. He was driving four hundred thousand men towards Steelhaven like a landslide that had forgotten how to stop, and his message was clear: *Wait for me, or die.*

"If I sit on that throne," Maren told his advisor Hadrian, "Kharic will tear this city apart to pull me off it. He has four men for every one of mine, and his men are killers while mine are... reasonable."

"So what do we do?"

"We act like guests," Maren said. "We camp outside the city. We leave the palace empty. We treat the Emperor's surrender not as a victory for me, but as a gift I am holding for the Hegemon." He managed a weak smile. "It is hard to kill a man who is bowing to you. I intend to bow very low."

So Maren Ashford did the unthinkable: he conquered the capital, and then he left it. He withdrew his army to the fields outside the walls, sealed the palaces, and waited in his tent for the storm to arrive.

It was the gamble of a gambler who knows his cards are weak, and that his only hope lies in convincing the other player not to call the bluff.

THE SMOKE OF THE HEGEMON

The peace of the captured Steelhaven ended not with a thumping vibration.

On the eastern battlements, the sentries—most of them men who had spent their lives measuring time by the growth of crops—stopped looking at the city. They looked at the horizon. It started as a low, subterranean thrum that rattled the loose mortar between the iron-slabbed stones. It was the collective weight of four hundred thousand boots striking the earth in a single, killing rhythm.

A former peat-cutter from Marsh gripped his spear, his eyes fixed on the horizon. The sky there wasn't grey with rain, but black with the soot of every village Kharic had burned to light his path. Then came the light—the cold, rhythmic flicker of a forest of iron spear-tips catching the dying sun.

There was no need to sound the alarm. The stone of the gatehouse was already beginning to pulse with the heartbeat of the arriving host. The Tiger was no longer on the road. He was at the wall. And the air was already beginning to taste like fire.

CHAPTER FIFTEEN

THE FEAST OF KNIVES

IN WHICH THE TWO RIVALS MEET AT THE MOST FAMOUS BANQUET IN HISTORY

The man who kneels lowest is the one who sees the daggers hidden in the dirt. Humility is not a weakness; it is a cloak that hides the teeth of a wolf until the moon is high enough to strike.

— Observations on the Western Marshes

OF KHARIC'S ARRIVAL

Twenty-one days after the fall of Steelhaven, Kharic Stormborn arrived.

He did not enter as a guest, and he did not camp in the fields. He rode straight for the palace gates at the head of five thousand iron-clad cavalry, ignoring the protests of Maren's sentries. The hooves of his warhorse clattered on the white marble, shattering the silence of the surrendered city.

Lucan, the former Iron Emperor, hurried out to meet him on the steps of the Grand Hall. He was still wearing the white robes of surrender, possessing the fatal naivety of a boy who believed that the mercy granted by one rebel applied to all. He knelt on the marble, bowing his head as the massive warhorse loomed over him.

"I greet the Hegemon," Lucan said, his voice trembling. "The city awaits your—"

Kharic did not dismount. He stared down at the young man, his eyes cold as winter frost. His hand moved to the hilt of his sword.

Sensing the shift in the air, Lucan looked up, panic seizing him. "Wait! I have surrendered! The war is over!"

Kharic paused, his blade half-drawn. "Over?"

"Yes! The Lord of Valdria accepted my submission three weeks ago!" Lucan cried out, holding up his empty hands as if they were a shield. "He swore an oath! He promised that I would be spared if I gave up the seals! I am a commoner now, guilty of no crime!"

"The Lord of Valdria," Kharic repeated. The name tasted like ash in his mouth. *Maren again. Always Maren.* Even in victory, the peasant had stolen the right to grant mercy.

Kharic looked around the courtyard, at the sealed doors and the quiet palace. "He promised you life?"

"Yes! He has pardoned me!"

Desperate to prove his worth, Lucan fumbled in his robes and produced the Imperial Heirloom Seal. He unwrapped it from its silk, held it up with shaking hands—the block of flawless white nephrite said to have been carved from the heart of the sacred mountain.

"Look!" Lucan cried. "I kept it for you! The Lord of Valdria refused it, but I kept it safe! I offer it to the true conqueror!"

Kharic snatched the seal from Lucan's hands. He held it up to the smoke-filled light, examining the intricate carving of the six dragons coiling around the handle. He turned it over to read the ancient inscription on the base: *'Having received the*

Mandate from Heaven, may the Sovereign lead an Everlasting and Prosperous life.'

"Everlasting and Prosperous," Kharic muttered, tracing the characters with a thumb stained by war. "A heavy stone for such light words."

He tucked the stone into his belt with a predatory arrogance, letting the heavy weight of the Mandate hang visibly from his hip. It was his trophy. The symbol of power was his.

"You have delivered the cargo," Kharic said, his hand resting on the cold white stone. "But the debt remains unpaid."

Shing.

Kharic drew his sword. The sound was sharp, metallic, and final.

"Maren Ashford collects subjects," Kharic said, his voice carrying to every corner of the plaza, ensuring every hidden scribe and spy heard him. "I collect debts. The Creedseat murdered my father. It murdered my uncle. It murdered the Six Kingdoms."

He looked down at the trembling Lucan. He didn't see a boy; he saw the living symbol of the tyranny that had destroyed his family.

"Your family owes mine a river of blood. And I am here to drink it dry."

"No—please—he promised—"

"Maren Ashford promised you a life in *his* world," Kharic raised the blade. "But you are standing in mine."

The blade fell.

Kharic beheaded Lucan on the steps of his own palace. The head rolled down the stairs, the white robes turning instantly red.

As Lucan's body slumped, the fold of his sash loosened. A heavy, dull object slipped out, bounced once on the marble step, and rolled into a pool of darkening blood. It gave a soft, final thud.

It was a lead coin. Ugly. Oily. Worthless.

Kharic glanced at it for a fraction of a second, sneered at the trash, and spurred his horse forward. He rode over the corpse, eyes fixed on the burning horizon, carrying the white seal of power, leaving the grey coin of fate behind.

OF THE THREE NEW MERCIES

Kharic wiped his blade on the white silk of Lucan's shoulder, the metal singing a low, mournful note. He did not look at the fallen boy; he looked up at the towering gold-and-iron gates of the palace. To Maren Ashford, this was a prize to be managed —a harvest for his new kingdom. To Kharic, it was a nest of vipers that needed to be smoked out.

"I am told the Lord of Valdria has granted this city his 'Three Mercies,'" Kharic's voice rang out, vibrating with a cold, terrifying authority. "He treats the Ironhold like a garden that only needs weeding. He is a farmer trying to domesticate a plague."

He turned to his primary generals—the Lords of the Storm —who waited on their horses like statues of lead.

"Maren offers the mercy of the living. I offer the mercy of the dead. Today, we grant this palace The Three New Mercies."

Kharic pointed his bloody sword at the Grand Hall.

I. The Mercy of the Root

"Fan out through every corridor, every harem, and every cellar. Every soul that carries the Iron bloodline—from the bastards in the kitchens to the dowagers in the high towers— is to be brought to the plaza. We shall grant them the mercy of an end. If a child bears the name, they die today. I will not have a new rebellion born twenty years from now because of a 'merciful' oversight. Root and branch, the Iron Tree must be felled so the world may finally sleep."

II. The Mercy of the Void

"Find the Hall of Records. We shall grant the people the mercy of forgetfulness. Burn the tax scrolls. Burn the genealogies. Burn every scrap of paper that Mordecai used to bind this world in debt. If it is written in the hand of the Ironhold, it is a lie, and the world must forget how to read it. Let no man be a slave to a dead man's ink."

III. The Mercy of the Forge

"Tear down the banners. Drag the Creedseat—that jagged monstrosity—into the centre of the courtyard with ten chariots. Build a pyre beneath it until the metal screams. I want the world to see the seat of the Emperors turn into a puddle of useless slag. If we cannot sit upon it as brothers, no one shall sit upon it as masters. We grant the Iron the mercy of the fire, that it may be forged into something humble once more."

Kharic looked back at the smoke rising from the city Maren had tried so hard to save.

"Maren Ashford gave them a second chance," Kharic whispered, his smile as sharp as a razor. "I am giving them an ending."

He spurred his horse forward, his hooves clopping over the marble steps, wet with the blood of the last Emperor.

"Begin the purge. Let the screams be the last music this palace ever hears."

THE WASTED CURRENCY

The army thundered past, eyes fixed on the empty Creedseat. Only Eldran Greymantle stopped.

The old strategist dismounted and plucked the dull object from the pool of royal blood. It was cold, greasy, and heavier than gold.

He wiped it on his sleeve. He didn't need to check the face. He knew the symbol; he knew the shape of the trap.

One eats, one is eaten.

He looked up at the gates where Kharic had vanished. The Hegemon had taken the Imperial Seal—the symbol of Rule— but left behind the Lead—the symbol of Ruin.

"I will keep it for you, my lord," he murmured. "Until the bill comes due."

He slipped the coin into his pocket.

OF NEW BANNERS

Then came the banners.

At Kharic's signal, the Black Iron standards of the empire— which had flown over the city for fifty years—were torn from the ramparts and cast into the mud. In their place, the royal guard hoisted the new sigil of the Hegemon.

It was a flag woven for conquest, not governance: a jagged silver lightning bolt striking across a field of blood-red silk.

The banner snapped in the wind like a whip, stark against the smoke-filled sky. It bore no crest of unity, no symbol of peace. It was the sigil of a storm that had finally made landfall. As it rose to the highest peak of the burning palace, it signalled to the million souls watching below that the age of Iron was over, and the age of Blood had begun.

For three days, the capital became a slaughterhouse. The

palaces that Maren had carefully sealed were looted; the archives Maren had protected were torched. The fire raged so hot that the night sky turned orange for miles.

Only after the butchery was complete, and the stench of smoke had replaced the smell of incense, did Kharic agree to meet the man who had arrived first.

OF THE FARMER'S BOW

The meeting did not take place in the Hall of State that Maren had so carefully preserved. Instead, Kharic summoned him to the ruins of the Imperial Garden, a place that had once been a miracle of botany and was now a blackened charcoal pit. Kharic had established his command post amidst the skeletal remains of the Royal Library, where the wind carried the charred fragments of a thousand years of history.

Maren arrived with only two guards. It was a calculated risk—a display of humility that bordered on a death wish. He found Kharic sitting on a block of scorched marble, using a scrap of fine, cream-coloured silk—likely torn from an Empress's gown—to wipe the soot from his greaves.

"You beat me here," Kharic said. He did not look up. His voice was a low, jagged rasp.

"I took a different path, Hegemon," Maren replied.

"You took an easier path." Kharic finally raised his eyes. They were bloodshot, rimmed with the red exhaustion of three days of systematic slaughter. "You avoided the hard fights. You courted the weak and made friends of the weary. I bled for every mile of the road, while you walked through the gates as if you were coming home from the market."

"I secured the city for you," Maren said, keeping his voice level. "I held the treasury, sealed the armouries, and kept the blood from the streets. I stayed outside the walls so that the world would see you as the only true conqueror."

Kharic let out a harsh, barking laugh. "You stayed outside because you knew if you stood in my way, my cavalry would have ground your 'New Army' into the mud before the sun set."

Maren didn't deny it. In the presence of a man holding a wet blade, silence was the only armour that worked.

Eldran Greymantle, standing in the long shadow of a burnt cedar, leaned forward. "My lord, the covenant was clear. The first through the gates—"

"The covenant was written for an empire that no longer exists," Kharic interrupted, his voice snapping like a whip. "I am the law now. And I decide what rises from these ashes."

He stood up, his massive frame towering over Maren. The scent coming off him was overpowering—a thick, cloying mixture of woodsmoke, ozone, and old, dried blood. He stepped into Maren's personal space, his hand reaching out to rest heavily on Maren's shoulder. His gauntlet was still stained with the life of the last Iron Prince, and as he squeezed, he left a dark, wet smear across Maren's clean tunic.

"The realm is vast, Lord of Valdria," Kharic said softly. "There are borders to pacify and ruins to rebuild. The West is a jagged place, full of peat and silence. It needs a ruler who understands the language of the mud."

The insult was precise. *You are not a king of men,* it said. *You are a king of dirt.*

"A man should know his place," Kharic continued, his grip tightening. "You have done... adequately. For a farmer."

Maren felt the weight of that hand—not just the physical metal, but the weight of the four hundred thousand swords Kharic held behind him. He thought of the "Three Mercies" he had posted on the city gates, now likely being torn down and replaced by Kharic's "New Mercies." He looked at the bloody handprint on his chest.

"I serve the realm," Maren said, bowing his head just low enough to hide the stillness in his eyes. "And I await the Hegemon's command."

Kharic smiled, satisfied. He believed he had not only dismantled an empire but had finally broken the spirit of the only man who might have questioned his ascent.

"Good," Kharic said, turning back to his maps. "Tomorrow, we feast at Swangate. Bring your generals. We have a new world to carve up, and I should like to see if your appetite matches your luck."

Maren bowed deeply and retreated.

As Maren walked away, Eldran Greymantle watched him go, his eyes narrowing as he studied the retreating figure. The old advisor turned to Kharic.

"He is too humble, my lord," Greymantle whispered. "He bows with the grace of a man who has practised his submission. A man who gives up a kingdom without a single scream is either a coward or a predator. And Maren Ashford is no coward."

Kharic waved a dismissive hand. "He is a peasant who looked into the abyss and realised he didn't have the stomach for the fall."

"No," Greymantle urged, his voice dropping to a low, chilling hiss. "He is waiting. He is hiding his claws in the muck. If you let him return to the West, he will be the ghost that haunts your dynasty."

Greymantle looked at the empty gate where Maren had vanished into the twilight.

"Tomorrow, at the feast... the farmer must not leave the table alive."

THE DEBT OF THE KINSMAN

The night before the banquet, a shadow detached itself from the mountain mist. It was Lord Glenn. He entered Maren's tent not as a commander of the Stormborn, but as a father who still remembered the warmth of a son he had once mourned as dead.

"Maren," Glenn whispered, his grey braid trembling in the lamplight. "My cousin's cup is filled with wine, but Greymantle has filled his ear with poison. There are five hundred axes behind the crimson silk. Do not go. If you go, you walk into a grave."

Maren looked at him, his eyes steady. "If I don't go, the world remains broken, Glenn. Tomorrow, sit where you can see my hands. If the General starts to dance... show me that your memory is as long as your shadow."

Glenn bowed his head, the weight of the debt pressing heavier than his armour. "The debt will be paid, Lord of Valdria. Tomorrow, my sword is yours."

OF THE INVITATION

Hadrian Narrowdale came to his lord with worry written on his face.

"Kharic has invited you to a banquet," he said. "At a place called Swangate, in the hills outside the city. He wishes to discuss the division of the realm."

"A banquet." Maren scratched his chin. "Well, the food's bound to be better than camp rations."

"My lord, he has four hundred thousand soldiers and cavalry camped outside the city. You have one hundred thousand. If he wishes to discuss anything, he can discuss it from a position of strength. The only reason to invite you to a banquet is—"

"To kill me?"

Hadrian Narrowdale nodded reluctantly. "It is the obvious interpretation."

Maren stared out the window in stillness, at the city he had conquered. Then he laughed—that sudden, unexpected laugh that so often disconcerted those around him.

"Well then." He shrugged. "Guess I'd better go see what he wants."

"My lord!"

"If I don't go, I look scared. My men start thinking maybe they should be scared too. Kharic's lot get cocky." Maren turned to face his advisor. "Besides, the man might actually want to talk. He's proud as a rooster, but he's not dumb. Fighting each other just helps the Iron bastards."

"And if it's a trap?"

"Then you make sure they pay for it." Maren clapped Hadrian Narrowdale on the shoulder. "Get Roland to round up an escort. Keep it small—don't want to spook anyone. And find out if Lord Glenn Stormborn is attending," Maren added. "Kharic's elder cousin. The one with the grey braid."

"The Kinsman? Why him?"

"Man owes me," Maren said, checking the edge of his dagger. "From way back. When Kharic marched his army through my marshes years ago, the column got separated in the fog. Glenn's youngest son wandered off the causeway. Kharic ordered the search called off after an hour—said one lost lieutenant wasn't worth risking the whole army in the dark. They left him for dead. I found the boy two days later, clinging to a root, and sent him home. Old Glenn never forgot who gave up on his son, and who brought him back."

OF THE BANQUET

Swangate was a hunting lodge in the hills above Steelhaven—a comfortable retreat where the Iron Emperors had once entertained guests in happier times. Kharic had chosen it for the banquet, and he had filled it with his most loyal retainers.

Maren Ashford arrived with only a hundred men, including Roland Knox and a handful of personal guards. He walked into the lodge as though entering his own home, showing no sign of fear or hesitation.

The Great Pavilion was a masterpiece of temporary decadence, a sprawling cathedral of crimson silk and gold-threaded canvas erected on the heights of Swangate. To the soldiers outside, it looked like a glowing jewel in the mountain mist; to those within, the air felt heavy, as if the oxygen had been replaced by the dry, metallic scent of whetted stone.

Maren didn't see them, but he felt the presence of the trap. Behind the thick, gold-embroidered velvet hangings that lined the inner sanctum, five hundred axes waited. Kharic's elite executioners stood in absolute silence, their breathing synchronised, their hands steady on the shafts of their weapons. They were a shadow-army, a wall of hidden steel waiting for a single, audible signal—the dropping of a malachite cup or the snap of a pendant—to turn the feast into a slaughter.

Kharic sat at the head of the table, the central pole of the pavilion rising behind him like the mast of a war-galley. Every flap of the canvas in the wind sounded like a muffled drumbeat, a reminder that they were all sitting in a cage made of silk.

The seating arrangement was a calculated insult. Kharic sat facing east, the position of an emperor, bathed in the light of the hearth. Maren was placed facing north, the position of a servant or a petitioner. It was a subtle declaration of dominance, loud enough to be heard without a word spoken. Maren took the seat without complaint, bowing deeply as he did so.

"Welcome, Lord of Valdria." Kharic said, rising to greet his guest. "I hope the journey was not too tiring."

"Nah, bit of a ride never hurt anyone." Maren took his seat, accepted a cup of wine, and waited.

Kharic gestured towards the crystalline decanter on the table. "This is the *Celestine Amber*—bottled during the last summer of the Old Kingdoms. It has a nose of crushed violets and the aftertaste of a fading empire. I was told you were a man of the vine, Maren. What do you think?"

Maren took a heavy, unrefined gulp, swilling the priceless liquid around his mouth as if it were common pond water. He swallowed hard and wiped his mouth with the back of his hand.

"It's alright," Maren said, leaning back with a grin that was far too wide. "A bit thin, maybe? Back in Marsh, we like a brew that bites back. Something you can chew on. This... well, it's a bit like drinking perfumed rain, isn't it?"

Kharic's lip curled in a micro-expression of pure, aristocratic disgust. He had offered a relic, and the peasant had treated it like a mistake.

"And the women," Kharic continued, his gaze drifting towards the imperial dancers who moved like silk ribbons through the hall. "I hear you spent three weeks in the capital and didn't touch the harem. My generals thought you were a saint. I thought perhaps you were just... selective."

Maren looked at the dancers—women whose beauty was legendary across five provinces—and his eyes widened with a raw, embarrassing hunger that made him look like a schoolboy. He looked back at Kharic, leaning in as if sharing a secret.

"To tell you the truth, Hegemon... I didn't know where to

start. They're so... clean. Back in Weed, I thought Celia was the peak of the world because she had all her teeth and a laugh that shook the rafters. But these ones? They look like they'd break if I breathed on them too hard. I spent half my time just trying not to trip over their silk tails."

Kharic didn't laugh. He felt a wave of reassuring pity. He had been worried about a rival; instead, he had found a man whose soul was still stuck in a village tavern, a man whose greatest ambition was to gawk at things he didn't understand.

The meal proceeded with elaborate courtesy—both men knew the forms of noble hospitality, even if neither entirely trusted them. They discussed the weather, the quality of certain leathers, the arrangements for managing the captured capital. They did not talk about what everyone knew would eventually be discussed: the future.

Finally, as the dishes were being cleared, Kharic raised the subject.

"The empire has fallen," Kharic said. He didn't say 'to us both'; his eyes suggested the victory belonged to the Stormborn alone, and Maren was merely a fortunate scavenger. "The question now is what replaces it. I propose that we divide the realm—I to take the eastern territories, you to take the western. Let there be two kingdoms instead of one, each independent, each free to govern as it sees fit."

"That's generous of you," Maren replied, wiping a stray drop of that 'perfumed rain' wine from his chin. "But here's a thought. Why split it up? Two kingdoms... they'll end up fighting sooner or later. One realm needs one man in charge. A man who can hold a sword and a mandate at the same time. And let's be honest, Hegemon—that man isn't a farmer from the marshes."

Everyone present understood what Maren was saying: he was offering to submit.

Kharic's eyes narrowed. "You would accept me as your Hegemon and Overlord?"

"I'd follow you. Bend the knee, all of it." Maren's smile was open, unthreatening. "You're the God of War best fighter any of us have ever seen. Stonedeer—you smashed them. Broke the empire's back. If anyone deserves to warm that metal throne and breathe that stale incense, it's you."

Kharic leaned back, swirling the wine in his golden chalice, his eyes fixed on Maren with a predator's curiosity. He looked at Maren's dirty fingernails and his awkward posture, and felt a wave of absolute, lethal certainty. This man didn't want the world; he just wanted to survive the night.

My scouts tell me you didn't even step foot in the Inner Treasury, Maren," Kharic said, his voice dropping into a dangerous, velvet growl. "They say the gold is still counted and the silk still folded. And the Creedseat... the very chair of the world... you left it cold and empty, as if you feared its touch. Why? A man like you does nothing for free. Even a wastrel doesn't find a mountain of silver and suddenly develop a conscience."

Maren looked down at his own calloused hands, then back at the Hegemon. "The treasures of the Empire are heavy, my Lord. Too heavy for a man of the marshes. I kept them for the only man whose shoulders are broad enough to bear their weight. I wanted you to find everything exactly as it was."

"Then what did you take?" Kharic snapped. "In those three weeks, what did you carry away in your pockets?"

"I took the only thing that doesn't melt in a fire, Hegemon," Maren said softly. "I took the hearts of the people."

Kharic laughed, a dry, rasping sound. "Hearts? You think a farmer's loyalty is worth more than the Imperial Treasury? I've heard of your 'Three Mercies.' Stellan called it statecraft. I call it the mercy of a woman. It is a weakness, Maren. It is the sentiment of a mother who cannot bear to see a hare killed. In this world, the only mercy that matters is the one written in steel."

Maren met the Hegemon's gaze, his voice a steady. "If that is a woman's mercy, then maybe the world has seen enough of men's 'justice'."

Kharic didn't respond. He looked at Maren—sweating, submissive, yet possessed of a strange, stubborn dignity. For a fleeting moment, Kharic felt a pang of something he hadn't felt since his uncle's death: Recognition. He saw in Maren a different kind of courage—the courage of the small. He felt a sudden, aristocratic disdain for the idea of killing him here. *To kill a man who cares for the weak is to admit I fear the weak,* Kharic thought.

"And what would you want in return?"

"Just what I've already got—my lands, my title. Let me run the east under your thumb. I don't want the bloody Creedseat. Don't want to rule the world." He shrugged. "Just want to keep my people fed and maybe find a bit of peace. That's all."

It was exactly what Kharic wanted to hear. Eldran Greymantle, watching from his place at the table, felt his unease deepen. This was not how ambitious men behaved. This was not how rivals for supreme power spoke.

But Kharic was intoxicated—by victory, by vindication, by the prospect of achieving all he had ever wanted. He raised his cup.

"Then let us drink to unity," he said. "To one realm, one ruler, one future."

The hall erupted in cheers. The banquet continued.

And in the shadows, Eldran Greymantle caught the eye of one of Kharic's generals and made a subtle gesture.

It was time for the sword dance.

OF THE DANCE

The entertainment that followed was traditional—musicians and performers demonstrating skills for the assembled nobles —but no one paid them much mind. The tension in the pavilion was a physical weight.

Then Ser Aaron Hestor rose, drawing his blade in one fluid, lethal motion. He began to dance—a complex series of movements that combined martial grace with a predator's intent. He whirled and thrust, his sword tracing patterns in the air like a calligrapher's quill, and with each rotation, he edged closer to where Maren Ashford sat.

Hadrian Narrowdale saw it first. "My lord—"

"I see it," Maren replied, his voice a low anchor in the silence.

The general's blade whistled within inches of Maren's throat, the steel flickering in the lamplight. But before the final, fatal strike could fall, Lord Glenn—the eldest of the Stormborn cousins—rose with a sudden, clattering ring of his silver cup. He drew his own longsword with a sound that sliced through the music.

"A masterful display, General Hestor!" Glenn shouted, his voice booming with a forced, desperate cheer. "But a solo dance is a lonely thing for a royal banquet. In the South, we say a warrior only shines when he has a partner to test his edge. Permit me to accompany you!"

Glenn didn't wait for permission. He moved with a speed that belied his age, his blade clashing against Hestor's in a shower of sparks. To the casual observer, it looked like a chore-ographed duet. In reality, it was a high-speed chess match; Glenn stayed positioned like a human shield, intercepting every strike meant for Maren's neck.

"Watch your footing, General!" Glenn grunted, parrying a

thrust that would have gutted Maren. "You're getting too close to the table. We wouldn't want to spill the Hegemon's wine."

Hestor's eyes were murderous. "Step aside, Old Man," he hissed under the ring of the steel.

"I find I enjoy the exercise," Glenn replied, his eyes fixed on the general's tip.

And then—just as the tension reached its breaking point—the flap of the tent exploded open.

Roland Knox shoved aside two guards who tried to cross spears to stop him. He crashed onto the floor, his iron shield slamming into the ground with a sound like a gong. He stood there, hair bristling, eyes wide and bloodshot, panting heavily, looking less like a man and more like a cornered bear guarding its cub.

Kharic stared at the intruder. Most men would have ordered the guards to kill him instantly. But Kharic Stormborn admired strength above all else, and he saw a mountain of it standing before him.

"Who is this savage?" Kharic asked, not with anger, but with curiosity.

"My shield-bearer, Roland," Maren said calmly. "He gets... protective."

"A fine beast," Kharic muttered. He picked up a massive flagon of unmixed wine—strong enough to knock out a horse—and shoved it across the table.

"Give him wine." Kharic commanded.

Roland didn't hesitate. He took the massive flagon, drained it in a single, terrifying gulp, and slammed it down. He didn't look at the wine; he looked at the shadows behind the curtains, where the light caught the glint of those five hundred hidden axe-heads ready to act.

"Good wine," Roland grunted. He turned his bloodshot

eyes to General Hestor and Lord Glenn. "But the floor is crowded. I think the music needs a drum."

Roland drew his own massive, notched broadsword. He didn't dance. He stood like a wall of iron between Maren and the rest of the room, his blade held low, ready to gut anyone who moved.

The moment stretched. The air in the hall grew heavy, suffocating.

Eldran Greymantle sat frozen, his eyes locked on Kharic's hand. He tapped his own garnet pendant against his cup— *Clink. Clink. Clink.*—a frantic, rhythmic signal that sounded like a ticking clock in the silence.

Do it, Greymantle's eyes screamed. *Drop the cup. Touch the pendant. Give the order.*

Berold stood by the tent flap, his arms crossed over a chest scarred by Ironhold lashes. A jagged brand—the mark of a 'Life-Eater'—crawled up his jawline, a permanent shadow on his face. He watched the necks of Maren's guards as if counting how many strokes it would take to clear the room, saw Greymantle's tapping of pendant, only waiting for the Hegemon to tap his.

"The Hegemon talks of glory," Berold spat quietly. "Mercy is a luxury for those who have never worn chains."

Kharic's hand moved towards the emerald pendant at his throat. General Hestor paused his dance, the blade hovering low, muscles coiled like a spring, waiting for the slightest twitch of his master's finger.

A bead of sweat rolled down Maren's temple. But Maren did not flinch. He looked at Kharic, sweating, ingratiating, submissive. He looked like a dog rolling on its back, exposing its belly.

Kharic's fingers brushed the cool surface of his emerald charm. He felt the ridge of the carving. One pull, and the floor would run red. One pull, and the threat would be gone forever.

But deeper than honour, there was pride. To kill a lion is a feat. To kill a dog that is already begging... that is merely butchery. Kharic looked at the brave savage Roland, then at the cowering Maren, and felt only disgust.

He is not worth the stain on my floor, Kharic thought. *Lions do not concern themselves with the death of insects.*

Kharic laughed—a genuine, booming sound that shook the silk walls of the pavilion. "Enough! This entertainment grows too exciting. Roland, Glenn—put away your steel. General Hestor, find your seat. Let us drink!"

Maren let out a long, shuddering breath, his shoulders sagging as if the weight of the air had finally lessened. He wiped a bead of sweat from his brow and gave a weak, flickering smile.

"My Lord Hegemon... you must forgive me," Maren stammered, his voice sounding thin and rustic. "My hands were made for the plough and the counting-frame, not for the parry. Seeing such... magnificent steel so close to my neck... it makes a simple man's heart skip beats. My Marsh-born soul isn't built for such 'exciting' hospitality."

Kharic looked at him with a mixture of pity and amusement. "You are a soft creature, Maren. But you have a loyal beast for a shield. Very well—no more steel. Let us have music instead! Something from the South, to soothe our guest's delicate nerves!"

Hadrian Narrowdale chose that moment to lean forward, his eyes glinting with a dry, lethal wit.

"A wise suggestion, Hegemon," Hadrian said, his voice smooth as polished opal. "Your hospitality is truly unparalleled. Most lords are content with a few servants to pour the wine, but you... you are so concerned for our safety that you have a few hundred axemen standing behind the curtains just to ensure the Lord of Valdria doesn't drop his fork."

Kharic's smile didn't vanish, but it froze. He looked at the heavy velvet hangings where the light caught the occasional glint of a hidden axe-head. He looked at Greymantle, whose face had gone from grey to a bone-white mask of pure, humiliated rage.

Hadrian raised his cup towards the shadows behind the silk. "Truly, such devotion to the guest is moving. But perhaps, since the music is starting, your servants could find a more comfortable place to wait? It must be terribly cramped back there, and we wouldn't want a stray axe to ruin the carpets."

Kharic let out a sharp snort of derision—not at Hadrian, but at the clumsy transparency of the trap he hadn't fully authorised. He snapped his fingers, a sound like a pistol shot.

"Out!" Kharic barked. "All of you. If I want a man dead, I will kill him myself, in the sun. I have no need for a chorus of blades behind curtains."

The curtains rippled. The axemen quietly retreated, their armoured footsteps creating a heavy, metallic thrum that vibrated through the floor like a retreating tide. Greymantle slumped in his seat, his assassination had failed. But the message had been delivered.

OF THE NATURE'S CALL

The sword dancers went back to their seats, the tension in the room remained brittle. Maren knew he had survived the immediate threat, but he also knew that Greymantle was whispering in Kharic's ear, and that Kharic's mood could shift like the wind.

Maren stood up, swaying slightly. He placed a hand on his

stomach, his face flushed—whether from the wine or a calculated performance, no one could tell.

"My Lord Hegemon," Maren said, his voice thick, seemingly from drink. "Your kind hospitality is... overwhelming. And your wine is stronger than the swamp water I'm used to."

He gave a pained, apologetic smile, playing the part of the rustic overflowed by noble luxury.

"I fear I must step out for a moment. Nature calls with some urgency."

Kharic looked at him with amusement. To him, this was just further proof of Maren's inadequacy—a man who couldn't even hold his liquor at a negotiation table. A weakling who needed a break from the pressure.

"Go, then," Kharic sneered, waving a dismissive hand. "Relieve yourself, Lord Maren. But do not take too long—we have maps to draw."

"I shall return before the cup is dry," Maren promised—a lie delivered with a bow.

Roland Knox stepped forward, his hand still resting heavily on his sword hilt. "I will escort my lord," the giant rumbled. "The paths are dark, and he is unsteady."

Eldran Greymantle opened his mouth to object—to insist that Kharic's own guards accompany them—but Roland turned his bloodshot, wolf-like glare upon the table. It was a look that promised immediate violence if anyone intervened. The guards stepped back. Kharic merely laughed and signalled them to pass.

"My lord," Eldran hissed, desperation cracking his voice. "He must not leave this hall alive. Kill him now."

Kharic's fingers tightened on the pendant.

And then he let it fall.

"No," he murmured. "Not as an assassin. If I defeat him, I

defeat him in the field, where victory has meaning. I will not win through treachery."

Eldran's face went grey. "You are making a mistake that will cost you everything."

"It may be. But it will be my mistake. My choice. My honour."

What followed was the culmination of weeks of careful preparation.

Hadrian Narrowdale had been working since the invitation arrived, deploying gold and promises throughout the Swangate complex. A servant had been convinced to leave a particular storage room unlocked. A stable boy had been paid to keep three horses saddled and waiting in an orchard beyond the pavilion's outer walls.

When Maren stepped away from the banquet hall, he did not go to the facilities. He turned left instead of right, ducked through a doorway that appeared to be a closet but actually connected to the servants' quarters, and found himself in a narrow passage lit by a single guttering torch.

Roland Knox was already there, along with two men who had infiltrated the Swangate staff weeks earlier. They handed Maren a servant's cloak—plain grey wool, forgettable—and led him through a maze of storage rooms and connecting corridors.

They emerged in a courtyard near the kitchens, where the chaos of food preparation provided cover for their movement. From there, through a gate that should have been guarded but wasn't, into the orchard where the horses waited.

The ride back to his camp outside Steelhaven took three hours. Maren pushed his mount hard, knowing that every moment increased the risk of pursuit.

OF THE MERCY OF A WOMAN

By the time Maren was safely within his own lines, surrounded by his one hundred thousand soldiers, the banquet had long since soured.

Back in the banquet hall, the music had not yet stopped. A group of court dancers, captured from the Imperial Palace and still draped in the gossamer silks of the fallen dynasty, moved in a hypnotic circle in the centre of the room. They were like captive butterflies, their movements a stark, haunting contrast to the mud-stained warlords drinking around the tables.

Kharic noticed the empty seat. The wine in Maren's cup was still swirling, but the man was gone.

"Where is the Lord of Valdria?" Kharic asked, his voice echoing in the suddenly quiet lodge.

Hadrian Narrowdale stood up, his face a mask of polite regret. He held a pair of cups made of fine tourmaline—a final gift. "My lord Maren has departed. He felt... unwell from the wine. He asked me to present these as a token of his eternal loyalty."

The silence in the hall was deafening. Kharic looked at the empty chair and let out a short, sharp laugh. "He ran. Like a thief in the night."

But Eldran Greymantle did not laugh. He stared at the empty seat, his face turning a sickly, bone-white. He walked over to Hadrian, snatched those cups, and smashed them against a stone pillar with a violent, desperate strength.

The sound of shattering precious stone was like swords clashing. The music died instantly. The imperial dancers froze in mid-step, their arms raised, their faces pale masks of terror. They stood like porcelain dolls in the wreckage of the feast, paralyzed by the sudden eruption of cold, murderous reality.

"Out!" Greymantle barked, not even looking at them. "Get them out of here!"

The women scrambled for the exits, their silk slippers clicking frantically against the stone, leaving the hall to the scent of spilt wine and the men who had just lost the world.

"Mercy of a woman!" Greymantle screamed, the words spraying from his lips like venom. "You mocked his heart, Kharic, but it is your own 'mercy' that has buried us this night! I am counseling a child who thinks he is a god!"

He pointed a trembling, skeletal finger at the Hegemon.

"Today, you have let the world slip through your fingers because you thought it was too small to grasp. Mark my words —we will all die captives of the Lord of Marsh. He didn't run because he was a coward; he ran because he is a survivor."

"He is a coward who ran from a fight!" Kharic shouted back, slamming his fist onto the table until the gold vessels rattled.

"And survivors, my lord," Greymantle retorted, his voice dropping to a low, haunting whisper, "have a way of lasting much longer than heroes. You have won the feast, Kharic. But you have lost the war."

Kharic stormed out of the hall, his red cloak snapping behind him like a dying flame. He ordered the banquet concluded and his army mobilised for the march east. But the air had changed. The chance to eliminate his rival before he became truly dangerous had vanished into the mountain mist.

They would meet again, these two men. And when they did, the calculus of the world would be written not in wine and fine stones.

CHAPTER SIXTEEN

A HUNDRED DAYS OF FIRE

IN WHICH INFERNO CONSUMES STEELHAVEN, KHARIC STORMBORN SHOWS THE WORLD WHAT VENGEANCE LOOKS LIKE

Stir the pot, stir the deep, While the Iron City goes to sleep. The silver's a juice, the gold's a broth, The sky is a piece of burning cloth. Don't blow on the soup, let it bubble and hiss, Give the pretty red flames a charcoal kiss. We're cooking the world, can't you see? But there's no more room at the table for me.

— *Fragments of a Poem by Edric The Secondborn*

OF THE CITY OF TEN THOUSAND YEARS

Steelhaven was not merely a city; it was a geography of arrogance.

Built by Seran the Unifier, the First Iron Emperor, it was designed to intimidate history itself. Its walls were sheer cliffs of black basalt that stretched for miles, so high that clouds often snagged on the guard towers. Its streets were paved with white stone brought from the conquered mountains of the West. The Great Hall of the Iron Creed—the heart of the palace complex—was said to be large enough to shelter an entire legion beneath its gilded roof.

Seran had decreed that this city would be the capital of the world for ten thousand generations. He had emptied the treasuries of six kingdoms to build it, believing that stone and geometry could grant immortality to his bloodline. It was magnificent. It was breathtaking. It was a monument to the idea that the Iron Empire was eternal.

Kharic Stormborn looked upon this grandeur and saw only a tomb.

He stood on the steps of that Great Hall, torch in hand, trembling not with fear, but with the dark ecstasy of vengeance.

"They built this to last forever," Kharic whispered to the wind. "Let us see how long it lasts against fire."

His orders were absolute.

First came the blood. Kharic's soldiers swept through the sprawling residential districts of the nobility like a plague. Every member of the Iron Clan—every cousin, nephew, and distant relative of the dead Emperor—was hunted down. Children were pulled from their hiding places in the ornamental gardens; women were slaughtered in their silk-draped chambers. The gutters of the Eternal City ran red, a grim offering to the ghosts of Kharic's father and uncle.

Then came the death of memory.

Kharic walked through the magnificent galleries, ignoring the pleas of the terrified courtiers. He looked at the tapestries that depicted the Empire's victories over his own people. He looked at the pillars carved from whole trunks of ancient mahogany.

He did not want to sit on the throne. He wanted to watch it burn.

He walked to the centre of the dais. There, coiled around

the legs of the Emperor's throne, were two massive statues of intertwining serpents—the "Divine Double" that Mordecai had made the realm bow down to. They were cast in solid silver, their eyes set with rubies, their scales detailed enough to seem wet. They were beautiful. They were the symbol of everything that had strangled the world.

Kharic looked at the snakes with a sneer of pure disgust.

"They worship the things that crawl on their bellies," he spat, kicking the silver snout of the nearest serpent. "Break them."

His soldiers hesitated—the fear of the serpent law was deep in their bones. Kharic didn't wait. He swung his warhammer, the "Stormbreaker," with a roar.

CLANG.

The silver head shattered, rubies skittering across the marble floor like drops of frozen blood.

"Look!" Kharic shouted to his men, pointing at the broken metal. "It does not bleed! It does not curse! It is just silver, made by men, to frighten children! There is no god here but Fire!"

The spell was broken. With a roar, his soldiers fell upon the throne room. They smashed the serpent statues, tore down the banners of the Coiled Path, and piled the wreckage onto the dais.

"Light it," he commanded.

He threw his own torch onto the Emperor's dais. The dry, ancient wood caught instantly.

As the flames roared upward, licking at the ceiling that had been painted to resemble the night sky, Kharic threw back his head and laughed. It was a sound of pure, terrifying release. The destruction of this beauty was sweeter to him than any wine, more satisfying than any woman.

He watched the "City of Ten Thousand Years" begin to die. It had stood for barely forty.

OF THE TITANS' FALL

In the days following the Feast of Knives, Kharic Stormborn stood before the Gate of the Eternal Iron and stared up at the monuments that had mocked his family for forty years.

The Twin Iron Titans rose two hundred feet into the grey sky, their hollow eyes gazing down at the conqueror who had come too late to claim the city himself. Maren had offered to let Kharic enter first—a gesture of courtesy that Kharic recognised as the calculated insult it was. The Lord of Marsh had already received the surrender, already taken the seals, already established himself as the city's protector. Kharic's belated arrival changed nothing except the degree of his humiliation.

But there was one thing Maren could not prevent.

"Pull them down," Kharic ordered.

The chains were already in place—his engineers had spent the night preparing, knowing what their lord would demand. Four hundred oxen strained against the ropes; three thousand men added their strength to the pull; and slowly, inevitably, the first Titan began to lean.

When it fell, the impact shook the earth for a mile in every direction. The statue burst open on impact, revealing what the chronicles would later record with bitter satisfaction: emptiness.

The great symbol of the Iron Creed's peaceful disarmament was hollow—a thin shell of metal wrapped around rotted wooden beams. The million confiscated swords had never been melted into monuments. They had been reforged into the weapons that killed Cherosian soldiers for forty years.

"Everything about this empire was a lie," Kharic said, as

the second Titan crashed down beside the first. "Even its promises were made of air."

He rode into Steelhaven over the corpses of the statues. Miles away, from the safety of his camp in the hills, Maren Ashford watched the dust cloud rise. He lowered his spyglass, his face pale.

"He is breaking the toys because he cannot break the boy," Maren whispered to Hadrian. "Let him destroy the stone. We will keep the hearts."

The war against the Empire was over. The war between victors was about to begin.

OF THE EXECUTIONS

Before the first head fell, Kharic stood before the Great Gate of Justice, where Maren's decrees remained inscribed on a simple wooden tablet.

He read the words—*Murder alone shall be punished by death*—and spat on the wood.

"A peasant's prayer," Kharic growled. He turned to the crowd of terrified citizens. "Your mud lord offered you mercy because he was afraid to judge you. I offer you the truth. In my realm, there are no mercies—there is only the Storm."

He snapped the tablet across his knee and tossed it into the nearest cooking fire.

The executions lasted three days.

Kharic was thorough. He had spent years compiling lists—names of officials who had served the Iron Creed with partic-ular zeal, names of executioners who had carried out its sentences, names of everyone who had participated in the machinery of oppression that had ground his family into dust. Now, with the capital in his hands, he worked through those lists with methodical precision.

Some of the condemned were clearly guilty—torturers, murderers, men whose hands were stained with the blood of innocents. Others were less obviously culpable—administrators who had simply done their jobs, soldiers who had followed orders, servants who had been in the wrong place at the wrong time. Kharic made no distinction. They had all served the order of the Iron that had killed his father. They would all pay the price.

"This is madness, my lord," Eldran Greymantle said, on the second day. "You execute men whose only crime was serving the old government. I have watched dynasties fall for such excess. You create enemies where you might have found servants."

"I don't want them to serve me. I want them to fear me."

"Fear is not enough to build an empire," Greymantle hissed, stepping over a pile of discarded imperial scrolls. "Do not mistake me for a man of sentiment, Kharic. I would have watched the Lord of Valdria bleed out on the floor of Swangate and slept like a babe. He was a rival; his death would have been a necessity. But these men? These clerks, these tax-collectors, these archivists? They are the gears. You are smashing the clock because you hate the time it tells. You kill the tools you will need tomorrow for an empire to prove you are angry today."

"I don't want to build an empire." Kharic's eyes were empty, hollow, consumed by the fire that had been burning since his uncle's death. "I want to destroy the one that killed everyone I loved. I want to make sure that nothing like it ever rises again. I want them to remember, for a thousand years, what happens to those who stand against the house of Stormborn."

Eldran Greymantle spoke no words. He had served the Stormborn family for decades; he had taught Kharic strategy and history and philosophy; he had believed, truly believed, that he was helping to shape a great ruler. But the man before him now was not the student he remembered. The man before him was something else—a blade tempered too hot, its edge turned brittle by the heat of its own making.

"And when the last of your enemies is dead?" he asked finally. "When there is no one left to punish? What then?"

Kharic did not answer, because he did not know. He did not want to think about a future that existed beyond his revenge.

The executions continued. On the morning of the third day, a young scribe named Lawren asked permission to finish copying a poem he had been working on—just twelve more lines, he said. The guards laughed and dragged him to the block anyway.

His quill was found later in the mud, the nib still damp with ink. When a curious soldier picked up the paper, he found the unfinished lines were not a lament, but an ode:

To the Storm that clears the sky, To the breaker of chains, To the King who brings the dawn...

He had been writing a poem of welcome for his executioner.

But the ink did not perish in the gutter. As the guards moved to the next row of the condemned, a trembling hand— an unnamed archivist, who had survived by hiding beneath a pile of discarded corpses—snatched the sodden parchment from the mud. He tucked it into his sleeve as he fled the smoking ruins of the city. Weeks later, that scrap of paper, stained with the soot of an empire, would be laid upon Markus Quillen's desk in the damp halls of Valdria. It was the first entry in a new ledger; the seed of a library that would eventually outlast the Storm.

OF THE GREAT BURNING

On the fourth day, Kharic raided the imperial tomb at Shadowmount.

The necropolis was the most sacred site in the realm—a geography of death meant to outlast the sun. Generations of artisans had laboured to create these underground palaces, filling them with treasures and armies to serve the Iron Emperors in the void. It was a place of silence, sanctity, and fear.

Kharic brought only noise and fire.

When his soldiers breached the massive iron seals, they found the rivers of mercury still flowing—a silver nervous system for a dead world.

"Poison," Kharic said, watching the toxic tide shimmer in the torchlight. "Just like his blood."

He ordered the channels smashed. The mercury spilt out, poisoning the soil for miles, turning the sacred valley into a grey, toxic swamp.

And the eight thousand Iron-Bound? The bronze soldiers that Mordecai had believed were immortal?

Kharic didn't fight them. He melted them.

He turned the tomb into a furnace, feeding the fires with the Emperor's own library. The bronze sentinels did not scream; they simply softened, slumped, and ran together into puddles of shapeless metal. The army that was supposed to guard the Emperor for eternity was reduced to ingots to pay for his destroyer's war.

Once the guardians were gone, the looting began. Gold and silver, silk and jade—artifacts of incalculable value were dragged into the light, piled in the courtyards like common firewood, distributed to soldiers who laughed as they draped themselves in the vestments of dead gods.

But stone and metal were not enough to sate Kharic. He wanted the man.

Seran the Unifier—the First Iron Emperor—was dragged from his sarcophagus of obsidian. The preservation oils had done their work too well; he was not a skeleton, but a leathery, yellowed caricature of a man, his face frozen in a command that no one obeyed.

Kharic hauled the corpse back to Steelhaven and hung it from the gates of the palace it had built. While the common people watched in horrified fascination, the Stormborn mounted a platform to deliver a eulogy of hate.

"This is the man who destroyed your kingdoms!" Kharic shouted, pointing his blade at the dangling, shriveled thing. "This is the man who killed your fathers and enslaved your children! He told you his line would rule until the stars grew cold!"

Kharic slashed the rope. The body fell. It hit the dust with the dry, hollow sound of a falling branch.

"He was wrong," Kharic said to the silence. "His throne is ash. His treasures are mine. And *this* is the fate of all who think themselves above the judgement of heaven."

The crowd did not cheer. The crowd stood in stunned silence, unable to process what they were witnessing—the systematic destruction of everything they had been taught to hold sacred.

Then came the fire.

Kharic ordered the torching of the Imperial Archives—the vast library that held the history, the laws, and the poetry of three hundred years.

"It is the ink of tyrants," he declared, tossing the first torch himself. "Let it warm the air."

The Everlasting Iron Palace did not just sit upon the earth; it sprawled across the valley like a sleeping dragon of wood and stone. Three hundred palaces were connected by the Cloud-Walks—covered bridges built so high on massive pillars that a man could walk from the North Ridge to Kingsriver without ever touching the ground. The roof tiles were not clay, but burnished copper that blinded the eye when the sun struck them. The pillars were not merely painted; they were carved from the sacred star-wood of the conquered South, inlaid with gemstone and gold.

Inside, the chambers were filled with the plunder of the Six Kingdoms. There were choirs of women who had not seen the sun in years, their only duty to sing for an Emperor who might never walk past their door. There were treasuries filled with pearls from the Eastern Sea and ivory from the Southern Jungles. It was a cage of impossible beauty, built to prove that the Iron Dynasty possessed everything under heaven.

Now it will all be ash.

As the flames consumed the palace, Kharic turned to Grey-mantle. "Seran the Unifier spent fifty years hunting us," Kharic said, watching the Creedseat turn black. "He killed my father. He burnt our libraries. He forbade our language. Because the oracles told him that '*As long as three embers of the Storm remain, it is the storm that melts iron.*' Kharic smiled—a smile that held no joy. "He should have killed us all when he had the chance." Kharic said, ignoring the look of horror on his advisor's face.

He watched the molten gold run down the scorched pillars like the tears of a dying god, and whispered to the ghosts in the smoke: "Father, Uncle... look. *This* is the melting."

The fire raged for three months. It turned the sky over Steelhaven a permanent, bruised purple. Ash fell like black snow on the shoulders of the weeping citizens. In those flames, the wisdom of an age was turned to smoke, leaving a scar on the memory of the world that would never heal.

Eldran Greymantle, watching from the edges of the crowd,

felt a cold stone settle in his stomach. He had seen many things in his long life. He had witnessed battles and betrayals, triumphs and tragedies. But he had never seen anything like this—this deliberate violation of every norm, every tradition, every boundary that separated civilisation from barbarism.

"You've gone too far," he whispered, though Kharic was too far away to hear. "You've shown them what you truly are. And they will never forgive you for it."

He was right, of course.

OF KHARIC'S CHOICE

When the fire finally died down, leaving the "City of Ten Thousand Years" a blackened skeleton, the generals gathered.

Eldran Greymantle pleaded with his lord one last time.

"Stay," the old advisor urged, pointing to the map. "Steelhaven is the heart of the world. It is fortified by mountains on four sides and fed by the endless fields of the central plains. He who holds this city holds the throat of the empire. If you leave, you leave the lock open for another thief."

Kharic refused. He looked at the charred ruins with disdain. To him, the smoke still smelt of the enemy.

"Stay here?" Kharic laughed, kicking a piece of charred rubble. "To possess the world and not return home to show it, is like walking through the dark wearing a robe of gold. Who would know? Who would admire?"

He turned his back on the greatest fortress ever built.

"I will return to Cheros," he declared, his eyes shining with a boyish, tragic pride. "I will rebuild my family's seat at Drumhold. I will rule from my home, where my ancestors can witness my triumph. I want the people who saw me leave as an exile to see me return as a King."

It was a choice that valued vanity over power, the applause

of the past over the security of the future. He chose to be a hero to his cousins rather than an Emperor to the world.

Before he departed, Kharic treated the geography of the realm like a gambler's pot. He stood before the charred remains of the Great Map and began to carve the world into pieces with his dagger. He granted the Silver Marches to Lord Berold, the Iron Hills to General Hestor, and dozens of other fertile provinces to cousins who had never seen a plough. He did not consult the tax rolls or the ancient boundaries; he simply gave, rewarding blood and loyalty with land he had not yet learned to govern. It was a grand, theatrical generosity—a victory for the Stormborn house, but a death sentence for the unity of the realm. Already, he was building a kingdom held together by debts and vanity, unaware that the men who cheered him today would be the first to bite when the gold ran dry.

Miles away, in the rebel camp, the news reached Maren Ashford.

Maren did not smile. He sat very still for a long time, then breathed a sigh of relief so deep it shook his frame. It was the sound of a man who had been standing on a gallows, only to watch the executioner walk away.

"He is leaving the fortress to live in a tent," Maren whispered to Hadrian, his voice trembling with disbelief. "He has thrown away the lock to the empire because he prefers the view from his porch."

Maren looked at the map—at the empty throne Kharic was abandoning.

"The Tiger is leaving the mountain to parade in the village," Maren said, a cold light entering his eyes. "From this day on, he is a guest in his own kingdom."

Maren didn't wait for the last of the smoke to clear. Even as he spoke, he was handing sealed letters to riders dressed as common peddlers. His movements were quick, surgical, stripped of the 'wastrel' lethargy he had worn at the banquet.

"Find Lord Berold," Maren commanded a scout, his voice a low, urgent rasp. "Remind him that the 'Count of Silver Marches' is a title Kharic wrote in ash, but a promise from Valdria is written in grain. And find the survivors of the Imperial Civil Service—the ones hiding in the cellars Kharic hasn't burnt yet. Tell them the Lord of Valdria has a use for their ledgers."

Maren turned back to the map. He looked at the gaps Kharic was leaving behind—the empty seats, the insulted lords, the abandoned roads. If Tiger was going home to show off his pelt; the Farmer shall stay behind to prepare the soil for a new, bloodier harvest.

Hadrian Narrowdale followed his lord in silence.

Kharic Stormborn would rule from Drumhold, surrounded by the ghosts of his ancestors. Maren Ashford would rule from wherever was most useful. The difference would prove decisive.

CHAPTER SEVENTEEN

THE CARVING

IN WHICH THE HEGEMON DIVIDES THE REALM AND MAREN ASHFORD ACCEPTS HIS EXILE

Gratitude is a tether of silk, easily broken by the weight of gold. Feed your hounds until they are strong enough to hunt the wolf, but leave them hungry enough to remember who holds the meat.

— The Principles of Statecraft

OF A SHEPHERD ON THE CREEDSEAT

The line of Iron Emperors had ended, but their steely ghost remained. In the centre of the ruined great hall, the Creedseat—that jagged mountain of black iron—sat empty, unaffected by the fire, a cold monument to a dead dynasty.

Behind the dais, a messenger from King Arion's court in Drumhold knelt in the soot, his fine silk tabard already stained with the greasy grey ash of Steelhaven. He held his breath, his forehead pressed against the charred floorboards, as he presented a scroll sealed with the intricate golden wax of the Celestine house.

Kharic took the scroll, his fingers blackened by the remains of the city he had just put to the torch. He unrolled it slowly. The parchment was scented with expensive lavender—a sickly sweet smell that fought against the stench of cold iron and charred bone.

"...to return the Mandate to its ancestral cradle," Kharic read aloud, his voice a low, jagged vibration. *"It is we, the King's righteous desire to move the seat of the Restoration to the Golden Palace of Steelhaven, that the people may once again see the glory of the Celestine Line reflected in the polished marble of the Capital."*

Kharic's eyes flicked further down the scroll. He paused, his grip tightening until the parchment crinkled.

"...And as sworn in our sacred covenant," Kharic continued, his voice dropping an octave, *"the Lord of Valdria, for his unmatched merit in the liberation of the realm, shall be duly invested as the King of the Central Plains, to rule the Heartland in our name."*

Kharic looked up from the letter. He looked at the shattered glass of the dome above him, through which the grey winter sky bled, those soot-covered pillars that had once been marble. He looked at the messenger, who was trembling so violently that the silver bells on his belt rang with a soft, pathetic chime.

Arion was writing from the safety of the east, still dreaming of silk and ceremonies, entirely unaware that the "Golden Palace" was now a hollow ribcage of blackened stone.

Kharic let out a short, sharp sneer—a sound like a blade catching on a bone. He tossed the lavender-scented scroll into a nearby pile of smouldering embers.

"The King wishes to reside in Steelhaven?" Kharic asked softly. For a moment, his face was unreadable, then a slow, terrifyingly pleasant smile spread across his lips—a tiger's grin.

"A righteous request," Kharic continued, his tone almost light. "A King should have his cradle, however scorched the earth may be. Go. Tell the Shepherd his wish is granted. Tell him that I shall announce the restoration of his capital and his royal seat at the Great Council, before every lord and king of the rebellion."

"Tell him, I will seal kings, messenger. I will seal many kings. I will carve this empire into so many thrones that the map will bleed ink." Kharic narrowed his eyes.

The messenger scrambled away, nearly tripping over his own finery in his relief. Kharic watched him go, the lavender-scented scroll still in his hand, before tossing it onto the cold, iron seat of the throne.

"Here, at least your hand that touched this paper touched the Creedseat."

OF HIS BLUEPRINT

Kharic was not a stupid man. He had spent his youth buried in the classic treatises of statecraft and the jagged annals of war, becoming, in his own way, a philosopher of power. Where others saw the Iron Empire as a triumph of absolute order, Kharic saw only a masterpiece of stagnation—a machine that had ground the spirit of the world into dust. He looked at the Creedseat, that high mountain of black iron, and saw not a throne, but a cage designed to turn noblemen into clerks, and clerks into the most meticulous of tyrants. To him, the realm's 'unification' under the Empire hadn't civilised the world; it had simply stifled it into a long, quiet surrender.

But his critique went deeper than the Iron Age. He looked back further, to the ancient Celestine dynasties—the legendary Old Order that preceded the Emperors. To the bards, that era was a lost paradise of chivalry; to Kharic, it was a structural failure. He believed the Old Order had collapsed not because it lacked virtue, but because it lacked a spine. It had been a body of eighteen limbs with no central heart to beat the rhythm of war. The ancient Kings had been High Priests of the sky who possessed the Mandate of Heaven but lacked the Scepter of Earth. Because there was no single Hegemon to command the world's steel and hold the leash of the armies, the kings and lords had turned upon one another, creating the very chaos that the Iron Emperors eventually quelled with their cruel, mechanical chains. To save the future, Kharic believed he had to become the guardian that the past had lacked.

His vision was dangerously ahead of its time: the Separation of the Mandate from the Sword. In Kharic's mind, the realm needed a Sovereign—a figure of pure, ancestral legitimacy who sat in the high gardens, performed the rites, and embodied the soul of the people. But that *Sovereign* must never touch the ledgers or the army. Beside him would stand the *Hegemon*—the arbiter, the guardian and the executor of the *Law*.

He sought to replace that self devouring machinery of the state with a living, breathing hierarchy of honour. Here are the three pillars of his noble, idealistic new world, drafted by the Hegemon himself.

I. The Ritual Sovereign: The Mandate of the Spirit

The King was to be of ancient lineage, and was to be the realm's symbol of High Order, a vessel of pure, ancestral legitimacy who existed above the grime of governance. He would be the Sovereign of the Spirit, tracking the celestial calendars, performing the high sacrifices, and bestowing titles with hands that remained unsoiled by the "dirty business" of war and coins. In Kharic's mind, the King was the sun—constant, radiant, and utterly untouchable—a moral compass meant to embody the soul of the people while the gritty realities of survival were handled by lesser, harder men. He was to be the Mandate of Heaven made flesh, kept "clean" so that the people would always have a dream to believe in.

II. The Hegemonic Arbiter: The Gavel of the Storm

Kharic decided to rule the Kings. He was to be the Gavel of Steel, the man who held the power so the Sovereign could hold the glory, ensuring that no single ruler could ever again grow powerful enough to become an Emperor. He would take the title of Hegemon—the Arbiter of the Sword—acting as the ultimate guardian of the status quo. By maintaining the realm's sole standing army under the permanent command of the Hegemon, he positioned himself as the storm that would descend upon any brother who dared to break the peace. If one king marched upon another king, it was not a matter for a courtroom, but for the Hegemon's justice.

III. The Covenant of Blood: The End of the Ink-Slingers

In his most defiant act, Kharic sought to abolish the "Web of Tax Collectors" that had strangled the old world. He loathed the central treasury, viewing the ledger as a more sinister weapon than the spear. In its place, he would establish the Covenant of Blood, where each King would pay a Tribute of honour—soldiers, grain, and horses—only when the realm faced a common threat. He operated on the fundamental belief that a man would fight a thousand times harder for a brother he loved and a land he owned than for a faceless tax bureau he feared. It was a trade of Ink for Oaths, a gamble that personal loyalty was a stronger mortar for an empire than the threat of a bailiff's knock.

The fatal oversight It was a cathedral of high principles built upon a foundation of shifting sand. In his quest to dismantle the machine of tyranny, Kharic had overlooked the quiet, tireless mathematics of the belly.

OF THE HEGEMON OVER KINGS AND EMPERORS

The night before the Great Council, Eldran Greymantle found Kharic by the high window of Summer Palace, looking out to the smoking ruins of Steelhaven at a distance. For nearly a hundred days, the Iron City had been a warning written in flame. From this height, the city looked like an open wound, the red glow of the embers pulsing like a dying heart.

"Emperor," Kharic whispered, the word sounding like a curse. "Emperor of Cheros. Lord of the World."

"You have earned the breath of it, my lord," Eldran said, stepping closer. "You broke the Iron at Stonedeer. You are the only man in that hall whose shadow reaches every corner of the realm. If you take the title tomorrow, the lords will kneel because they have no other choice. You could build a dynasty that mocks the one you burnt."

Kharic finally turned. The firelight from the window caught the hard, tragic lines of his face.

"My grandfather died in a hut in the marshes, dreaming of the old flags," Kharic said. "He didn't hate the Iron Emperors because they were cruel. He hated them because they were arrogant. They took the title *Emperor* to place themselves above the gods and the old kings. They turned free lords into slaves and history into a lie. I did not break their chains only to forge a heavier one for my own neck."

"My lord, noble ideals are poor mortar for a new house—" Eldran urged.

"If I take the crown I just shattered," Kharic's voice dropped into a register of cold, absolute conviction, "then every drop of Torian's blood was spilt only to change the name of the tyrant. I would rather be the man who restored eighteen kingdoms than the ghost who owned one. Let the kings have their crowns. I will be the Hegemon—the shield that ensures they never have to fear an Emperor again."

Eldran felt a chill that had nothing to do with the night air. It was the most noble thing Kharic had ever said. It was also the most foolish.

"And the taxes, my lord? The law? Who decides the boundaries when these eighteen brothers begin to bite one another?" Eldran asked.

"They will bring their problems to me," Kharic said, looking back at the map. "And I will judge. Not as a master, but as a father."

A father with a bloody sword, Eldran thought. Kharic was trying to purify the machine of empire by giving it a different name. He wanted the obedience of kingdoms without the 'sin' of the crown. He was but a King Arion with teeth—just as disconnected from the earth as the old puppet.

"And if goodwill fails, my lord?"

"Then they will remember why I am called the Storm," Kharic replied, his hand resting on his blade.

Eldran bowed his head, realizing the tragedy was already set. Kharic was trading the security of the future for the applause of his ancestors.

"As you wish, I will prepare the proclamation."

Eldran left him alone with his principles and his map, wondering which would burn first.

OF THE CARVING OF EIGHTEEN KINGDOMS

It was in the depth of winter when Kharic Stormborn summoned all the rebel lords to the Great Council at the Summer Palace.

While the rest of Steelhaven was a blackened skeleton, the Summer Palace remained an obscene miracle of preservation. To reach it, the lords had to ride through miles of "black snow"—falling ash that coated their furs and choked their horses—only to pass through a gate of polished white marble into a world where the fire had never touched.

The shock was physical. The air inside the palace walls didn't smell of burning mahogany and dead men; it smelt of blooming winter jasmine and expensive sandalwood. The lords of the rebellion, men who had lived in rain-soaked tents and slept on stone for years, found themselves walking on silk carpets so thick they silenced the clatter of their armoured boots. They stared at the ceiling-high mirrors of silvered glass, seeing their own haggard, soot-stained faces reflected against a backdrop of gold-leafed pillars and unfaded tapestries.

Every uncharred beam spoke of a reminder of the Empire's wealth, and every lord in that hall—from the highest King to the lowliest bandit—felt a sudden, sharp hunger. They hadn't just come to be free; they had come to possess this.

They came in their hundreds: kings and generals, nobles and warlords. They moved through the lush, heated galleries with a predatory stillness, their eyes darting from the moon-stone vases to the heavy silk hangings, expecting rewards and justice for their merits in having served the rebellion.

At the centre of it all, beneath a dome of glass that showed a sky clear of smoke, Kharic sat upon a temporary dais. He looked less like a liberator and more like the architect of a dream they were all afraid to wake up from.

Maren Ashford did not arrive alone. He entered the hall flanked by his inner circle and eight Marsh-guards—men who looked like dark stains against the palace's gold-leafed pillars. They stood in a tight, silent formation, their broad-bladed axes held at an angle that whispered of execution, not ceremony.

Maren walked through the gauntlet of Stormborn soldiers with a calmness, as the lords cheered with a toast of fine wine. He knew why he was safe today. Kharic had spent the morning weaving a tapestry of 'restored honour.' To kill Maren now, in the temple of his own new order, would be to burn that tapestry. Kharic was a man who would rather lose an empire than lose the argument that he was the most honourable man in it.

Eldran Greymantle watched from the side, his stomach churning.

"The Iron Creed is dead," Kharic announced from the great throne. "The world that existed before I drew my sword no longer exists. We have the obligation to create something better."

He paused, letting the words settle.

"Since King Arion is a true descendent of the House of the ancient Celestine Kings, he is now to proclaim his new title King Arion the Righteous, the King of Kings. All under heavens shall pledge loyalty to the him. King Arion is to hold court here at this Summer Palace. It is a place untouched by the fire, where he may look upon his realm without needing to rebuild a palace."

He turned to his guards. "Send a messenger to Drumhold, find the King and tell him this and embark on His Majesty's journey here. Order the scholars to write long poems about him. Make the people cheer for him. And tell him that I shall soon return."

The gathered lords, Maren included, exchanged glances of stunned disbelief, unable to comprehend a conqueror who viewed the crown not as the ultimate prize, but as a shackle to be discarded.

Everyone knew King Arion was merely a figurehead to rally the traditionalists into the Rebellion because of the harmless old man's distant relation of the ancient Aurelian kings and Cheros royalblood. But the devil, as always, was in the details.

Kharic Stormborn did not want a king. He wanted a mask.

"I have decided to restore the realm into the Old Eighteen Kingdoms, and many more Lords and Counts. Each of you will govern your own domains, subject only to my authority."

The lords knew in that moment that the war had not ended. It had merely changed players.

A murmur ran through the hall. Eighteen kingdoms, plus city-states meant that every significant lord would receive something. The tension in the room eased. Beside Maren, Roland Knox grinned, adjusting his sword belt.

"He's trapped, boss," Roland whispered, his voice a low, jagged rasp. "He hates your guts, but he's got the whole world watching. He has to give us the Heartland. The Covenant is the only thing keeping these eighteen bastards from turning on each other. If he robs us, he robs everyone's trust."

Markus Quillen stood on Maren's other side, his face pale but his eyes sharp behind his spectacles. He didn't look at Kharic; he looked at his ledger, his quill poised like a dagger.

"He must honour the King's word," Markus muttered, more to himself than Maren. "The Central Plains are the only provinces capable of feeding an army of our size. Kharic knows that if he pushes us to the fringes, he creates a famine we'll be forced to solve with steel. Even a Stormborn can't be that foolish. He'll give us the Heartland to keep us quiet."

"What title will you take, then?"

"The Hegemon, of Cheros and of the Realm" Kharic traced the borders of the old kingdoms on the map. "First among equals. The sword that protects the alliance, not the hand that crushes it." He looked up. "Kings keep their crowns, their lands, their dignity. Let them rule their own people in their own ways."

" All armies answer to me. All lands are divided by me." He glanced at the lords.

"To ensure peace," Kharic continued, his eyes scanning the crowd, "the Heartland surrounding the ruins of Steelhaven must be guarded by men who know the terrain."

He gestured to the three men standing in the shadows—the surrendered Iron generals: Jared Steelbane, Sylvanus, and Holten.

"I name you The Three Shields," Kharic declared. "You shall rule the lands of the old Ironhold. You will guard the ashes."

Kharic was giving the most strategic lands to the very enemies they had just defeated. Lord Berold's face went from purple to a ghostly white; he looked at Steelbane—a man he had spent three years trying to kill—and saw the traitor's hands already reaching for the map.

Kharic began to bestow the names of the other kingdoms, his voice gaining speed as he felt the mounting rage in the room. He was a man burning his bridges while he was still standing on them.

Then came the final blow.

"Maren Ashford."

The hall went silent. By rights, the man who entered the capital first should have been King of the Central Plains. Roland puffed out his chest, waiting for the title.

Kharic looked down from his seat, a cruel smile playing on his lips.

"The Lord of Valdria has shown a great fondness for the wet earth of the west. It seems fitting that he should remain where he is most comfortable."

Kharic unrolled the map and pointed to the desolate, mountain-ringed province on the far western edge—a jagged tooth of land trapped between the eternal snows and the Three Shields.

"I name you King of Westmarch. It is a rugged land, isolated and wild. But best of all, it includes your beloved Valdria. Since you rose from that very mud, you shall rightfully rule over it."

Roland's hand flew to the hilt of his sword. The veins in his neck bulged like cords. This was never a name of an old kingdom; it was a geography of despair. Westmarch was the realm's mountainous swamp, a jagged throat of land choked by impassable peaks and filled with bandits and poisonous pests that even the Iron Empire hadn't bothered to conquer fully. it was a prison sentence. Beside him, Markus went pale, staring at the map. He saw no cities, no trade routes, only the impassable mountains that would lock them in forever.

To get there, Maren would have to march through the lands of the Three Shields—his enemies. Once inside, the mountains would swallow him. He would be a king of mosquitoes and outlaws, locked behind a wall of Iron generals, forgotten by the world he had just helped to save.

"He's burying us alive," Roland hissed, the sound of his blade half-sliding from its scabbard a sharp, metallic warning in the hushed hall.

Even the crackle of torches sounded like bones breaking.

It was a blatant betrayal. To send the conqueror of Steelhaven out into the wilderness, to the boondocks was an insult so profound it demanded blood. All eyes turned to Maren. His generals were trembling with rage. The gathered lords held their breath, expecting an explosion—expecting Maren to demand the justice he had been promised.

"As I have suggested at our celebration, a kingdom in the west. Look at us, Maren," Kharic sneered, his voice dripping with contempt. "A peasant made king of the spear-carriers. How the world turns. May your House reign over a thousand years."

Roland took a step forward, a growl rising in his throat.

Maren placed a gentle hand on Roland's arm, stopping him.

Then, Maren smiled.

"The Westmarch," he said, his voice steady, carrying across the hushed hall. "I am honoured by the Hegemon's generosity."

OF THE COVENANT
OF ETERNAL PEACE

"Before we drink," Kharic said, his voice dropping into a ritualistic boom that echoed off the draped curtains, "we bind the world."

He drew his greatsword, its edge shimmering like trapped lightning. With a swift, practised motion, he drew the blade across his own palm. He held his hand over a silver basin, letting the heavy, crimson drops fall into the wine within.

"This is the Covenant of the Storm," Kharic announced. "We swear two oaths this day. First: that we shall hunt the remnants of the Iron Empire to the ends of the earth. No magistrate shall breathe; no fortress of the Shadowhand shall stand. We scour the metal from the soil until the world is clean."

He looked at the eighteen kings, his eyes burning with the fever of a prophet.

"Second: that there shall be Eternal Peace between these eighteen houses. The borders I have drawn are sacred. The blood in this bowl is the blood of brothers. If any king among you raises a sword against another, he is no longer a king—he is a traitor to the Covenant, and I, the Hegemon, shall be his executioner."

One by one, the lords stepped forward. They cut their hands. They added their life's blood to the basin. When it came to Maren, he did not hesitate. He felt the sting of the knife and watched his blood mingle with the men who had just robbed him of his victory.

Maren did not wait for the council's feast. As he walked from the marble gates of the Summer Palace, he felt the first flake of black snow touch his cheek—bitter, burnt, and real.

CHAPTER EIGHTEEN

THE ROAD TO WESTMARCH

IN WHICH A YOUNG OFFICER OFFERS ADVICE MAREN ASHFORD DID NOT ASK FOR, BUT DESPERATELY NEEDED

I am told that I am now the 'Queen of Westmarch.' It is a title that sounds less like a rank and more like a chronic respiratory condition. This is appropriate, as the local atmosphere is essentially a thick, grey soup that one must chew before swallowing.

My silk slippers have committed suicide; they are now indistinguishable from the peat. Meanwhile, Maren—my dear, industrious husband—looks as though he has finally found his natural habitat. He spent the afternoon in a state of near-erotic excitement discussing the 'load-bearing capacity of silt' with a man who appears to be made entirely of compost. I was promised a man of 'Destiny' and some 'Heavenly Mandate'; instead, I find I am married to a glorified gardener who treats a drainage ditch with more reverence than he ever gave the Imperial Seal.

— Fragments of the Diary of Lyra, Queen Consort of Westmarch

OF THE SOIL'S CHEMISTRY

The mountains were shedding their winter skin, but it was not a graceful transition. It was a violent, weeping thaw.

The air was a thick, freezing soup of mist and wood-smoke. Above the column, the ancient pines groaned under the weight of the last, wet snow of February. Every few miles, the silence of the high passes would be shattered by a sharp, bone-cracking *snap*—the sound of a hundred-year-old branch finally surrendering to the slush. Occasionally, a whole tree would lose its footing on the saturated slopes, tumbling into the ravines with a muffled, distant roar that sounded like the earth itself was sighing in exhaustion.

Below, the road had ceased to be a road. It was a river of grey slurry, a churned-up mess of half-melted ice and bottomless mud that seemed to possess a hungry, malicious intent.

Those newly made banners of the King of Westmarch, until recently vibrant and stiff with the wind of rebellion, now hung like sodden rags from their poles. The soldiers did not look at the horizon. They looked at the heels of the men in front of them, their boots making a wet, rhythmic thwack-slop that echoed the beating of a tired heart. They were no longer the liberators of the realm. They were an inconvenience being swept into a dark corner of the map.

Behind the vanguard, the "Royal Carriage"—a gilded relic Maren had insisted on bringing from the capital—groaned as its wheels sank axle-deep into the mire. Inside, the atmosphere was sharper than the wind outside.

Lady Lyra pulled back the silk curtain, only to be met by a wall of slate-grey mist and the smell of wet wool. She looked at her husband, who sat across from her, his face a map of exhaustion, his hands still stained with the grit of the road.

"And that white Seal, Maren?" Lyra asked, her voice a thin, cultivated blade. "The Spirit of Bryn. The only thing that separates a Sovereign from a common thief. Did you at least have the sense to pack the Mandate of Heaven before we were chased into the clouds?"

Maren didn't look up from his mud-caked boots. "Kharic has it. He liked the weight of it on his belt."

Lyra let out a jagged, bitter laugh. "He liked the weight? You broke the greatest city in the world, and you gave away the Mandate because it was *heavy*?"

"I gave him a target, Lyra," Maren said softly, finally meeting her eyes with that terrifying, peasant stillness. "Every lord in this realm is going to be staring at that white stone. While they are busy looking at the sun, they won't notice the man standing in the shadows. I'd rather have a sharp shovel than a heavy stone."

He looked back out the window at the long, dejected line of his men.

"Do you feel it, Maren?" Lyra asked, her voice a low, cultivated rasp. "That is the sound of the world forgetting you."

Maren didn't turn his head. His eyes were fixed on the line of the hills. "The world has a short memory, Lyra. That is its only virtue."

"Virtue?" She let out a jagged, bitter laugh. "Look at you, Maren. First you were just a headman of Marsh. Then the 'Lord' of Valdria. And King of *what* now? What's clinging to your boots? Bushes and quags?"

She leaned forward, her eyes bright with malice.

"What is your next title, *Prophet of the Peat? Emperor of Valdria*? With that cesspit village as your capital, I bet? Oh, yes, I can see it now—'*The Rise of Valdria*'. The bards will sing of how you conquered a bog."

She spat the words out like they were spoiled wine.

"It's a joke, Maren. A rise from the gutter into a deeper pothole. Look at this place! It's no kingdom; it's a drowning accident. *You* were the man who broke that Dragon Gate, that kid surrendered to *you*, and now you are a chieftain leading a trail of wodewoses into a swamp. What are you rising towards? A better class of mud?"

She leaned out further, the spray of the road hitting her pale face. "Kharic didn't give you a kingdom. He gave you a cage with no bars. He gave you a title so heavy it will drown us both, and you... you accepted it with a thank you."

Maren finally pulled his pony closer to the window. His face was a map of exhaustion, but his eyes held that terrifying, peasant stillness that always made her blood run cold.

"Kharic Stormborn gave me what he thinks is a grave," Maren said softly. "He understands the geometry of power, Lyra, but he doesn't understand the chemistry of the soil."

"And what is the chemistry, my Lord of Toads?"

"In the capital, everything is iron and stone. It breaks. But mud... mud swallows. It waits. It adapts." Maren looked back at the long, dejected line of his men. "They aren't cattle, Lyra. They're seeds. We are going to a place where no one will watch us, no one will tax us, and no one will expect us to survive. Let the world laugh at the 'Rise of Valdria.' I'd rather they laugh than look too closely."

Lyra stared at him, looking for the man she had married in the gilded halls of the capital, but she found only a stranger with dirt beneath his fingernails and a crown of rain.

"You're a fool, Maren Ashford," she whispered, closing the curtain. "You're taking us to a place where even the bog-wights are hungry."

"Then we shall feed them," Maren muttered to the grey wind.

OF WORDS UNKEPT

The Westmarch was the most remote, most impoverished, most strategically worthless territory in the entire realm. It was cut off from civilisation by impassable mountains, accessible only through narrow passes that could be blocked with minimal effort. It was, in every meaningful sense, a prison—a place where a man could be sent to disappear without the inconvenience of actually executing him.

And Maren Ashford, by any reasonable measure, deserved better. His forces had captured Steelhaven—had been the first rebel troops to enter the capital, had accepted the surrender of the imperial garrison while Kharic was still parading his victory over the remaining Iron troops after Jared Steelbane's surrender. By rights, he should have received one of the prime territories: the rich plains of the central provinces, or the prosperous cities of the south.

Instead, he was being exiled to a frozen wasteland.

"You should have challenged him," Roland Knox growled. "You had troops in the city. You could have—"

"Could have what? Started another war? Challenged Kharic to single combat?" Maren shook his head. "He wanted me to protest. He wanted an excuse to strip me of what little he was offering. By accepting gracefully, I've denied him that excuse."

"But the Westmarch is worthless! It can barely support a village, let alone a kingdom. You'll starve within—"

"I'll survive." Maren's voice sounded amused. "I've been surviving my whole life, Roland. I survived being a farmer's son in a world ruled by nobles. I survived the conscription that was supposed to be my death sentence. I survived the rebellion that should have killed me a dozen times over. The Westmarch is just another obstacle."

"And Kharic? You're just going to let him insult you like this? Let him treat you like a—"

"Kharic has shown everyone exactly what he is." Maren's smile faded, replaced by something harder. "He's shown them that he rewards loyalty with contempt, that he punishes success with exile, that he sees allies as threats rather than assets. Every lord in that hall watched him humiliate me, and every lord in that hall is now wondering if they'll be next."

He rose from his seat and walked to the window, looking out over the city he would soon be leaving.

"Kharic has won the war. But he's already losing the peace. He's making enemies of the people who should be his closest allies. He's showing everyone that his word means nothing, that his gratitude is worthless, that serving him brings only danger."

"And how does that help you?"

"It helps me because I'm going to do the opposite." Maren turned back to face his advisors. "I'm going to go to the Westmarch, and I'm going to build something there. I'm going to treat my people fairly, reward my followers generously, keep every promise I make. And when Kharic's kingdom starts to crumble—when his allies turn against him, when his subjects rebel, when everything he's built on fear and vengeance falls apart—I'm going to be there. Ready."

"Ready for what?"

His smirk won him followers and enemies in equal measure.

"Ready to pick up the pieces."

OF BURNING THE BRIDGES

The march west took five weeks.

When the last soldier had crossed the Great Gorge—the

only chokepoint connecting Westmarch to the rest of the world—Maren stopped his horse. He looked back at the wooden trestle road clinging to the cliffside. To the soldiers, this road was the only umbilical cord connecting them to the civilization they had just left behind.

"How do we defend it?" Maren asked, his voice tight with the stress of exile. "If Kharic changes his mind, he can march his iron cavalry straight into our bedrooms."

"We fortify the heights," Roland Knox suggested. "We turn the pass into a slaughterhouse."

"Kharic has more men to lose than we have arrows," Markus Quillen muttered. "A fortification is just a tomb we build for ourselves."

"Then we burn it."

The voice came from the rear, sharp and insolent. A young, lanky officer named Xander stepped forward. He stood there with a piece of straw between his teeth, looking at the Great Gorge with a strange, detached clarity.

"Burn it?" Maren rounded on him, his face reddening. "This road took the Empire thirty years to build. It is our only way back. You want me to break my own legs and call it a strategy?"

"The road is not a path, my lord. It is a leash," Xander said, his voice flat. "Kharic is a wolf. As long as that road stands, he knows you are thinking of the return. He will watch you. He will fear you. And eventually, he will kill you."

Xander stepped closer, ignoring the dark looks from the other generals.

"Burn the road. Show the Hegemon that the King of Westmarch has no ambition but the mud. If you destroy the way back, he will turn his back on you to fight the other kings. And while his back is turned... you grow your claws."

Maren let out a harsh, mocking laugh.

"You're a fool, Xander. You're asking me to become a prisoner in my own kingdom." Maren turned to his guards, his temper flaring. "Strip this boy of his rank. If he loves the mud so much, he can spend the rest of the march counting grain sacks in the rearguard. Get him out of my sight."

Xander didn't argue. He didn't beg. He simply spat the straw onto the ground, gave a curt, mocking bow, and walked away into the mountain mist, his silhouette disappearing among the supply wagons.

OF REGRET

Silence fell over the cliff edge, broken only by the whistling wind. Maren was still fuming, staring at the path Xander had taken.

"Arrogant brat," Maren muttered. "Counting rice is too good for him."

"Actually," Hadrian Narrowdale said softly, stepping forward.

The strategist had waited until the young officer was gone before speaking. He looked at the road, then at Maren, his expression profoundly serious.

"The boy is a genius, Maren. Every word he said was correct."

"Hadrian, not you too—"

"Think, my lord," Hadrian interrupted, his voice gaining iron. "Kharic is consumed by pride. To him, burning the road is not just a tactical move—it is an act of absolute, public submission. It is the ultimate white flag. It is the only thing that will make him feel safe enough to forget us."

Hadrian pointed into the abyss.

"By destroying the bridge, we buy the one thing we need most: Time. If we keep the road, we invite a siege. If we burn it, we win a year of peace to build an empire Kharic won't see coming until it's at his gates."

Maren looked at the road. The anger in his eyes was replaced by a slow, cold realization. He looked back at the supply train where Xander had vanished, but the boy was already gone.

"I've made a mistake, haven't I?" Maren asked quietly.

"A significant one," Markus Quillen added, his voice filled with a sudden, sharp anxiety. "That boy... I've been watching his ledgers. He doesn't just count grain, Maren. He sees the rhythm of the entire world."

Maren sighed—the sigh of a man who realised he had just thrown away a diamond thinking it was glass.

OF THE ABYSS AND THE ASHES

"Burn it," Maren ordered. "Burn the road."

When the flames took hold of the oil-soaked timbers, the sound was not a crackle but a scream. As the first massive section of the trestle road plummeted into the mist-choked abyss, the echo rattled the canyon for a long time, as if the very bones of the earth were shuddering at the finality of the act.

Lady Lyra stood by the door of the gilded carriage, her fingers gripping the damp velvet of the frame so hard her knuckles turned the colour of bone. The orange glare of the conflagration washed over her pale face, reflecting in her eyes like a dying sun. She didn't look away as the wood groaned and snapped. To her, this wasn't a tactical maneuver; it was a public execution of her past.

She reached down and touched the hem of her silk gown, now heavy with the grey slurry of the road and stained beyond repair. For months, she had clung to the hope that this was a temporary detour—a brief, muddy nightmare before they returned to the chandeliers of Steelhaven. But as the bridge fell, she realised that Maren hadn't just burnt a road; he had burnt the only version of her that she recognised.

"Look at it, Lyra," Maren said, his voice reaching her through the roar of the fire. He didn't look back at her; he was staring into the West.

"I am looking," she whispered, her voice barely audible over the snapping timber. "You've finally done it, Maren. You've traded the stars for the mud."

She didn't wait for his answer. She stepped back into the dark interior of the carriage and pulled the curtains shut, choosing the suffocating silence of her cage over the sight of her husband's victory.

Roland Knox stood at the cliff's edge, the orange light dancing across his heavy plate. He was a man built for the charge, and a charge required a path. He watched the only umbilical cord to the world turn to ash, his knuckles whitening on the haft of his warhammer. He didn't speak, but his eyes—usually narrowed in search of an enemy—were wide with a sudden, raw reverence for the wilderness they now called home.

As the torches were thrown and the gigantic ancient timber structure began to crash into the abyss, Markus Quillen did not watch the fire. He turned his horse and galloped towards the rearguard, calling Xander's name into the dark.

But the rearguard was empty. The boy had taken his pack and vanished into the moonlit mountains.

Across the gorge, on the lands they were now abandoning, three sets of eyes likely watched the rising smoke. The Three Shields—Steelbane and his fellow shields—were already at their posts, silent jailors in a kingdom of ash. This fire was Maren's signal to them: *I have entered the cage, and I have melted the lock from the inside.*

Markus looked at the vast, dark wilderness of the West. He felt a sudden, sober premonition. The road to the East was gone, but the man who knew how to lead them back was gone too.

"Find him," Markus whispered to the wind, a sharp, cold anxiety cutting through his voice. "I don't care if you have to ride through the night or turn over every stone in the West-march. Do not let that boy reach the border with hatred in his heart. If he leaves us now, this abyss we just created will one day become our grave."

The wind swallowed his words, and for a moment, the only sound was the crackling of the dying bridge. Markus looked at the vast, dark wilderness, feeling the weight of the silence. But then, the silence broke. It wasn't the sound of an army, but the heavy, rhythmic thud of a single pair of boots against the freezing stone.

OF THE GHOST IN THE MIST

The smoke from the burning bridge was still thick enough to taste when a shadow detached itself from the ancient pines.

Roland Knox leveled his warhammer, his breathing heavy in the cold air. "Halt! Show yourself!"

The shadow didn't halt. It moved with a slow, heavy confidence that seemed to vibrate through the very rock of the cliff. Out of the slate-grey mist stepped a man who looked less like a human and more like a fragment of the mountain that had decided to go for a walk. He was a head taller than Roland, his shoulders like oak beams, his beard a matted catastrophe of frost and peat.

He smelt of wet earth, bog-iron, and the bedrock loyalty of a man who had waited six months for this moment.

"I heard," the giant rumbled, his voice sounding like boulders grinding together at the bottom of a well, "that the Hegemon gave my brother a cage."

Maren pushed past his guards. He didn't look like a King in that moment; he looked like a man seeing his own soul reflected in the dark. "Beric."

Beric Durrant grinned, revealing teeth that looked like they had been sharpened on river stones. He stepped forward and gripped Maren's forearm—not a courtly greeting, but the "Marsh-brother's" latch.

"The 'Three Shields' are watching the road, Maren," Beric said, gesturing with a massive thumb towards the abyss behind them. "But they're looking at the empty sky. They aren't looking at the deep ways. My boys have been in these mountains since the first snows. We've cleared the bandits from the Oakhaven Pass. We've mapped the hidden granaries in the bogs. We've even started the drainage on the Valdrian dikes."

Beric leaned in, his eyes bright with a cold, predatory joy.

"You're not alone in the mud, headman. I brought five thousand 'rats' with me. Farmers who forgot how to fear, and veterans who forgot how to lose. We've been waiting for you to close the door."

Beric looked at the flaming ruins of the bridge, then back at the long, shivering line of Maren's men. He let out a low, jagged laugh.

"Kharic thinks he gave you a grave. He doesn't realise he just gave us the only fortress in the world with no back door."

Maren felt the warmth of the grip, the solid, unmoving weight of the giant beside him. Lyra's words about the " Rise of Valdria" being a joke suddenly felt thin and fragile. Kharic had the Mandate, and Kharic had the Seal, but Maren had the man who knew how to turn a swamp into an anvil.

"Marsh-brothers," Maren whispered, returning the grip.

"Until the end," Beric promised.

Neither of them looked at the silk cord hanging from Maren's belt, or the shadows that would one day turn this reunion into a tragedy.

For now, in the freezing mist of Westmarch, the mud was finally beginning to hold.

EPILOGUE
THE KING IN THE WATER

Kharic is a violent boy, yes, but he understands the geometry of power. He gives me the title, and I give him the blood. It's a perfect circle, really. A man of my lineage provides the soul, while a man of his... utility... provides the hands. It's quite sophisticated, if you have the mind for it.

—From the unfinished memoirs of Arion the Righteous, The Geometry of Sovereignty

The carving was done. The lords had departed to their new kingdoms. The fires of Steelhaven had finally burnt themselves out, leaving only the soot-stained skeleton of an empire to be claimed by the winter wind.

King Arion of Cheros, the Righteous—the newly anointed "King of Kings"—travelled northwest towards his designated capital.

He moved with a small, ceremonial escort, his heart heavy with the realisation that he was being sent to a gilded cage in the countryside. But at least, he told himself, the war was over. At least the Stormborn had kept his word about the crown.

"A tragedy, really," Arion remarked, his breath misting in the cold air. "The boy has the arm of a god, but the soul of a vandal. Did you see the West Barrier Gate as we passed? All that white marble from the Bryn quarries, scorched black. He could have spared the Great Hall. One cannot hold a proper coronation in a charcoal pit."

He turned to the lead oarsman, looking for a sympathetic ear.

"He thinks he is being grand, I suppose. 'The Storm.' But a true Sovereign knows that you do not burn the foundations of the house you intend to live in. Such a waste of perfectly good masonry. Don't you agree?"

The oarsman did not answer. He didn't even look up. He simply signalled the others.

They rowed in silence.

At nightfall, the procession halted at Coldmirror Lake, a black, glacial body of water nestled in the jagged foothills that marked the final border before the Westmarch. The water was unnaturally still, reflecting the grey sky like a sheet of polished steel. To the west, the mountains of Maren's new kingdom loomed like a wall of dark, indifferent teeth.

A group of riders met the procession. They wore no banners, no sigils of the Stormborn or any known house. They were draped in the rugged, mud-stained furs of mountain men, their faces hidden behind heavy, frost-rimmed cowls.

"The bridge ahead has collapsed under the thaw, Your Majesty," the lead rider said, his voice a muffled, gravelly rasp. "The way is blocked for carriages. But there is a barge waiting to take you across the narrows. It is the only path left before the snows return."

Arion, frail and trusting, stepped onto the flat-bottomed boat with only two attendants. He gathered his heavy ceremonial robes—embroidered with the golden phoenix of his ancestors—and looked down at the water. He saw his own reflection staring back: a king, crowned and glorious.

"It has been a peaceful day," Arion remarked, his breath misting in the cold air. "The gods smile upon our journey."

The oarsmen did not answer. They rowed in silence until they reached the centre of the lake, where the water turned from blue to absolute black, indicating the crushing depth beneath. Then, the oars stopped. The silence of the mountains was absolute.

"Why do we stop?" the old King asked, a tremor of fear finally cracking his voice.

The lead man stood up. He did not bow. He reached into the bottom of the boat and lifted a heavy iron anchor. It was rusted, ugly, and terribly solid—a brutal contrast to the King's silks. He stepped towards the King, the iron chain rattling like a serpent across the wood.

"Wait! I am the Sovereign! I am the Righteous!" Arion stumbled back, his golden robes catching on the rough timber. "Who sent you? Is it the Hegemon? I have his word!"

"The Hegemon?" the man laughed, a dry, hollow sound that seemed to come from the depths of the lake itself. He grabbed Arion by the throat, forcing the old man to his knees. "The Hegemon is a dreamer. But our master—the Lord of Valdria—is a man who knows the value of a clean slate."

Arion's eyes widened. "Maren? No... he wouldn't..."

"He sends his regards from the West," the man hissed. "He says the mud is getting hungry for a better class of blood."

With a brutal, clinical efficiency, he clamped the iron shackle around Arion's thin ankle. The metal was colder than the lake. Arion looked towards the western peaks—the very place Maren Ashford was currently marching his army—and saw only the indifferent mist.

"For the Lord of Valdria!" the man shouted, his voice echoing off the cliff walls.

He shoved the heavy iron mass over the side.

For a second, the chain pulled tight. Arion screamed—a thin, high sound that was cut short as the weight jerked him off his feet. His golden robes, meant to display his majesty, now acted as a shroud. The silk filled with water, dragging the "King of Kings" into the black heart of the lake.

There was a splash. A frantic struggle of bubbles. Then, the water returned to glass.

The men in the boat watched the surface until the ripples faded. The reflection of the King was gone, replaced only by the grey, empty sky.

"It is done," the leader said. He did not reach for a seal or a letter. He simply signalled the oarsmen to turn the boat towards the shadows of the shore. "Leave the Westmarch badge on the landing. Let the escort find it when the sun goes down."

He looked at the dark water one last time, his expression unreadable behind the cowl.

"Tell the world," he whispered to the wind, "that the era of the Shepherd has ended, and the era of the Mud has begun."

The boat disappeared into the mist, leaving the King of Kings at the bottom of the lake at the foot of that vast, mountain-locked basin—a world of fog and fertile mud that would now be hunted for his murder."

APPENDIX I
TALES OF THE COUNTLESS

History is a ledger written in the blood of the many to honour the names of the few. These fragments are the marginalia of the war—the records of those who lived, starved, and survived while the Great Men played for thrones. One sought renown; another, a crust of bread; all sought a world that had not yet turned to ash.

OF THE EARTH

THE UNNAMED MOTHER

She never knew her name would be remembered.

She was a farmer's wife from a village that doesn't appear on any map—a woman of some thirty years of age, with three children and a husband who had been conscripted into the Imperial army five years ago and never returned. She survived as peasant women had always survived: through labour, through endurance, through the grim determination to keep her children alive one more day.

Then the war came to her village.

It began with soldiers—not Imperial soldiers, but rebels, men who wore the badges of the southern resistance and spoke of liberation and freedom. They requisitioned food from the village stores, took the livestock that had been carefully hoarded against the winter, promised to repay everything when victory was achieved.

Victory never came—at least not for her village. The rebels moved on; the Imperial response arrived a week later. Soldiers who wore different badges but behaved much the same way: requisitioning, confiscating, punishing anyone suspected of collaboration with the enemy.

When the smoke cleared, her home was ashes. Her eldest son was dead, killed trying to protect the family's last pig. Her two remaining children clung to her skirts, too traumatised to cry.

Years later, a scholar collecting testimonies from the war years would find her in a refugee camp near the southern border.

"What do you remember most?" the scholar asked her. "From those years?"

She thought before she answered.

"The hunger," she said at last. "The cold. The look in my children's eyes when they asked me why the soldiers were burning our home, and I had no answer to give them." She paused. "The lords fought their war, and we paid the price. That's what I remember."

"Do you hate them? The lords, the rebels, all those who made the war?"

"Hate takes energy. I don't have energy to spare on hate." She smiled thinly. "I'm too busy surviving. The lords make their decisions, the armies march back and forth, the great events of history unfold. And we survive. It's not much, but it's what we have."

THORNBURY: THE OLD FARMER

When the war began, Thornbury was seventy years old. Three times in his memory, armies had marched through his village. He had no use for politics, no interest in ideology. All he wanted was to tend his fields and die in peace.

But the war gave him no such choice. When the armies came this time, they came with an offer: join us, or refuse and face the consequences. Thornbury chose to fight. Not because he expected victory, but because his sons were fighting, and he couldn't let them face it alone.

He survived the war, against all probability. He lived to see the victory celebrations, to witness the establishment of the new order, to return to his village and find it still standing.

"Was it worth it?" his grandson asked him once, years later.

Thornbury considered the question for a long time. "I don't know," he said at last. "The lords who rule us now seem much like the lords who ruled us before. The taxes are different, but they're still taxes. The soldiers are different, but they're still soldiers."

"Then why did you fight?"

"Because sometimes you have to." The old man looked out at his fields—green again, productive again, proof that life goes on regardless of who sits on which throne. "Because there was a moment when I had to choose, and I chose the side that seemed... better."

"Was it better?"

Thornbury smiled—a weary, knowing smile. "Ask me again in twenty years. Maybe by then we'll know for certain."

THE UNNAMED SOLDIER

He had a name once. But he lost it somewhere in the war.

He had enlisted young, driven by the recruiters' promises of glory. Instead, he had found mud, blood, and endless tedium. When the rebellion came, he found himself on the losing side—because that was the uniform he happened to be wearing.

At Stonedeer, he was captured. The enemy commander—a young lord named Maren—offered the prisoners a choice: join us, or face execution. Most chose to join.

So the nameless soldier became a rebel. He wore their colours, marched under their banners, fought against the men who had once been his comrades. It was strange, at first—the disorientation of changing sides. But eventually, it became normal. Soldiers adapt, or they die.

In the peace that followed, he was given a small parcel of land. He married, raised children, grew old in the quiet obscurity of his duty.

His grandchildren sometimes asked about the war. He told them sanitised versions—heroes and villains, battles won and enemies defeated—but never the truth. Never the screaming. Never the smell of blood. Never the faces of men he had killed who looked no different from men he had served beside.

Some truths are too heavy for children to bear. And some truths, he had learned, are too heavy for anyone.

PIP: THE SCAVENGER

After the battles, the scavengers came.

They always did. Farmers from nearby villages, refugees from cities that no longer existed, the desperate who had learned that dead men have no use for their possessions. They crept onto the field in the grey hours before dawn, when the soldiers were too exhausted to post proper guards.

The boy was twelve years old. His name was Pip, and he had not eaten in three days.

Tonight, he was looking for boots.

His own had worn through weeks ago. The mud of the battlefield squelched between his bare toes as he picked his way among the bodies, avoiding the groans of the wounded, ignoring the stench that would stay in his nostrils for years.

He found a soldier whose feet were roughly his size. The man was dead—probably—his chest pierced by something sharp and final. Pip knelt beside him and began unlacing the boots.

The dead man's eyes opened.

"Water," he rasped. "Please. Water."

Pip froze. He had a waterskin—half-full, precious—tied to his belt. The dying man's eyes were fixed on it with the terrible intensity of ultimate thirst.

Neither of them moved.

Then Pip untied the waterskin and held it to the soldier's lips. He watched the man drink—watched the convulsive swallowing, the momentary peace that washed over the ruined face.

"Thank you," the soldier whispered. "Thank you. I... I have a son. Your age. Tell him... tell him his father died..."

The words trailed off. The eyes went blank.

Pip finished unlacing the boots. They fit well enough.

He never learned the soldier's name. He never delivered any message. The son—if there was a son—would never know what happened here, in the mud and blood of a battlefield that would be ploughed under within the year.

But as he walked away, his feet warm for the first time in months, the boy felt a strange grief. For the man whose boots he wore. For all the men who lay on this field, having died for causes they barely understood.

The war went on, and the great men continued their struggle for crowns and glory. And the boy survived. That was what the powerless did. They survived.

OF THE MINDS

FRAGMENTS FROM ELDRAN'S SECRET JOURNAL

Recovered from a locked cedar chest in the ruins of the Summer Palace. The ink is smudged with what appears to be wine—or salt water.

"Tonight, the Hegemon spoke of his 'Three Pillars' as if they were etched in the firmament. He looked at me with those eyes of trapped lightning, expecting a reflection of his own fire. I gave him a bow and a smile, but my hand shook as I held the candle.

He wants to build a world of heroes, but heroes are like stars—they are beautiful to look at, but they provide no warmth to the man shivering on the ground.

Kharic's first error is the Sovereign in Silk. He believes that by keeping Arion or his heirs 'pure' and 'untouched,' he preserves the soul of the realm. He is wrong. Power is not a relic to be kept in a velvet box; it is a living, predatory thing. By denying Arion the ledgers and the coins, he has not made the 'King of Kings' holy—he has made him desperate. A desperate man with a high title is a seed of rot. Arion will soon realise that the incense of the Summer Palace does not fill a stomach, and he will begin to trade his 'ancestral legitimacy' to the highest bidder behind the Hegemon's back.

His second error is his own role as the Hegemonic Arbiter. Kharic wishes to be a 'Father' to eighteen kings. But he forgets that a father's authority rests on the fact that the children cannot leave the house. In this new world, the 'children' have their own walls, their own spears, and their own hungers. When the first dispute over a border or a water-right reaches the Summer Palace, Kharic will be forced to strike one of his 'brothers' to save the peace. In that moment, the illusion of the Arbiter will vanish, and the lords will see only what they have always feared: an Emperor who refuses to wear the mask.

His final error—the one that will drown us all—is the Covenant of Blood. He has abolished the 'Web of Scribes' because he loathes the coldness of the ink. He thinks that Oaths are a stronger mortar than Taxes.

It is a noble thought, but a foolish one. Oaths rely on memory, and memory is the first thing to fail when the crops wither. A tax-clerk is a nuisance, but he is a predictable nuisance. He ensures that when the North freezes, the South provides. By cutting the 'ink-slingers' out of his empire, Kharic has performed a miracle: he has created a body without a nervous system. He will not know the realm is dying until the limbs start falling off.

I see the way he looks at me now. My silences are becoming too loud for him. My 'prudence' is starting to taste like 'disloyalty' in his mouth. He is a man of the Storm, and a storm does not want a mirror; it wants an echoing thunder in its praise.

I write these words because I can no longer say them. I fear that the day is coming when the Hegemon will look at his oldest friend whom he call *Father*, and see not a counsellor, but a crack in his cathedral. And when that day comes, I know which of us the Storm will choose to break first."

MARKUS QUILLEN: THE ADMINISTRATOR'S ORIGIN

Long before he became the most powerful administrator in the realm, Markus Quillen was a junior clerk in the Imperial tax bureau. He had chosen the position not out of love for the Empire, but because it was the only path available to a bright young man with no family connections.

Before the examinations, he had been trained in the militia like most boys who could not afford exemption: spear-drills at dawn, bruised knuckles, the dull endurance of formation marching. He learned how to hold a line, how to strike without flair, how to keep his breathing even when the man beside him panicked.

But when the Empire offered him ink instead of iron, he took it without hesitation. Violence was immediate, and therefore honest. Administration was slower, quieter—and it lasted.

For fifteen years, Markus had served faithfully. He had collected taxes, maintained records, and compromised his principles in a thousand small ways. Then came the incident at Millbrook.

He was sent to seize the last seed grain from a starving village. The regulations were clear. But standing in the mud, looking at the hollow faces of the farmers, Markus refused.

He fled south, carrying nothing but the clothes on his back and the skills in his mind. When he encountered Maren Ashford's growing movement, he recognised immediately what it lacked: organisation.

Markus built the administrative apparatus that made victory possible. He designed the supply systems, the communication networks, the financial structures.

"Administration is war by other means," he once wrote. "Every bushel of grain that reaches our soldiers is a victory; every message that arrives on time is a triumph. The battles are dramatic, but the logistics are decisive."

THE SIEGE OF COLDWATER: MARKUS QUILLEN'S CRUELTY

But Markus Quillen was not merely an administrator. In the

fourth year of the war, he proved he could be as ruthless as any general.

The fortress of Coldwater had resisted siege for three months. Its commander, Lord Tarkus the Younger—son of the man who had crucified the villagers at Gallows-Cross—had supplies to last two years. The rebel army was bleeding men to attrition and disease. Something had to change.

Markus studied the fortress. He studied its water supply.

The Coldwater River ran through an underground channel, providing the garrison with unlimited fresh water.

"We can't poison it," Roland Knox had said, when Markus raised the possibility. "The channel is too deep, the flow too fast."

"I don't intend to poison it," Markus replied. "I intend to redirect it."

For six weeks, using miners and engineers, he dug a new channel that would divert the river away from Coldwater. When the diversion was complete, he gave the order to open it.

By the third week, the garrison was rationing. By the fourth week, men were dying of thirst.

Lord Tarkus sent an envoy to negotiate.

"Surrender unconditionally," Markus told the envoy, "or watch your men die one by one."

The envoy's face went white.

"Your commander," Markus continued, his voice as flat as a tax assessment, "crucified sixty-three people in Gallows-Cross. Including a seven-year-old girl named Bird, who sang beautifully. I have decided to give him exactly as much mercy as he gave her."

Coldwater surrendered the next day. Lord Tarkus was captured and executed.

When Maren heard what Markus had done, he summoned his administrator.

"Did you have to?" Maren asked. "There were other ways—"

"Other methods would have cost us two thousand more men," Markus interrupted. "Men with families. I traded the comfort of our enemies' deaths for the lives of our soldiers." He paused. "If that makes me a monster, then I am a monster. But I am a monster who serves you, and our monsters need to be more effective than their monsters."

Maren weighed this. Then he nodded.

"Don't tell me about it next time," he said. "I need to think we're better than them."

"You won't hear about it," Markus agreed. "But it will happen again. Because that is what administration requires."

It was a truth that the songs rarely mentioned. But it was the foundation upon which everything else was built.

HADRIAN NARROWDALE: THE DIPLOMAT'S BURDEN

The man who would become known as Hadrian Narrowdale was born in the service of the old Celestine kings. Bearing the fallen kingdom Narrowdale's name, his family had survived the Iron conquest by bending the knee, and Hadrian had learned the subtle arts of negotiation at his father's side.

By thirty, he was an accomplished Imperial diplomat. But he found himself using his skills to maintain a system of oppression—persuading conquered peoples to accept their subjugation, negotiating treaties that favoured Imperial interests at the expense of justice.

When the rebellion came, Hadrian saw a chance to use his abilities for something he actually believed in.

In the rebel camp, he found his true calling. The cause needed a voice. It needed a negotiator who could forge alliances and reconcile factions. But he also provided something else: a conscience.

"The difference between a revolution and a coup," he told Maren once, "is what happens after you win. A coup replaces one tyrant with another; a revolution changes the rules of the game. We can win every battle and still lose the war if we forget what we're actually fighting for."

THE COALITION OF VIPERS: HADRIAN'S MASTERPIECE

But diplomacy, Hadrian knew, was not always about ideals. Sometimes it was about destruction.

In the sixth year of the war, Maren faced an impossible situation. Three major warlords—Lord Varen of the Iron Mountains, Lord Cassius of the Coastal Province, and Lady Vermillion of the Western Reaches—had formed an alliance against him. Individually, each was manageable. Together, they commanded armies that outnumbered Maren's forces two to one.

"We cannot fight them all at once," Roland Knox reported. "If they coordinate their attack, we will be overwhelmed."

"Then we ensure they do not coordinate," Hadrian said, his voice carrying the quiet certainty of already having seen the outcome. "Division is cheaper than battle."

He travelled to each of the three camps, ostensibly as an envoy seeking peace.

To Lord Varen, he revealed that Lady Vermillion had been corresponding secretly with Maren, offering to betray the alliance. He produced letters as evidence, beautifully forged by artisans Hadrian had cultivated over years.

To Lord Cassius, he revealed that Lord Varen was planning

to assassinate both of his allies. He had intercepted messages —also forged—that laid out the plan in detail.

To Lady Vermillion, he revealed that both Varen and Cassius considered her the weak link, the one they would sacrifice first.

None of it was true. All of it was believable.

The Coalition of Vipers collapsed within a month. Lord Cassius attacked Lord Varen preemptively. Lady Vermillion withdrew her forces. Lord Varen, fighting a war on two fronts, sent desperate messages to Maren offering to switch sides.

Hadrian accepted his surrender graciously. Then he arranged for certain damaging documents to be "discovered" by Lady Vermillion—documents that proved Varen had been working with Maren from the beginning. She attacked Varen's weakened forces, destroying what remained of his army.

By the time the dust settled, two of the three warlords were dead—killed by each other—and the third had surrendered unconditionally.

"How'd you know it'd work?" Maren asked.

"I knew them," Hadrian replied simply. "I knew their fears, their ambitions, their suspicions. I simply gave their suspicions... evidence."

"You destroyed three armies without drawing a sword."

"Words are more dangerous than swords, my lord. A sword can only kill one man at a time. The right words can kill thousands." Hadrian sounded utterly devoid of pride. "That is why you pay me."

Maren studied his advisor. "Ever think," he asked, "what happens if someone uses your tricks on me?"

"Every day," Hadrian replied honestly. "That is why I make sure you never give me reason to use them in that direction."

It was not a threat. It was simply the truth.

BEROLD THE BRANDED, LORD OF WHITECROFT

Berold was a creature of the dark, forged in the granite quarries of the North. His face was bisected by the purple brand of a "Life-Eater"—the Imperial mark reserved for those whose crimes were too great for the rope, intended to mark them as property of the state until death.

When Kharic Stormborn broke the empire, Berold didn't just break his chains; he turned them into weapons. He led a vanguard of three thousand convicts—the "Stone-Eaters"—who fought with the frantic, suicidal desperation of men who had already looked into their own graves. He was Kharic's "Hammer," the man who personally executed the *Mercy of the Root*, ensuring that not a single drop of royal Iron blood remained to reclaim the throne.

Berold's disdain for Maren Ashford was pathological. He mocked Maren's "farmer" origins at every council, sneering at the smell of marsh-water on the Lord of Valdria's boots. This was not the hatred of an aristocrat; it was the arrogance of the damned. Berold believed that the only legitimate path to power was through the Baptism of Pain. He had survived the brand, the lash, and the mines; he had "bought" his nobility with his own skin. To him, Maren was a fraud—a commoner who had climbed to the top through cunning schemes, womanly mercy and agricultural ledgers rather than the edge of a blade.

AARON HESTOR: THE OLD SOLDIER

Aaron Hestor had been a warrior since before most of the men he commanded were born.

He had served under Kharic Stormborn's grandfather in the final war against the Iron Empire—the catastrophic defeat at Thornfield that had broken Cherosian resistance for a generation. He had watched the lord he served cut down by Imperial cavalry; had fought his way out of the rout with a handful of survivors; had carried the body of his master back to Cheros for burial.

In the years that followed, he had lived in quiet obscurity —a minor lord on a minor estate, nursing wounds that never quite healed. He watched the Cherosian nobility decline, their lands parceled out to Imperial favourites, their pride systematically broken.

When young Kharic Stormborn raised his banner, Hestor was the first to answer.

He answered because honour demanded it. Because if Cheros was destined to die, he wanted to die with it, sword in hand, facing the enemies he had spent a lifetime hating.

What he found in Kharic's army gave him hope he thought he had lost.

"You remind me of your grandfather," Hestor told the young Hegemon one night by the fire. "He had the same fire in his eyes—the same conviction that the world could be reshaped by sheer force of will."

"And look where it got him," Kharic murmured, sharpening his blade.

"Yes. But he died free," Hestor replied. "He died fighting for what he believed in. There are worse ends for a warrior."

"I'm not planning on dying," Kharic said, testing the edge of his sword. "I'm planning on winning."

Hestor smiled at that—the smile of an man who knew the cost of such promises. He knew that the boy before him was dangerous, perhaps even doomed. But he would serve him to the end. Not for victory, but for memory.

LORD GLENN STORMBORN: THE KINSMAN

Glenn was never the thunder of his clan; he was the steady rain that kept the earth from blowing away. As the elder cousin to Kharic, he served as the conscience of a house that had forgotten how to feel.

His tragedy was one of competing loyalties: he loved the Stormborn name, but he feared the Stormborn fury.

His life was defined by a ten-year-old ghost. When Kharic abandoned Glenn's son to the rising tides of the Western Marshes, it was Maren Ashford—a mere patrol captain then—who pulled the boy from the muck. Glenn never forgot. At the Swangate Pavilion, when General Hestor's blade sought Maren's throat, Glenn rose to dance. He did not dance for a crown; he danced to pay a debt, shielding the mud-lord with the silvered steel of a Stormborn prince.

CASSIUS JONN: THE UNTRUSTED SHARP

Cassius Jonn joined the rebellion for the simplest of reasons: he wanted a world where a man was judged by his victories, not his pedigree.

As the youngest son of a minor noble house, he was a man of "near-blood"—close enough to power to see it, but too far away to ever touch it.

He rose from obscurity to command ten thousand men

through sheer, clinical competence. While Berold fought with the rage of a branded slave, Cassius fought with the precision of an architect. He was the man who turned Kharic's wild "Storms" into actual military campaigns.

The Tragedy of the Middle: His greatest burden was his past. Before the war, he had shared bread and wine with a young, low-born guard named Hans Xander. They had discussed strategy by firelight when no one else would listen to them. Now, with Xander serving in Maren Ashford's army, that friendship has become a noose.

Every time Cassius suggests a cautious maneuver or a strategic retreat, Greymantle whispers that he is *thinking like a marsh-man*. He is a man who builds a throne for a master who suspects him of wanting to steal it.

"We bleed for him," Cassius whispered to his lieutenants as the wind whipped the crimson banners of Swangate. *"I have mapped every hill from here to the sea. I have won him the East. And yet, when I speak, he looks at me suspiciously. Kharic wants a world of heroes, but heroes don't build empires—soldiers do. And soldiers need to be trusted."*

He served loyally, but the bitterness is a slow-acting poison. He saw Maren Ashford—that "mud farmer"—treating his generals like partners rather than servants. Cassius Jonn did not want to tear down the sky; he just wanted to be allowed to hold it up without being accused of trying to drop it.

OF THE QUILL

THE CHRONICLER'S INK: THE TRUTH IS A SOFT STONE

Chronicler Caelen had spent forty years in the sub-vaults of the Great Library, and his fingers were permanently stained with the grey-black ink of the Imperial Record. He was the man who turned events into eternity.

He had written the history of the Battle of Red Sands three times.

The first version, written in the heat of the moment, was a record of catastrophe: four legions slaughtered by a desert storm and incompetent scouting. It was a story of blood, sand, and screaming.

The second version, ordered by the Ministry of Stillness a week later, was a record of "Strategic Realignment." The legions had not been slaughtered; they had "ascended into the Emperor's memory" after achieving a vital objective that was too secret to name.

The third version, the one currently being etched into the obsidian tablets for the centennial, did not mention a battle at all. It spoke of a "Bountiful Migration" where the soldiers had laid down their iron to teach the desert tribes the art of the plough.

"The truth is a soft stone, Caelen," Mordecai the Shadow-hand had told him during his last visit, leaning over the scribe's shoulder with a scent of bitter almonds. "A skilled craftsman does not leave the rough edges for the public to trip over. He polishes it until it reflects only the light we choose."

Caelen looked at the tablet he was currently carving. It was an account of the Great Famine in the Eastern Gully.

In reality, ten thousand had died of starvation because the

grain had been seized for the Emperor's bronze-casting foundries. In Caelen's current draft, it was described as the "Year of Sacred Fasting," an empire-wide spiritual exercise designed to purify the soul from the distractions of the flesh.

The scratch of his chisel felt like a knife in his own marrow. He realised then that he was not just recording history; he was murdering it. Every adjective was a burial; every omission was an execution.

When the Iron Empire finally fell—when the fires of Kharic and the mud of Maren finally reached the vault—they would find a library filled with a thousand years of perfect, unblemished lies. They would find a world where no one had ever bled, no one had ever hungered, and the Emperor had never aged.

Caelen dipped his pen into the ink and began to write the history of the Siege of Steelhaven. He did not mention the smoke. He did not mention the smell of burnt mahogany and dead men.

He wrote that the sun had simply chosen to set early that day, out of respect for the Emperor's afternoon nap.

He wondered, as he blew on the drying ink, if anyone would ever find the small, hidden scrolls he had tucked into the hollows of the pillars—the ones written in his own blood, recording the names of the mothers, the scavengers, and the soldiers who had actually lived.

Probably not. In the Iron Empire, the ink was always heavier than the soul.

OF FINE ART

ART OF THE IRON-BOUND: THE MAKING OF A MONUMENT

General Ulric did not struggle. To struggle was to invite an imperfect finish, and in the presence of the Shadowhand, imperfection was the only true sin. He stood on the obsidian dais, his ceremonial armour stripped away to reveal the map of scars he had earned in the Emperor's service. He was fifty years old—a masterpiece of survival, about to be retired into eternity.

"Keep your chin up, Ulric," Mordecai whispered, adjusting a heavy iron shackle around the General's neck. "We wouldn't want the bronze to pool unnecessarily around the throat. It ruins the silhouette."

THE BAPTISM

The vat was suspended above him by chains of black iron. Inside, the bronze was a churning, liquid sun—a heavy, golden soup that had been fed a steady diet of charcoal and bellows for three days. It hummed with a low, predatory heat.

The process was handled with the clinical efficiency of a royal tailor:

The Foundation: First came the feet. The pour was slow—a deliberate tide of fire. When the liquid metal met the soles of his feet, Ulric's body attempted to perform the biological ritual of screaming, but the Shadowhand had already placed a gag of salt-soaked silk in his mouth.

The Ascent: The bronze rose. It claimed his shins, then his knees. It was a strange, heavy intimacy; the metal didn't just burn the skin—it replaced it. It sought out the pores, the creases of the joints, and the old sword-wounds, filling them with the weight of an era.

THE INTERNALISATION

The true craftsmanship happened at the chest. As the bronze reached his heart, the technicians tilted the vat to ensure a sudden, decisive rush. The metal poured over his shoulders, a molten cloak that draped itself with perfect gravity.

Then came the "Internalisation." A funnel of tempered glass was forced into the gap of the gag.

"Take a deep breath, Ulric," Mordecai said with a thin, appreciative smile. "This is the last promotion you will ever receive. From General of the Flesh to Commander of the Void."

The air in the foundry did not smell of burning flesh; the heat was too intense for that. It smelt of ozone and copper, a clean, metallic scent that masked the atrocity occurring within the mould.

The molten bronze was poured down the funnel. It was a surgical strike against the lungs. The liquid fire raced down the windpipe, mapping the bronchial trees in a fraction of a second, turning the soft, wet sponges of his breath into a solid, unyielding statue of metal. The internal and the external met at the ribs, fusing the man into a singular, seamless piece of hardware.

THE POLISH

Within minutes, the heat began to bleed away into the cold obsidian floor. The red glow faded into a dull, authoritative brown.

Ulric remained. He was standing exactly as he had been: chin up, shoulders back, one hand forever reaching for a sword that was now part of his thigh. He looked magnificent. He looked reliable. He looked like a man who would never ask for a raise, never plot a coup, and never fail a patrol.

Mordecai walked around the new addition to the Eight Thousand, tapping the bronze chest with a manicured fingernail. It gave off a high, clear ring—the sound of a bell that had nothing left to say.

"A bit stiff in the expression," Mordecai noted to the head caster, "but the posture is impeccable. Move him to the third row, behind the archers. And do try to keep the dust off him; the Emperor hates a dull soldier."

OF MAGIC

THE SIN-EATERS OF CHEROS

From the eye-witness testimony of a palace page, recorded after the fall of the Cheros capital

King Arion could not look at the Hegemon without seeing the three hundred thousand ghosts of Stonedeer—a visceral nightmare that made the King's silk robes feel like sandpaper against his conscience. His solution was characteristically elegant, hideously expensive, and entirely useless: he hired the Sin-eaters.

In a windowless cellar beneath his court in Drumhold, Arion sat behind a lavender-scented silk screen, watching three hollow-eyed men from the furthest marshes prepare to digest the Hegemon's divinity. The table was set with a perverted banquet: loaves of black barley kneaded with the soot of burnt granaries, and bowls of wine thickened with salt and copper filings to mimic the metallic taste of a dammed river.

The first man took a bite of the "Bread of the Breach" and immediately began to vibrate with the frequency of a falling city. His jaw locked with a sound like a snapped axle. As he choked, he did not gasp for air, but let out a high, metallic whistle—the exact, haunting pitch of an Imperial bronze signal.

The second man drank the "Blood of the River Isldra" and was instantly claimed by the Storm. He did not merely vomit; he stood rigid as a black, oily bile, smelling of ozone and ancient rust, geysered from his throat to coat the palace stones in a slick of liquid regret.

The third man, the oldest of the three, merely stared at the final dish—a heart of raw ironwood meant to represent the Hegemon's pride. He looked towards the King's silhouette and spat out a mouthful of teeth that had turned to silver.

"One does not eat a storm, Majesty," the man rasped with a terrifying, bloodied grin. "One only provides it with more things to break."

Arion, trembling, ordered the cellar scrubbed with lye and paid the survivors in gold, but the cleansing failed.

Kharic remained a God of War, and Arion remained a man who believed the moral rot of an empire could be cured by a sufficiently traumatising dinner service.

THE ALCHEMIST'S DEBT

Months before the Iron Emperor's final breath, Mordecai the Shadowhand had visited a cave on the eastern coast, where the sea churned grey and angry against the rocks. There, he met the man the legends called the Alchemist. He had not come seeking the Elixir of Life; Mordecai was too pragmatic to believe in fairy tales. He had come to buy a truth.

The Alchemist sat amidst a chaos of boiling retorts and glass vials filled with liquid silver. He didn't look at Mordecai. He was staring into a bowl of mercury, whispering to the fumes.

"The Emperor wants to know if he will live forever," Mordecai said, his voice cutting through the bubbling silence.

The Alchemist cackled—a wet, rattling sound. "Live? The Red King is already in the putrefaction! The sulfur eats the soul, little shadow. He seeks the *Rubedo*, the reddening, but he is stuck in the *Nigredo*! Black rot! The vessel cracks!"

He looked up then, his eyes milky and blind, seeing things that were not in the room.

"Iron is a fool's salt," the Alchemist gibbered, dipping his fingers into the toxic mercury. "It pretends to be solid, but it screams when the air touches it. Rust! Rust is just the iron trying to breathe, trying to return to the dirt. Your Emperor has built a cage of metal, but the Salt... the Salt of the Sea remembers the shape of the mountain before it was stone. The dissolution comes!"

He reached into the bowl and pulled out a glob of quicksilver. It writhed in his palm like a living thing.

"He wants the sun, but he is only the fuel," the Alchemist whispered. "But you... you are the Crucible. You wish to hold the fire without burning? You wish to be the glass that watches the world melt?"

He held out a small, jagged pill. It wasn't round; it looked like a gallstone cut from a god.

"Swallow this. It is the Fixation of the Volatile. It will grant you the endurance of the cold stone. You will not sleep until the debt is settled. You will be the statue that walks while the flesh of the world sloughs off."

Mordecai did not hesitate. He swallowed the pill. It tasted of bitter salt and sour rust, a cold fire that seemed to map the veins in his chest with liquid silver.

Then, the Alchemist grabbed Mordecai's hand with a grip like a bird's claw. He pressed a heavy, cold coin into Mordecai's palm.

"Payment for the ferryman," the madman hissed. "Keep it. Study it. It is the shape of the world."

Mordecai looked down at the coin. It was not gold, nor silver, but a strange, heavy lead that felt oily to the touch. Stamped upon its face was not a king, nor a god, but two serpents, distinct and terrified, knotted together, each devouring the tail of the other in a loop of eternal, suffocating hunger.

"One eats, one is eaten," the Alchemist chanted, turning

back to his boiling phials. "The perfect circle. The infinite trap. Go now, Architect. Go and build your ruin."

When Mordecai left, he found his hands were stained with silver. No matter how hard he scrubbed, the metallic scent remained—and the image of the two snakes burnt in his mind.

APPENDIX II
FOUND FRAGMENTS

Fragment Recovered from the Great Library of Draconia, circa 300 years post-Fall

———

Gentle Reader, take heed! Thou holdest in thy hands a most curious relic—a traveller's missive from an age of Iron and Ash. Though time hath nibbled the edges and the ink hath faded like a dying sun, we present here the geography of the Great Age. Marvel at the follies of the ancients!

A GAZETTEER OF THE OLDE EIGHTEEN KINGDOMS

Greetings, bold traveller! Hast thou a yearning for adventure and a sturdy pair of lungs? Then tarry a while and peruse this most spirited summary of our fractured world! Though some say these lands be haunted by the ghosts of kings, we say they are merely ripe for a most memorable holiday!

I. THE HEARTLAND: THE SEAT OF RUIN

In days of yore, this was the pivot upon which the world turned. Now, 'tis but a graveyard for giants.

STEELHAVEN

Once the world's most radiant pearl, this grand old city now wears a most fashionable coat of permanent soot! While the basalt walls remain quite black following the Hegemon's thorough toasting, the soil beneath is still the finest in the realm for growing a bumper crop—provided thou dost not mind the occasional rusted helmet in thy furrow!

THE THROAT

Behold the legendary western gateway! Where once six kings were barred by iron and blood, thou mayest now stroll through with nary a challenge. The great gates swing most merrily in the wind, creaking like a dead man's laughter, offering a truly brisk and unguarded passage for any wandering soul!

THE THREE SHIELDS

Do stop by and wave to our "Kings of Penance"! These three surly Iron generals have turned jailor-extraordinaire, keeping a most watchful eye upon the western mists. 'Tis a marvel of military hospitality, though they do tend to be a bit prickly if thou shouldst mention the word "surrender" in their presence.

———

THE SUMMER PALACE

A most eerie and enchanting garden retreat! Nestled by the Mirror Lake, 'tis the perfect spot for quiet contemplation. The flowers bloom in most unusual shades of mourning, and 'tis whispered the very air holds the lingering, desperate breath of King Arion himself—truly a sensory delight for the morbidly inclined!

II. THE WEST: THE SOVEREIGNTY OF SILT

A place for those the world wisheth to forget. Do not journey hither without a stout heart and high boots.

THE WESTMARCH

For those seeking true isolation, the Westmarch is a rugged paradise of peaks that tickle the heavens! While the roads have been most inconveniently turned to ash, the view of the abyss from the cliff-side is simply unparalleled. Just remember: once thou art in, the mountain hath a most permanent way of keeping thy company!

VALDRIA

Frogs, peat, and hidden bounty await in this misty village! Though the world mocks the "Lord of Toads," the valleys here are secretly fat with the forgotten harvests of the West. 'Tis the perfect spot for a traveller who enjoys a thick shroud of fog with their breakfast and doesn't mind a bit of mud between the toes!

THE GREAT GORGE

A canyon of most dramatic proportions where the sun is but a fleeting memory! Since the grand bonfire of the plank roads, it hath become a most splendid impassable monument. A limb severed from the world's body, it offers a breathtaking lesson in the finality of a well-placed torch!

Shouldst thou find thyself lost in the Great Gorge, do not panic! Simply wait for the fog to lift; though it rarely doth, the silence is quite peaceful for one's final moments of reflection.

COLDMIRROR LAKE

Famous for its island temples and morning mists that dance upon the water. 'Tis a serene freshwater sea with a most royal history, being the very site where a "King of Kings" took his final and most permanent retirement dip amongst the reeds!

III. THE EAST: THE STORM'S CRADLE

Where the canals flow with water and the courts flow with pride.

DRUMHOLD

Enter the dark stone heart of Olde Cheros! This commercial hub is brimming with ancient pride and the Hegemon's glittering gold. It sits upon a most invitingly flat plain—easy to reach, easy to see, and, alas, quite easy for a hungry wolf to wander into should the mood strike!

ALDORIA

A land of salt, shimmering silk, and most clever scholars! The Gilded Athenaeum is a must-see for those who prefer philosophy to pikes. They have gold enough to buy the very stars, though they seem to have misplaced the steel required to keep them!

IV. THE NORTH: THE FRACTURED SHIELD

A land where the wind biteth harder than any blade.

NORDHEIM

A brisk and bracing realm of bitter snow! The folk here are as hardy as the frost and twice as solitary, guarding the world against horse-lords with a most chilly determination. 'Tis far too cold for any sensible conqueror, making it the safest spot for a very long winter nap.

DRAGONSPIRE

Horses and arrows galore! This north-central plain is home to the realm's swiftest cavalry. They possess a most charming habit of making the Hegemon look over his shoulder, as their arrows fly straight and their riding tactics are delightfully barbarian-chic!

GRANDSMARK

The world's favourite doormat! Being as flat as a pancake and twice as tempting, everyone of importance hath walked across its fields at least once. With infantry as stubborn as stone and diplomats with silver tongues, they've made a most profitable habit of surviving everyone else's wars!

———

SORROWFEN

[A large, dark stain—perhaps wine, perhaps old blood—obscures three lines here]

————

[The final page of the folio is badly scorched, as if used to kindle a fire. The handwriting changes here from the elegant script of the Antiquarian to the frantic, sprawling hand of a man in a great hurry.]

...and should thy travells take thee past the last marshlight of Valdria, thou shalt find a most curious valley where the wind never bloweth and the birds refuse to sing! The locals call it the Vale of Stillness, and it is said to be the final resting place of the—

[unintelligible]

—stay not the night! I thought them statues, mere monuments of bronze to honour the old wars. I even dared to tap the chest of the one in the third row, the one with the high brow and the empty sockets. It rang like a bell, just as the guide promised! But then, in the absolute quiet of the moonrise, I heard it.

APPENDIX III
THE ORCHID PETITION

Document found amongst the charred remains of the Orchid Pavilion, never delivered.

THE HUMBLE SUPPLICATION OF THE LAST SCION TO THE RESPLENDENT HEGEMON

To the Most August and Heaven-Anointed Stormborn, the Zenith of Terrestrial Valour and Arbiter of the Iron Realms,

Whereas the Celestial Mandate, in its inscrutable and circuitous orbit, hath seen fit to withdraw its luminescence from the House of Iron and bestow its meridian glory upon Your Grace's person; and whereas the terrestrial tides have ebbed beneath the weight of Your Grace's inexorable justice, I, Lucan, the unworthy remnant of a fallen sun, do prostrate my spirit before the altar of your mercy.

It is written in the *Tractates of the Golden Age* that the virtuous conqueror is he who seeketh not the erasure of the past, but the harmonisation of the new order with the ghosts of the old. Be it known to Your Grace that I hold the Great Seal —the Untainted Eternal Stone of the Realm—in trembling trust within the Orchid Pavilion. The Lord of Valdria, in his rustic humility, hath declined to touch this sacred weight, stating that so hallowed a stone must only be received by the hand of the true Phoenix. Thus, I remain here, a gaunt shadow in a garden of fading blossoms, clutching the Signet to my breast and awaiting the thunder of Your Grace's arrival to surrender it. I do humbly beseech Your Grace, upon the receipt of this jasper, to permit this withered branch to retire into the shadows of the Western Glebe.

My heart yearneth no longer for the clamour of the Creed-seat, nor for the leaden weight of crowns. I seek only the tranquility of the Ancestral Farm, there to devote my fleeting hours to the study of the Celestial Orbs and the Precession of the Equinoxes, seeking in the stillness of the stars a geometry more stable than that of men.

Let it be known that I offer not a challenge, but a silence. I would live as a common scholar, tending to the cenotaphs of my line, ensuring that the spirits of the departed do not wander the realm as restless shades to disturb Your Grace's peace. May the gods grant Your Grace a thousand winters of prosperity, and may the name of Stormborn be etched upon the black basalt of history as the one who spared the lamb to prove the majesty of the Lion.

— *Inscribed by the hand of Lucan, Son of Stillness, in the Year of the Final Sunset.*

ABOUT THE AUTHOR

Nolan R. Highmoor is an author and creative developer fascinated by the recurring cycles of history and the heavy price of power. When he isn't chronicling the rise and fall of dynasties, he lives in Middle Tennessee with his family and two cats—who, much like the characters in his novels, frequently plot to overthrow the established order.

www.ingramcontent.com/pod-product-compliance
Lightning Source LLC
Chambersburg PA
CBHW030730310726
48969CB00005B/1171